the ABCs
OF Spellcraft

the ABCs OF Spellcraft

COLLECTION
VOLUME 1

JORDAN CASTILLO PRICE

jCPBOOKS.com

First published in the United States in 2019 by JCP Books
www.JCPBooks.com

ISBN 978-1-944779-09-2
First Edition
Also available in audiobook

DEDICATION

Quill Me Now is the first book in The ABCs of Spellcraft series, but it got its start as a simple writing challenge: start a story with the line *Nothing good ever came of a valentine*. And thus, the Bad Valentine collection was born. Four writers wrote four very different Valentine's Day stories. And all of those tales are dear to our hearts.

Special thanks to my fantastic writer friends, Dev Bentham, Clare London and Jesi Lea Ryan, whose enthusiasm and support made Bad Valentine (and, thus, The ABCs of Spellcraft) a reality.

CONTENTS

QUILL ME NOW

DIXON

1

"Nothing good ever came of a valentine," Sabina declared with great vehemence and utter conviction. "You hear me, Dixon? Nothing."

I love my cousin. I do. But there's opinionated...and then there's Sabina. I said, "You haven't even heard the details."

"I don't need to, either. Everyone knows those contests are a bunch of baloney."

"Who's everyone?"

She ignored the question. "And this 'big prize'... what's it even supposed to be?"

I squinted at the fine print. It was smudged with barbecue sauce, but if I held it up to the light, enough came through for me to get the gist. "A thousand dollars."

Sabina waded through the furniture we were saving for someday. She squeezed between two heavy oak dressers, veered around a massive roll-top desk, climbed over a pile of boxes, and worked her way into our kitchen. It was really just an old utility sink and a microwave perched on top of a mini fridge, but both of us liked to keep up the illusion that we still lived in an actual house, not just a hastily converted attic. She attempted to clatter some dishes to demonstrate how ridiculous she thought my idea was, but we'd sold the maple kitchenette on Craigslist to keep creditors off our backs. And since the only flat surface to slam her mug against was a vinyl card table, it just gave off an unsatisfying thwack. She filled the mug with water and stuck it in the microwave, then crossed her arms, turned to me and said, "A thousand dollars for a few lines of schmaltzy poetry?"

"The verse doesn't have to rhyme." I slid the ad across the table for her to look at.

Sabina ignored it. "There's no possible way anyone could afford to pay that kind of money to produce a valentine."

"But Precious Greetings is the biggest card company in the state."

"Even if every lovestruck dope in the city bought one, they'd barely recoup their outlay. Plus, who spends money on paper cards anymore when everything's digital?" She slammed down a box of hot chocolate with an even quieter thwack, then glared at the microwave as if it would heat her water faster. "You're just the type to fall for this kind of scheme, too."

"What's that supposed to mean?"

"A soft touch. You're always giving your spare change to that wino down by the underpass. And he probably lives in a cushier place than we do."

Well, no argument there.

No one would ever take Sabina for a soft touch. As we were growing up, strangers usually thought she was a boy. The weird, too-short haircuts from my Aunt Rose and hand-me-down clothes from me didn't help. Nowadays, the ratty denim vest and bleach-tipped fauxhawk tomboy look were entirely deliberate. Plainly female...and no one pegged her for a pushover.

Not like me.

Trustworthy. Sensitive. *Nice.* This was the opinion strangers formed of me before I even said hello. I guess I just had one of those faces.

"Who sends valentines these days, anyhow?" Sabina went on.

"Obligated spouses? Sappy girls swooning with unrequited love? Slimeballs looking to get in someone's pants? Screw valentines. The world is better off without them."

My cousin wasn't usually so negative—though I'll admit, she was never really a happy ray of sunshine—but the two of us always had each other's backs, and I'd been counting on her support. I was pretty sure this argument had nothing to do with valentines. She was just upset that I'd finally given up on the family Spellcraft business.

The microwave beeped, and she savaged open a cocoa packet and dumped it into her mug. "If you're so hell-bent on writing something—"

"Sabina...."

"—then maybe you should write something that actually matters."

She gave her hot chocolate a vicious stir, and a slurry of hot water and half-dissolved powder slopped over the side and splattered on the ad. I tried to yank it away, but too late. It was one of those local ads you find printed on the back of a sales register tape, along with coupons for oil changes and ads selling more ad space, and the ink from the front was already bleeding through.

Luckily, before I said something I'd regret, my phone chimed. Saved by the bell...or in this case, the WheelMeal delivery app. "Gotta go," I said, and left my cousin fuming in the kitchen.

Write something that matters...talk about a low blow.

I jogged down the stairs, lost in my own thoughts, not stepping as carefully as I usually do. Our downstairs neighbor pounded on the wall so hard, the pictures hanging in the stairwell rattled. Mr. Greaves didn't like hearing footsteps. Or music. Or especially laughter.

Technically, Mr. Greaves was our tenant, so you'd think Sabina and I would be in charge. But because the apartment we'd cobbled together in the attic wasn't exactly legal, Mr. Greaves used our situation to his advantage to throw shade a normal tenant would never get away with.

All the artwork that used to decorate the main house now hung in the stairwell, stacked railing to ceiling, four or five pictures high, up one side and down the other. It was the easiest way we could figure to store them while we rented out the downstairs.

I paused at the bottom step and looked up at a picture of Uncle Fonzo. It was a Sears portrait taken sometime in the early seventies when hair was side-parted, sideburns were bushy, and fashionable clothing was plaid. Uncle Fonzo wouldn't let Mr. Greaves walk all over him like we did. But he wasn't around to put the guy in his place, was he?

Not that Uncle Fonzo was dead or anything. Just that nobody knew where he was. And yet, he was everywhere. From the house, to the car, to the crippling debt.

Since Sabina could walk to work, I drove the car, a powder blue Buick with bald tires and an unfortunate tendency to stall at stoplights. But it was the only car I had, plus it was paid for. And it started, mostly, so I didn't complain.

While I waited for the engine to warm up, I thumbed open the WheelMeal app and checked the delivery. It was on the east side of Pinyin Bay at the very edge of my zone, and normally I'd let someone else pick it up. But not only did I need the money...I needed time to cool off. I couldn't afford to snap at Sabina. She was my most solid ally.

The thing was, she knew I was sensitive about my writing. Our whole family knew—and it was no big secret. In fact, if there were people living on the moon, I'd be surprised if they hadn't heard about the giant fiasco.

My whole life, I'd had a way with words. Not spoken, but written. I'd always known how to set just the perfect tone and evoke any emotion I chose with a well-turned phrase. Everyone held me up to be an aspiring Scrivener, the golden boy, the one with all the talent—the one who'd finally help the Penn family make their mark in the Spellcraft circuit. And then...to be the only one I'd ever personally known to fail the Quilling Ceremony?

Beyond humiliating.

Even worse than the lime green WheelMeal visor I wore to

make the deliveries.

I stopped off at Bam Burgers to pick up the order, which was supposed to be ready by the time I pulled up...but of course, it wasn't. Bam Burgers usually ran late, but tonight, they were in rare form. I opted to wait inside. I burn through less gas that way.

As I crammed myself into the sea of hopeful diners waiting for a table to open up, I glanced up at the ill-conceived piece of Spellcraft that was responsible for all the congestion. To the Handless—the uninitiated—it would just look like a kitschy little piece of artwork—a quick painting of a table with burger, fries and drink, and arched over the top of the scene, the words "Come for the Food, Stay for the Atmosphere."

But I knew it for what it was. Spellcraft.

Poorly worded Spellcraft, at that. Because of the words the Scrivener chose, no one ever wanted to leave. The waitstaff got stuck refilling drinks all night, and regular customers resorted to carryout. But even the carryouts felt compelled to linger, chatting with old acquaintances or striking up new ones in the lobby. And amid the chaos, harried staff handed out orders seemingly at random. The customers who got home to find the popcorn chicken where the cheese fries should've been came back to fix their orders and got sucked right back into the fray.

Could I get away with knocking that failed bit of Spellcraft off the wall and "accidentally" stepping on it hard enough to smudge out the image? Maybe. But it wouldn't get me my order any faster. Plus, all the Handless would wonder why the WheelMeal delivery guy was flailing around.

I sighed. Funny, how I still thought of myself as a Spellcrafter. Even now that it was obvious the Penn family's Scrivener talent skipped me entirely.

I'd spent the last year doing my best not to think about it, but sitting there staring at the lousy spell, I couldn't help but mentally re-Craft the words. *Come Hungry, Leave Happy* had a nice ring to it. Not only would it encourage repeat business, but once people were done eating, they'd actually make room for more customers.

But what did I know? I was just the guy in the lime green visor.

I got the order with no time to spare and high-tailed it out to the car, half expecting to be caught stepping too loudly and hear Mr. Greaves pounding his complaint somewhere in the distance. On paper, WheelMeal didn't pay too bad, a guaranteed ten dollars an hour, plus tips.

Unfortunately, you only got that ten dollar guarantee if you met a number of criteria, and one of those was delivering the order in half an hour or less. Not a problem...if the food is waiting for you when you get to the restaurant, like it's supposed to be. But, like a failed piece of Spellcraft, the "on paper" bonuses were nothing more than a colorful idea and a few nice words.

The tips weren't really all they were cracked up to be, either. "You'd make better tips if you flirted a little," Sabina always told me. "You're cute—you should definitely flirt."

As if wearing a lime green visor wasn't awkward enough.

I found my delivery address without too much backtracking and hurried up three flights of stairs. By the time I got to the top, I was winded, but I'd made it, by the skin of my teeth.

Until I stood there in the hallway for nearly three minutes waiting for the customer to open the door.

I gave a polite tap and called out, "WheelMeal!"

"Just a minute," came a man's reply—directly from the other side of the door. I didn't think much of it, initially. For all I knew, he was naked and needed some time to pull on a pair of shorts. Although I didn't hear any sounds of shorts rustling. But they could be very quiet shorts.

Although, the more I pondered it, the more I thought...wouldn't you put some clothes on if you'd just ordered food? Maybe the customer had his evening routine down to a science, I decided. Maybe he put in his Bam Burger order and had just enough time to get home and shower before the food showed up.

But if that were the case...why was he right there on the other side of the door? It must be Sabina's flirting idea that had me convinced I'd caught the customer in the act of pulling up his pants.

Would it be weird if I flirted with a guy who was just naked a few minutes ago? I didn't want to come off like I was desperate—I just wanted a bigger tip.

Needed a bigger tip, was more like it. Because thanks to that crappy Spellcraft at Bam Burger, no way was my hourly minimum gonna happen. Fine. I could flirt. I was perfectly capable of flirting. I've been told I have very nice eyelashes.

My app figured out what the customer was doing a split second before I did. I hadn't yet figured out how to mute all the dumb sound effects that the user interface made—you'd swear they were thought up by a teenaged boy with a lowbrow sense of humor—and so it was with a tinny sad-trombone sound that my phone informed me my delivery was late.

Just as the wah-wah faded, the customer opened the door. Fully dressed. And smirking.

I said, "Did you just make me wait for two minutes so you could mark me as late?"

"Nothing personal." He grabbed the Bam Burger bag from my unresisting hand. "When your food's late, you get 15% off your next order."

He shut the door. No tip. Not even a thank you. I stood there and stared at the closed door and wondered if it would've mattered if I'd managed to flirt.

Probably not.

I sighed and trudged down the stairs. Between the lack of a tip and the fact that he'd marked me late, all I'd earn was two dollars for the whole delivery, and I strongly suspected the Buick ate most of that in gas. And when I checked the WheelMeal app to see if there was another delivery I could grab to make the whole outing worth my while, there was nothing.

Unfortunately, the app prioritized drivers who were on time. Nothing personal.

I slipped behind the wheel of the Buick, logged out of the app, and wondered how it was that my life had taken such a dismal turn. Scrivening runs in families. Both of my parents, my cousin and

Uncle Fonzo all had the gift. Three of my four grandparents had it (God rest their souls). And the fourth, Papa Tobar, made such exquisite apple turnovers, no one held his lack of talent against him.

All the odds were in my favor. It was presumed I'd join the family business just as soon as I earned my quill. We were all so sure of my talent, I'd even taken some gap years after college, bummed around Europe with a knapsack over my shoulder, seen the inside of many a youth hostel, and cried over the blue-eyed French boy who proclaimed his undying love but ditched me at the bus station with a stubborn case of mono. Only when my tame bout of wanderlust was exhausted did I come back home....

And discover I was no Scrivener after all.

The smell of the Bam Burger lingered in my car—and something else, too. I retrieved it from the floor. Just a menu that had fallen from the bag, with that terrible Spellcraft slogan front and center: Come for the Food, Stay for the Atmosphere! It wouldn't influence reality as digital typography on a printed menu, of course. It was just an attempt at pretending the thing hanging in the dining room was a slogan, not sorcery.

I turned it over in my hands despondently, then realized something else was stapled to the bag: a receipt. And while the WheelMeal app prides itself in customer and driver anonymity, the Bam Burger ordering system did not. There was the order: Bam Burger Supreme, no onion, extra mayo, with a side of fries and a diet cola. And there below it?

The customer's name.

Brad.

Did Mr. Cheater look like a Brad? Yes. I could see it.

And I could see myself lettering that name in my best Scrivener-trained calligraphy.

The thing about Brad, when he acts like a cad, it comes back to burn him...but twice as bad.

Spellcraft doesn't have to rhyme—but when it does, it's epic.

It wasn't the rhyme that was unusual about that particular

Scrivening, though, but the inclusion of a proper name. Uncle Fonzo always told me, "If you pen someone's name in a spell, it's got just as much chance of working as any other Spellcraft. But actually doing it? Felony. Even if it's only designed to clear up someone's pimples. People say it's a matter of public safety, a precaution against a badly-worded spell misfiring." He gave me that knowing look of his. "But you and me...we know different."

"The Handless are scared of anything they can't control," I said. So cocky. So oblivious.

"Especially Spellcraft, kiddo. Especially Spellcraft."

I had no idea what it would be like for my Spellcraft misfire. And I never would. How...fortunate for me.

I tucked away my brief daydream about getting even with Brad where I kept all the rest of my unfulfilled fantasies. There were so many, you'd think I'd have nowhere left to store them anymore. I guess they don't take up much space. Either that, or I had a vast capacity for disappointment.

I tossed the paperwork onto the passenger seat and figured I might as well head home. Sabina's remark about writing something important still stung, but we Penns are a tight-knit clan. Hearing about how Brad bilked me out of my ten bucks would be a bonding moment that would leave the two of us united against a common foe. Doubly so considering he hadn't even tipped.

But as I started up the Buick and peered out at traffic, debating the wisdom of saving a few minutes by pulling a U-turn, the menu beside me settled with a quiet rustle of paper, snagging my attention.

I glanced down and saw it had fallen on its side, with the receipt flipped over to reveal the printing on the back. More ads. A dollar off a car wash. Pedicures, buy one, get one half price.

And a certain greeting card contest with a thousand-dollar prize... with a deadline, I now realized, of midnight.

2

Over the course of a normal day, most people will find themselves needing to write something at least once, even if it's as dull as a shopping list. But while the majority of adults know how to write, it's another thing entirely to have a *talent* for writing.

And that's aside from being able to Spellcraft.

My family's shop, the Practical Penn, sat in a strip mall between a dollar store and a carryout place that sold take-and-bake pizzas. Pro tip: you can't cook those pizzas in a microwave unless you want to give your jaw a really solid workout. Practical Penn's business hours varied, depending on my mother's mysterious circadian rhythms—on a bad day, she's awake several hours before dawn—but it was a safe bet that no one would be there at this time of night.

During my sporadic pitstops home throughout my gap years, I spent my time learning the business end of the shop, since everyone expected that someday it would be mine. It wasn't a gender thing. Sabina had made it clear since she was in zit-cream and braces that she wanted nothing whatsoever to do with spreadsheets and marketing. I might have been full of myself back then, but I'd been more amenable to doing all the boring jobs that came with owning a business...until it became clear that I could never aspire to anything more.

I still had a key. And I still had an office. But in the pit of my gut, I knew that someday my parents would retire, Sabina would need to hire more Scriveners, and I would eventually discover some stranger had taken up residence behind my desk.

For the time being, though, the desk was mine. And I would use it to win that thousand dollars if it was the last thing I did.

Getting into the right frame of mind was a challenge. Every time I thought I found the right words, they slipped away to the sound of a sad trombone. I was overtired and desperate, and I found it challenging to reach for a valentine sentiment that wasn't trite, forlorn, or downright cynical.

It took every last second I had, but eventually I came up with a phrase that didn't feel entirely contrived.

Love lets the heart soar free.

I was so wrapped around my own axle I couldn't tell whether it was optimistic or just plain weird, but time was running out. Ever since I could hold a crayon, it was presumed I'd do everything longhand, so I'm a terrible typist. In fact, I still had the Penn family callus—right hand, middle finger, first knuckle—that resulted from thousands of hours of perfecting my letterforms. I barely had time to call up the Precious Greetings website, peck out the words, and launch the entry before the clock struck twelve.

Okay, nothing actually struck. But the digital clock in the upper corner of the screen went from 11:59 to 12:00 right after I hit *send*.

Afterward, it seemed like there should have been some sort of fanfare...but there wasn't. Just me, sitting there alone in the dark, in the office I no longer wanted, yet desperately missed.

If I were a drinking man, it would've been the perfect setting for me to break out a bottle of booze, just me listening to the HVAC system wheeze by the dim glow of the emergency exits at midnight. I even knew where my father kept a little something, though I strongly suspected it was peppermint schnapps...and it would take a lot more than a customer failing to tip for me to get drunk on syrupy, boozy mouthwash.

I was so convinced I was completely and utterly alone, though, that when a new email chimed, I jumped so hard I nearly tumbled out of my chair. Rattled, I looked at my inbox and saw the sender was Precious Greetings, and immediately chided myself for being ridiculous. Obviously, no one was sitting there going through the contest entries at midnight. It must be an autoresponder telling me they'd received my entry. Nothing more.

Dear Mr. Penn,

Thank you for your entry to the Greet the Day Valentine contest. We were very impressed with your entry—

Was it just wishful thinking? The more closely I read the message, the less automated it sounded.

—and note that you have a local residential address. Our staff would be interested in meeting you in person.

Tomorrow morning, in fact (or today, technically, since it was now 12:03.) Bright and early. Nine o'clock.

If this was an autoresponder, it was doing a pretty darn good job of looking like an actual email from a real person. And then I saw it was signed by the founder of Precious Greetings himself— Emery Flint.

Very impressed. That's what the email had said. They were *very impressed* with my entry. *He* was very impressed with my entry. I couldn't recall the last time anyone had been *very impressed* with me, let alone the CEO of biggest greeting card company in the state, but it was definitely sometime before my Quilling Ceremony failed.

The next morning, Sabina had left for work by the time I squeezed out from between the floor-to-ceiling bookshelves that divided my "bedroom" from the rest of the attic. I was glad. I know that deep down inside, she wanted what was best for me. And in her fantasy world, that meant me somehow finding a way to take the test again. I'd pen a pithy bit of Scrivening—*Second time's the charm!*—and take my rightful place at Practical Penn.

Thing was, I'd never known anyone to fail the Quilling Ceremony, but I'd never even *heard* of anyone trying a do-over. Failing the first time around was devastating enough, not to mention the fact that I'd ruined the other half of the spell—the precious, magical half.

I wasn't sure exactly what I was dressing for that morning, but I figured it was hard to go wrong with a bow tie. I come from a long line of snappy dressers, after all. With my shoes shined, my tie tied and my dark hair artfully tousled, I headed off to Precious Greetings with butterflies in my stomach and a spring in my step. And I kept my fingers crossed that I wasn't reading too much into a cleverly worded autoresponder after all.

3

〜

The Precious Greetings Card Company was everything I hoped it would be...and more. It was a lot like a Spellcraft shop, actually, but without the anxiety that the slip of a pen could result in a bunch of customers refusing to leave your restaurant until you chased them out with a fire extinguisher.

No, at Precious Greetings, all they endeavored to create was something to bring a smile to the recipient's face. Well, the security guard at the gate probably didn't—but he did check me off a list of preapproved visitors and let me in.

At the building's grand entrance, the ubiquitous Precious Greetings-sponsored mascot, the Pinyin Bay Perch, greeted the visitors. The 6-1/2 foot tall plushy fish was a staple at all of the city's sporting events, tourism commercials and mall openings. It never occurred to me the Perch hung out anywhere between appearances. He (or she) waved at me listlessly. I waved back—though I wasn't sure the person inside the costume could actually see me—and stepped inside.

An imposing front desk barred my way, with an equally imposing receptionist who gave me a "look" when I said I had an appointment. Stern, middle-aged...in fact, she would've made a pretty convincing dominatrix. She subjected me to a long, cool scrutiny that had me fidgeting in place, but she did pick up her phone and let someone know I was there. Once she announced my name and said Mr. Flint would see me, I treated her to my most winning smile.

She didn't smile back. Oh well.

The reception area led to a broad workroom that contained desk after desk of artists and writers painting and penning the next big greeting card hit. I paused for just a moment to soak up the atmosphere. The air smelled of cellulose and India ink, and dust motes floated in the thin rays of sunlight eking through the smudgy skylights overhead. Conversation was muted, and the overall mood was serious, even intense. To the uninitiated, greeting cards might seem like so much fluff—but I could totally tell, these folks meant business.

I must have expected Emery Flint to be larger than life, too, because I was surprised when he came out to greet me and he was the same unremarkable height as me.

But what he lacked in tallness, he made up for in extremely strange hair. Close cut, old-fashioned, and slicked back severely from his brow. A wig? That was my first thought, though if it was indeed a wig, the hairline was really well made.

"Thank you for coming, Mr. Penn. I'm sure you're very excited to get a firsthand look at the top greeting card company in the country." Actually, I was pretty sure Hallmark held that slot, but I wasn't about to contradict him. "As you can see, Precious Greetings employs the top echelon of artists and writers. People come from far and wide to ply their trade at my not-so-humble shop."

Our footfalls rang alarmingly in the cavernous room. In the far corner, a quiet cough escaped one of the employees. A fountain pen scratched on a sheet of paper. In fact, it was so uncannily quiet, the father in I got, the more I worried I might be breathing too loudly.

Mr. Flint led me to an office graced by floor-to-ceiling windows that looked out over the bullpen, his greeting card domain. The room was somehow gray and somber at the same time as being brightly lit—so much so that my eyes watered a little. But he could see every last corner of the room beyond, while the employees, should they look up, would mostly be looking at their own reflections.

Beyond the glass door, though, the office was anything but quiet. I've never heard—or seen—so much noise condensed into such a small space. Noise...and movement. Because there were more tanks and cages in that room than there were in the reptile room of the Pinyin Bay Zoo. I'd always been soothed by the sound of crickets chirping. But when I realized they were only there to be food for lizards and toads, I found their song less than encouraging.

Interspersed with all the cages, in a mish-mashed jumble, dozens upon dozens of greeting card characters leered out from the cacophony. Easter Bunny. Santa Claus. And, of course, the ubiquitous Cupid.

"Have a seat." Mr. Flint indicated a very stiff looking chair, then glanced behind me and added, "And don't mind Yuri."

I presumed he was talking about the massive white cockatoo grooming itself on a perch beside his desk...until a huge man peeled out from behind a coat rack. Well over six feet tall, shaved head, bulging with muscle and covered in tattoos. The type of guy you'd cross the street to avoid late at night.... Unless you're into that sort of thing, in which case, he had really striking hazel eyes. He wore an off-the-rack suit that could barely contain him. Its fabric stretched precariously across his biceps and chest, and when he folded his arms in front of him, I was worried he'd split a shoulder seam.

"Yuri is head of security here at Precious Greetings," Mr. Flint proclaimed. "It's a sorry state of affairs when a greeting card company needs hired muscle. But the theft of intellectual property is always a concern—and Precious Greetings really is that popular."

"Oh," I said stupidly, recalling the height of the chain link fence.

Mr. Flint settled behind his desk and steepled his fingers. "Now, just to be clear, you are a member of the Penn family that owns Practical Penn Spellcraft?"

"Well, yes, but I don't actually work there."

"No matter, I won't hold it against you. And Fonzo Penn—you're related?"

"He's my uncle."

"Ah! How's old Fonzo doing these days?"

"Well, he's been traveling." Nice euphemism. "So, I don't really get to, uh...anyway...."

"Now, this entry you created, it has the mark of some very promising writing."

I stared hard at his hairline. I didn't think it was a wig.

"*Love lets the heart soar free.* The wording is very concise. Does what it says on the tin. Specific enough to evoke the holiday, general enough to appeal to a broad audience. Plus, it's something I haven't seen before, and it would pair well with a few different styles of artwork. These are the types of things we look for at Precious Greetings."

But no one's hair really was that particular brown, the color of the second darkest crayon in the box. And real hair didn't have that strange luster.

"Of course, when you have as much experience as I do, you can always tell amateur writing from professional. Please don't take that as an insult. In the greeting card business, you need to develop a thick skin."

Or maybe it was just that his eyebrows didn't really match his hair. They were half a shade lighter and had an almost greenish undertone.

"At any rate, why don't we move on to the written portion of the test?"

"Test? What test? I thought this was a contest for a greeting card slogan."

"Oh. Yes. Indeed, it is. But if you don't take the grand prize, there may be something we can offer you as a runner-up. For entrants with potential, there may be future opportunities, but we need to vet those entries thoroughly. Make sure they haven't been plagiarized from somewhere on the web. Nasty business, plagiarism."

"Oh, right. I see." I shifted in the seat that really was as uncomfortable as it looked. "But I would never...."

"The only way to be entirely sure this greeting was created by you, and you alone, is to administer an in-person test. Surely, you understand."

Well, I guess with a thousand dollars on the line, I couldn't afford to say no. "Okay."

Mr. Flint gestured to Yuri. "An image to inspire another verse from Mr. Penn?"

Wordlessly, the outrageously muscled, tattooed man turned to a folder, drew out a single sheet of heavy paper, and set it in front of me on Mr. Flint's desk. It wasn't just any old image. The paper was fine watercolor stock, and the image was an intriguing, gestural piece of work. If I weren't so baffled by the fact that I was supposed to come up with a greeting card sentiment on the spot, I might've had a flashback to my Quilling Ceremony. "Are you sure you want me to mark up this beautiful artwork?"

"It's just a copy," Mr. Flint said.

I held up the paper to the light. The texture was definitely that of a richly colored gouache on cold-pressed block. "This is an original," I said. "I'm sure."

"It's a proprietary inkjet technology," Mr. Flint reassured me. "Entirely new. People are into handcraft these days. You can charge more for a greeting card that appears to be hand-painted."

Wow, I could swear I was holding an original watercolor.

"Were we to hire you at Precious Greetings, give you a chance on the writing staff, you'd need to follow orders explicitly and learn from constructive criticism. This is my company, after all, and it's my job to carry the vision. It's all part of the job."

And, in fact, one of his eyebrows was slightly higher than—wait, what was that about putting me on the staff? I did my best to block out his weird hair, and leaned forward in my seat. "I'm totally open to criticism," I said. "Not a confident bone in my body."

Mr. Flint smiled. One of his eyebrows quirked strangely. "Good, that's good. I look for employees who are willing to set aside their egos and learn."

Nope. No ego whatsoever.

If a thousand dollars would be a huge blessing, imagine the impact a permanent, full-time job would have! I was brimming with so many questions I could barely contain myself. But Mr. Flint was unwilling to share any more details until I'd passed this test of his.

He slid a fountain pen across the table, and I turned it around in my hands. Thanks to their potential to leak and blot and otherwise create very inky messes, fountain pens aren't too common anymore. But I'd used many a fountain pen, since Spellcraft families have a tendency toward exotic writing instruments. Apparently not as exotic as this one, though. Instead of the normal bronze writing nib, this one had a hollow tip that looked an awful lot like a hand-cut quill from a feather. "How unusual," I murmured. "I've never seen a—"

"This will be a timed trial," Mr. Flint said abruptly, and glanced at his watch. "When you're ready...."

"But what's the greeting?" I asked. Mr. Flint seemed puzzled, or at least I think he was. Hard to tell with the way his eyebrows were canted. "Get well soon?" I suggested. "Mother's Day? Another Valentine?"

The cockatoo gave an edgy chuckle that sounded eerily like a human laugh, though it cut off just as abruptly as it started.

Ignoring the bird, Mr. Flint nodded gravely. "Ah—you've passed the first portion of the test. Obviously, you can't write a sentiment without knowing which occasion it's meant for!" He laughed a bit too loud, and I forced myself to join in, though mostly I just felt nervous. "Tell me, what does it look like to you?"

I swallowed hard and wondered if this was part of the test as well. I looked down at the painting—and hard to say *exactly* what it might be, but it was difficult to pull my eyes away. The colors were rich and lush, yet tasteful and subtle. Wet-on-wet technique yielded gorgeous gradations of color, purple to red to orange—while other strokes were hard-edged and defined. I turned it around, unsure which was way was up, but as I considered the beautiful image in its various orientations, eventually I saw, within the deft, colored strokes, a road. "A congratulations card? The type of thing you would send someone when they get a new job?"

Mr. Flint drummed his steepled fingers together, one pair at a time. "That sounds absolutely perfect. Begin."

Well, okay... What do you say to somebody who gets a new job? *Good for you. Now you don't have to deal with jerks who claim you're late when you're clearly on time.* Okay, no. That was way too personal.

Or was it?

All the best! Maybe someday you can move out of your uncle's attic.

No, not that.

Here's to no longer having to wear a lime green visor.

That one might work if I changed the visor to a name tag, but the tone was all wrong for such a serious painting. Creating greeting cards might not be exactly the same as Spellcraft, but despite the fact that I wasn't Crafting, I couldn't shed my inherent respect for a beautiful piece of art. I ran my fingertips over the nubby texture of the paper—just enough tooth to capture the paint vividly—and softened my inner focus. Aside from the obvious hallmarks of success that would mean something to me—living in a real house again; having respect from my customers; waking up to face the day without an impending sense of dread—I let the concept broaden. It had been an awfully long time since I felt successful, but I gave it my best shot.

When I opened my eyes, the painting filled my field of vision, once I let the cluttered office recede into the background, at least. The road could be leaning toward a sunset, retirement, the end of a fruitful career... But I didn't think so. Something in the way the purple bled into the subtle rosiness of the reds told me this was a sunrise. A beginning. A fresh start. I felt that old familiar tingle in my arm, the one I used to think meant I was Spellcrafting, and I allowed the words to flow.

May your feet set you on the path to success.

I almost second-guessed myself, thinking it might be too preachy, or perhaps too vague. But I'd already penned the words. And so, I simply sat down the scratchy fountain pen and hoped it was enough.

"All done," I said.

The cockatoo chuckled, then fell silent.

Mr. Flint had been watching me eagerly. He picked up the sentiment, then turned it this way and that. His eyebrows screwed up. Maybe. And then he stood abruptly. "Thank you very much for your time, Mr. Penn."

"Is that it? When do I know—?"

"We'll be in touch."

"If you have any feedback about how I could improve—"

"Yuri will see you out."

And with that, I suppose I was dismissed. The massive, silent, tattooed man detached from the wall, inserting himself between Mr. Flint and me, and with only his strikingly hazel eyes, gestured toward the door.

Guess it was time to go.

For such a huge man, Yuri walked silently. Maybe he'd had a lot of practice navigating such a stunningly quiet workplace. I'm not sure if it was eagerness I was feeling or anxiety over the prospect of winning the thousand dollars—either that, or one of the available staff positions, and so my whispered words just tumbled out into the stifling silence. "Have there been many other contestants?" I asked Yuri. "Do you think I have a chance? Because greeting cards seem like simple things, but they're actually pretty difficult to do just right. And if I have competition, I guess it's best for me not to get my hopes up. And not to toot my own horn, but I think I did pretty well. If that painting was supposed to be a road. Do you think it was a road?"

My babbling had carried us all the way past the receptionist to the front door. Yuri crossed his arms, and beneath his ill-fitting sport coat, muscles bulged hard enough to strain the polyester blend while tattoos peeked out at the collar and cuffs.

"Forget about the job." Oh…he had an accent. A lyrical Russian accent. "Precious Greetings is not the place for a nice boy like you." He stepped forward, into my space, and I realized he was wearing cologne. Not a lot of men can carry off a fragrance, but the resinous hint of cedar emanated from him in a deliciously tantalizing whiff, briefly there, then gone. And before I could close the space between us to try and identify the notes of the cologne, he poked me in the chest, sending me staggering back a couple of steps, then pulled the front door of Precious Greetings shut.

The electronic lock gave a loud click.

I stood there, peering through the locked door, searching for his eyes. I thought I caught a glimpse of him looking at me with a cryptic expression on his face that was oddly tender. But then the clouds overhead shifted, and all I could see was my own reflection in the glass. I looked to the Pinyin Bay Perch for guidance, but all he did was shrug.

I thought the interview had been going well, at least until I was done writing the sentiment. And then it seemed like something had shifted. Hopefully Mr. Flint hadn't thought I'd been cheating last night. What I wrote today seemed pretty promising to me—but it wouldn't be the first time I'd been guilty of hubris.

Like when I decided to take the Balthazar Expressway to deliver an order of hot wings to the south side. What was I thinking? If that customer marked me late, it wouldn't be for a coupon—it would be because I deserved it. I finished that thankless delivery, then accepted another. It was either ferry meals all over the city, or face another long day pounding the pavement. And by pounding the pavement, I mean trying to find something on Craigslist that was anything more than a weird pyramid scheme. Eventually, I did manage to deliver a few orders on time, but no matter how eager, friendly, and charming I attempted to be, I didn't receive more than a three-dollar tip.

Did they not see I was wearing a bow tie?

By the end of a lackluster lunch and a dispiriting dinner, I pulled up to my uncle Fonzo's house well after dark, barely fitting behind our tenant's car, which was taking up two spaces, and thought back to the remark Yuri had made—such an odd thing to say—that Precious Greetings was not the right place for a "nice boy" like me.

If not, then where *did* I fit in?

4

I'm sure anyone born into a family business is expected to take up the reins once they're old enough to settle down. The Penn family certainly presumed Practical Penn would eventually fall to me. My family is a pretty easygoing bunch. My folks had been not simply tolerant, but downright indulgent about me "finding myself." I'd put off my Quilling Ceremony until I was nearly twenty-six years old—because maybe what I really wanted to do was design men's outerwear or curate a wine subscription or study contemporary European pottery.

One day out of the blue, though, Uncle Fonzo sat me down and told me in no uncertain terms that I needed to quit screwing around. Life was short. And while Scrivening might not be seen as a particularly cool endeavor, nothing compared to the feel of the Spellcraft tingling down your arm.

Uncle Fonzo was my sponsor—not only was he the patriarchal Hand of the family, but he was like a second father. He was the one who'd rented out the gazebo at Parliament Park. He was the one who'd arranged for the most important local Spellcrafters to be there. And he was the one whose Spellcrafting quill would allow the Quilling Ceremony to bring me one of my own.

There was no room for improvisation in the traditional Quilling Ceremony. The words are always the same. Given that I didn't have to come up with a pithy saying on the spot—and that I'd always presumed I'd be a Scrivener—I wasn't particularly anxious. A little nervous that my first official Spellcraft would look pretty, maybe. But I'd practiced the letterforms in pencil enough times to ink them in my sleep.

Axioms are axioms for reasons. Pride goeth before a fall.

I accepted my uncle's quill from the oldest practicing Scrivener in our circuit, Morticia Shirque, and heard the traditional phrase in her gravelly old-lady voice. "Dixon Penn, do you promise to keep the Spellcraft within your own family, to abstain from sharing our secrets with the Handless?"

"I do."

"Do you acknowledge that words have power?"

"I do."

"And are you ready to let Spellcraft flow through you?"

"I am."

She placed the first element of the Spellcraft, the *Seen*, in front of me. "Then take up the quill of your family's Hand and Scribe your first Crafting."

I looked down at the small watercolor—a squiggle, which was probably supposed to be a feather. Practical Penn Seens are notoriously abstract, even to the point of being ugly, but that was a minor aesthetic consideration. What mattered was that they always worked. With the sort of gravity you'd expect for the occasion— but no lack of overconfidence—I penned the traditional phrase, *I choose the quill and the quill chooses me.*

While eagles were occasionally spotted around Pinyin Bay, they don't seem inclined to participate in Quilling Ceremonies. No, I'd be more likely to have a hawk or a Canadian goose drop a feather on me. I'll admit, I was hoping for a swan—despite the fact that I'd never spotted one in the wild—but the quill truly does choose the Spellcrafter. Case in point: despite the fact that they can't fly, some poor turkey lost a tail feather to an errant breeze during my father's ceremony and it practically flew up his nose. If you've ever heard one of his dad-jokes, you'd definitely agree he couldn't have found a better match.

I finished the final stroke and set down my uncle's quill. And with that, all the Scriveners there, plus all their extended families, looked up into the sky expectantly. And looked. And looked.

...and looked.

Sabina was the first one to realize the Quelling Ceremony had failed. She makes this funny strangled sound when she cries. Disbelief rocked Uncle Fonzo—I couldn't count the number of times he demanded, "What do you *think* happened?" And as for me, given the fact that I'd spent my whole life worrying that being a Scrivener would prevent me from pursuing other lines of interest, once I realized there was no quill for me, I found myself feeling unexpectedly bereft.

After the debacle, my parents insisted they loved me just as much—but it was clear the Penn family simply wasn't the same. Uncle Fonzo left on a spur-of-the-moment trip the very next day... and never came back. Every now and then, Sabina gets a postcard from some tacky, oversized roadside attraction—from a giant smiling peanut in Georgia to an oversized moose in Canada. But there was no way to write back and tell him that we missed him. Or that his house was on the verge of foreclosure. Or that every time I picked up a writing implement, I was ashamed I'd let him down.

My disappointment was no longer fresh. But on nights like this, it was definitely persistent.

When I finally got home that night, I trod carefully on the stairs so as not to wake Mr. Greaves, and was surprised to find my cousin sitting up at the kitchenish card table waiting for me. "Where was your last delivery?" she asked with forced lightness. "New Jersey?"

"I doubt the Buick could make it that far."

Sabina might have pooh-poohed my attempt to win that contest, but it was impossible to stay mad at her. I pulled out a chair, and we both winced as it squalled against the floorboards. We braced ourselves, but there was no ceiling pounding. This time, anyhow.

"Look," she said, "I didn't mean to be such a downer before. You'd be great at writing greeting cards—in fact, I bet you'd be the best writer they've ever had. You've always been good at anything you set your mind to."

Well, I *had been*. Once.

"Y'know, Dixon, maybe there's a reason your Quilling Ceremony didn't pan out."

"Right. Because I didn't inherit the talent."

"No...." Sabina waggled her finger at me. "Because the Scrivening and the Sight can't coexist in the same human consciousness."

Otherwise, I'd be a god...and then I'd really make that guy Brad sorry for marking me late. I sighed. Scriveners were uncommon, but Seers were downright rare. "I think we would've noticed by now if I had the Sight. For one, I'm right-handed."

"Are you? Or did the family just train you to use your right hand because they *presumed* you'd be a Scrivener like the rest of us?"

"Listen," I said, "it's late...."

Sabina ignored my attempt to fend off the conversation. She'd been waiting all night to talk, and she wasn't going to let me rest until she said what she had to say. "I remember when you came out—it was Sunday dinner and the whole gang was there. I was just fourteen, but I'd always suspected you were gay. You were just too damn nice to be a straight guy."

"Um...thanks?"

"You hear about families losing it when their kids come out to them, but I'll never forget what your mom said."

Actually, neither would I. *What a relief. Now you can find yourself a handsome Seer and settle down, so I won't have to worry about you when I'm dead and gone.*

I'm told that Handless families usually want sons, someone to carry on their family name. Not Scriveners—when they have kids, they hope for daughters. The best a male Scrivener could hope for was to pass on his talent. But any offspring who managed to loop a Seer into the family would secure the future of the entire clan.

Neither science nor medicine had ever quite figured out what made Spellcrafters tick, but the working theory was that Scriveners—male or female, always right-handed—carried a recessive gene on the X chromosome, which made the Scrivening run in families. Seers—left-handed and always male—cropped up with no apparent rhyme or reason. It was thought the trait must be a mutation of a Y chromosome, though the specific gene involved was yet to be pinned down. And just like it took two hands to tie a shoelace, it took a Scrivener and a Seer working together to Craft a spell.

Sabina cleared the remains of her cold take-and-bake pizza from the card table and set a blank piece of paper in front of me. "The family never made any assumptions about your sexuality. But Scrivening? They figured it was a given."

She pulled out a plastic sandwich bag, but the thing inside was no sandwich. It was a piece of foil with a few smears of color on it. "Oh no." I swallowed hard. "You didn't."

"I only took a few dabs."

"Oh my God."

"Calm down. No one will even notice it's gone."

Hopefully not. Rufus Clahd, the Seer at Practical Penn, was beyond particular. He was around my parents' age, but somehow his sense of fashion never evolved beyond the eighties—and though his mustache and aviator glasses had come back in fashion, no one would ever mistake him for a hipster. He'd go for days on end without speaking to anyone, then suddenly blurt out the accusation that everyone was ignoring him. If he knew Sabina was not only pawing through his paints, but *stealing* from him? He could easily pack up his stuff and leave. Seers were rare, and he could find a new job before the day was out. And it might take months for our family to find a new Seer—if we were lucky enough to replace him at all.

My failure to earn my quill was a disappointment, sure, but the family business chugged along without me. If we lost our Seer, though....

"What's done is done," Sabina said decisively. "I can't put the paint back in the tube. So, make it worth my while, Cuz." She slid a coffee mug full of water toward me and dropped a paintbrush in. "I believe in you. Just try."

True enough, if Rufus knew his paint had been tampered with, it wouldn't matter whether or not I dabbled with them now. And while there was no chance whatsoever I'd paint a Seen (since I was most definitely not a Seer), if Sabina saw me try and fail, hopefully I'd never have to hear about it again.

The Sight is mysterious, but it's hardly complicated. The Seer would dab his brush in paint, clear his mind of all thoughts, and let the magic come to him. I'm sure anyone is capable of making marks and squiggles on a page—that was all Rufus Clahd's ugly doodles looked like. But only a Seer could capture the elusive gesture it takes to fashion Spellcraft.

I wet the paintbrush, then looked across the card table at my cousin. She'd washed out her fauxhawk, and her peroxide blonde hair hung, straight and fine, in her eyes. She was almost twenty-four, but she looked like a teenager tonight. Vulnerable and young. "What do you want to Craft?" I asked her. "You're the Scrivener."

She laughed nervously, as if she could make a joke out of it, but the Crafting she came up with was dead serious. "I want our house back."

I glanced at the floorboards as if I could see crabby Mr. Greaves sprawled out in the master bedroom where Uncle Fonzo should have been snoring away. It was definitely no joke. Sabina and I both wanted nothing more than to see that moving truck pull up and get the irritated canker downstairs out of our lives for good.

A more frivolous guy would dash off a quick gesture à la Rufus Clahd and be done with the whole thing. But even though I didn't have the talent myself, I held a deep respect for Spellcraft. Sure, most people thought of the art in the same vein as Magic 8-Balls and Ouija boards, but I saw the Craft as my family's legacy. And as crappy of an evening as I'd endured, as weary and broke and all-around disappointed as I felt, I couldn't just phone it in.

I pictured our house as it used to be, with Uncle Fonzo here. Not a silent shell with the two of us gingerly skulking around in the attic, but a home. Full of music and family and the smell of my mom's famous cheeseburger casserole. I held that feeling, and then I pictured it swelling, lighting my body up from the inside. Starting from my heart, then growing, spreading, until the energy of *home* reached my hand. I poised the brush above the paper, and Sabina whispered, "Left hand."

Oh, right. I switched hands, called up my image of our house the way it used to be, then touched the brush to the paper.

Nothing.

Not that I'd expected anything...or, at least, I *thought* I hadn't. But even in my failed Quilling Ceremony, I'd felt a little something. Maybe not the "tingle" Uncle Fonzo always talked about, but a spark of excitement when I touched my pen to the Seen. I'd felt it even when the words I'd written fell flat on the page. Even when my words just sat there like so much dead ink.

Now, in our makeshift apartment, I did my best to create a small painting. But I was no artist...especially left-handed. All my life, I'd been exposed to the types of paintings that would light up under a Scrivener's touch. They weren't necessarily works of art. But they contained a special "something." Always. The lopsided house I was currently trying to paint was clearly no Seer's work. But I dutifully tried, nonetheless. I added a reddish stroke for the chimney and a cheerful yellow rectangle for each window, doing my best to imagine the house as it used to be when Uncle Fonzo was still here, brimming with laughter and light. And I slid the drawing across to Sabina.

Sabina shook the painting dry, then took up her quill, a long raven pinfeather that came to her at the tender age of seventeen at the completion of her own successful Quilling ceremony. Frankly, I thought it bordered on heretical for Sabina to use her quill on my silly left-handed painting that was clearly not an actual Seen.

But before I could voice my trepidation, Sabina was already inking her Scrivening.

There's no place like home.

Phrases become cliches for a reason. Often, they make extremely effective Spellcraft. In this case, though? We were probably lucky that my stupid little painting was as magical as a gum wrapper. Because as Scrivenings went, the phrase was far too inexact to be effective. Not only were no two homes exactly alike to begin with, but there was certainly no place like the half-finished attic where we currently lived. A Scrivening like the one Sabina had just written could very well leave us squirreled away in the attic forever.

"Nice try," I told her anyway. She didn't need a lecture on Spellcraft from me.

Particularly since I had no quill of my own.

YURI

5

"How disappointing." Flint glared at the tiny bit of Spellcraft. "I thought we'd finally found our new Scrivener."

I shrugged—no answer was often the best answer, and it has never been safe for me to say what I really thought.

America was supposed to be different.

What a joke.

Flint never minded my silence. In fact, I think he preferred it. With no one to contradict him, he could pontificate for hours in his grandiose bubble of self-importance. Meanwhile, I stood by and fantasized about the satisfying crunch his nose would make when it connected with my fist.

Too bad the time for fighting my way out of the situation was long past.

And now I was stuck listening to this.

"Scriveners are a dime a dozen." Flint waved his hand and the gecko in the tank beside his desk scampered behind its driftwood to hide. "It makes absolutely no sense. Unless the attraction Spell is tapped out."

It wasn't. I wanted to shrug—to let him think the Crafting was no good. But my muscles seized up, and the desire to speak burned in my belly. I might be able to hold out for a minute or two, but no longer. I've timed it. The quicker I answered, the more natural it would sound, and I was too proud to let him know how deeply I was under his control. Pride was a poor substitute for freedom, but it was all I had. "The Spell is fine."

Flint tipped back in his chair, which gave off a metallic squeal. Meringue puffed up her yellow crest and imitated the sound. I handed her a peanut from my pocket to shut her up. Once she got going, she'd squeak and creak all afternoon until you provided her with a distraction. Plus, I got some satisfaction from seeing her fling bits of shell around her perch.

Flint ignored her, like he ignored all his acquisitions once the shine wore off. "The kid's from the Penn family and everything. Their Scriveners run three generations deep. How is it even possible he can't Scribe?"

My insides clenched as I thought of all the ways that question could have landed. "Genetics," I said. It was fortunate Flint was so careless with his words—when Dixon Penn Scribed, his right hand sparkled like it was covered in glitter—but anything was *possible*.

"Just my luck. I somehow managed to pull in the one family member the talent skipped."

Good thing he hadn't phrased that statement as a question. The Crafting's failure had absolutely nothing to do with luck. Once I got a look at Dixon—the way he sparkled with innocence and goodness—there was no way I'd let Flint sink his claws in.

Flint sighed. "Maybe I shouldn't have let Dolores go."

I rolled my eyes. "Dolores was so old she could hardly hold a quill."

"There's always duct tape. D'you think she'd come back if I offered her a bonus?"

Once Dolores Tran found a loophole in her contract, she'd moved to Maple Heights and changed her phone number, so I highly doubted she was in any hurry to resume her relationship with Precious Greetings. But I couldn't be absolutely *sure*.

I shrugged.

"Yuri, are you positive the Spellcraft is still working properly? Reaching halfway around the world for you had to use up a lot of power. Take a better look and make sure."

I didn't want to touch the nasty little thing, but I had no choice. Even as I considered shrugging and giving him another bland reassurance that the Crafting was fine, shooting pains sparked along the muscles in my back, and my arms began to cramp. I struggled to turn away, briefly, but it was no use. The only way I could move was toward the Spellcraft.

I pulled it from its place among all the clutter. For such a tiny slip of paper, it was very heavy on my soul. The square of cardstock was the size of a sticky note. The Seen painted on it was a lopsided red arch—a magnet, I supposed—and the Scrivening read: *Magic Draws Magic*. Dolores's penmanship was shaky. Her fingers were all twisted with arthritis, but Spellcraft flowed through them just the same. I never learned who the Seer was, but it didn't matter. Before Flint had Spellcraft in his arsenal, he used trickery and blackmail to get what he wanted. I knew plenty of men like him in Russia. If he needed a Seen, he'd find a way to get one. Just like he'd eventually find a way to replace Dolores.

I held the stiff square of paper to the light, sideways, so I saw it only in two dimensions. Like hot asphalt, the surface of the paper distorted the air above it. "Still good," I said shortly.

"If you say so." Flint gave a negligent toss of his hand. "Then put it back where it belongs and update the website with a Mother's Day contest. There's bound to be a real Scrivener out there dumb enough to take the bait."

I tucked the tiny square back into the corner of a mirror frame. The reflection of my eyes in that mirror looked blank. A carefully cultivated neutrality. Bits of Spellcraft were hidden throughout the room, endowing Flint with everything from stamina, to luck, to the ability to stick to his Keto regimen. There was only one Crafting I cared about—the one that stole my will, that reduced me to nothing more than Emery Flint's puppet. I knew it was there somewhere. But Flint had declared I wouldn't be able to find it. And thanks to the power of the Casting—*of my own damn painting*—no matter how hard I looked, it was nowhere to be seen.

DIXON

6

Even though I'd been up early and run myself ragged making deliveries, when my head hit the pillow, I found myself staring sleeplessly at the ceiling slats, thinking about how I might have phrased that particular Scrivening. *Home is Where the Heart Is* might seem like a cute sentiment, but there's too much potential for serial killer action. *Bless this House* was potentially harmless, though in the hands of a clumsy Scrivener, it might leave people sneezing. I could have written *Love is the Heart of this Home*. Though without Spellcrafting ability behind it, they'd be nothing more than pretty words.

It had been a while since I'd lain awake creating Spellcraft in my mind. I blamed the pop quiz at Precious Greetings for getting the wheels turning again—wheels I'd presumed were permanently stuck. By the third or fourth or twenty-fifth time I checked my email the next morning, I still hadn't received any word from Precious Greetings. That didn't stop me from suggesting some new phrasing for the painted road Mr. Flint had shown me in his office.

Enjoy your new journey.
Follow your own path.

Find delight wherever life takes you.

Just to name a few. Because who's to say that persistence wasn't another thing I was being tested on. Right?

I started off my day's deliveries with a tandoori chicken from Curry Favor that left my car reeking of garam masala, but I hardly noticed the smell. My brain was still churning on potential greeting card verses. I checked my phone, and checked it again, but Mr. Flint still hadn't returned even one of my emails. And then I started worrying that I was coming off a little too eager.

Especially with the one I'd sent in the middle of the night.

My own road, studded as it was with WheelMeal deliveries, was nowhere near as promising as the watercolor painting I couldn't put out of my mind. I detoured from my latest route and pulled up alongside the Precious Greetings studio. It hulked beneath a lowering gray sky, industrial brick, the opposite of welcoming. But if I was simply persistent and polite, surely Mr. Flint would be willing to let me plead my case. My name was still on the good-list, but unfortunately, I couldn't make it past the receptionist without a prior appointment.

If my time at WheelMeal had taught me anything, though, it was that there's more than one way into a building.

I went around back, and sure enough, there was a weathered, sagging picnic table surrounded by cigarette butts. All I needed to do was act casual until someone came out for a smoke, and then come up with a clever excuse as to why I was lingering around outside. Luckily for me, no one has ever been intimidated by me, and so I parked myself at the picnic table, picked a splinter out of my slacks, and waited.

There must've simply been too many entries. With a thousand-dollar cash prize, of course there were. And Emery Flint would get back to me just as soon as he'd been through all of them and seen that mine was definitely the best. I checked my email— nothing new. Right. But surely he would get to it soon. And then....

The back door opened with an ominous creak, and I turned. Out trudged the Pinyin Bay Perch, in all its plush, mascot-like glory.

It proceeded to tear off its own head.

The man inside the striped brown and yellow costume was gray. Gray hair, gray stubble, even a somewhat gray pallor. He squinted up at the gray sky as if the dim, overcast light hurt his eyes. And then he shuffled over to the far end of the picnic table, pulled out a cigarette from somewhere on his costume, and lit up.

"Hi," I said. "I'm Dixon."

The man in the headless Pinyin Bay Perch costume smoked listlessly. "TGIF."

"Actually, it's Thursday."

He took a drag of his cigarette and gave a smoky sigh.

"So...you work at Precious Greetings. That must be exciting."

The man sniffed a silent laugh. A stream of smoke curled from his nostrils.

"And you're a professional mascot. That must be a fun job."

The man said nothing, just shook his head vaguely. Well, I couldn't really blame him. After all, who would really want to share the lowdown about working at Precious Greetings with a total stranger? This guy had no way of knowing that I was a team player. Supportive, enthusiastic.... Actually, that would make a really good email. I pulled out my phone to compose yet another message to Mr. Flint while the Pinyin Bay Perch stubbed out his smoke, stood up and headed back into the building. I was so involved in my email that I barely had time to register what was happening, but at the last second, I hopped up out of my seat, scrambled up behind the Perch, and managed to sneak my foot in the door just before it closed.

I caught the tail end of the gray man turning down the far end of the hall. He'd taken no more notice of me following him in than he had of me talking to him at the picnic table.

Guess he wasn't a people person.

I got my bearings, figured out where Mr. Flint's office was most likely to be in relation to where I was. If I could avoid the dominatrix receptionist, it would be smooth sailing. Casually, I strolled around the perimeter of the quiet workroom, keeping my eye on the reception desk all the while. I was nearly home free when I rounded a corner and found myself face to face with a tall, imposing, tattooed wall of muscle.

Yuri.

He seemed as surprised to see me as I was to see him. He wore black leather driving gloves and a tweed overcoat big enough to wrap around me twice, though he could barely button it across his broad chest. In each hand, he held a canvas bag of groceries, bulging with fruits and vegetables. Leafy celery greens, a big purple cabbage, a bundle of parsley, and even a whole pineapple.

"That's some produce," I said conversationally.

He rolled his eyes. "The boss is on a juicing kick. Don't get me started."

"Juicing. Right. That sounds very healthy. I love juice. Orange juice, apple juice, cranberry juice...."

"Stop talking. Unless the next words out of your mouth are a very good explanation as to what you think you're doing here."

"I had an idea. Inspiration, really. I'd like another chance at that test. I think I could really nail it."

"Trust me...." He backed me into the wall, chest to chest, with a bulging bag of veggies blocking my escape from either side and his spicy cedarwood fragrance welling up between us. "You don't want to nail anything here."

Oh, I wouldn't say *that*.

His fathomless hazel eyes bored into mine, and my heartbeat did a little syncopated flip. I couldn't tell if he was threatening me or flirting with me. But it must be wishful thinking—the flirting part. Right?

I swallowed nervously. "It's just that I don't think I showed myself in the best possible light yesterday."

"You showed yourself, all right." Yuri was less than a hand's breadth away from me, and his closeness was making my knees go all to jelly. He shifted the heavy bags, so he was carrying both in his right hand. A grapefruit bounced out and rolled away in a bid for freedom. "And I'll tell you now what I told you then. This is not the place for nice boys like you."

"I'm hardly a boy—how old are you anyway? You can't be more than a few years older than—hey, watch the sleeves. I had this jacket specially tailored."

My snappy taste in clothing failed to impress him. Unceremoniously, he grabbed me by the arm, dragged me down the hall, past the formidable receptionist, and out the front door. He didn't let go until I was at the foot of the imposing gray stairs. "I'm not telling you again," he said. "Go away. And don't come back."

7

Throughout the day, I kept myself logged into my WheelMeal app and managed to do a handful of deliveries—some of them on time. But the whole encounter at Precious Greetings kept gnawing at me. My ideas were good. I knew they were. I was an enthusiastic go-getter. So, what was with the silent treatment?

When I got back home that evening, I stomped up the stairs so hard, Mr. Greaves punctuated each one of my steps with a pound of his own on the other side of the stairwell. But I didn't have time to worry about him. I was too caught up in Precious Greetings.

I found Sabina surfing the web at the far end of Uncle Fonzo's couch. It was a hideous plaid thing known as the "davenport," older than the two of us put together, but impervious to random spills and strangely comfortable. "Something doesn't add up," I declared.

Sabina pulled out her earbuds. "Isn't everything logged in that app? Times, GPS, everything?"

"Not WheelMeal—Precious Greetings."

"Oh no. You didn't enter that stupid contest, did you?"

I climbed over the end table and squeezed onto the davenport.

Even though no one in our family has smoked since we kids were still in grade school, every now and then, a faint whiff of cigar surfaced. I found it comforting, as if my uncle was still puttering around the house with a stogie clamped between his teeth. "A handful of words, a thousand dollars. Of course I entered that contest. Not only that, but I went to Precious Greetings and met Emery Flint himself.

Sabina snapped the laptop shut and gave me a wide-eyed look. "You didn't."

"I did."

"No offense, but you've always been a total dilettante. If you haven't been distracted by some other shiny object yet, you must really want this."

"I do—I can't stop thinking about it. I even made it to the second round of the contest. But like I said, something just doesn't add up. Everybody who works there is weirdly standoffish. And he has a security guard, a big Russian guy whose muscles have muscles."

"Is he cute? Does he have an accent?"

"This isn't funny, Sabina."

"You're such a sucker for accents."

I ignored the remark. It might be true, but it wasn't the point. "There's too much security. Everything is locked up so tight, you'd swear they were printing money, not greeting cards."

Sabina's dark eyes flashed, and I knew I'd managed to reel her in. Then again, between the two of us, I'd always been the instigator. That time when she was eight and I was eleven, and the two of us got in trouble for selling fake Spellcraft charms at school? Yeah, that was me. Sabina just got caught up in all the excitement and didn't stop to think about what would happen once the Spellcraft revealed itself to be a bunch of childish nonsense.

"I'm sure no one gets away with printing money these days," Sabina said, "what with all the anti-counterfeit measures in place, but I'm sure there are plenty more scammy things you could print. Coupons maybe? Gift certificates?

I didn't actually think counterfeit items were being printed…

Although, given that special proprietary ink they had, maybe they really were doing something that wasn't on the up-and-up. "Like you said before, more and more greeting card companies are going digital these days. Maybe they had to start doing something shady to make ends meet."

Sabina nodded eagerly. "And maybe that contest you entered was all part of the scheme somehow. Maybe they were looking for people they could lure into their shady business, and they saw how squeaky clean you are...."

"Not *that* squeaky clean." Spellcrafting families did have a reputation for a certain amount of hustle, after all.

"We need to take a look for ourselves," Sabina decided. She stepped over a coffee table on its side and climbed around an exercise bike with half her laundry hanging off it. "Well, what are you waiting for? Don't just sit there. Let's go."

It had seemed like such a good idea at the time—these things Sabina and I cooked up often do—until we got to Precious Greetings and found the massive chain-link fence surrounding the building closed and locked. We circled the perimeter and discovered a gap between two sections of fencing where the ground had settled. Sabina is a tiny slip of a thing, and she squeezed through the bars like a contortionist. I, however, was not so limber.

"There's no barbed wire at the top," she said helpfully. "And it's not electrified. What are you waiting for? Climb."

Although there was nobody there to see me but her—that was bad enough. I climbed that fence, albeit with the grace of a drunken three-legged sloth. Sabina had the grace not to laugh... too much.

I dropped the last few feet. My hands smelled like galvanized metal and I'd split the knee on my favorite skinny jeans, but my heart was pounding with more than just exertion. Precious Greetings lay ahead of us, dark and quiet, just waiting to give up its secrets. "The windows look awfully high. How are we going to see in?"

"Don't worry, Cuz, I got this." Sabina pulled out her wallet.

Behind the various maxed out credit cards was a tiny slip of paper. Thick. Textured. With a watercolor rectangle...and some hand-drawn lettering.

"You carry a Scrivening with you?" I asked. "If you ever got arrested, the judge would have a field day with that." Spellcraft might be technically legal. But law enforcement went hard on anyone who kept it on their person.

"Don't be such a baby. It's not like we're going to get caught."

I recognized Uncle Fonzo's calligraphy immediately. It was big and bold, and he crossed his T's with a certain flourish. It read: *Persistence opens all doors.* I supposed that rectangle could be seen as a door... Among other things. Definitely Rufus Clahd's work. "When did your father give you that?"

"After the fourth or fifth time I lost my keys and woke him up after midnight. Pretty handy, huh?" She felt all around the door-jamb, whatever she could reach, and poked and prodded the bulletproof glass door panels.

"That might work with a flimsy home lock," I said.

"A door is a door."

"This was a bad idea."

"Persistence," she said. "It's genius, when you think about it. Because otherwise, doors would just be flying open left and right as I walked by. But the way Dad Crafted this, I've got to do some fiddling first." And fiddling she did. She rattled and shoved and jiggled, but while I was discouraged, Sabina simply kept trying. And just as I was tempted to call it a night and go back to the Buick, I heard a tiny, yet satisfying click.

"Ta-da!" she said happily.

"That thing really works?"

She grinned. "Like a charm."

"Then how come you made me climb that stupid fence? Was it just to see me squirm?"

"No, silly. The fence is closed with a *gate*, not a door."

Well, she had me there. Spellcraft could be really persnickety.

We crept past the reception desk, and I stole a look at the family photos tacked discreetly to the bottom of the stern receptionist's computer. She was in a few of them, but only holding up big puff-ball of long-haired guinea pig for a selfie. Others were of the rodent, solo. In a tiny cowboy hat. Eating a stalk of celery. Lounging in the grass in a glamour shot pose.

Interesting. But it shed no light on Precious Greetings. "What is it we're looking for, exactly?" I asked.

"It's like porn, Dixon. We'll know it when we see it."

We crept into the workroom, row upon row of desks all silent beneath the yellow safety lights by the exits. Practical Penn had a similar silence late at night after my parents clocked out. And yet, there were subtle differences. Rufus Clahd's desk was a riot of paint and color. Notebooks, pens, and other office supplies littered the various workstations. Half-done projects lay everywhere.

But not at Precious Greetings. Every desk was as clean as if it had just been hauled in from the showroom.

"Does anyone actually work here?" Sabina asked.

Hopefully so. Otherwise, I'd fallen victim to a frighteningly realistic hallucination. The two of us circled around one of the desks to get a better look at it. I captured a few eraser crumbs on my finger. "Look at this—someone's been here."

"Then they must lock up everything at the end of the day. Funny that they're more careful with their greeting cards than we are with our Scrivenings."

Half-done Spellcraft wouldn't do anyone any good. Maybe there was more black market value to a partially done greeting card.

"Just keep looking," Sabina said. "Anything might be important. Once we take a good look around, we just have to connect the dots."

Funny how hard it is to locate a dot when you simply don't see any. But while I couldn't see much, I did hear something. The gentle scrape of shoe leather on floorboards.

I glanced up just in time to see a figure emerge from the hallway, safety light glinting off his oddly-quirked eyebrows.

I grabbed Sabina's arm and yanked. She looked up, startled, and gave a tiny squeal. Then we both ran like all get-out.

The broad, empty desks formed a maze in the dim safety light, and we scampered through it like a couple of long-haired guinea pigs in cowboy hats. We spilled out the far end and sprinted toward the door. I heard the other knee of my jeans rip—at least they were even now. And, bonus! I could bend my knees a heck of a lot better. We outpaced Emery Flint easily, being both younger and fueled by terror—Sabina with a not-so-legal Spellcraft in her pocket, me mortified at the probability of him recognizing me. We were well ahead of him when we got to the fence and Sabina squeezed her way through. But as she did, I realized something. I would get over my mortification a lot more easily than she would do a jail sentence for the Scrivening that got us through the doors.

"Come on, Dixon," she whispered breathlessly.

With a sad smile, I pulled the car keys out of my pocket and handed them through the chain-link.

"What is this?" she snapped. "Climb."

I shook my head. "He's right behind us. And there's no sense in us both getting caught. Go."

Sabina would've stayed—she's loyal to a fault. But I clasped her fingers through the chain-link and said, "Please? For me? Go."

"Jerk," she muttered. But by the time Emery Flint caught up with me, the Buick's tail lights were receding through the trees.

"Keep your hands where I can see them," Mr. Flint said, "and no one needs to get hurt."

Dutifully, I surrendered, and a flashlight beam played over my face. "Wait a minute. Dixon Penn—is that you?"

I'm sure the wince I gave him in return was very becoming. "Just following up...did you get my email?"

Mr. Flint dropped the flashlight beam so it was no longer shining directly in my face. I tried to back up. The chain link fence behind me bowed a little, but held firm. "I could call the cops and have you prosecuted for trespassing."

"I'm sure the cops don't want to be bothered over a simple misunderstanding. Honestly...I was just really pumped up about that contest."

"You don't seem to be able to take no for an answer—so let's settle this once and for all. One more test. And if I'm not blown away, then you stop pestering me for good. Deal?"

I was getting another chance at the thousand bucks? I could barely contain myself. "Deal!"

He pulled out his phone and made a quick call—*I need you at the office. Yes, now*—and then walked me back to the workshop with a firm hand on my elbow. Inside the menagerie, the animals I'd seen before were asleep, while some new creatures had come out of their plastic foliage—a huge moth fluttering against the side of its tank; a hedgehog rummaging through his wood chips; a troupe of tiny frogs the size of my thumbnail that filled the office with a midnight chorus. I attempted to charm Mr. Flint by asking questions about his exotic pets, but he had one word for me, and one word only. "Sit."

I sat.

Behind me, bird toenails clacked. The massive cockatoo pulled its head out from under its wing in annoyance, frilled its yellow crest, and began gurgling like a backed up water fountain. It was a disconcerting sound, but it filled the awkward silence until the door opened, and Yuri stepped in.

He was dressed in another suit that strained across his broad shoulders, this one tobacco brown, his ubiquitous leather gloves, and a slightly wrinkled dress shirt that couldn't quite button around his thick, muscular neck. I knew just the place to find clothing in unusual sizes. But judging by the disgruntled look he aimed at me, I suspected he wasn't interested in the name of my tailor.

"What is this?" he said...the accent was truly droolworthy.

"The Penn boy has convinced me to give him another chance at the exam."

"Don't be stupid," Yuri said—to his boss, or to me? "You already saw he's not...qualified."

"And yet, he just can't seem to stay away. That tells me he might have what it takes after all." Mr. Flint swept a hand through his hair—if it was a piece, it was truly good...except the way the color didn't quite match—and then flicked open a binder.

"Fine." Yuri snapped. "I'll go get him a *picture*."

"I don't think so." Mr. Flint was taking some kind of tone, though I had no idea what it might mean. He pulled a square of watercolor block from the binder and slid it across the desk to Yuri. "I'd like something fresh. Here. And Now."

Yuri was glaring so hard at his boss that when he reached into his pocket, I half-expected him to pull out a sockful of pennies and whap Mr. Flint upside the head. But what he came up with instead was a tiny metal box, scuffed and battered. A miniature paint set—one that had clearly seen plenty of wear and tear. The paints were mostly used up, some only thin slivers of pigment clinging to the edges of the pans, and the brush was smaller than his index finger.

Still glaring, Yuri took up the paintbrush in his gloved hand, grabbed the cockatoo's water bowl and dipped the bristles. "What is the sentiment?"

Flint's right eyebrow canted alarmingly. "How about a wedding? The type of card you'd give someone as they're embarking on a fresh, new relationship...one that will last a lifetime."

Yuri and swirled the tiny brush in a pan.

"Without the gloves," Mr. Flint said.

Yuri glared even harder and removed his gloves. His hands and fingers were covered in tattoos. I tried to read the words inked across his fingers but gave up when I realized the letters were Cyrillic. But then I saw something much more personal and telling: the colorful stain of paint pigment around his nail beds.

"Left-handed," Flint added.

Maybe Yuri's just ambidextrous, I told myself. But the way my pulse was going haywire—the way the very air in the room seemed to crackle with anticipation—I could hardly deny what my heart already knew.

I was in the presence of a Seer.

8

Staring at Mr. Flint the whole while, Yuri swirled the brush in a pan of brown paint that was little more than a crust in the corners. He scowled so hard his thick eyebrows drew entirely together, and then he placed the brush on the paper—left handed—and swept it across in a graceful stroke

Mr. Flint planted his hands on his hips and looked down at the small painting eagerly. "A knot? How...romantic."

"Maybe you would prefer a ball and chain."

Flint chuckled stiffly. "Russian humor. Ha ha. No, I'm sure this will do quite nicely." He pulled a heavy keyring out of his pocket and selected a tiny key. He opened his top drawer, pulled out a metal cashbox which he opened with another key. Inside that was a locked bankers bag—yet another key. And once that was unlocked and unzipped, he withdrew a silk-wrapped bundle which he conferred to reveal...a fountain pen.

The same pen I'd taken yesterday's test with—the fountain pen with the nib that looked suspiciously like a feather quill. Obviously because it actually *was* a feather quill. A quill that had once belonged to a Spellcrafter.

It's Spellcrafter tradition to bury the dead with their quills—at least that's how my grandparents were sent off. But I suppose a desperate family could stand to make a few bucks by selling one. It didn't seem like there'd be much of a market, though. Spellcraft was genetic, passed from parents to children. It's not like you could just pick up a quill on eBay, watch a few YouTube videos, and get Crafting.

At least, I didn't *think* so.

As soon as Mr. Flint unwrapped the fountain pen, Yuri snatched it away. There was a red dot of color on each of his cheeks, and his eyes roiled with fury. He was so angry he was shaking. And when he turned to hand the pen to me...he dropped it on the floor.

"Idiot," Flint yelled.

Yuri bent to retrieve the pen, and snapped, "It's fine." And maybe it was. But while he was crouched over, out of Mr. Flint's line of sight, he slipped another fountain pen from his sleeve and tucked away the one that had been kept under lock and key. With a look in his riveting hazel eyes I can only describe as pleading, he handed me the switcheroo and said, "Good luck."

Obviously, he didn't want me to Craft anything for Mr. Flint— and given how hinky the guy was acting, I could see why. But all the subterfuge was unnecessary, since I'd never Scribed a word in my life. At that point, all I wanted to do was jot down some kind of semi-coherent sentiment and get the heck out of there without anyone calling the cops.

Unless the thousand dollars was still on the table.... No, there was no thousand dollars. Was there? Probably not.

"Well?" Flint said. "It's not getting any earlier."

Right. I settled my butt cheeks in the seat, sat up straight, cupped my hand around the tip of the fountain pen to disguise the fact that it was not the modified nib, and penned the first phrase that popped into my head.

A Perfect Union.

As Scrivenings went, it wasn't bad. No loopholes for things to go horribly wrong, like the Bam Burger spell that forced them to pry their customers off the tables with crowbars. Really, I would've made a pretty good Scrivener...if it weren't for the fact that the elusive Spellcrafting "tingle" my uncle told me about was entirely absent.

Then again, what could I expect when I was writing with a mundane pen—which Yuri snatched away from me, and deftly palmed. I'm not sure which quill made it back into the locked bag in the locked box in the locked desk. All I knew was that all eyes were on the fake Scrivening...which Mr. Flint plucked off the desktop with gusto. He held it up triumphantly and asked me, "*Who* do you work for?"

"Um...WheelMeal?"

One of his eyebrows twitched. With pointed emphasis on a different word, he asked, "Who do you *work* for?"

I shook my head helplessly and repeated, "WheelMeal."

"Who do you work *for*?"

"Look," I spluttered. "I'm not proud of it, okay? But I've put in applications all over town and it was the only place I got past the first interview."

Before Flint could ask the question any more weirdly, Yuri said, "I told you he was no Spellcrafter. If he carried the talent, do you think his family would have him delivering burritos?" He plucked the paper from his boss' grasp and tossed it on the desk as if he was dealing a particularly odious hand of poker. "There's no magic here. Satisfied?"

"If you know what's good for you," Mr. Flint said to me, "you'll get out of here and never come back. No more phone calls. No more emails. I don't want to see your pathetic, hopeful face here ever again. Got it?"

"So, what you're saying is, I didn't win the prize?"

Flint rubbed his face in his hands. When he looked up, one of his eyebrows was slightly lower than the other. He gestured to Yuri and said, "Toss this useless nitwit—get him out of my sight."

Yuri hauled me up out of the seat by my armpit and wasted no time dragging me toward the door. My feet were hardly touching the ground, bicycling along without actually propelling me forward. But Yuri didn't really need my help. For such a big guy, he moved really fast.

Before we crossed the threshold, though, Flint told me, "One peep about this to anyone, and you'll regret it. Remember, we know where you live." I wasn't so sure I believed that...until he added, "You wrote it on the entry form. Oh, and Yuri—just in case the kid gets any funny ideas about talking, make sure you give him a good pounding."

My armpit was really smarting by the time we got through the bullpen, but I was so terrified, I barely noticed. "That pen he had under lock and key—was that an actual Scrivener quill? It looked like a quill. Can I see it? Because I've never seen anyone modify—"

"Stop talking."

"It's almost like he thought I was a Scrivener, y'know? As if I'd be driving for WheelMeal if I could be Spellcrafting instead—"

"Stop. Talking."

"I'm sorry, I'm just nervous—you can't blame me for being nervous when you're—"

Yuri spun me around and slammed my back into the wall beside the reception desk. The photos of the guinea pig trembled. He mashed his huge hand over my mouth—it smelled of leather. "Listen to me, Dixon, and listen good. We need to get out of here before he gives me any more orders. Get it?"

I nodded and said, "Got it." The words were pretty muffled.

Yuri dragged me out the door and down the stairs, then shoved me into the passenger seat of a battered pickup truck. The gate was open. Gravel kicked up as he floored it and put as much distance as possible (as quickly as possible) between us and Precious Greetings. And while I had a million and one questions, by that point I was so baffled, I no longer knew what to say.

You know the type of person who talks just to fill the silence? That was definitely not Yuri. He gripped the wheel tightly in his tattooed hands, glaring hard at the road ahead of us. Seething, he stuck to the back streets, guided mostly by moonlight and instinct. Pinyin Bay is not a huge city, though the outskirts sprawl into patchy expanses of bluffs on one side and cornfields on the other three. Yuri drove toward the water. Over the summer, it would be bustling with tourists who were too frugal to make a trip to the ocean. But in February, the eponymous Pinyin Bay was entirely deserted.

Back at Precious Greetings, I thought Yuri had been helping me, at least that's how I'd interpreted the look he gave me when he bent over and switched the pens. But now? Maybe I should've been less turned on and more freaked out. Why bring me to a deserted beach if not to fit me with a pair of concrete shoes? When he slammed the car into park and killed the engine, I said, "It's a little chilly for a swim, so I'm just gonna—"

Yuri climbed out, stomped around to the passenger side and yanked open the door. "Get out of the truck. And don't make this any harder than it already is. It will only be more difficult if you struggle."

My life flashed before my eyes—mainly the part where I wasted so much time delivering food when I could've been doing pretty much anything else. What a disappointment. "Listen, you don't have to do this."

"Yes. I do." He grabbed the entire back of my shirt in his meaty hand and hauled me up a walkway toward a tidy row of beach houses. They were tiny clapboard things, touristy vacation cabins with colorful gingerbread trim tacked around the windows and roofs, but shuttered with utilitarian plywood for the winter...all of them except one.

Yuri shoved open the door and dragged me in behind him. There was no wheelbarrow or sack of concrete—what a relief—but the interior was still nothing like I expected. Sure, it contained all the sorts of kitschy, beachy nick-knacks you'd expect to find in a tacky weekend getaway cabin. But they were all piled in the far corner in an unceremonious heap.

The rest of the dinky beach house was spartan. One room, none too large, served as living, eating and sleeping quarters, plus a bathroom off the side that was so narrow, Yuri must've had to back in and hope he didn't need to turn around. The bed took up most of the floor space, made up tight with a woolen army surplus blanket and a single flat pillow. I got up-close and personal with the bed when Yuri pitched me across the room like a bag of trash aimed for the top of an overflowing dumpster. I bounced once, then settled, staring up at the cedar-paneled ceiling in a daze.

I have taken a punch exactly one time in my life. I was eight. And Melissa Dombrowski's seven-year-old fist packed a huge wallop—though when little Sabina joined in the fray and threw dirt in her eyes, Melissa cried a lot harder than I did.

At any rate, I'm not sure if it was the flood of adrenaline that preceded my imminent thrashing that inspired a string of associations, or if bouncing off the mattress had managed to shake an idea loose.

*Get him out of my sight...*check.

*Toss him...*ditto.

And give him a good pounding.

I swallowed hard.

Yuri had removed his jacket, presumably to keep me from bleeding all over it, but if I was right about my suspicions, maybe the situation had another way out. "Say, Yuri." I thought I sounded pretty calm for someone who'd very nearly mastered flight. "Do you *want* to do every last thing Mr. Flint tells you to...or do you *have* to?"

"I don't know what you're talking about," he claimed. Not only was his delivery entirely unconvincing, but when I watched him really carefully, I could've sworn I saw the subtle glimmer of Spellcraft dancing along his lips.

Either that or he was wearing shimmery lip balm. But he really didn't seem like the type.

I eased myself off the scratchy blanket and sauntered up to Yuri as my best charming self—not that being charming had gotten me very far lately, but there was no time to dwell on that. I looked up at him through my eyelashes in a way that was anything but demure, and said, "I'm on board with the pounding...so long as you still respect me in the morning."

His hazel eyes went wide, and for just a second, I thought I might have entirely misread the way he'd been looking at me. But then his nostrils flared, and when he grabbed twin fistfuls of my shirt, it wasn't to pitch me across the room this time, but to drag me into a deep, searing kiss.

Flirting has always been a little hit-or-miss for me, and that moment when I realize someone likes me back is always filled with a squirmy and precarious eagerness. There's always the chance, however slim, that the body language, the banter, the pheromone cloud—or whatever subtle clue I think I've picked up on—was nothing more than my own wishful thinking. When Yuri kissed me, not only was I flooded with relief, but with yearning.

Sure, I'd manage the occasional hookup now and then. But I hadn't had a serious boyfriend since undergrad, a relationship that fizzled when we tried to take it long-distance, though even now he'll occasionally throw a "like" my way on Instagram. It wasn't that I didn't *want* to be with someone. Settling on my futon at night, staring up at the rafters and wondering how I'd ended up where I was? Beyond lonely. But how could anyone possibly take me seriously—a college-educated delivery boy who lived in an attic—until I turned my life around?

I might be trapped in a truly underwhelming circumstance, but Yuri was trapped in Spellcraft. Which made my own situation seem a heck of a lot more surmountable. Not only that—but it gave me the chance to play the hero for a change. Yuri searched for words, then sighed in frustration. Obviously, he couldn't talk about it—but that was fine. I've been told I'm able to talk enough for everybody.

I drew him down to the edge of the mattress and knelt beside him, facing him with my whole body, and took him by the shoulders—wow, they were solid—then told him, "Listen, Spellcraft can be tricky, but it's not set in stone. People need misfired Craftings untangled all the time." Of all the Penns, Uncle Fonzo was actually the most adept at Recrafting a Spell, but even so... "I've got a family full of Scriveners who can turn this around."

"Certain things are not so easy," he said under his breath.

"Well, sure." I traced the edge of his ear with my fingertip and he shivered. A black smudge of ink had leaked from the fountain pen and wicked into the callus on the knuckle of my second finger. You'd never know I hadn't picked up a real pen in months. "Nothing worth doing ever is."

I trailed my ink-stained fingers down his jaw and turned his face toward mine.

"Now, I know you can't confirm or deny anything, but if you truly are compelled to follow Mr. Flint's orders to a tee...you won't be able to think straight until you serve up my pounding."

"This is not a game," he said raggedly. His pupils had dilated and his whole body was tense.

"You're right." I slid my hand down his broad chest and fit my mouth against his, speaking in a whisper against his lips. "It isn't."

9

As much as all the major elements of my life had conspired to leave me mired in discouragement, I'm really an optimist at heart. Case in point: Sabina teases me relentlessly for keeping an extra-large condom stashed in my jacket pocket.

But who's laughing now?

Actually, not me. I was too busy having my back exfoliated on the world's roughest blanket...and loving every deep, shuddering thrust. The tiny cabin was chilly, but Yuri radiated so much body heat it warmed up fast. And as we moved together with my legs clasped around his lower back and our bodies grinding together, we even managed to work up a sweat. I wished it could last forever—or at least all night—but I was so taken by the emotion in his eyes, I couldn't help but be swept away in the heat of the moment. If I'd figured my lousy living situation took me off the market, Yuri must have despaired of ever enjoying another human touch. And yet, there we were. Moving together in that age-old rhythm, reaching not just for satisfaction...but connection.

I'd always thought there couldn't be anything worse than failing a Quilling Ceremony. But being forced into a magically indentured servitude, Spellcrafting under duress? I'd rather deliver gyros for chump change.

I'm a sucker for big, brawny guys anyhow—but add that spark of intelligence, some roughness around the edges, and a hint of magic? Yowsa. Good thing I wasn't on top—I would've finished before we even got started. And by the time Yuri dug his big hands into the rough blanket on either side of my head, balled it up in his massive fists while his whole body bucked into me and his breathing staggered, I was flying high enough to get off from nothing but the sweaty brush of our bellies.

Even though we were both wrung out and well satisfied, I felt a pang of loss when Yuri pulled out and rolled off me. That, and a momentary stab of alarm. While the two of us did the horizontal tango, he'd well and truly rocked my world—but what if he'd only been following a magical directive? If I'd taken an already bad situation and used it to my advantage, I'd never forgive myself.

Maybe I should've just let him beat me up.

Yuri glanced over at me. "What is this face?"

"Just...free-floating anxiety."

He cupped my jaw, then ran his thumb along my lower lip... and I hoped my worries were for nothing. Because yes, he had to "pound" me. But nothing required him to touch me afterward.

"Dixon. I need you to write something. Will you do this for me?"

Writing? That would be no problem. It was obvious, though, that what he wanted was for me to Scribe. "I know you can't say it, not in so many words. But what you're asking me to do? I would if I could, but I simply haven't got the gift. The talent runs in my family, but it managed to skip me. And that's just the way it is."

Trailing a caress across my chest that left me shivering in the cedar-scented dimness, Yuri salvaged his jacket from the floor, pulled out the modified fountain pen, and pressed it into my hand.

"Yuri...."

"Try," he murmured. "For me."

He poked through my pockets and came up with a stray receipt, then dug out his battered metal paintbox and slipped on a pair of glasses off the nightstand. (Glasses? As if he could possibly be any more adorable.) Perched naked on the edge of the mattress, hulking, tattooed and criss-crossed with old, faded scars, Yuri was the absolute picture of concentration. He smoothed the receipt over his knee, dampened the tip of the minuscule paintbrush on his tongue, and captured a trace of gouache.

On YouTube, I've watched Seers create miniature scenes so detailed it looked like you could step right inside and inhabit them. The recordings were time-lapsed, and spanned hours, even days. In person, I'd watched Rufus Clahd paint his misshapen, clunky strokes that somehow managed to capture enough magic to Craft with. But watching Yuri work was fascinating.

He peered at the slip of paper with a grim intensity, sifting through his internal landscape, filtering the image, perfecting it. And only when he fully grasped the essence of what he wished to convey did he touch brush to paper. As gestures went, it was bold. All-in. And at first I thought it might be nothing but a gray stroke on a white field.

But then I looked closer.

The stroke itself was too dry to be solid, and where the sable of the brush had split, gaps appeared in the paint. But Yuri had varied the pressure so those gaps opened and closed like tiny white islands in the stroke. In the center, he'd lifted off entirely, allowed the paint to spatter, then continued the stroke to the other side of the receipt. He handed it to me. I stared for a moment, and then what I was actually seeing clicked.

Not just an artfully-rendered chain—but a broken one.

As a rule, Seers call the shots. And if a client wants them to Craft something that rubs them wrong, all bets are off. How long had Yuri been bound to Flint, forced to See whatever Craftings were demanded of him? He couldn't tell me, not in so many words. But in the simple gesture of that chain, I saw it must have been quite a while. "Even if I had the ability to Scribe, whatever it is that's holding you back came first. In the hands of a good Scrivener, maybe it could be unmade. But I've never heard of one Crafting being negated by another."

"I knew a man in the old country who could do it. The *volshebstvo* was strong in him."

Yuri must've missed the part where I held no *vols*...omething at all.

Or maybe it just felt better to hope than to admit defeat. He took my hand in his and ghosted a fingertip across the first knuckle of my middle finger. His cuticles were stained with pigment, my callus with ink. It was the match my mother had dreamed about ever since I defied the dinner table to give me flak about my big announcement. A Seer and a Scrivener. But this Scrivener had no talent, and the Seer was magically bound to someone else.

Yuri took my hand in both of his as if it was something fragile and precious, and said, "Please. Try."

I'm not religious. But it felt profane to take up the mangled remains of another Scrivener's quill and pretend to Scribe onto an actual Seen. Even so, with Yuri watching me, brittle with hope, I felt I had to at least make the effort, even if it was only to show him that what he wanted simply wasn't possible. We could bring the Seen to one of my family members who actually had it in them to Craft, but none of them had ever undone someone else's Scrivening by Crafting something new. Not even Uncle Fonzo.

I pulled on my jeans and took the receipt over to the counter-top of the tiny kitchenette. Once I brushed away a few crumbs, I smoothed the paper flat. It was tempting to simply tear off the bandaid—write the first thing that popped into my head and declare, "See? I told you it wouldn't work." But I'd have to look into Yuri's earnest face as I said it. And so, I couldn't just pretend to try.

I shook out my writing hand, took a steadying breath, and cleared my mind until all it held was the image of the breaking chain. So much easier than trying to make sense of one of Rufus Clahd's distorted blots. I could practically see it coming to life, a painted chain pulling taut with a quiver—and snap! Both sides fall to the ground. It wasn't just my overactive imagination—it was the power of Yuri's painting.

What a shame to waste it on such a hopeless endeavor. But even as I despaired, words floated to the surface of my mind in that way they occasionally do, when I used to practice with the expectation I'd ace my Quilling Ceremony and take my place in the family business. I was so caught up in the fantasy that we'd actually create something that I felt the tingle in my writing hand—the one that meant nothing more than wishful thinking—as I penned the words: *Free in Body, Mind and Spirit.*

There were too many strikes against us. Even had I actually been a Scrivener, it was a long shot to hope any new Spellcraft could override what came before. I gave Yuri a sidelong glance just in case some miracle happened, and by the strength of his Seen alone, a few hopeful words could set him free. He picked up the receipt, stared at it—attempted to absorb it. "Nothing."

My heart sank. I snatched the paper from him and balled it up, but he stopped me. "Just hold onto it." He tucked the wad into my jeans—right into that tiny little pocket where nothing really fits. "A little something to remember me by."

"I'm not leaving you," I told him. "I'm going back to find the Crafting. The only way is to unmake it."

"Don't be stupid. Go back to your shop and forget about me."

No. Despite the fact that I couldn't help Yuri myself, I was determined to undo whatever malignant Spellcraft had been done. Moral, upright people tend to look askance at Spellcraft. Even when it's done to the utmost ethical standards, people see it as cutting corners, like buying a cake at a grocery store and claiming it's your grandma's recipe.

Spellcraft might influence, but it should never command. No shop worth their salt would actually Craft something that impinged upon a specific person's freedoms. So, if we could just get our hands on the Crafting, someone in my family would surely be willing to unravel the magic.

"Can you tell me what happened to the Scrivener who wrote the Spell that's holding you?" I ventured.

Yuri's jaw worked, but he didn't answer.

"Okay, maybe not. But whatever the reason, if Flint is trawling for a Scrivener, it means someone else runs the risk of getting scooped up under false pretenses. Probably someone I know. I might not have inherited the gift—but I'm not Handless. Scriveners are still my people."

"You are determined to go back to Precious Greetings." It was more of a statement than a question. "No matter what."

"I'm just not willing to walk away from this." Not if it meant leaving Yuri behind.

"The next time Flint gives me an order, he will not be so sloppy about it."

"Then we'd better make sure there *is* no next time."

YURI

10

Back in Russia, where every gay person is a "pervert" who's fallen victim to a pedophile's propaganda, this was how I always imagined it would be once I got to America. A society swimming in gallons of soda and covered in big box stores? Sure. But somewhere I could be who I really was without fear of finding myself on the wrong end of some corrupt policeman's nightstick.

Except I wasn't really free. I'd just experienced a few moments of something that disguised itself as freedom. And all the while, I was only skirting the edges of Emery Flint's commands.

Dixon was the first man I'd made love to on American soil—and if that was the only thing we shared, it would be plenty. But he was also the first man to put his lips to mine like his whole heart was behind the kiss. And the first one to break in pleasure at just the feel of me inside his body.

Maybe this was what it was like to grow up without stigma and shame.

Though when I looked at Dixon and saw the fierceness in his dark eyes, I knew it was more than just a different set of circumstances.

He was special.

Unfortunately, Emery Flint was also in a class of his own. I thought all Americans were gullible and soft—chum in the shark-infested waters of reality, bobbing in the waves, waiting to be gobbled up.

Again, I was wrong.

Every time I tried to tell Dixon he was in danger—to get as far away from Emery Flint as possible—my tongue froze, and the words died before I could speak them aloud.

As we approached the building, I tried to figure out some way to warn him without actually speaking the words. Euphemisms are powerful things. But even those locked me up tighter than a jar of paint with the lid crusted on. And all I could do was sit in my dread, and hope I could manage to distract Flint well enough for Dixon to get away.

"So, what's the deal here?" Dixon asked.

Precious Greetings was nothing more than a front for Emery Flint to run illegal Spellcrafting. He lured in unsuspecting Scriveners and Seers, and exploited their talents for both his gain, and his sickening sense of shrewd entitlement. He forced us to Craft things that would land us in prison for sure—and while American minimum security incarceration was nowhere near as bad as a Russian penal colony, I for one did not want to end up behind bars. Or worse, deported. And now Flint's Scrivener was gone, and he was desperate for another.

That's what the deal was. I longed to tell Dixon. But all I could do was shrug.

Dixon batted his eyelashes and gave me a look that was part conspiratorial, part seductive, and tapped his earlobe. "You can whisper it to me if you want."

Oh, I wanted to do *many* things. But Flint's Crafting wouldn't allow it.

"How about I try to guess—and if I just so happened to figure out what's what, maybe you could remark on the weather. Let's see... Mr. Flint is in witness protection. New name, new identity, new hair—that's where the toupee comes in."

Actually, the hair was real. I snorted.

"No? Maybe he's got amnesia—and all the Spellcrafting is some way to try and regain his lost memories. Or else...ooh, wait, I know. Secret twin."

"This is no laughing matter." Vague enough to evade the bonds of Spellcraft locking me down? Apparently. But no less true.

Dixon took my hand in his and threaded our fingers together. It might seem like a small thing. But it was a small thing I never thought I'd experience. The men I knew in Russia might kneel down and unzip your fly—but they'd never hold your hand. It should have been a happy moment; instead, it was bittersweet.

I couldn't let Flint sink his claws into this tenacious young man. I refused. Though when my body allowed me to let us into the darkened Precious Greetings studio to find the Spellcraft holding me captive, I had to wonder if maybe I was not actually rebelling, but playing right into my enemy's hand.

DIXON

11

Breaking into Precious Greetings was a heck of a lot easier now, since Yuri had the keys. But he seemed pensive and discouraged, even though I was confident I could set things right. Maybe I couldn't personally unmake the Spellcraft holding him hostage... but I could ask my parents to help. Running to Mom and Dad might not make me look particularly sexy...but if it could help Yuri, I'd do it in a heartbeat.

"Okay," I said, "I know you can't tell me anything, so I'm just gonna spitball out loud. Mr. Flint might be carrying around the Crafting itself, but I don't think so. Because he's tied to the spell, but he's not actually the subject. And it's not on you, either, because you're a Seer, and if you had easy access to it, you might 'accidentally' use it for scratch paper in such a way that you negate the magic. So, the next logical place to look is his office."

Yuri couldn't answer. But I liked to think he looked pleased with my powers of deduction.

Even without Emery Flint inside, the office was active 24/7. It was just a few hours before dawn, but the nocturnal critters were still rustling around, while the diurnal ones were annoyed with our intrusion. "I don't suppose you can throw me a hint," I said with my most winning smile.

Yuri looked at me blandly.

"That's fine. I love a good puzzle." I started at Mr. Flint's desk, but the drawers were locked, and Yuri's keys didn't fit. I pondered the lock, stumped, then realized a bit of reverse psychology might help me figure things out. "Say, Yuri, do you suppose you can pry this open?"

Yuri grabbed a letter opener off the desk—it looked like a miniature sword—and jammed it into the seal.

"Never mind," I said. Because if he was able to try, then that wasn't where the Crafting was hidden. I cast around, overwhelmed by the sheer busyness of the room, the terrariums and aquariums, the decorations and doodads. Every surface was covered in color and texture, and dozens upon dozens of words. Samplers and motivational posters warred with framed sentiments and calligraphy. So many trite, kitschy sayings, I might never spot an actual Spellcraft among them.

But maybe I could recognize Yuri's painting.

From afar, many miniature scenes looked like they could've originated in that tiny, battered Russian paintbox. But up close, none of them held the confident elegance of Yuri's hand. I scanned carefully, up, down and across, inching my way along the wall. Something chittered at me—oh God, Mr. Flint had an actual monkey in his office. And it really stunk. But I kept my eyes on the prize and continued searching for Yuri's work.

"Can you tell me if I'm warmer? No? That's okay—got to be here somewhere." I picked my way through an ant farm, a case of taxidermy butterflies, and some truly sappy kitten paintings. I scoured that room from end to end and top to bottom. But when it was all said and done...nothing really spoke to me. "I don't get it," I finally admitted. Yuri stood with his back to the door and his massive arms crossed, but said nothing. "This is the logical place for him to keep it. Unless it's just not scary...enough."

As I finished the thought, my gaze fell on a terrarium. A small, plain thing—unassuming, really, compared to the other exotic habitats all butting up against one another. Just a glass cube with some dry moss, a hunk of driftwood and a shallow bowl of water.

And in the background, a small laminated card. I couldn't tell what the painting was from where I stood. But even from across the room, I could see the painting was colorful and confident and gestural. My mouth went dry, and I swallowed against my sudden nervousness. Even before I saw it up close, I knew in my gut it had to be the thing I was looking for: Yuri's Crafting.

Hopefully he hadn't been instructed to dismantle anyone who happened upon it.

"Maybe you want to leave the office?" I was aiming for a playful tone, but mostly it came out strained.

"I believe in you, Dixon."

I peered through the glass. The hermit crab, or whatever it was, had burrowed under the driftwood, leaving the Spellcraft in plain sight. I could see where it could easily be mistaken for a greeting card—that's exactly what it looked like. A valentine. With a red heart that looked like it was soaring, and the simple words, "Be Mine."

I might not be a Scrivener, but even I could see the tiny card was crackling with Spellcraft. "Okay, then. Here goes nothing."

The terrarium was thick and sturdy, with a door in the lid for feeding and cleaning that was held shut with a simple latch. It wasn't even locked.

Maybe that should've been my first indication that it wasn't quite what it seemed. But I was so focused on retrieving that tiny magical valentine, I didn't realize what was happening until an alarm blared, emergency lights flooded the dim room, and the top of the terrarium snapped shut, trapping my hand inside.

The alarm was loud—so loud I nearly wrenched my shoulder trying to cover my ears. At that point, I realized two things: one, apparently I'm very sensitive to loud noises. And two, the terrarium must've been bolted down, 'cause that thing didn't even budge.

I wasn't the only one none too keen on the bleating alarm. The stinky monkey started shrieking, baring its tiny yellow fangs in an unsettling grimace. The cockatoo stuck its crest straight up and began bobbing like a punk rocker in a mosh pit.

And the driftwood inside the terrarium trembled as the creature beneath it was roused.

Yuri was across the desk from me—no more than a couple of yards away—but all he could do was stand there stiffly as if even breathing was difficult for him. He squinched his eyes shut and shouted over the alarm, "I am not telling you this specifically, just making conversation—I happen to know a few things about tarantulas."

Oh crap.

I watched in horror as, inches from my poor, exposed right hand, one fuzzy leg probed the gravel—then another, then another, as an impossibly big, hairy, spiderish body squeezed out from beneath the driftwood.

Yuri called out, "Tarantulas don't attack unless they're threatened."

There were plenty of spiders in the attic. Sabina enlisted me to kill them on a weekly basis. I never thought I was scared of them... until now. Suddenly, every spider death in which I'd been a culprit was coming home to roost. I tugged hard on my arm, twisting and pulling, but my hand was well and truly trapped.

"If a hypothetical person wished to be ignored by a tarantula, they should stay as still as possible."

I pulled harder, but it was no good. My hand was clamped just below the wrist bone, and unless I could dislocate my thumb, no amount of yanking would help me.

The tarantula, meanwhile, must have mistaken my hand for a pale, fleshy, five-legged playmate. It tiptoed over and began to circle beneath it while I splayed my fingers and did my best to keep them out of reach. I turned my head away, so I didn't need to see the massive spider considering my hand.

"Tarantulas have poor vision," Yuri announced, as if he was giving an eighth-grade science report, "but the hairs covering their bodies are very sensitive. They explore their world by the sense of touch."

I told myself the shrilling alarm totally covered up the high-pitched whine that was suddenly escaping my throat.

"This hypothetical person I have never met who didn't want to threaten a tarantula should stop moving their hand around," Yuri said urgently.

"But...it's...touching...meeeeee."

It was just a poke of the foot—nothing worse than being prodded by a cotton swab. And yet, some primitive part of me was going into full-on *OH GOD SPIDER* meltdown mode. Luckily, the creature soon grew bored with poking at me, and paused to itch at its butt with one of its hind legs.

Yuri, however, looked distinctly unhappy about this.

"When certain species of tarantula feel threatened, they kick barbed hairs off their back to ward off the threat."

My hand began to prickle. "Oh, come *on*."

"Species which do this are not as venomous as others," Yuri said helpfully.

"It's venomous?" I shrieked, *waaay* louder than the alarm, and started hauling at my arm for all I was worth.

It was then that Emery Flint sauntered in, treating us to the world's most patronizing slow-clap—one which hopefully wouldn't provoke the threatened tarantula into an all-out venomous attack.

"And here we are again," Mr. Flint crowed to Yuri. "You, me, and a decidedly unmolested Dixon Penn."

"Oh, I molested him, all right," Yuri said quickly, and then flushed redder than the scarlet gouache in his paintbox.

Mr. Flint's whole face registered shock—all but his eyebrows, which merely went a little cockeyed. "Really? Well, I'll be. No wonder you were so keen to take any work visa you could find." He gave me the side-eye. "And no wonder this little weasel was able to turn you against me. Don't worry, I forgive you—but I won't make the mistake of abandoning you to his dubious charms again. Come on, Yuri, let's shut off this alarm before my head splits open."

Yuri glowered like he'd enjoy nothing more than watching that exact thing transpire, but when Mr. Flint turned to leave me there with my hand stuck in the tarantula trap, he followed without a backward glance.

"This is so not fair," I told the gigantic, venomous, itchy-haired spider. "I don't care if it was a twisted bit of Spellcraft that brought Yuri and me together. It doesn't matter whether or not I can Scribe—I think we'd be good together anyhow. In fact, I *know* we would. But if Mr. Flint doesn't have Yuri kill me outright, at the very least, he'll make it so we never see each other again. And all I'll have to remember this night by is...."

The lousy wad of failed Spellcraft in my pocket.

I dug it out—awkwardly, with my left hand straining to reach my right pocket—and eased open the crumpled ball of receipt paper with my thumb. Yuri's painting was inspired, and my calligraphy wasn't half bad. *Free in Body, Mind and Spirit.*

If only our attempt had worked. If only I'd inherited the Craft. If only I wasn't stuck in this ridiculous....

My gaze fell on an electrical cord that connected the base of the terrarium to an outlet on the wall. I'd presumed it was for the heat lamp. But the sensor that clamped the jaws shut must've been powered by something too. It was a real stretch—I very nearly dislocated my shoulder reaching with my right foot for all I was worth—but on the third try, I snagged the cord and yanked it from the wall.

With the alarm still shrilling and every last animal in the menagerie either hiding or screeching, the tarantula tank went dark and the lock sprang open. But before I yanked my hand out of that den of itchiness for good, I made sure to snag the thing I'd been after in the first place: the tiny bit of magic—one simple image, two simple words—binding Yuri to do the bidding of Emery Flint.

Laymen think getting rid of Spellcraft is as easy as tearing up the Crafting. Not so. Uncle Fonzo once told me, "You think Spellcraft lives in pictures and words? That's only part of it. The rest of the magic is in the skill of the Seer and the intent of the Scrivener. And those things don't go away so easy."

Destroy a Crafting, and you might release the magic. But there was also a chance of it sticking around permanently. The only sure way to dispose of Spellcraft for good was to Uncraft it first. In the case of a misfired Crafting like the one at Bam Burger—*Come for the Food, Stay for the Atmosphere*—I'd simply add the line, *Leave with a Smile.*

Since I wasn't a Scrivener, though, my ideas didn't matter.

In this case, my best bet was to replace the Crafting with a decoy and smuggle out the tiny card so someone competent could undo it. I sat down at Mr. Flint's desk, grabbed one of his business cards from a bronze holder, flipped it over to the blank side, and jabbed my palm with the dull letter opener until I drew blood. With just a few smears, I approximated Yuri's soaring heart painting. The color would be a lousy match as the blood dried and turned brown, but it didn't need to fool Mr. Flint forever. Just long enough for me to smuggle the real Crafting out of there.

I flapped the card in the air, hoping for my blood to dry just enough for me to add the lettering, and cast around for a pen.

And found nothing.

I was seated at a desk. How could there not be a single pen in sight? Papers, sure. Plenty of papers. I scattered them all over searching for something to write with, but came up with nothing I could use while the alarm bell bleated. Rubber cement, sticky notes, an "insult of the day" calendar, a tiny pencil sharpener, even an inkwell. But no pen. Then I thought back to the modified quill Flint had produced from the locked pouch in the locked box in the locked drawer. Yuri still had the real quill—but he'd swapped another fountain pen in its place. If I could just get to that—

I was going at the locked drawer for all I was worth when a shadow loomed overhead. When I jerked back in surprise, something bounced off my head, then dropped to the desk in front of me.

A single white feather.

The cockatoo landed clumsily on the desk, crest high, bobbing up and down and whooping along with the alarm. It would be some sort of poetic justice—or maybe just irony—if I managed to slip this trap with an actual feather quill. But you can't just pluck a feather from a bird and write with it. The tip has to be cut to hold the ink properly. I knew full well how to cut a nib. I'd practiced so many times I could do it in my sleep. But without a blade....

The cockatoo flapped its wings. Papers rustled, and the tiny pencil sharpener tumbled across the desk. The tiny plastic pencil sharpener with the even smaller metal blade inside.

That would do.

In mere moments, I'd crushed the pencil sharpener between my molars and freed the minuscule blade. It was so small I could barely hold it, but it was enough to take to a feather and create a pen.

I thanked my lucky stars for the inkwell. Even though the gouge on my palm had already clotted over, it really stung. Not to mention the itchy spider fur. Once I inked my quill and made a few preliminary test strokes, I studied the Crafting that bound Yuri to get a feel for the lettering. The penmanship was shaky and awkward, but I should be able to mimic it well enough to pass from across the room. With my plan in place, I set the tip to the fake Seen. But when my quill touched the cardstock, my hand erupted in tingles. At first, I took it for an allergic reaction—the onset of severe anaphylaxis—but when my throat didn't close, I realized the tingling had nothing to do with the tarantula fuzz.

My feather might not have dropped from the sky at my Quilling Ceremony...but this was definitely no ordinary feather, and it fit in my hand as if I'd been born to hold it. I looked at the bird in wonder, hoping to share this joyful moment of revelation. It kept right on bobbing and weaving, dancing its loopy bird-dance and shrieking along with the alarm.

I couldn't be entirely sure that I wasn't just having a hallucinatory dream brought on by tarantula venom. But if I truly was the Scrivener now that I always thought I would be, I couldn't Craft alone. The Spellcraft would be no good on my bloody heart. It would only work on a real Seen.

I spotted the receipt—Free in Body, Mind and Spirit—and briefly considered adding Yuri's name. I discarded that idea just as fast. The way I'd Crafted the rest of the Scrivening, putting his name on it could very well kill him. No, if I wanted to free Yuri, the only way to do it was to unmake the Spellcraft that bound him to Emery Flint.

With trembling breath, I cleared my mind and studied the Spellcraft I'd liberated from the tarantula tank, much more carefully now than I had when I'd just been making a quick duplicate.

Be Mine.

The only word I could think of that started with *mine* was *mineral.* And while I didn't think Spellcraft was powerful enough to turn Yuri into a pillar of salt, I couldn't risk it. Okay, add something to the front instead. *Maybe mine?* No, too vague.

Never be vague in your Crafting, Uncle Fonzo used to say. *The magic is wily—and vagaries are where the failure slips in.*

Okay.

Breathe. Think.

Be Mine. Be Mine....

Be. Mine.

The alarm stopped, though the cockatoo kept right on bobbing and shrilling. He wasn't nearly as loud, but it meant Mr. Flint had turned off the alarm and was now coming back toward me—unless I could stop them by thinking of a word other than mineral that made the Scrivening read something else. But try as I might, nothing made sense. I racked my brain until I saw two men emerge into the bullpen, heading right for Mr. Flint's office—where surely he'd tell Yuri to wring my neck, and force him to carry that memory with him for the rest of his life.

I was just about to settle for Maybe Mine—though who knew what it might result in—when I realized the letters of the penmanship were far enough apart for me to sneak letters both in and around the words. Just as Mr. Flint crossed the bullpen, I dipped the fresh, white quill again, and with the Spellcraft raging through my veins, set pen to paper.

YURI

12

When Emery Flint shielded the alarm from me with one hand and keyed in his code with the other, I wanted nothing more than to grab that finger and snap it right off. But even though I was trembling with the urge to hurt him, all I could do was stand by and watch.

The noise died down, and Flint turned to me with a self-satisfied grin. "Never fear, Yuri—I won't make you do away with your new playmate. Contrary to popular belief, he's actually pretty valuable. Sometimes the road to success has a few pitstops along the way. It's all about patience—being in it for the long game. Fonzo Penn should've been the answer to my prayers—the most slippery Scrivener Pinyin Bay has ever known. But he'd rather gnaw off his own quill then partner up with me? So be it."

I've never met Fonzo, but I suspected I'd be able to relate to the man. However he fell in with Flint—if his best option now was to abandon both his family and his quill, his other choices couldn't have been good.

Flint turned away and began striding across the bullpen. "I got his quill," Flint went on, "I've got his nephew...and maybe the kid can't Scribe himself, but we can use him to pull the daughter in."

I hated Flint. I always had. But now the urge to rip him limb from limb was so strong it might very well kill me. Except....

When I closed the gap between us...when I flexed my fingers and anticipated how satisfying it would be to sink them into his arrogant throat...the painfully stiff pins-and-needles feeling I'd get when I so much as *thought* of going against him was entirely absent. Which could mean only one thing.

Dixon Penn had done it.

Somehow, I was free.

It seemed like there should have been some external cue—fireworks. Or at least a burst of light. But Flint just went on as if I was still frozen in his web of magical compulsion.

"That Dixon kid might not be the sharpest rock in the box...but I'm sure he'll make excellent bait."

I straightened my fingers experimentally. Clenched my fist. Then, as we approached the office, took a few long strides and overtook him.

It must have been the sound of my footsteps that alerted him something wasn't quite right. When he spun around to face me, I pinned him to the floor-to-ceiling window with my arm across his throat. I pressed, hard, and imagined the feel of his windpipe collapsing like the core of a paper towel roll. He struggled and scratched, and his feet scrabbled against the linoleum. One of his ridiculous eyebrows dropped off and landed on my sleeve. But I held fast. I was so full of pent-up anger, it was as if I'd been storing it up all these many months, just waiting for somewhere to release my fury.

"Let...go...of...me...."

The words were a dry wheeze. And they held no power over me at all.

I thrust my face into his and said, "You are not now, nor will you ever be, a Spellcrafter. And if you ever try to control me again, I will show you exactly what it means to be Handless."

DIXON

13

"So…" I murmured. "His *eyebrows* were fake." Somehow, I'd totally missed that. Guess it's not something you see every day. "And what about the first Seen I wrote on, the one that didn't Craft—did you paint it right-handed?"

Yuri looked pretty pleased with himself. "I did. And I kept my gloves on, too."

Mr. Flint's office lit with the wan sunlight creeping over the horizon. The Pinyin Bay Perch costume was slumped in the corner, looking deflated, or possibly just hungover, without an actual person inside. While the animal menagerie squawked and screeched (or in the itchy tarantula's case, hid in his gravel) Yuri and I stared out at the bullpen where Mr. Flint was trussed to one of the drafting tables like a sacrificial virgin. Yuri had been eager to exact a very personal revenge, but I'd managed to convince him it wasn't worth the risk of him harming his hand.

Seers are so few and far between, after all.

Yuri stroked his chin-stubble and said, "Flint thought Spellcrafting was something he could learn, if only he found someone willing to teach him."

"Good luck with that. Any oath-breaker who went around spewing secrets to the Handless would not only get themselves in trouble, but their whole family."

Yuri shifted uneasily.

"And the eyebrows?" I prompted.

He made a vague gesture. "His lessons were less than successful."

What I wouldn't have given to be a fly on the wall the day he blew off his own eyebrows for good. "So, when he figured out Spellcraft wasn't learnable, he moved on to entrapping Crafters—and that's how you ended up here?"

Yuri nodded sadly. "Just like you. *Magic draws magic*—once you were in the spell's influence, you couldn't stay away."

Good thing. Who else would've had the inspiration to change *Be Mine* to *Able and Determined*? So much better than *Be Mineral*.

"Funny, how the Crafting knew I had the gift, but my Quilling Ceremony was a total flop. What are the chances?"

Yuri looked pointedly out the window, and I realized that for someone who'd just defeated his mortal enemy, he was acting awfully subdued.

"Yuri?"

He reached into his coat and drew out a fountain pen—the pen Flint had used to try to trick me into Scribing for him—and handed it to me. He said, "It's impossible to Scribe without a quill."

Obviously. That was Spellcraft 101. Yet I had the sense Yuri was trying to get me to infer something, but without actually coming right out and saying it. My Quilling Ceremony. The pen. The fact that he couldn't bring himself to meet my eyes.

"You're holding the oath-breaker's quill," he said softly.

I suppressed a shudder. "That's awful. His poor family."

"Dixon..." His hand fell to my knee, and it occurred to me that his voice was filled with a deep sorrow. And of all the clues, it was the sadness in his tone that caused all the pieces to fall into place.

I dropped the fountain pen as if it was venomous, this horrible mangled thing that had once carried my birthright.

My failed ceremony.

Uncle Fonzo's relentlessly repeated question.

What do you think happened?

Well, now I knew, didn't I? Scribing that traditional Quilling phrase had felt like writing the empty sentiment with the switcheroo pen. Just words—nothing more.

You'd think the most painful betrayal would come from a lover. But no, it was family.

"Don't blame your uncle," Yuri said. "You see how easy it was to fall into Flint's trap."

I swallowed hard. I'd been advocating to bring the authorities down on Emery Flint's head. "But if we call in the police, then everyone will know. My family—" Cast out of the Spellcrafting community, just as surely as the tip of Fonzo's quill had been castrated to make the freakish hybrid pen. "My parents will lose the business," I whispered. "And all their friends. They'll lose everything."

Yuri gave my knee a squeeze, not so much in reassurance— actually, it kind of hurt—but to pull me out of the shock. "Only if word gets out."

"But how could it possibly stay a secret? If we file a report of illegal Spellcrafting, everyone will know Uncle Fonzo leaked our secrets to a Handless."

"In Russia, the police were all corrupt. I had no use for a bunch of bullies with their hands out for bribes." He took *my* hand in his— my right hand, his left—and a tingle raced up my arm that had nothing to do with how sexy I found his tattooed fingers. "It's better to handle this ourselves. No cops. Just you and me. Do you agree?"

"In theory, sure."

"No theories." He raised my hand to his lips and brushed a kiss across my knuckles. My whole body lit up. "Close your eyes, Scrivener, and think about what he's done to you and yours. What words come to mind?"

Revenge would be an understandable motivation, but when I considered the word, it didn't quite fit. I went through a few others, trying them on and shedding them just as quickly, like so many pairs of jeans in the world's most esoteric fitting room. "I don't want to get back at him," I said finally. "I just want to make it right."

Another tingle rippled down my arm, and Yuri shivered. "Then that is exactly what we will do."

He let go of my hand and pulled out his tiny paintbox, borrowed a water dish from the tank of a sleeping tortoise, and set to work. Moments later, he slid a miniature painting over to me—a painting of a fish. I didn't understand, not intellectually, anyhow. But my heart recognized its rightness.

The inkwell was nearly dry, but there was enough ink to pen a line or two. Good thing. Only weirdos make a habit of Scribing in blood. I thought through my letterforms and set the cockatoo quill to paper, and before I could second-guess myself, I Scribed the phrase *Recompense and Justice*. Our two original halves, image and word, Scrivening and Seen, became a single, focused Crafting— and only then did I recognize the tiny, gestural painting for what it was.

"Is that the Pinyin Bay Perch?"

Yuri smiled grimly. "As you say in English: Keep your friends close, and your enemies closer."

When I squinted at the painting, I marveled at the resemblance he'd been able to capture in such a small image. The striped markings. The matted fuzz of the plush material. But the most impressive detail of all was the Perch's expression. It was some- where between confused and surprised—thanks to the addition of a cockeyed pair of greenish-brown eyebrows.

14

~~s~~

Because of our Scrivening, the wheels of justice turned with
blinding speed. Bright and early the next morning, Bayside
Savings and Loan came collecting on a late repayment, and by the
end of the week, Precious Greetings was up for auction.

Yuri and I sat in the battered pickup truck and watched the
Pinyin Bay Perch wandering back and forth on the side of the road,
at the highway entrance ramp between the two busiest service
stations on that side of town, holding a sign that read, *Business
Liquidation Sale - Everything Must Go.* It was unseasonably warm
for Valentine's Day, and surely Emery Flint was sweltering inside.

Good.

Yuri brushed his pigment-stained fingertip over the inky callus
on my knuckle. "Will you bid on the business? With everything
he's stolen from your family, you could have it for a song."

"I thought about it long and hard." I managed to keep from
snerking over my choice of words, though I couldn't quell the
impulse to glance toward Yuri's fly. "In fact, I've been thinking
about lots of things. My family is beyond ecstatic. Not only that

I'm a Scrivener myself, but that I've found a special someone."

Yuri might look mean enough to send a tarantula packing, but at the mention of my family, he paled. "What did you tell them?"

"Nothing. Yet. But my mom can't help but notice the fact that I've been smiling so much my face literally hurts."

He let his breath out carefully. "It will take some time for me to get used to people of that generation accepting me...accepting *us*."

"Accepting? They're beside themselves with joy that I've snagged a boyfriend. Just wait till they find out you're a Seer." I gave a contented sigh. "I suspect I could very well end up the new owner of Precious Greetings if I chose that route. Or I could let my folks start grooming me to take over Practical Penn. Heck, maybe I could even merge them both. But if these last few days have taught me anything, it's that there's more to life than Crafting spells for money. I could make a real difference in the world, but not if I'm cooped up behind a desk."

Yuri slid me a knowing look. "Or maybe you'd rather charge someone ten times as much as a freelancer to undo a bad Crafting."

I gave him my best innocent smile. "But that's half what you'd pay at one of the bigger shops." Though all the Bam Burgers I cared to eat had also been a wonderful incentive.

Fine. Specializing in Uncrafting *was* pretty lucrative. And I definitely needed the cash if I ever hoped to get rid of our thumpy tenant. But that wasn't my main motivation.

Spellcraft was volatile and unreliable—and the Handless only tolerated it with the same long-suffering distaste they usually reserved for ambulance-chasing lawyers—but it was my birthright. And, damn it, I was good at it. After everything I'd struggled through to finally claim my quill, though, I wanted to be more than just a Scribe for hire. Especially since my Craftings could have such profound effects elsewhere, righting the subtle wrongs of the world.

Was our first official Spellcrafting—*Recompense and Justice*—entirely legal? With the right lawyers and a sympathetic judge, we'd probably get away with a stern warning. I hadn't specifically named Emery Flint, after all, and it could certainly be argued that sometimes, an eyebrow was just an eyebrow.

My second act as a bona fide Spellcrafter was to defuse the Crafting that was drawing unwary Scriveners and Seers to Precious Greetings. *Magic Draws Magic.* The malformed magnet behind the words could be none other than a pilfered Rufus Clahd painting—yet another way in which Uncle Fonzo had bent the rules. But how annoyed could I realistically be over his dubious choices when, ultimately, his involvement with Precious Greetings led me to Yuri? I changed the last word to "Magically"—making it a rather weird and obvious statement instead of a command—and gave it to Yuri for safekeeping. I suspect he might have eaten it to ensure it didn't fall into the wrong hands again.

I looked at Yuri out of the corner of my eye as he watched Flint caper for the passing cars. Yuri simply sat—cool and collected, muscular and tattooed. And above it all, profoundly vigilant, taking everything in with his shrewd hazel eyes. There was zero doubt in my mind that if I hadn't intervened, there'd be no more Emery Flint to drag through muck—just shreds of bone and gristle, and a stray prosthetic eyebrow.

I liked to think I was a good influence on Yuri. He wore his freedom well. As if he could sense my satisfaction washing over him, he turned to meet my gaze and gave my Scrivening hand a tingling squeeze.

One Scrivener, one Seer...and one heart.

Together, we were unstoppable.

ALL THAT GLITTERS

YURI

1

Pinyin Bay was both everything I thought it might be, and nothing whatsoever like I expected. It was a small American Midwestern city in a fly-over state, where traffic moved slowly and strangers always insisted on smiling. But I'd learned the hard way not to underestimate the damage a smiling man was capable of inflicting.

Pinyin Bay in the winter was also colder than St. Petersburg, and even as February turned to March, my little lakeside cabin was frigid...but I couldn't really complain about that these days.

"I've got a surprise for you," Dixon sing-songed from the bathroom.

I'm sure he did. I frankly never knew what he was going to come up with next. I pulled the blankets around me to stop my body heat from escaping. "A good one, I hope."

"Not just good...." He elbowed open the door and struck a dramatic pose. "But sparkle-licious."

He flung a hand high, one foot forward, one foot back, arching his spine like a showgirl. Dixon Penn wasn't just confident—he was ludicrous.

And I was captivated by him anyway.

It wasn't his body, and it wasn't his looks, either. It was the sheer audaciousness in the way he approached everything. Including the two of us. Together. Especially the two of us, together.

"What do you think?" he said playfully.

"I think you will freeze your balls off unless you come to bed."

"We wouldn't want *that* to happen. I've been getting so much use out of them lately." He tiptoed forward on the cold wooden floor and struck the pose again. "But, seriously—do you like it?"

His nipples were stiff with the cold. Stiff, and alluringly pink against his winter-pale skin, surrounded by whorls of dark chest hair that circled them like a night sky by Van Gogh. I was well acquainted with the way they'd feel against my tongue—but I was suddenly aching to remind myself anyway. Just in case I'd forgotten some very important detail.

"Yuri..." he used his exasperated *Yuri*. I pretended not to notice. "Not up here." He framed his nipples briefly, then pointed toward his crotch. "Down there."

Light from the bedside reading lamp reflected from his pubic hair in tiny glints of pink and silver.

"You put glitter in your...?"

He struck another pose. "And I shaved it into the shape of a heart. See? Uh, well, I guess it only looks like a heart if I'm standing with my thighs pressed together. And my dick is tucked between them. Except I was kind of excited, and the more I handle it, the less tuckable it is."

"Funny how that happens." I peered at his handiwork and saw part of his treasure trail was now stubbled. And the whole bush was somewhat misshapen...and sparkly. Very sparkly.

"It's called Glee Glitter. Not only is it edible—it tastes like cotton candy."

"Oh, does it?" I said skeptically.

Dixon peeled back the covers and slipped into bed, staring me straight in the eyes, then scaled my body like he was working his way across a fallen log. Whenever I thought I'd learned the extent of his shamelessness, he still managed to surprise me—in the best possible way. He straddled my shoulders, poked me in the chin with his stiffening dick, and said, "Why don't you find out?"

He shrieked with delight when I pushed up from under him and practically threw him into a backward somersault. The bed groaned, but held. Its rough wooden frame had taken plenty of abuse from the summer tourists—from obese fishermen to families with small children playing trampoline—but after I met Dixon, I had to reinforce the lumber with additional support brackets and longer screws.

Though it could be argued that long screws were the problem to begin with.

I pinned him on his back with his knees around my neck and pressed my forehead to his. "I'll taste your Glee Glitter when I'm ready. And not a moment sooner."

"Ohmigod, Yuri, you're *so* butch." He laughed as he said it, as if he was making a joke. But like most humor, it carried more than just a kernel of truth. I was not the type of man you'd want to keep around for more than a dirty hook-up. But instead, he was drawn to me like a planet orbiting a star. A disarmingly adorable planet. I gazed down into his eyes as we grappled for better leverage (whatever we were currently doing—apparently we hadn't quite yet decided).

His eyes were the darkest brown, nearly black—even in the sunshine, but especially inside the dim cabin. Show me a fair-haired Scrivener, and I'll show you bottle of peroxide dye stashed under the bathroom sink. Scriveners all come from the same stock: black-haired, brown-eyed people too clannish to risk diluting their gene pool. Dixon looked nothing like the thick, ruddy, pale-eyed men I'd been with back in Russia.

And that was how I liked it.

When I pinned him down, he never struggled. Instead, he devoured me with his dark, mischievous eyes while he luxuriated in whatever we were doing at the moment. Rough, tender, impulsive or absurd. He was eager to explore every facet of lovemaking.

I was mistrustful, both by nature and experience, but even so, I couldn't help but indulge him. And while I wouldn't say the edible sparkle tasted exactly like cotton candy, it was definitely more palatable with a bit of salt to cut the sweet.

As we finished, he kissed the taste of himself from my lips—or maybe he was re-introducing me to my own flavor—and then nestled his dark head in the crook of my shoulder with a sweaty, contented sigh. "I could do this all day."

"Good thing you didn't freeze your balls off."

"Too bad I said we'd be there by six."

For all that Dixon tended to flood me with information, he also had a habit of presuming I was privy to his thoughts. Either that, or he just lost track of what he'd actually told me and what he'd only been thinking. But he'd been scoping out various business opportunities for us ever since we agreed we didn't want to Spellcraft for anyone else, and it was high time something finally came through. "Where do we need to be?"

"Dinner—the best chicken and dumplings you've ever had. Bar none. Because my mom uses those great big flaky buttermilk biscuits, you know, the kind that come in the can—"

"Dixon...?"

"Do you have those in Russia? Biscuits in a can? Do you even call them biscuits, or do you think biscuits are cookies, like Brits? You know what I mean, though—the ones that scare the bejeezus out of you when they pop open and they're all big and squishy inside? I guess they're technically just biscuit *dough* until you actually bake them—"

"Dixon...."

"When I was little I used to chase my cousin all over the place with those half-open cans because they scared her so much when they popped, and once I made her wet herself—oh God, don't tell Sabina I told you that, she'll totally die—"

"Dixon!"

He shut up, finally, but his dark eyes were startled and wide. I pried him off me—we were somewhat stuck together—and turned him onto his back, pinning his wrist to the pillow so he'd stay right there and look at me when I spoke. "Why is *your mother* making us dinner?"

"Because ever since Dad melted her favorite Tupperware in the oven, he's only allowed to cook on the grill, and it's too cold out for grilling."

Oh, Dixon Penn is adorable all right. But I'm no pushover, and I wasn't about to let him think he was getting away with anything. I glared at him until he squirmed in my grasp...and finally, he relented. "What's the big deal about meeting my folks? We're an official thing. Right?"

He knew there was no one else. I grunted a reluctant affirmation.

"And so, you were bound to see them sometime. Pinyin Bay's not that big."

Maybe not.

Still, he grossly underestimated my how much I truly hated playing nice.

2

"**U**nfortunately, Sabina can't be there. Which is a shame, because Sabina has this dessert thing she does with marsh-mallows and coconut and green Jell-O. Do you have Jell-O in Russia? I'm sure you do, but it's probably called something else. Anyway, she's taking these mandatory classes in defensive driving to get her traffic ticket reduced, which is totally not fair. It's not her fault the Buick's gas pedal sticks."

Dixon had been talking nonstop since we pulled away from the cabin to the point where he steamed up the windows. I turned up the blower.

"And, no pressure, but it's always been Mom's dream that I'd end up with a Seer. Don't worry—I didn't tell her about your talent. I know you're traumatized after what happened with Precious Greetings."

"*Traumatized* is a bit...exaggerated."

"It's okay, Yuri, you can feel your feelings in front of me. I mean, heck, you feel everything else." He was batting his eyelashes. I could tell from the corner of my eye, but I pretended not to notice. "I just want you to be prepared. My mother is profoundly sentimental. Don't be embarrassed if she gets all schmoopy on you."

I was unfamiliar with the word, but that was fine. Dixon's ideas were a constant patter. It was a stream one could dip into and out of at will and still end up at the same location.

"And my father...let's just say I think the term 'dad-joke' was coined specifically for him. He's the life of the party. Whatever you do, though, don't pull his finger."

When I first came to the United States, it was disconcerting to see everyone constantly baring their teeth in bizarre and inappropriate smiles. We Russians only smile when we mean it...and I've never had much to be happy about. But when Dixon smiled at me, he wasn't just trying to coerce me into liking him. No, he exuded joy. And so it didn't surprise me at all to find out he'd come from a loving home where his mother was kind to him and his father knew how to laugh.

One where I'd fit in like a bear in a rabbit hutch.

Dixon's family lived in a part of town where lawn ornaments never got stolen, though you couldn't say the same for cars. I left my truck unlocked anyway. It was more rust than metal now. And no matter how many times I cleaned it, when it was above freezing out, I still got an occasional whiff of the dead squirrel I'd found in the glovebox.

His parents' place was a small, square, no-nonsense tract house with vinyl siding and a shockingly green plastic wreath hanging on the front door...which was also unlocked.

"Hello-o! We're here!" When Dixon burst through the door, the smell of cooking hit me in a blast of humidity. Chicken and fake butter, rounded out with apples and cinnamon and something that was browning on the verge of being burnt. The home inside was cluttered with bric-a-brac and far too many pieces of furniture. Not antiques, unless you counted the 70s wicker furniture that was starting to unravel. It was as if no one could bear to throw anything away, even though it was pressboard, plastic and veneer.

"Hey, Dad!"

Dixon's father sat in a faded recliner with his feet up and a newspaper in his hands. When Dixon greeted him, he let one corner of the paper droop and assessed the two of us over the top. He looked like Dixon—brown hair, dark eyes—but with high widow's peaks and extremely deep frown lines. "Took you long enough."

This was the family's source of dad-jokes? If he was kidding, he had a phenomenally dry sense of humor. While I tried to determine if it was sarcasm or true annoyance, Dixon kissed the top of his head, then gestured at me with a sweep of his hand. "This is Yuri, obviously. Yuri, this is my father, Yoska—everyone calls him Johnny—whoa, do I smell what I think I smell?"

"Your mother pulled out all the stops and made her Dorito green beans on the side."

"Best day ever!"

As Dixon enthused about dinner, his father eyed me over the top of the newspaper. Was I supposed to shake the man's hand? Refuse to pull his finger? I was in the dark as to the Penn family traditions. Spellcrafters are insular, and the ones I knew in Russia would only meet with me for as long as it took to do our Crafting. They'd never invite me into their homes, let alone introduce me to their families. Johnny narrowed his eyes, then flicked up the newspaper barrier between us.

How soon would I be able to go back home?

I followed Dixon into the kitchen, which was just as cluttered as the living room, and hot enough to steam a dumpling. His mother was at the counter, chopping parsley very loudly with a knife that was bigger than her arm. To say she was a stout woman would be putting it kindly. She was very nearly spherical, with apple cheeks and black-dyed hair teased and sprayed into an improbable shape. I would have taken it for a wig, if it weren't for the half-inch of gray at the roots. She wore a T-shirt with the words *Mama Bear* stretched across her wide bosom.

"Mom!" Dixon rushed her, nearly impaling himself. They hugged each other fiercely. "Mom, Yuri. Yuri, the most awesome mother in the world, Florica."

Dixon's mother glared at me as if she'd found the perfect place to sheathe her knife—directly in my chest.

"Do they have Doritos in Russia, Yuri?" Dixon asked, but before I could answer, he had his head in the oven. "Apple turnovers? Ma, you've outdone yourself!"

"They're frozen," she said gruffly.

"Not anymore." He pulled them out with an oven mitt and set the tray on the butcher block to cool. "Actually, the green beans are just the way I like 'em, too—y'know, with the crunchy little brown tips—I say, let's eat."

With lots of fussing and jostling, Dixon herded me over to the dining room, which had one too many chairs jammed up to the table, despite the fact that there were only four of us. It was set with random foods. Not only the chicken covered in canned biscuits, and green beans with crushed, orange-powdered corn chips on top, but lima beans studded with chopped hot dog, a plate of saltines, a bowl of pickle slices and a can of aerosol cheese.

Dixon plunked himself down at my side and squirmed with eagerness on the edge of his seat. Florica slammed a plate of folded bologna on the table while Johnny glowered. Once all the "courses" were set out, Florica picked up a serving spoon...and Dixon gasped.

"Mom! What the heck is that?"

She gave his father an exasperated sigh and said, "I told you he'd make a big deal out of it."

Out of...what? No idea. But my policy has always been to keep my mouth shut and play along until I figure things out.

Dixon sprang out of his chair and plucked the serving spoon from her hand. "You can't serve it without the red spatula."

"Dixon—"

"No, It's bad luck."

"I'm sorry, Dixon, I know how attached you are, but I haven't seen the spatula since Christmas. Now let go of the spoon or the casserole will get cold."

"But we *all* love the red spatula."

"We looked," his father said. "You think we haven't looked?"

Dixon set his jaw. "Well, look again. This is our first dinner with Yuri, and it would be bad luck to start off on the wrong foot."

Florica shook her head and muttered something about the Dorito topping going soft, but she pushed herself away from the table and said, "Fine. We'll take one last look. You search the dining room with your father. Yuri can help me in the kitchen."

As I pried myself out of my seat, I wondered if the whole setup was some kind of bizarre American prank. But given the high flush on Dixon's cheeks and the frantic way he began tearing through the sideboard...I didn't think so.

3

The steamy kitchen smelled of cheese powder, corn chips and singed apple turnovers. I kept an eye on Florica and she kept one on me. "Might as well make yourself useful and look up high," she said, and began turning out the drawers. The Penn family owned a startling number of can openers. I went through the highest shelves in the pantry—not that it was a logical place to put a spatula. Perhaps I thought I would understand Dixon better by seeing what his family kept on their shelves. But the contents were just as baffling as he was, rows of generic canned goods with faded, dusty labels covered in neon "closeout" and "half off" stickers.

I was still wondering if this was some kind of hazing ritual when I overhead Dixon's father telling him, "Calm down, kiddo. How about this? I'll run out to the store and get us a brand new red spatula."

"But it's not the *lucky* red spatula...."

If the gruff tenderness in Johnny's voice and the distress in Dixon's were fake, the two of them should have been actors, not Scriveners. As if she'd somehow read my mind, Florica said, "I suppose you know we're a Spellcrafter family. Practical Penn. That's us."

"I know."

"And I suppose you have all kinds of notions about what that might mean."

I had many notions, of course. But not the ones she might think.

I realized Spellcraft was deceptively powerful.

I suspected a good Scrivener could work wonders.

And I knew that outsiders—the Handless—were both fascinated and repulsed by Spellcraft magic, even as they scoffed about it and made it the butt of their jokes.

"I'll tell you something," Florica said. "People might look down their noses at Scriveners. But you'd be wise not to underestimate my son."

I'd circled around the kitchen to search the top of the refrigerator, which was covered in old cookbooks, oily dust, and a broken fortune cookie still in its wrapper. "Did you know Spellcraft was illegal under Soviet rule?"

Like most Americans, she got her knowledge of my homeland primarily from cold war spy movies. "That's a bit extreme."

My gaze fell to the refrigerator door. It was crowded with cheap plastic magnets shaped like various states, menus from at least four different Chinese restaurants, and a truly bizarre shopping list. "Even now, it's unusual for someone to hang a sign on their shop and proudly declare what they do. Who they are."

"Well. This isn't Russia. And Spellcraft might not be the world's most glamorous profession, but don't go thinking my son will give it up to go do something more exciting with you. He's worked long and hard to be a Scrivener. And if you can't handle that—"

I checked the freezer—which, other than some ice cube trays and a box of waffles, was empty. But when I closed the door, my eyes returned to the grocery list.

It looked like it had been there for ages. The paper was a torn scrap with a coffee ring in the center. It read:

FLOUR
FAMILY SIZED
FISH STICKS
KIELBASA FETA CHEESE

I should count myself lucky that whatever dish was comprised of these ingredients was not on tonight's menu. But when I began to turn toward the cabinets, I found my gaze drawn back to the list.

Why was it written that way, with the family-sized fish sticks on two lines, but the sausage and cheese on one? And other than the coffee ring, the paper was bright white, and very thick. Quality paper. Cotton rag, by the looks of the torn edge. Not the sort of thing most people use to jot a quick note.

But definitely the sort of thing to hold a Crafting.

My vision shifted, and I saw the brown circle wasn't a coffee stain after all, but a distorted circle of golden brown watercolor. The words seemed to vibrate—some at a different frequency than the others. And as if they'd just lit up to my inner eye, I saw the Craft cunningly hidden within the words.

FL **OUR**
FAMILY SIZED
F **IS** H STICKS
KIELBA **SAFE** TA CHEESE

Dixon's relentless optimism was one thing, but I'd been dreading meeting his parents—worried that I would find a couple of soft, weak, gullible fools. Easy prey. But when the hidden Crafting revealed itself, I saw they were clearly shrewd enough to handle themselves—and they had the good sense to realize that Spellcrafters couldn't afford to be too trusting.

"Tell me something," I said. "Is there actually a lost spatula, or is this some kind of test?"

Dixon's mother blinked. "Of course there's a spatula."

I drew my paintbox from my pocket and set it beside the charred turnovers. "Then, if it's here to be found, I will help you find it."

Her eyes went wide when I pulled out the tiny notepad I carried everywhere these days—just in case—and she realized what I was doing. I cupped my hand beneath the tap to capture a bit of water, wet my brush, and cleared my mind.

When I was a young man (and my Seens would fail as often as not) I would try to picture a thing in my mind and copy it to the page, until an old Scrivener helped me find my inner sight. She drove a hard bargain, too. In return for this education, I painted her a thousand small Seens over the next few years.

Florica was not unlike my old mentor.

I didn't try to picture a spatula. I focused on Dixon instead. His distress. His hope. His fear that his loved ones' fortunes hinged on a random bit of "luck." And when I had the feeling fixed firmly in my mind, I swirled my wet brush against the red paint and set the bristles to paper.

When I was done...it certainly did look like a spatula.

My composition was strange, however, with the painting all on one side rather than the middle, but I no longer question these things. I slid it across the butcher block and told Florica, "Find it."

She scrutinized the small painting, then my face. And without mentioning anything to her husband and son, she slipped out of the room, returning shortly with an inkwell and a case that contained a long white plume. Before she dipped her quill, she leveled a hard look at me—one that told me if I wasn't legit, if I was trying to make a fool of her, I would no longer be welcome in her home.

I held that cool gaze for a moment, then nodded.

She closed her eyes and allowed words to come to her in much the way I did my painting. She considered them for a long moment. And when she was finally satisfied, she opened her eyes, turned the Seen on its side so the spatula was at the bottom, and in simple, precise penmanship, wrote, *Luck, Laughter and Love.*

I would have written, *Look, there's the spatula.* In Russian. This is why I'm no Scrivener.

As Florica's Scrivening meshed with my Seen, the power of Spellcraft played across the back of my neck like a gentle breeze. The whole kitchen held its breath as the two of us looked expectantly at this thing we'd made together. And whether or not the spatula ever turned up, I'd shared a secret of utmost importance with Florica. A profound secret that could mean as much to her family as Dixon finally receiving his quill.

Her words had a chance to succeed where mine might have failed. They were general enough to embrace many possibilities. This was important, because sometimes what is lost can't be found again, not in the way we hope. If the spatula had been accidentally thrown away some months ago, it would be out at the Pinyin Bay landfill by now. And while Spellcraft was certainly a deep and mysterious power, it couldn't make a hunk of plastic erupt from the ground and fly across the city.

As surely as I felt the magic course through me, though, Florica had felt it too. And her voice sounded different when she said, "I've always been partial to Seens that actually look like something."

We both reached for the Crafting at the same time, then both pulled away with a huff of embarrassed laughter. The small paper fluttered to the floor. "I'll get it," I said, and knelt down to retrieve it...and saw a hint of red plastic peeking out from between the range and the cabinet.

I pulled out the cobweb-covered spatula and handed it to Dixon's mother, who took it from me with no surprise at all, and then held her hand out for the Crafting. She turned on the stove's burner, then touched the corner to the flame. I must have looked worried, because she said, "Most people keep Spellcraft around forever. But not me."

"I thought it was dangerous to destroy a Crafting."

"Only if you're trying to reverse the spell when you really need to Uncraft it. This is different, though. I have a theory that once the Crafting has done its job, the magic wants to be free again."

Clearly, Florica Penn was a wise woman. And I still had so much to learn.

A curl of smoke rose from the Crafting as she dropped it to the surface of the stove. The paper flared, browned, and collapsed. Florica wiped away the ashes with a bright yellow sponge, then handed me back the spatula and said, "You should be the one to make Dixon's day. I think you've earned it."

The bottoms of the biscuit dumplings were still raw—everyone else just scraped off the doughy parts without comment—but Dorito green beans, it turns out, are edible.

"A Seer," Johnny murmured, while Dixon squirted aerosol cheese on a piece of bologna and topped it with a pickle slice. "And how did the two of you meet, again?"

Before I could figure out where to even start, Dixon kicked me under the table and said, "The internet."

His parents nodded sagely. And I supposed, in some small way, it was true. If he hadn't entered the online Precious Greetings contest, we might never have crossed paths.

Johnny helped himself to more lima beans, taking care to capture some extra bits of hot dog. "Do you need a job, Yuri? I'm stuck in a contract until our Seer wants out..." he gave me a shrewd little smile. "But with your help, we can Craft a little something to make an early retirement seem pretty appealing."

That was entirely illegal. Even here.

I liked the way the man thought.

"Yoska," Dixon's mother scolded. "Isn't it obvious now why Dixon hasn't come back to work with us? The boys are freelancing."

"Oh, sure, Practical Penn might not have some fancy foosball table or staff retreats or beard glitter." *What?* "But what about stability? No one respects a side hustle as much as I do—honest. I'd even write a special freelancing clause into your contract...so long as you agree to a non-compete agreement."

Dixon rolled his eyes, not dismissively, but with adoring tolerance. "I love you, Dad, and I know you only want to make sure we're both provided for. But I've gotta figure out my own way." He grabbed my hand and squeezed it for emphasis. "Me and Yuri."

I've seen plenty of strange things over the course of my life, but

I wasn't sure which part of that exchange was more surreal. Dixon saying "I love you" to his *father*? Taking my hand right in front of him? Or Johnny tearing up, claiming to have something in his eye, and reeling off to the bathroom?

Dixon and his mother kept on eating, totally unfazed. Florica said, "Of course, if Yuri needs a work visa, we'll put him on the books."

Dixon gave a happy wriggle. "You're the best, Mom."

As the night wore on, I realized I was no longer so eager to leave. That Dixon's father did indeed crack jokes, though they were stealthy and dry, and that his mother's fierce scowl protected a tender heart. When we climbed back into the pickup truck, Dixon was uncharacteristically silent, and I watched his eyes flick back and forth as he replayed our first family dinner with a faint smile.

It had been a long time since I cared what someone else thought of me. I knew the Penns would embrace me as a fellow Spellcrafter. Just the fact that I was not Handless would have been a relief, but a Seer? Practically unheard of.

And yet, I'd been worried I would screw everything up, despite the magic. After all, the last time I'd visited my own mother, she'd told me, *Bring a girl home with you next time...or don't come back at all.*

Scriveners were a clannish bunch, all right. And I'd never realized how much I'd longed to be included.

"Yuri? What are you thinking?"

I cleared my throat. Twice. Then gruffly said, "That went well."

"There was no doubt in my mind they'd adore you as much as I do. But I wonder what Dad meant about the beard glitter—um...oh."

"Oh?"

Dixon looked entirely too innocent—but he was staring at my chin. I yanked down the rearview mirror to see what he was looking at. When I tilted my head, by the dim light of the cab, I could just make out tiny glints of pink and silver in my stubble.

I'm not one to blush...but I wouldn't have been surprised if the edible body glitter singed to a crisp like the Doritos on his mother's green beans.

"I can always put some glitter in my 5 o'clock shadow the next time we go there," Dixon offered. "Make them think it's something all the cool kids are up to these days."

I shook my head, put the truck in gear and headed back to the cabin. "Never mind. I have a feeling it would take a lot for your parents to disown me."

And not just because I was a Seer, either. But because I made their son happy.

TROUBLE IN TACO TOWN

DIXON

1

Do animals feel sentimental about their homes?

I imagine they must. So many of them are built with their own little paws or claws or...whatever is on the ends of those eight horrible little tarantula legs. But what actually constitutes a home? Take, for instance, the terrarium in my lap with the wonky little stick insect inside. He was part of the menagerie collected by Emery Flint, the previous owner of Precious Greetings—the menagerie that now needed to be re-homed.

I don't know if Sticky Stickerton was born in captivity or captured in the wild. Heck, I don't even know where these little critters would roam free. But I do know that ever since he was bought and paid for by Mr. Flint, this little plastic box was all the home he'd known. So, did he care if we moved him from Precious Greetings to my parents' rec room? Hard to say.

Also, I wasn't sure it was "he." But, you know. Stick insect. They must all be "he"s.

I rode in the passenger seat of Yuri's pickup truck while he followed my cousin Sabina in the Buick, and she followed my parents in their Monte Carlo. The convoy snaked through the streets of

Pinyin Bay, on a mission to make sure that none of the creatures had to suffer for Mr. Flint's mistakes. The Bay County Zoological Society only had space for some of the animals—and I thank my lucky stars the tarantula was one of them—but we were still working on finding a forever home for a dozen toads and salamanders, a sugar glider, several hermit crabs, three lovebirds (who am I to judge?), and the cockatoo. There were some Madagascar hissing cockroaches too...but I think they "accidentally" met up with the bottom of my mother's shoe.

We pulled up in front of my folks' house. Sabina ran up the front stairs to open the door, while Dad, Yuri and I formed a chain to hand off the habitats and cages. Mom supervised—she's good at that. And together, the five of us got all the animals inside before anything caught their death in the chilly March air.

"What happened to the monkey?" Dad said.

My mother didn't bother to hide her relief. "The zoo took it, and good thing. Those animals are constantly throwing poop."

"But they're very smart. We could have trained it to only throw poop at people we don't like."

"Says the man who couldn't train his philodendron."

Mom had a point. That plant had formed a weird blob in the living room corner that no one dared look at too closely for fear of being sucked into another dimension, never to return.

My parents have been together for over thirty years. They have an understanding. Dad pushes the limits, and Mom pushes back, and the two of them always meet somewhere in the middle. Hopefully Yuri would eventually get the dynamic. So far, I pushed and he grumbled—but eventually caved in.

Then again, maybe I shouldn't look a gift dynamic in the mouth.

My parents' home is pretty cozy. Even though they'd shifted around a lot of stuff in anticipation of fostering the menagerie, we still found ourselves with floor-to-ceiling cages in teetering stacks. The frogs all went quiet, and the lizards went ballistic.

"We don't have room for this," my mother said. "You kids have to take something."

Erm...they'd seen the attic Sabina and I called home. Heck, they were the ones who'd helped us convert it. And Yuri was living on borrowed time in an off-season vacation rental.

Yuri said, "This could all be solved by putting the cages outside and leaving them unlocked."

Such a kidder. I said, "I'm sure if we just categorized everything by its sleep cycle and stacked the cages better, they'd fit, no problem." I glanced down at a two-gallon tank where black ribbons swirled through the fronds of fake neon plants. "So, are leeches diurnal?"

My parents exchanged a glance with "down the toilet" written all over it as Sabina struggled through the front door with a blanket wrapped cage half as tall as she was. I hurried over to help her set it somewhere, though we ended up crab-walking around the living room at least four times before we finally admitted defeat and put it on the couch. A hiss sounded from inside, and I wondered if one of the cockroaches had made it out of Mr. Flint's office after all. But no. It was just the big, white cockatoo, Meringue.

"Whatever you do," I said, "make sure this bird gets a really good home. She deserves it."

My parents squeezed into the living room to have a look at the creature who'd single-handedly changed the course of my life. The bird took one look at them, ruffled her crest, and said, "Dirty Scribblers."

Awkward silence.

"I didn't realize she could talk," I eventually said.

Yuri shrugged. "She usually doesn't."

Talk about getting off on the wrong foot. The last customer who uttered the word Scribbler in my mother's presence found himself confessing all his indiscretions in his sleep, "Since he's so fond of the sound of his own voice," Mom had said. He was in divorce court within a month.

I tugged the blanket back over Meringue's cage and said, "Y'know what? I think I've got just the spot for her. C'mon, Yuri, let's go."

YURI

2

No one was more shocked than me to hear that bird speak. I've always been partial to her, but only because she was so good at annoying Emery Flint. There was no doubt where she'd picked up the phrase "dirty Scribblers." Flint muttered it all the time. But she'd never repeated it for him—at least, not in front of me.

The Handless can be funny about Spellcrafters. We are the first ones they turn to when they have a problem too strange (or embarrassing) to solve with conventional means. But they're quick to forget who helped them, to make us the butt of their jokes. Scriveners and Seers become "Scribblers and Hacks." It made them feel better to mock what they didn't understand.

I say, let them laugh. It's so much easier to pick off your enemy when they underestimate you.

Before Dixon's mother could pluck the cockatoo and add it to a casserole, I hefted the cage and turned toward the door. "Wait," she said grudgingly, and for a moment I thought she'd had a change of heart. "It's cold out there. Throw another blanket on it first."

Even an inconvenience was an opportunity for Dixon to find something to be delighted about. "I can't believe it," he called from the back of the linen closet. "You still have my favorite quilt!"

Oh, I believed it. The Penns clearly never threw anything away.

Dixon strode into the living room wearing the duvet like a cloak, and gave it a whirl. Sparks of static crackled in the polyester. I caught a salamander tank that very nearly ended up on the floor. A massive houseplant in the corner rustled. The blanket was printed in bright primary colors with a superhero character: Wonder Woman. Dixon struck a tacky pose, which I found disturbingly alluring. "I haven't seen this thing in years. Just think, if it weren't for Meringue, who knows how long it would've stayed in the closet."

The bird groomed her wing, unimpressed.

We said our goodbyes, wrapped the cage in Wonder Woman, and headed off for the apartment. The blanketed cage sat between us in the truck like a bulky third person, and I couldn't see Dixon's expression when he spoke. "Meringue's cage is gonna be a tight squeeze—and I've priced the storage units around here, they're ridiculous. How mad do you think Uncle Fonzo will be if I get rid of a few pieces of his furniture? I can totally replace them when he gets back."

Yet another example of how different Dixon is from me. I would never presume the man was coming home. Frankly, I wouldn't even put money on him turning up alive. "Do what you have to. Fonzo will understand."

I didn't know the man, but he might understand. Or he might not. One thing was for sure—I should've understood him. The two of us had each found ourselves trapped by a man looking to exploit our talents. But I was alone in the world with nothing to lose. Not Fonzo. When I saw the damage he could've done to his family, a family he should have cherished and protected at all costs, I was none too eager to make his acquaintance.

"Maybe I can get rid of his grandfather clock," Dixon said. "I'll bet someone would buy it—it only runs a little slow. Maybe Uncle Fonzo wouldn't even miss it. He's got this uncanny ability where he always knows what time it is, within half an hour, give or take. It's like a superpower."

"Impressive."

"And he probably wouldn't miss the tube TV. The remote hasn't worked in years. Although he might be sentimental about it, since it was a prize for guessing the number of jellybeans in a jar at the rent-to-own furniture store. Maybe guessing numbers is a super-power, too."

Or maybe he used a bit of Spellcraft to come by his guess.

"Ooh. I know. The end table he set fire to when he fell asleep with a lit cigarette almost looks like an antique—"

"I'm sure you will make the right decision," I said abruptly. Because plugging my ears wasn't an option while I was driving. According to Dixon, Fonzo had been gone since the failed Quilling Ceremony. Well over a year. At some point, Dixon would think of him less often as new memories began to overtake the old ones, and eventually he'd stop glancing out the window to see if his uncle had finally come home.

And I could keep him busy until then.

We pulled up in front of the hulking two-story home that Fonzo had left behind—along with an old Buick, a distraught daughter, and a crushing debt. The birdcage was not terribly heavy, but thanks to the Wonder Woman blanket, I couldn't see around it. Dixon acted as my eyes, backing along in front of me with a series of enthused directions. "Okay, there's a step. And another step. And that one feels a little soft, but don't worry, it should totally hold you—"

"Just tell me when I'm at the top."

I took a jarring step, and he said, "You're at the top!"

Beneath the Wonder Woman blanket, Meringue grumbled, "Dumb Hack."

Dixon struggled to wrangle open the inner door while he held open a screen door that was determined to snap shut. "This would be a lot easier if Sabina helped."

"We will manage." I squeezed in sideways with the cage. The stairway leading up to the illegal attic apartment was lined with paintings and photographs on both sides, and I had to back up the stairs to avoid knocking anything off with the birdcage. Dixon was coaching me with a running stream of encouragements, which I tuned out since he couldn't see which stair I was on any better than I could. I made it to the top without dropping anyone or tumbling back down, but then had to balance the birdcage on my knee while I opened yet another door.

"Hello-o!" Dixon called past me. "We saw the Buick, Sabina—we know you're here. Would it kill you to lend a hand?"

There isn't exactly an entryway in the attic Dixon shares with his cousin, just heaps of displaced furniture. I turned in a circle, looking for somewhere to set the tall birdcage, but every surface was already occupied by vases and lamps and boxes and bins.

Beyond the wall of clutter, Sabina sat, very still, at a card table in the area designated as the "kitchen."

"Seriously," Dixon called over. "Don't break a sweat or anything."

I might not have known Dixon's younger cousin long...but I knew it was unusual for her not to give back as good as she got. While Dixon crashed through the attic, hastily righting some things as he knocked others down, I nudged aside a crate of books, set Meringue's cage on the floor, and approached the table. "Sabina?"

She looked up, glassy-eyed, as if she'd only just noticed the two of us were there. In her hand was a postcard she held by a single corner. She flapped it up and down a few times and said, "Funny...I usually have some reason or other to think about my dad. But today, in all the excitement, he didn't come to mind... not even once."

I held out my hand, and she surrendered the postcard. It read: *Sabina—miss you, darlin'! Be good and don't stay out too late. And never run from a fat cop, he's more likely to shoot than give chase.*

-Dad

I handed it back to Sabina. She chafed away a tear with the side of her hand. "Not even *once*. Is it crappy of me that I forgot about him?"

Dixon squeezed past a set of filing cabinets stacked three-high and plucked the postcard from my hand. "Look at the postmark—this was just mailed yesterday. I don't have a day job anymore, and neither does Yuri. There's nothing stopping us from hitting the road right now and tracking him down!"

If Fonzo Penn wanted to be found, he'd make contact with a phone call, not a tacky postcard with no return address. But before I could say as much, Dixon turned his earnest, dark-eyed gaze to me while his cousin held her breath...and I couldn't bring myself to crush their dreams.

The postcard was traditional Americana, a painting of a road winding gently through a tall pine forest...with something that looked like five-meter-high taco poking out from behind the trees. I was sure I must be seeing it wrong. But with the title Taco Town, Minnesota curving beneath the shell...apparently not.

DIXON
3

"And so that's when I told her, I don't care if that dress is made of curtains, this is only Pinyin Hill, it's not like you're traipsing through the Alps—say, Yuri, d'you hear that sound?"

He sighed. "I've been trying to tell myself it's nothing...but it's been happening since Dubuque."

I paused my story and the two of us gave an extra hard listen. It wasn't precisely a grind. Maybe more of a rattle? Or kind of a clinkety-clink. Whatever it might be, it was coming from beneath the truck.

That couldn't be good.

Yuri pulled to the side of the road. Gravel crunched under the tires. There was no one for miles around, unless you counted the pasture dotted with cows. And even they were pretty far away.

We both got behind the truck and crouched to peer beneath it. I didn't particularly know what I was looking at, but it seemed like the thing to do, plus it was always fun to watch Yuri being all butch. He didn't really need to do much more than stand there to be the manliest guy in the room, but to see him looking knowledgeably at a motor vehicle made me all giddy inside.

"It's the muffler," he said.

"I take it we need that part?"

"Technically, no. But it will be an unpleasant few hours to get where we're going without it. Hand me the duct tape."

I dug the big silver roll out of the toolbox in back. "You realized you haven't said it yet, don't you?"

"Said what?"

"The name of our destination."

He took the duct tape and began tearing off long strips, cutting them with his teeth.

"C'mon, Yuri," I teased. "I'll bet it would sound exotic in your accent. And maybe even a little dangerous."

"Taco Town?"

I hugged myself with glee. Only Yuri could deliver that phrase with such sardonic disbelief.

He narrowed his eyes at me briefly, then set about strapping up the dangling muffler with yards and yards of tape. "Hopefully that will hold it until we can find a more permanent solution."

I glanced at the bulge in his pants. Not *that* one, but the square bulge in his pocket where he kept his tiny paintbox. "Maybe we should just make sure."

He straightened up and brushed gravelly snow off his knees. "You know better than that." He gestured toward the cab with his head. "It's getting late. Let's go."

He pulled out onto the road, and it seemed like the duct tape was doing its job. The engine was a bit louder now, but nothing was pattering against the undercarriage like a giant castanet. In another mile or two, he said, "Your quill is so new it's still warm from the bird. You still see Spellcraft as the answer to everything."

"Not *everything*." Just most things. "Plus, I grew up in the Craft. It's not as if I'm a total rookie."

"But the shine has not worn off." His voice went soft. "Try to keep it that way."

"What is it about machines, anyhow? My folks usually turn away customers looking for that sort of thing, but they've never given me a straight answer as to why."

"Too many moving parts. Too much that can go wrong. Spellcraft was born in a time before machines. It hasn't adapted well."

Born? *Whoa.* Mind blown. "Spellcraft deserves an honorary birthday! With sheet cake! And male strippers dressed like cowboys! How old do you think it is? I guess it couldn't be any older than the first writing, could it? Even so...."

Unfortunately, the origins of Spellcraft were lost to the ages. Although Scriveners made their living by writing words and phrases for the Handless, they were adamant about passing on their traditions orally—or not at all.

It took us three tries, but we finally found the road to Taco Town just after moonrise. It was a little touristy place like Pinyin Bay, except the trees were taller and the lakes were smaller...and at the end of the main drag, instead of a boardwalk with a few carnival rides and a fishing lodge, there was a hill topped by a moderately large taco.

Yuri put the truck in park, squinted through the windshield, and said, "Huh."

We'd expected there to be a giant taco. We hadn't expected it to be swarming with birds.

Unfortunately, there was a gate across Salsa Lane and it was locked up tight, so we couldn't drive any closer. But that was probably for the best. Nighttime was really dark in Minnesota.

We circled back around to the only motel in town, a 50s roadside two-story affair with a central courtyard and a flickering neon sign that read *Masa Motel*. The parking lot was full of cars, and we ended up wedging into a spot by the dumpsters back behind the pool.

I slung my messenger bag around my shoulders, climbed out of the truck, and got my bearings. When we cut across the courtyard, I realized what I'd initially taken for a kidney-shaped pool was actually no kidney at all, but a taco. How delightfully kitschy. Too bad it was too cold for swimming. And the pool was drained, except for some traces of snow at the bottom.

As we strolled across the courtyard, I looped my arm through

Yuri's. The way his outrageous biceps squish my fingers never gets old. And the way he tenses up—like the KGB's gonna leap out from behind the nearest stationary object and read him the riot act for being gay—is less and less pronounced these days.

The last few weeks, we'd spent most nights together at Yuri's cabin. Don't get me wrong, it's the most charming little hideaway you could ever hope for, and it leaves us both smelling like the cedar wood chips in the gerbil cage we'd inherited from Mr. Flint... which is a lot more pleasant than I just made it sound. Anyway, the cabin is ah-MAZE-ing. Even so, the bunk leaves something to be desired, and I was eager to see Yuri sprawled out on a nice big bed. Wrapped in a fluffy white robe. Watching me with smoldering bedroom eyes. Easing open the terrycloth tie....

"Dixon."

"Um...yes?"

"What now?"

Oh, right, we'd need to check in before anyone could tempt me with an open robe. Yuri paused at the office door, where a hastily scrawled *No Vacancy* sign was taped to the glass.

I said, "If we're really nice, maybe they'll make room for us."

Yuri gave the jam-packed parking lot a sidelong glance.

I forged ahead. "Mom always told me, you never know till you try."

"Your *mother* said that?"

Actually, now that I thought about it, my mother's actual advice was, *If you don't get what you want, force it out of the weakest link.* But I'm sure someone's mom said that first thing at some point.

The motel lobby was done up in a decor that was part southwest Aztec, part northern pine. It was all a little worn and faded, but the triangular shapes complemented each other really well. But it was hard to really get a feel for it with all the boxes.

It looked like a delivery person just dumped a shipment in the middle of the floor and took off. The boxes were stacked all around the concierge desk—brown corrugated cardboard printed all over with beans, and happy smiling cartoon faces. Pinto beans,

I presumed...until I stole a look at one of the labels.

"Yuri? Do they have tofu in Russia?"

"Russia and China share a four-thousand kilometer border."

I had no idea how long a kilometer might be—but it sounded pretty impressive anyway.

There was a call bell on the lobby desk, and I gave it a few dings... and then a few more, just to make sure whoever was on-duty heard me. I was pondering what tofu borscht might taste like and whether I should try dinging louder when a woman in a square-shouldered pantsuit came out and said, "Are you here with the gluten-free tortillas? It's about time!"

She seemed pretty ticked, so I plastered on my winningest smile. "Sorry, no. Just passing through town and hoping to find a room."

"Can't you read? We're booked solid!"

"But we've come such a long way."

"What difference does that make?"

"Look, if it's a matter of waiting for the maids to finish changing the sheets, we can just hang out in the lobby."

She planted her hands on her hips and glared. She had an impressive glare, with good eye contact and expressive eyebrows. "Look how late it is. The sheets were all changed hours ago. And the rooms are full. Every last one."

I skootched a bit closer, leaned in conspiratorially, and said, "Listen, I know how these things work. There's an extra ten-spot in it for you if you can hook us up. Promise, I won't mention it to the owner."

"I am the owner!" She pointed at the name tag on her lapel. *Olive - Owner.*

Guess I couldn't argue with that.

"I've been up since dawn," she said, "and I've still got a million things to do. Unless you've got a gross of gluten-free tortillas for me—in which case, I'd give you my own bed—then go get a room in Grimford and let me get back to work."

I looked at Yuri hopefully. Who's to say what he kept in his truck? But he gave his head a subtle shake.

As Olive turned to leave, I pulled out my phone and said, "Wait—before you go—can you just tell us if you recognize this man?"

As a visual aid, Sabina had sent me the best pictures of her father she could dredge up. Although my uncle Fonzo is a handsome guy, the most recent shots weren't flattering. He looked kind of sweaty and dyspeptic in the one we'd finally decided on—he might have been recovering from the flu. But it was, unfortunately, the most current likeness.

Annoyed, Olive gave the phone a cursory glance, then paused and looked closer. Her mouth opened. Closed. Then compressed into a tight line as she turned on her heel, and stomped off.

"Well, that was weird." Maybe Olive remembered a vacant room that had somehow slipped her mind.

While I wandered through the boxes, Yuri pulled out his phone and did a little recon. "We're in the middle of nowhere. Grimford is over an hour away, and the nearest gluten-free tortillas are in a health food store in Minneapolis. And it doesn't open until morning."

"Honestly, I don't know what they expect all the third-shift celiac folks to do when they're in urgent need of a late-night burrito. There's a business opportunity if ever there was one. Say, maybe I should see if Olive would like a hot tip for a nifty side-hustle."

Yuri slid the call bell out of reach. "If there's no room, no amount of sweet-talking will make one appear. If Grimford has a vacancy, we should book it now and hit the road before it gets any later."

As we headed out, another customer was just climbing out of a bright orange, double parked VW Beetle with the vanity plate BUGGIN. I paused to hold open the door. She was probably my mom's age, a full-figured Black woman with her hair in a smart twist. She wore khaki head to toe, with lots of cargo pockets, an impressive utility belt, and sturdy brown boots. She looked like she was dressed for safari, or at least a segment on the local news where she'd hold up moderately exotic animals from the zoo and hope they didn't pee on her.

Maybe she'd be interested in taking some salamanders off our hands....

"If you need a room," Yuri told her, "don't bother. The place is full."

Safari Lady planted her hands on her hips and glared at the back of the *No Vacancy* sign. "But I've come such a long way."

I shook my head sadly. "That's exactly what I said."

"The nearest motel is in Grimford," Yuri said.

"Unbelievable! I passed through Grimford an hour ago." She whipped out her phone. "I'll bet there's a YourBNB that's closer."

Ooh, good idea. I did the same, and found a cute little coach house just a few minutes away. Not only did it have a really good star rating, but there were jacuzzi jets in the bathtub...and I could think of a few interesting diversions that involved me, Yuri and several simulating jets of water. But when I tapped to create a booking, the status changed to *unavailable.*

Safari Lady pocketed her phone and said, "Well, that worked out for the best. Not only was the place I found cheaper than this motel, but there's a jacuzzi tub. I'm off to treat myself to a good, long soak."

As I watched her pull out of the lot in her bright orange Bug, it occurred to me I should've asked if she'd be willing to share. Maybe she was in the market for something other than gluten-free tortillas—something that Yuri and I would've been able to barter. Oh well, maybe next time. I told Yuri, "We made it to Taco Town, anyhow. And there's a flashlight in the glovebox. Might as well jump the gate on Salsa Lane and get a look at the Big Taco."

4

At the foot of Salsa Lane was a low, flat-roofed chain of souvenir shops done up trading-post style, with a taco stand on one end, a T-shirt pagoda on the other, and a tanning salon in the center. Despite the fact that it was now getting on toward most peoples' bedtimes, the T-shirt pagoda still had a light on. Not only that, but there was someone there scraping bird poop off the plate glass window: a middle-aged guy with a thick red mustache. He was all in hunter's plaid, right down to the wool cap with ear flaps. He paused in his scraping as we got out of the truck and called out, "Store's closed. Come back tomorrow."

His scraping had revealed an array of Taco Town postcards in the window. I took a look, and there it was: sun-faded, but definitely the same one Uncle Fonzo had sent. And better still, inside the store, beside a mannequin in a Taco Town visor, was a Post Office service window. Talk about luck! "Actually," I said, "I'm looking for someone. Maybe you can help? I'm sure it's unlikely you'd remember every single customer...." Crickets chirped. "But we think he may have sent a postcard within the last few days."

I pulled out my phone and flashed the picture, and the guy said, "Oh, I remember that character, all right." He offered his hand and said, "Reginald." We shook and introduced ourselves, then he said, "I'm not surprised trouble's following him. We should have known his claims were too good to be true. But when your town's livelihood is on the line, you'll believe anyone who gives you hope."

He invited us into the shop, which was brimming with brightly colored Taco Town tchotchkes and smelled like wet corn chips. There was a staff break room in back, an afterthought of a room with a kitchenette, table and couch. Yuri and I settled at the table while Reginald set out three taco-shaped mugs and put on a kettle.

While our tea steeped, he launched into a story. "It all started with a lousy review on Yelp. Someone said our Big Taco looked more like a hunk of roadkill, and the town took a referendum to refinish the finish—a finish that's done the Taco proud for a good many years, I might add. But when we had restorationists come in from St. Cloud and take a look, the price they quoted us would've wiped out the town's treasury."

Reginald pulled off his earflap hat and swabbed his brow with it. He was bald except for a ring of red hair around the edges and a little tuft on top.

"Well, then this Fonzo character came rolling into town—if that's even his real name."

I opened my mouth to say, Of course it is.... But Yuri nudged me with his knee, and I kept quiet.

"Yep, there he was, in a powder blue convertible, with a sharkskin suit and his hair slicked back all fancy. He saw the crowd around the Big Taco, and he took a look himself. And once the restorationists were on their way back to St. Cloud, he took me aside and said to me, 'What if you don't need to fix that Taco?'

"'Of course I do,' I told him. 'Up close, you can see it's got some major problems.'

"We looked at the Taco together for a good long minute, then he said, 'Is that adobe?'

"I was excited, because most people think it's just concrete or maybe stucco. 'Yep,' I told him. 'That *is* adobe. Not to be confused with adobo.'"

No doubt it was the same line he gave all the tourists—he paused as if he was expecting a laugh. I managed a weak titter. Yuri narrowed his eyes—Russian humor is different, no doubt.

Reginald went on. "He took a good look at the adobe, then said to me, 'The natural world is full of wonder. What if I told you I can help the Taco fix itself?'

"I know I'm coming off as the world's biggest patsy now, but you'd have to know this Fonzo character. He had a certain way about him."

I did know him. And I would have to agree.

"Maybe if he didn't come to us on the tail of those restorationists, the price he quoted would have been crazy. But after hearing what those crooks from St. Cloud wanted, this guy's price seemed like a bargain. So once I paid him, he went up there with a bucket of water, threw in some pine cones he'd gathered from the woods, and painted it all around the base."

Spellcraft was so much easier when you could just come right out and tell your client your actual process consisted of writing words on a slip of paper.

Yuri steepled his fingers. "When did you first notice something was wrong?"

"I had my eye on the Big Taco—even though the guy told me I probably shouldn't watch, I couldn't help myself. I love the Big Taco. And I was excited to see the moment where our fortunes turned."

In the distance, birds called.

Reginald sighed. "It's not as if birds never perch on the Taco. They do. Even with all the trees in the world at their disposal. There's even a stubborn robin that builds a nest inside the lettuce topping every spring. We've got all kinds of birds around here, but I remember the one that showed up after the pine cone treatment 'cause I'd never seen one like it before. I was excited—can you believe that? When it was just the one, I was actually excited...."

He shook his head and set out the tea. I took a sip. It was

good—what made it into my mouth, anyhow. The taco-shaped mugs were adorable, but they weren't exactly conducive to drinking.

"Within the hour," he said, "there were two. Then ten." He gestured in the Big Taco's general direction. "And now look what we've got on our hands. You know what the funny thing is? Those damn birds shouldn't be here. We looked it up. The crested carrion titmouse is only found in New Mexico...and once in a while around Wichita, depending on the migration patterns and the jet stream. And just our luck—those birds are rare. Someone posted a picture of them on Facebook and it went viral, and before we knew it, Taco Town was crawling with birders."

I said, "I'll bet that was good for business."

"Ha! That's exactly what *we* thought! Those people rolled into town just like the birds. One or two, then little clusters, then a whole flock. There was a steady stream at the motel, checking in all day long, one after the other, until every room was full. And the next morning, Olive served her famous huevos rancheros at the breakfast buffet...and all hell broke loose. The birders went nuts. Yelling, crying, carrying on. One of them tied herself to the chafing station in protest, and another one scrawled *Bird Murderer* in yellow paint all over the parking lot."

I'll bet that was a sight to see. "We were just over at the motel. How did we miss the graffiti?"

"Well, it rained a few hours later and washed the paint away, but that's not the point. It was some fine print on the motel's paperwork—more of a slogan than an actual binding legal statement, but one of those nasty birders was a retired lawyer, and he threatened to sue...."

Yuri scowled. "What was this 'fine print'?"

"Satisfaction guaranteed or your next night's free." Sloppy wording—not unlike a lot of the wonky Spellcraft I run across. "Some long gone ad man probably liked the way it rhymed. Anyhow, when the birders spotted the guarantee, they all extended their bookings by a week, then complained about the food so they could weasel out of paying for the second night. And once Olive caved in to that, they started complaining about everything from the towels to the toilet paper just to see how far they could take it."

Yuri stood and strode to the window and edged aside the blinds to check out the Big Taco, looking dashing and dangerous, like a secret agent in a blockbuster action thriller. The Taco's silhouette was visible against the starlit sky. Above, titmouses—titmice?—glided in lazy circles. "All it would take is someone with good aim and a shotgun to give those people a reason to leave."

"My thoughts exactly!" Reginald cried. "But the darn birds are endangered—and if we shot 'em out of the sky, those egg-sympathizers would turn us in faster than you can say 'over easy.'"

I wasn't entirely sure Yuri meant killing the birds, not the birders, but I gave him the benefit of the doubt.

Reginald said, "Obviously, those creeps in Udderville sent that Fonzo character to sabotage the Taco."

I really wished he'd stop calling my uncle that. "And they would do that because...?"

"Because they're jealous—always have been. Their Mother of all Udders attraction isn't half as popular as the Big Taco. But now that it's being picked apart by the crested carrion titmouse—which we can't even shoot because they're endangered...." He shook his head sadly. "All because of one lousy review. And that Fonzo character."

Before I could let Reginald know I'd had quite enough of his "character" rigmarole, Yuri cut in with, "We want to get to the bottom of this as much as you do. When was the last time you saw him?"

"Running off with Taco Town's hard earned cash!" Reginald was obviously very invested in being angry, but the steam went out of him quickly and his shoulders slumped. "I haven't seen the guy in a few days, but I can ask around in the morning." He took a final slug of his tea. Half of it dribbled down his neck. "I should've known there was no such thing as a self-fixing Taco."

Since the couch pulled out and the motel really was full, Reginald offered to let us stay in the break room. I wanted to be upset about the whole "character" remark, but decided anyone nice enough to give a couple of strangers somewhere to stay couldn't be all that bad.

And besides, I did have to admit...my Uncle Fonzo had always been quite the character.

YURI

5

Dixon slept like a baby while I struggled to ignore the metal bar beneath my back. Had his uncle merely swindled the town out of its money with grandiose claims and then abandoned it to let nature take its course? Or was there Spellcraft involved?

I would presume he was Scribing again, if not for the fact that Dixon now had his quill. You couldn't just pick up another magical quill at MallMart. And even if he did manage to lead a flock of crested carrion titmouses to a rare and tasty meal, I doubt one of them had bestowed him with their plumage. Not only was it unheard of for anyone to have a second Quilling Ceremony, but the birds were far too small to produce a sizable enough feather.

I rolled to face Dixon. Even in his sleep, a faint smile curled the corner of his lips. Who knew what Dixon Penn might dream about? It was difficult enough to comprehend how his conscious mind worked.

His uncle was clearly no good, but Dixon idolized the man. How many rambling stories had I heard about Fonzo's exploits? Too many to count. I'm not one to make a moral judgement about right and wrong. I have never been what you'd call a law-abiding citizen myself. It was the way in which Fonzo worked his game that got under my skin.

Fonzo Penn was a con man. A swindler. All charm and no substance.

And, again, I've never been one to balk about bending the truth to suit my own needs. It made no difference to me if Fonzo took advantage of the Handless.

But I couldn't get past the fact that he'd done it to his own flesh and blood by falling in with Emery Flint.

What he'd done to his nephew.

Dixon's thick, dark eyelashes fluttered open and the faint almost-smile broadened into a full-fledged grin. "Yuri Volnikov.... Are you watching me sleep?"

I aimed for a playful tone so as not to broadcast how concerned I felt. "I would be a foolish man to not keep an eye on you."

"Adorable." He launched himself out of bed, calling over his shoulder, "I was tempted to do the very same thing last night once you nodded off, but I'll admit, the allure of the after-hours souvenir shop was too much. While you were out like a light, I had a look around." His voice had been growing fainter, but was now getting loud again as he circled back toward the break room. "And you'll never guess what I found."

I waited for him to announce his discovery.

He poked his head through the doorway and flashed an eager grin. "C'mon. Guess."

"I have no idea."

"Yuuuuuri...."

"Fine." I guessed the first thing that came to mind. "You found a gun."

"A taco gun? That would be totally cool—would it shoot little tacos, or shoot various toppings *onto* tacos?—but, no, that's not it. Drum roll, please!"

I did no such thing.

Dixon made his own drum roll sound with his mouth, then swung through the door with a flourish and said, "Puppets!"

I would have thought it unlikely that American puppets would be as creepy as the misshapen, moth-eaten monstrosities used by my childhood teachers to "encourage" the class to learn multiplication (but instead only encouraged horrible dreams of those tiny felted hands touching my feet where they stuck out from the blankets). But I was wrong.

He thrust a nightmarish creation into the room with a wedge of cheese for a head.

"I'm Mr. Big Cheese," he declared in a falsetto voice as he flapped the mouth-slit open and closed. "And I can't wait for you to meet all my friends—"

I grabbed the thing off his hand, yanked open the freezer, threw it inside and slammed the door shut.

Dixon blinked. "Wow. You could've just mentioned you were sensitive about puppets."

Before I could insist I was not "sensitive," a frantic pounding on the outside door startled us both, followed by indistinct yelling.

Dixon made a startled, eager "oh" face, then dashed out of the room to see what was going on.

I followed him out to the front of the shop, where a small, stout man was pressed against the glass door. He was backlit by the parking lot security lights, so he couldn't see past his own reflection...though not for lack of trying. His nose has flattened into the glass, leaving an oily smear behind. "I know you're in there, Reginald. Open up—it's Wendall." *Knock-knock-knock.* "Come on, it's important!"

"This is none of our business," I said, but Dixon was already clicking open the locks.

"You heard him, Yuri. It's *important.*"

He swung open the door, eager to help. Wendall blinked at Dixon. "You're not Reginald."

"Nope."

He turned and looked at my truck in confusion. "And I suppose that's your truck."

"Yep."

"Don't you know how much healthier it is to walk?"

He was one to speak about health. He was winded just from sprinting through the door.

But before Dixon could regale him with the tale of our journey, he sighed and said, "Never mind. Sorry to bother you. I'll go try to catch him at home."

"Maybe we can help."

Dixon was always saying such things. I had no idea why.

"Are you postal employees?"

As surely as if he'd already blurted it out, I knew immediately that Dixon would agree. Like most Spellcrafters, he had a malleable concept of the truth, and if his curiosity was piqued, he'd say whatever it took to hear the man's story. Before he could make the ludicrous claim we were off-duty mail carriers, I said, "No. We're not."

Wendall looked around the empty souvenir shop with its shuttered postal window. "Are you sure?"

And now it was Dixon's turn to stop *me* from speaking my mind. He said, "What's so important that you need a mailman at this hour, anyway?"

Wendall wrung his hands. "I run the taco factory on the other side of the hill, and I realized this morning that a shipment got out that shouldn't have made it past quality control."

Dixon's eyes went wide. "You ship tacos through the mail?"

Wendall laughed nervously. "Oh no, we don't make actual tacos at the taco factory. We make snow globes." Of course they did. "With tacos inside. It's a state-of-the-art process, totally automated. I run the machine myself. But I guess that's not always a good thing. I didn't realize the machinery was on the fritz until a box broke open and I noticed something went wrong with the taco mold."

Shaking his head, Wendall sat on the edge of a tomato-shaped ottoman and said, "I'm sure it's my own fault. A big order came in, so I hired that guy to tune up the machine. It worked great for about a week—"

"What guy?" I asked.

"A traveling mechanic—he happened to be sitting at the counter in the coffee shop when the order came through and I was wondering aloud how I'd ever managed to fill it given the amount of raw materials I had." Wendall's brow furrowed. "Huh. Maybe it wasn't a coincidence."

As a rule, I try not to roll my eyes. It undermines my natural authority. But some days it was a real struggle.

Wendall said, "At first, I couldn't believe my luck. The tune-up wasn't cheap, but it eliminated a lot of waste, and I got that big order out, no problem. The machine even ran a little faster. Plastic needs a certain amount of time to cure, though, and now the tacos don't look right anymore. I have my reputation to think of. I can't let this get out. But a bad batch went out last night, and I need it back."

He looked forlornly at the postal window, which was clearly closed. Dixon said, "Well, if it's locked in there, it's not going anywhere, right?"

That observation seemed to be some comfort. "True. I'll just sit here and make sure I talk to Reginald first thing."

While I went in back and folded up the couch, Dixon chatted with his new friend. But there was little to learn...other than the fact that this so-called "traveling mechanic" had dark eyes, dark hair, and a way with parting people from their money.

I found some instant coffee in the break room and made us each a cup. I'm not sure if Dixon was questioning Wendall on purpose, or if the meandering conversation was just more of his stream of consciousness. I sipped my coffee and listened, and found out that Taco Town was off the beaten path, but occasionally some intrepid connoisseur of Americana would mention it in a magazine article or blog post, and they'd get enough visitors to see them through another season. The permanent population was less than two hundred people, and growing smaller every year as people died off and teenagers left for college. For every one that came back with a future spouse, three more fled for good.

I knew more about Taco Town than I ever wanted to by the time

Reginald finally showed up. "A souvenir seller and a postmaster," Dixon said with reverence. "Talk about having it all."

"I need that box back I dropped off yesterday," Wendall said.

Reginald stroked his chin. "You've already mailed it—it's not yours anymore. Tampering with the US Mail is a federal offense." Both men looked very grave...for all of two seconds. Then they both laughed, and Reginald clapped his friend on the shoulder, and said, "C'mon, let's take a look."

Wendall was practically tap-dancing with anxiety as Reginald unlocked the mailroom. Behind the door, a small basket of postcards waited to go out, a pile of bills, and a single small box marked *perishable*. No snow globes.

"Oh, great," Wendall said, "you pick now to become efficient?"

Reginald took the insult in stride. "You might want to check over by Vanessa's farm. Sometimes when she picks up late, she doesn't drive out to the main hub in Fairmont till the next morning."

"Give her a call and tell her I'm coming by," Wendall called over his shoulder as he sprinted out the door, moving fast on his stumpy legs. He darted out to the parking lot, did a little hop, then turned around and stuck his head back inside and said, "Say, this would go a lot faster if you guys could give me a lift."

DIXON

6

Taco Town was not exactly a thriving metropolis, and we pulled up at the farm in just a few minutes. I was struck by how neat and orderly the greenhouses were—not that I consider myself a horticultural expert. But there was a tidiness to the farm that made it seem more like a storybook scene than an actual agricultural operation, despite it being the dying end of winter with traces of snow underfoot and bare trees all around.

Even the cars were parked neatly. A pickup truck, a little hatchback, and a mail truck with its steering wheel on the wrong side, all of them lined up precisely beside the main greenhouse building.

The structure's walls were clear flexible plastic, with condensation beaded thick on the inside. But we could see through it well enough to spot a person moving among the plants. Wendall burst through the door without even knocking. Yuri and I exchanged a glance and a shrug, and followed. Inside, the greenhouse was still cool, but the way the early morning sun was beaming through the panels, I could tell it would warm up fast. It smelled like spring— soil and moisture and green growing things. As far as I was aware, I didn't have a green thumb myself, but you never know. I'd never really tried my hand at gardening. But the enticing springtime scent of the greenhouse had me thinking it might not be a bad hobby....

A middle aged woman with strawberry blonde hair stood in the center of the greenhouse. She wore a postal uniform with a spotless white lab coat over it. She was as neat and tidy as the rest of the farm, right down to her shoes—which were so shiny I could practically see myself in them from a half dozen yards away. "Wendall," she called over, "look at my tomatoes!"

Yuri and I shifted our attention to the veggies in question...and, wow, those really were some tomatoes. Not only were they red and ripe, and not only were there positively scads of them, but they were huge. Seriously huge. The size of my head.

"Yeah, they look great," Wendall said distractedly. "But what can you tell me about my package?"

Vanessa crossed her arms and drawled, "Excuse me?"

"The taco globe package that went out last night. Have you delivered it to Fairmont or is it still in the truck?"

"Off the top of my head? I have no idea. Late last night, I picked up a second delivery, and maybe it's in there, maybe not."

Wendall took a lurching step toward the door like a dog trying to get someone to throw a tennis ball, hoping Vanessa would follow. But Vanessa didn't budge. "I'm not looking for your package until I'm done harvesting."

Wendall finally did the first thing Vanessa asked of him when he walked through the door, and took a good look at her tomatoes. So many tomatoes. He groaned. "But that'll take all morning."

"Not if you get a move on. Plus, it's a good thing you brought friends." She pointed out some bushels, then took a tomato in hand and demonstrated. "Twist, then pull. It's better if you leave the stem intact."

How exciting—I'd never picked a tomato before—but before I could grab a bushel, Yuri snagged me by the shoulder and gave his head subtle shake. I mouthed the word *why?* and he made a little painting motion.

Spellcraft? What gave him that idea? Maybe they were just really nice tomatoes. Ripening all at once. To gigantic proportions. In the middle of March in Minnesota. Overnight.

All right...I could see where Spellcraft *might* have been involved.

Wendall grabbed bushel basket and started power-picking the tomatoes none too gently. "I don't understand. Just last week you were complaining that your crop wouldn't ripen."

"Well, I must have complained in the right place. Because a traveling botanist overheard me down at the diner—what are the chances?"

Yuri gave me a meaningful look.

Okay, fine.

Vanessa went on. "He came and checked out the whole operation, and you know what he determined? The soil was deficient in minerals. All this time, I'd been fertilizing with nitrates, but what it needed was rock water."

Wendall, Yuri and I all mouthed the words *rock water*.

"It's true," Vanessa said. "I'll show you." She led the three of us to a rain barrel in the corner and heaved open the lid. We all peered inside. Arranged in a circle at the bottom was a handful of fist-sized rocks. "The botanist put this together for me, and after the very first irrigation I had results. Not only did the most stubborn green tomatoes start showing hints of yellow, but some of them even doubled in size overnight."

Yuri seemed particularly unimpressed. "And how much did this traveling botanist charge you?"

"What difference does it make? Just look at this crop! And now that my mineral problem is solved, all my future crops will be just as bodacious. Frankly, I think I got the better end of the bargain."

Yuri's not one to argue. He simply turned his attention to one of the massively overburdened tomato plants and studied a ripe, heavy globe. I joined him, and he cocked his head in its direction. I took a better look, and when the sunlight hit the skin's surface just right, the subtle sparkle of Spellcraft revealed itself. But even if the traveling Spellcrafter was responsible for the bumper crop, and even if Uncle Fonzo just so happened to be passing through Taco Town, I didn't buy that the two things were necessarily related. Because it's not as if the members of my family were the only Spellcrafters in the world. Besides, Uncle Fonzo's quill was back in the attic. Just before we left, I'd hidden it under the bread box for safekeeping.

I turned to Vanessa and said, "I, for one, think it's great. And don't let on about the rock water—keep your horticultural edge. After all, if your competitors got wind of your secret sauce, pretty soon everyone would be doing it, and that'd just drive down the price of tomatoes."

Vanessa's eyes went wide. "That's exactly what the botanist said! And, y'know, he actually looked and sounded a lot like you."

I didn't need to glance at Yuri's expression to sense the I-told-you-so. "Come on." I shoved an empty bushel basket into his hands. "These tomatoes won't pick themselves."

While Wendall tried to get Vanessa to change her mind and look for his package, Yuri and I went to the far corner of the greenhouse and got picking. "Most Spellcrafters look pretty much the same to the Handless," I told Yuri—and that was the truth. Whatever common ancestors we had, there was a particular something about most of us that made us easy to spot, if you knew what you were looking for. "But even if my uncle did manage to find another quill, I don't see what's got you all hot and bothered. Okay, maybe the snow globe machine is on the fritz—but you said yourself, Spellcraft and machinery don't always mix. And the tomato lady seems happy."

Yuri gave a grunt and snapped a huge tomato off the vine. But he couldn't disagree.

Personally, I was excited. If Uncle Fonzo did have a new quill, then chances were, we'd catch up to him as he made his way through the back roads and small towns looking for ways to help people with their problems. Towns where no Spellcrafters lived, and the types of problems that were best fixed with the pen could still be found. It was just a matter of figuring out which way he was headed.

I filled bushel after bushel as we worked our way down the rows until my hands hurt from picking. Wendall was still complaining, but Vanessa stood firm. "How about this?" Wendall suggested. If the box is already gone, I'll get my kid to come help you while I go after it. He's got a much stronger back then I do."

"Call Harvey before we look. If the box is gone, he takes your place—and if it's still here, you both work."

She drove a hard bargain, but in the end, he made the call.

Wendall's son was a younger, geeked-out version of him. Genetics really can be pretty amazing. Harvey wasn't quite as rotund—yet—and his hair was bright ginger without any grays. He wore perfectly round glasses with dark plastic frames and a tweedy jacket with elbow patches over a too-tight sweater vest. An impressive camera hung around his neck. "I was just out getting some shots of the new stop sign over by Fourth and Colby."

"Harvey works for the Taco Town Tribune," Wendall said proudly.

When Harvey got a load of the tomatoes, he did a double-take. "I thought you said your plants wouldn't ripen!"

Vanessa risked a small glance at her rain barrel, then said breezily, "Oh, that was just me being impatient. Obviously, this year's crop is doing just fine."

"Fine?" Harvey said. "These are amazing. Look at that one—it's as big as my bowling ball."

"I can't take all the credit—I had a botanist's help."

"The dark-haired guy, came through town last week? He was really something else. Actually finished a Taco Tornado—that's an eating challenge of twenty tacos in twenty minutes—but he wouldn't let me post his picture on the diner wall. Said he didn't want to unseat the reigning champion. A real class act."

"That's him," Vanessa agreed.

"Even if you turned to him for outside advice, it's still your greenhouse. Can I get a picture for the Tribune?"

Vanessa glanced toward the rain barrel again. "I don't know...."

"With you in it, obviously."

Vanessa blushed and patted down her pristine white coat. "But I'm such a mess."

"C'mon, Vanessa—you know how seriously the paper takes our produce. I'll bet you and your tomatoes make the front page."

She primped her hair. "Well, if you really think so."

Ignoring Wendall, who was having a flailing-arm meltdown by the door in his urgency to get to his box, Vanessa allowed his son to pose her for the photo op. Harvey stood her in front of the tallest tomato plant, which towered over the petite postal carrier. He handed her a bunch of lush, ripe tomatoes, and instructed her to cradle them in her arms like she was holding a bouquet. All that was missing was a tiara.

"That's perfect," Harvey said, "just perfect. Now, look over here—that's right—and give me a nice smile."

The sun shone through the greenhouse, dazzling Vanessa, but she gave a tenuous smile. I stood tall and began to clap, cheering her on. And once I elbowed Yuri hard enough, he did the same. Although I don't think he knew the slow clap had a sarcastic connotation in English.

As we clapped and whistled, Vanessa gained confidence, shifting her shoulder to face the camera with a smile growing broader and more sure. "That's it," Harvey said as his shutter clicked. "Fantastic. Just wait till the town sees this."

The smile finally reached Vanessa's eyes as a single leaf dropped from the towering plant. It floated down gently on a warm updraft, unnoticed by both the photographer and his model. But it seemed like such a strange time for a leaf to fall. Maybe it's the Spellcrafter in me, but I can't afford to miss any details. Yuri, too. I felt him stiffen beside me...right before all hell broke loose.

Explosions on TV are loud. But gargantuan vegetables? They just make a wet squelching sound.

The tomato directly over Vanessa's head burst in a stunning explosion of ripe, red juice. It deluged her fair apricot hair, sliding down like something had been disemboweled directly overhead. The guts stood out vividly on her pristine white lab coat. But that single tomato was only the opening volley. Soon another burst, and another. Throughout the greenhouse in a series of squishy pops, the overstrained tomato skins gave up the ghost in a cluster of soft detonations. Harvey tried to backpedal, but he slid on the jellied insides of all the victims and tumbled inelegantly out of the way.

The blowup lasted several long minutes. When the juicy red globes were finally done exploding, not a single plant was left standing. All was silent but the plunk and splatter of tomato guts dripping from the plastic ceiling.

We slipped and slid and skidded over to Vanessa...who, in her shock, was moving in slow motion. Which didn't make it any better to see the dismay registering on her face in excruciating detail. She burst into tears just as we reached her. Yuri recoiled as if he'd just now discovered his kryptonite.

"Hey, it's okay," I said, but tomato guts were dripping into my hair, her crop was ruined, and it probably wasn't okay. I was just about to offer to help her clean up—but unfortunately, it looked like it would take a while. And we were so close to finding my uncle.

Wendall slipped and slid over to Vanessa and took her by the arm. "Come on, let's get you cleaned up." And together, like a pair of toddlers learning to ice skate, they made their way out the greenhouse door.

Once they were gone, Yuri muttered, "It's bad enough Fonzo took their money."

"Wait, what?"

He pressed his lips together is if he regretted he'd said anything.

"No, go on," I insisted.

I didn't actually think he would elaborate, but he squared his broad shoulders and said, "It's one thing for him to promise something he can't deliver, and another to completely destroy someone."

"Hold on, buster. First of all, we don't know for a fact that this is anything more than an accident. And second, how can this be my Uncle's work if he doesn't have a quill?"

Yuri's eyes went hard. "We both know how far someone will go to get a quill."

Oh no he *didn't.* I was a heartbeat away from cracking open a can of Penn family whoop-ass when Harvey called out, "A little help, here?"

Yuri strode over to where Taco Town's photojournalist was still flailing in tomato guts. Luckily, Harvey had landed on his butt, so his fancy camera was still intact. As if the full-grown man weighed no more than an empty tomato bushel, Yuri plucked him off the mushy ground and set him on his feet.

I almost allowed my anger to crank down a few notches...but then Yuri said, "The stranger who ate all the tacos—do you still have his picture?"

Harvey seemed puzzled, but since Yuri had just come to his rescue, he shrugged and took a look. "If I haven't switched out my memory card.... Hold on. Yep, you betcha. Here he is."

Yuri looked down at the viewfinder, then at me—and by the look on his face alone, I knew I wouldn't like what I saw. But you never know. It could have been some other Spellcrafter. I stuck my hands in my pockets, crossed my fingers, and faced the music.

The viewscreen on the camera was tiny, just a couple of inches, and the picture was somewhat confusing with all the piñatas and sombreros and Minnesota Vikings gear cluttering up the shot. But when I finally picked out the figure in the center of the frame grinning over an empty taco platter, there was no denying it.

At least Uncle Fonzo looked happy.

I was about to insist the photo didn't prove a darn thing (despite the fact that it pretty much did) when Wendall and Vanessa made an appearance. Wendall had a stack of T-shirts in his hands with a Fajita Farms logo. He passed one to each of us and said, "It's too cold to go outside in a wet shirt." Yuri nearly refused, and I'll admit, I was tempted, too. I have my image as a natty dresser to consider—but I reckoned it was best to come out of the fiasco with my nipples intact.

Even if I had no intention of letting a certain someone near them. At least until he apologized.

Once we were all in our new Fajita Farms shirts, Vanessa took stock of the greenhouse with the glazed, stunned expression, then sighed and said, "Okay, Wendall, let's look for your package."

Her mail truck was surprisingly full, but between the four guys, we had it unloaded before long. Especially since Wendall was working faster and faster the farther down he got without finding his box. But then, there it was, at the bottom of the heap. A battered box with one corner crunched in, the tape splitting, and a big oil stain on the bottom. A box marked *fragile* in at least a dozen different places.

Wendall cocked his head. "Wait a minute...." He pulled out a pocket knife and slit open the box. Styrofoam popcorn scattered as he pulled out a snow globe, then peered inside. "I must've had my boxes mixed up. This is from a batch I ran last week. They're perfectly fine." He turned to Vanessa. "Got any tape?"

"No can do. You opened it, it's yours."

They both launched into some nonsense about postal regulations, but I had no desire to stand around and listen to them arguing—not when I was busy brewing up an argument of my own.

I gave Yuri a cool look, then turned and headed back to the truck, fully expecting to lay into him once we were alone. But then Wendall snatched up the box of snow globes and came running after us. "Hold on! Can you give me a lift to my shop?

And even though the annoyance was thick enough to cut with a fork, Yuri gave his head a small, dismissive nod, and said, "Fine. Get in."

YURI

The You-Make-Um factory was a sprawling corrugated metal building with a pair of wooden Indians flanking the door. Apparently, political correctness was not a pressing concern.

"Back when my dad ran the business," Wendall said, "this parking lot would be full of workers. We'd make taco T-shirts, print taco postcards, and stamp taco fridge magnets. Nowadays, there's no one around to fill all the jobs, and besides, it costs barely half as much to outsource and have it all shipped in. All we've got to make onsite is the snow globes—that's our most popular souvenir. We're the only shop in the whole country that manufactures a taco snow globe."

Imagine that.

He let us into the building, which was crowded with machinery and supplies. Dixon was uncharacteristically quiet as we took in the layout, angry with me for speaking my mind about Fonzo, though as he took in all the equipment, his chilly annoyance began to thaw. Printing presses, silkscreen, embossing stamps—the work stations hugged the perimeter of the building, all of them silent and abandoned. All save the single large monstrosity in the center.

"Here she is," Wendall declared. "Globe-O-Matic. Taco Town's pride and joy."

"I thought the Big Taco was the town's pride and joy," Dixon said.

"Well, sure, aside from that. This is a close second." The machine was a massive metal box, the size of my cabin, with a clear plastic hopper on top filled with colorful plastic beads. With a flourish, Wendall pulled a huge lever on the side, and the monstrosity chugged to life. As gauges swung back and forth and colored lights lit, the raw plastic was funneled down a confusing series of tiny chutes. "The base of the globe feeds in here, glass there," he shouted over the noise of the machine, and gestured to a looping tangle of conduit. "And here's the impressive part. Pressurized water flows through these lines. It cools down the hot taco and fills the globe—double duty! Then a robotic arm screws it all together, and they come out fully assembled."

He smiled expectantly while the machine groaned and wheezed and clattered. Dixon was fascinated. I was just eager to find the next road out of town before yet another person fed him a sob story he couldn't resist. And when I thought the whole contraption would finally exhaust itself and fall to pieces, a chute opened up, and a snow globe rolled into a box of packing foam. Wendall pulled it out and handed it to Dixon, and said, "There's something off about the taco, but I can't quite put my finger on it."

Dixon's eyebrows shot up halfway to his hairline. After an awkward pause, he said, "Yeah, me neither."

Wide-eyed, he handed me the globe. Inside, the specks of sparkling glitter settled to reveal a plastic vagina.

I handed it back and said nothing.

Wendall said, "Quality control was so much easier when I had a bigger crew, and I could supervise instead of running the equipment. But now it's just me, a couple of gals who moonlight at the call center, and Harvey when he's not chasing down a story. I'm sure it just needs to be calibrated."

Something needed to be tweaked, all right, but I doubted it was his equipment. "Machines like these are delicate things," I said. Americans find me very wise when I state the obvious, and Wendall was no exception. "We should take a look around and see if there's anything you might have missed. A plugged vent, maybe, or a loose connection."

"Absolutely," Dixon agreed. "Fresh set of eyes can't hurt."

Another obscene snow globe tumbled from the chute. "You'd do that?" Wendall asked. "Take a look around? Thanks, guys! Thanks a bunch!"

I can handle a screwdriver as well as anyone else, but when I got closer to the massive snow globe maker, I wasn't looking for mechanical defects...I was searching for evidence of Spellcraft. Amid the vibrations and the steam and the chatter of the tiny nubs of plastic, I found exactly what I was looking for. When I looked at the machinery just so, the air around it wobbled as if I was viewing a reflection in a trembling bead of mercury. There was nothing mechanically wrong with the equipment. The problem was a Crafting gone wrong.

Or, perhaps, gone right...depending on the intent behind it.

Spellcraft might be technically legal here, but the government put more rules and regulations on it than legalized gambling. Any Crafting designed to actively harm, defame or impinge on another person was a serious enough offense to carry a prison term. Preferable to Russia, where large men in plain uniforms would simply come by and crush your hand. Still, nothing I would have risked.

Spellcraft was obviously in play, but that knowledge didn't help me locate the Crafting itself. I ran my hands around the frame, singed my fingertips on the metal casing of the plastic-heating element, but came up with nothing. As I began to worry how obvious it would be that I was just going through the motions of troubleshooting the machine, Dixon sidled up next to me. He pitched his voice barely above the rattle of the machine and asked, "Did I ever tell you how much I like corn?"

"I don't...think so."

"Well, I do. I love it. Crazy about it. Especially canned corn.

There's something about the bite, and the juiciness, and the milky, watery corn taste...anyhow. Mom used to get mixed veggies in these big, industrial-sized cans. Peas, carrots, green bean fragments, and corn. And whenever mixed veg was on the menu, Uncle Fonzo would sort all the corn out of his veggies, knock our plates together, and shove the kernels over to me. Claimed he didn't care for it. But once I was walking down Main Street and I saw him in a diner—you know the one, with the big chicken wearing a hat painted on the window? There was this group of Spellcrafters he used to meet up with twice a month. I wasn't spying. Really. I just happened to notice what was on his plate: chicken fried steak, mashed potatoes, and canned corn. And he was eating it. And not like he was just forcing it down, either. And I realized that all these years, he didn't give me the corn from his mixed veggies because *he* didn't like it...but because I *did*."

Maybe so. But all it proved was that the man could be generous with his corn.

"Here's the thing," Dixon said. "Obviously, tomatoes don't explode on their own. And, yes, I thought they seemed a little sparkly. And, yes, my uncle did come through Taco Town. But why would you presume he was sabotaging the city? He's the one who taught me to Craft, after all. Maybe there was another Spellcrafter here before him, and maybe he was trying to set things right."

I couldn't deny his argument was all very logical. But I also couldn't deny the feeling I got: that something was just not right, and Fonzo Penn was written all over it.

If any Spellcraft was hidden in the factory, I should be able to find it. It took focus, will, and always a bit of luck, but whatever it was that allowed me to paint my Seens also let me see the magic of Spellcraft dancing around a bit of Crafting. The factory was large, though, with a discouraging number of places in which to hide a small slip of paper. Dixon and I split up in hopes of finding the thing. We searched for most of the day, until our stomachs were growling and our feet were sore.

Unfortunately, if a spell was indeed to blame, we couldn't find it. I was about to suggest we pack it all in and start fresh in the morning when Reginald the Postmaster skidded into the room and said, "Guys, you won't believe it, but I think our luck has turned. The birds are flying away!"

DIXON

I climbed into the truck, at a loss for words. The scrap of paper I'd found tucked inside the factory's fusebox was heavy in my pocket. I couldn't deny who'd done the Spellcraft—the Crafting was strange, but the penmanship was unmistakable, so I could hardly be mad at Yuri for being right. But Yuri didn't know Uncle Fonzo like I did. If my uncle put a Crafting on something, there was a darn good reason. For all we knew, these people in Taco Town had a comeuppance due. Maybe they drove a giant sausage out of business. Or maybe a giant waffle. I had no idea, but I did know it wasn't fair to point the finger at my uncle without knowing his side of the story.

Salsa Lane was open now. We pulled up at the top of the hill beside Reginald. Yuri cut the engine, turned to me and said, "You haven't said a word. All the way here." He frowned. "What is it?"

"Overwhelmed, I guess. All those coochie snow globes." I forced a laugh. "Just...wow."

I don't think he bought it, but before he could ponder my reaction too closely, Reginald staggered out of his car, then froze directly in front of us, staring up at the Big Taco. He stood perfectly still, transfixed. And then he fell to his knees and burst into tears. "It's ruined!"

My heart sank. "I know, I know," I said to Yuri, low enough that Reginald wouldn't hear it through the closed windows...and all the wailing. "It's probably another Crafting gone berserk." When Yuri raised an eyebrow and I realized I hadn't mentioned the Crafting in the factory, I hastened to add, "Or the *first* Crafting gone berserk. Who knows which order they would have been done in...if there even was more than one, that is."

Yuri cut his eyes to me briefly. He was so not buying it.

Best not dig myself in any deeper. "Here's the thing, Yuri—I just need you to have some trust, at least a little bit—if not in my uncle, then in me. I need us to be on the same side."

Yuri stared through the windshield, eyes narrowed, and said nothing.

I said, "Even I'll admit—it looks bad. But before you jump to any conclusions, let's see what was actually written." I slid my hand across the seat and brushed my pinkie alongside his. It's natural to me to touch people. I was raised by an affectionate family. But Yuri can be surprisingly disarmed by the tiniest displays of affection, and just this subtle nudge was enough to make him give my uncle one more chance. Grudgingly. But he relented, and that's what mattered.

"Fine," he said. "Let's hope we find a Crafting...this time."

"*Totally*," I said, and hopped out of the truck before he noticed me obsessively patting down my pocket to make sure the snow globe factory's Crafting was still there.

The Big Taco perched at the top of a scenic hill as if a massive lunch lady had reached down from the sky and placed it there for all of Minnesota to behold. It was a proud taco, as tall as a Winnebago and nearly as long. Its base was constructed of rough-hewn Northern Pine, log cabin style. And the Taco itself was....

I paused and squinted at its crumbling veneer. "What's this made from again?"

"Adobe," Reginald reminded me through his tears as Yuri hauled him to his feet. "When Pedro Johansen moved to this area, it was nothing but forage land for the local dairy farms. But Pedro had a vision. A marriage of North and South, like his parents...but in terms of cuisine. You might be surprised to hear it, but back then, this part of Minnesota wasn't exactly a thriving metropolis."

Yuri refrained from noting that we could literally hear cows mooing in the distance.

"I know what you're thinking," Reginald said. Given that I was mainly wondering where the Spellcraft was hidden, I highly doubted it, but I didn't correct him. "Does Minnesota really need *another* ode to the taco? I say we do. Sure, maybe people think it's ridiculous. And maybe what we're doing here won't put men on the moon. It doesn't cure cancer and it can't plug the hole in the ozone. But in Taco Town, we make people happy." He choked up, briefly, then pulled himself together and added quietly, "And I think that counts for something."

As he knuckled away a tear as if it was just a stray bit of dirt in his eye, it occurred to me the same could be said for Spellcraft.

"Someone needs me by the store," Reginald claimed. From our vantage point on the hill, we could see there was clearly nobody around but us, but we didn't call him on it. It was a grown man's prerogative to hide his tears from the world.

Once he scampered back down Salsa Lane, Yuri surprised me by grabbing the front of my jacket and hauling me up against his massive chest. While I stood on tiptoe, he mashed his forehead against mine, filling my vision with his huge, solid presence. And when he spoke, his breath played tantalizingly across my lower lip like Spellcraft tingling through my nervous system when I composed an original saying. His voice was low. And intense. And sexy. "I am always on your side, Dixon Penn. Never doubt that."

I fully expected him to release me and leave me wobbling around, weak-kneed, in the shade of the Big Taco. But instead of letting go, he pulled me even closer and pressed his lips to mine in a fervent kiss. Stubble scoured my chin as he thrust his tongue into my mouth, and my whole self went pliant and willing. I've had boyfriends before who felt compatible, but never like this. In every way, it seemed like Yuri and I were complete opposites—and yet we were less like antagonists, and more like a couple of kids keeping a see-saw going so both of us could play.

Maybe Spellcraft is less like roadside attractions and more like sex. Sometimes you take, and sometimes you give. And when you're really lucky, you get to do both. Public displays of affection were definitely not Yuri's thing, so when he assailed me with his big, hard body and stole my breath away with his fierce kiss, I knew he really freaking meant it.

Yuri was both predictability and thrill. He was safety and danger. He was the guy my mother had warned me about, and the one she always hoped I'd end up with. He backed me into the Big Taco, cupping my head in his massive hands, and kissed me so thoroughly I was glad for the pitted adobe at my back keeping me upright. Yuri filled my senses, all bristle and muscle and cedar-scented wool. Need roared through my body—and even in broad daylight on the most prominent hill in Taco Town, I was ready to satisfy it.

Yuri was, too. With a desperate grunt, he bumped his groin against mine...well, more like it hit my waistband while I rode his thigh for dear life. We might even peak that way—up on Taco Town's peak—and I didn't care, even if it meant I'd have to do some creative repositioning of my winter coat, then clean up in the bathroom at the nearest gas station. The most exciting part? When Yuri's breath quickened and his teeth clashed with mine, I knew he wanted me just as savagely as I did him. Like a promise of what he'd do the next time we had fewer clothes between us, he thrust his hips at me again....

And the adobe made a sound like a hundred knuckles cracking.

Yuri reeled back, bulging and dazed. I snapped my arms out sideways to keep the Big Taco together. Never mind that if it actually toppled, it would crush me. I wasn't making good decisions—all the blood my brain needed for thinking was currently trapped down the inseam of my left pant leg.

It wasn't the whole Taco in motion, though, just a section behind my back. Yuri grabbed hold of me and pulled me out of harm's way. And when he dragged me away from the crusty adobe, a squared seam line appeared in the finish...and out swung a secret door.

YURI
9

I was off my game—stupid with lust, and my protective instinct in overdrive—when the adobe-covered panel popped open. Dixon's first impulse, naturally, was to lunge toward it. And mine, just as naturally, was to grab a handful of his jacket and rein him in.

"A secret door!" he chortled. "I'll bet there's treasure inside. Gold nuggets. Or gold doubloons. Or a golden antique tortilla press!"

I held back a sigh and considered letting him go before his running in place kicked up a dust cloud. Where else would the key piece of Spellcraft be hidden, if not within the main attraction itself? Besides, this was no dangerous metropolis—it was Taco Town. Then again, considering the tomato bloodbath, we couldn't be too careful. I moved Dixon out of the way... "Hey!" ... and had a look.

It was dim inside the Taco, with the only light filtering in through the doorway and the small holes made by the crested carrion titmice. It took my eyes a moment to adjust—but when they did, the sight of a clown looming in the shadows purged all traces of the excitement we'd stirred up with our kisses...until I realized it was just a mannequin. An ugly clown-painted mannequin holding a sign that read, *Welcome to Taco Fest*.

In all, the narrow space was about the size of my truck, and it was crammed full of painted plywood. Dixon crowded in behind me with a gasp. "Oh wow, I always wondered where neighborhood carnivals went when they weren't being carnied."

Of course he did.

We searched through the plywood for Spellcraft, picking up splinters in our hair and clothing, and a particularly annoying shard in my thumb. Dixon was even willing to search the clown. But we turned up nothing.

"Maybe there's no Spellcraft to find," he said. "Maybe there's just something in Taco Town's water that makes it look all sparkly."

He was reaching, and we both knew it. The town was crackling with *volshebstvo*. And if there was malicious work to be Uncrafted, Dixon was the man to do it. "Dixon—it is obvious the titmouses didn't pick Taco Town at random. Just like the tomatoes didn't randomly explode." I had hoped to spare him, but maybe it was for the best he got a good look in the cold light of day at what his uncle had left behind...or the dim light leaking through the holes in the Big Taco. I drew out my paints and said, "I would never Craft something new to change another man's magic. But I am willing to try to expose it."

Dixon's breath caught in the way it did whenever I opened my paintbox. Sometimes I thought he was more excited to see me open that box than he was when I opened my fly. This was not necessarily a bad thing. People are attracted to each other for many reasons. It might as well be a reason that can't fade as surely as looks eventually will.

I drew a bottle of water from his knapsack and a small, blank card from my opposite pocket, cleared my mind, and sent my focus outward to encompass all of Taco Town. The people so desperate to preserve their livelihood. The disasters falling like dominoes in Fonzo's wake. Dixon's pathetic hope that everything would somehow manage to turn out just fine. I held these ideas in my mind for a moment, then dabbed my brush, and painted.

Yellow-brown, some orange, some blue-gray. A dark speckle that was a smattering of birds against a blue sky. And a scattering of white spots that only appeared once I was done painting, thanks to contaminants trapped between the paper and paint that caused a pattern of resist. I squinted at a beam of light knifing through a hole, and saw the sunbeam was dancing with motes of dust. I flapped the small paper and considered the flaw. The Seen felt no less potent to me...as if there really were no accidents.

Once the surface was dry enough for ink, I handed it to Dixon. He turned it this way and that, not critically, but with fascination. Dixon has seen many paintings in his life. Not only in his family shop, but in his travels through far-flung cities. And even with so many works to compare to, he continues to find subtle nuances in mine.

"It's Taco Town in all its magic," he said wistfully. "Do you think there's magic to this place, aside from just the Spellcraft turning the town upside down? Sometimes I wonder if memories count as magic. Or whimsy. Or fun. They're intangible things, and yet they're so...present."

His voice had gone soft as he spoke in this rare moment of introspection. It suited him, this glimpse of his serious side, a side which still managed to be so enviably full of wonder. But it was tainted by the fact that he'd soon need to face up to exactly what his uncle had done.

Dixon carried his quill and ink at all times—he'd even half-joked about bringing it to bed. All Scriveners value their quills, but after his horribly failed Quilling Ceremony, Dixon was even more fanatical about the instrument of his Craft. I could relate. I was able to paint a Seen with anything that would leave a mark, and still I felt attached to the miniature travel set I kept in my pocket.

I no longer painted for my own amusement, but Dixon practiced his calligraphy every day, even if it was just a series of loops and flourishes in ballpoint pen on the side of a paper bag. He had the most breathtaking writing I'd ever seen, even compared to the decrepit Scriveners I'd known in Russia who'd been honing the skill all their lives—maybe because it felt somehow more youthful. Maybe because it wasn't yet jaded.

Dixon brushed dust from the edge of a collapsed carnival game, then placed the fresh Seen on the precarious surface. His focus went soft and he stilled, searching inside with a deep sense of respect, even gratitude. With purpose. When he opened his ink, dipped his quill, and set pen to paper, his lettering flowed unusually small. And yet, it didn't feel at all cramped. Instead, it was delicate, like the finest lace.

Crafting calls crafting
What's hidden is seen
Magic stands revealed
Above, below, between

The first line would have been sufficient, but Dixon Scribed with not only the enthusiasm of a brand new Scrivener, but the confidence of someone who'd come to the skill later in life, armed with more experience and depth. Instead of creating loopholes in which the Crafting could go awry, this elaborate Scrivening amplified the Spellcraft power I'd begun to harness in my painting, then cinched it elegantly in its intricate web of words.

And as Dixon inked the final flourish, he smiled—but not his usual broad, open smile. This was a secret smile: quite aware of exactly how much power he'd so masterfully wielded, and pragmatically satisfied.

I was unexpectedly moved that my own contribution had helped to elicit that expression. But before I could revel in my own self-satisfaction, I felt the power of the *volshebstvo* blow through me like a gust of arctic air across the Baltic.

The Big Taco rocked as if it had been hit by a physical wind. Inside, all the pressboard and plywood creaked louder than the hull of a great ship, and adobe dust fell like hail. Dixon's eyes went wide, showing white all around, and he snapped his quill back into its rigid case before it came to any harm.

He was not the only one to react.

I flung out my arms to shield him with my body, spanning the width of the Taco. Crumbs of adobe bounced from my shaved head as I braced myself against a collapse, but once the Spellcraft was done rushing through the structure, everything settled as if nothing had happened.

"Wow," Dixon said. "That was close."

But as I straightened, I felt the subtle precursor of movement—and barely had time to brace myself again as something big toppled against my back. I tucked Dixon into a protective embrace as the two of us went down hard, him under me, and stiffened to take the brunt of the impact. A Seer should be more protective of his hands—and I didn't care in the least. We fell to the floor with the breath knocked out of us, clasped together as desperately as we'd ever been in bed, and just as winded.

Dixon's eyelashes fluttered against my cheek as he opened his eyes. "Yuri? How is it you're grabbing my junk with both your hands behind my back?"

Whatever had fallen on me was no mere plywood. In fact, the way it hugged my body curve for curve, it could only be one thing.

I threw it off with a noise of dismay, shuddering all over.

The clown toppled onto its side, leering, and its red rubber nose bounced away.

"Now there's a three-way I'll never forget," Dixon declared, then cocked his head to match the angle of the mannequin sprawled on the floor. "Hey, look! There's something shoved up its nostril."

Luckily, he was eager to see. I couldn't bear to touch the thing.

It had to be Spellcraft. I knew without even bothering to check and see if the air distorted around it.

Dixon retrieved the Crafting, pushed into a sitting position and unrolled the paper carefully. I crouched to one side, keeping as far from the toppled clown as the cramped space would allow. Queasy excitement churned through my belly. This would be the moment in which his uncle's sabotage would come to light, and while I didn't exactly revel in the pain it would cause Dixon once his idol fell from grace, in some sense, I was eager for this Fonzo character to get what he deserved.

Dixon smoothed the paper over his knee...and stared at it, brow furrowed.

The Crafting was upside down. Not only that, but it was in a language other than my native tongue, and the lines were rough and splotchy. It took me a moment to decipher. When I did, where I'd expected to find the Scrivening that caused the ruin of Taco Town was written, instead, a single word.

Revivify.

DIXON
10

Of course, I could deduce the meaning of the word *revivify*. I supposed we should be grateful it didn't raise any zombies.

Frankly, the Crafting left me with way more questions than answers, not just because of the obscure vocabulary, either.

We scrambled out to the truck, covered in adobe crumbs. Yuri seemed more pensive than usual. I was just confused—and gritty. A fine layer of dust coated my teeth. When we climbed into the cab and I pulled out my water for a swig to wash away the adobe, a telltale slip of paper stuck to the bottle fluttered to the seat between us...the Spellcraft I'd found at You-Make-Um.

The one I'd been carrying in my *pocket*, not my bag.

It was a lot like the Crafting we'd found shoved up the clown's sinuses. The same hot-pressed cotton rag paper used in all the Spellcraft my family's shop created. The same weird blob of watercolor from Practical Penn's Seer, Rufus Clahd. And the same penmanship, too. I'd recognize it anywhere. It was not just the hand that had taught me to write, but the Hand of my family.

Uncle Fonzo.

And yet, like the other Crafting we'd just discovered, it was nothing like Uncle Fonzo's typical spells. I've never known a Scrivener to pen a single word. Not that it couldn't work, technically. But it was definitely weird. Word choice, meter and penmanship all contributed to a Scrivener's signature style. Uncle Fonzo had a tendency to write the sort of upbeat phrases you'd find in a fortune cookie, like the lockpick Crafting my cousin Sabina carried, *Persistence opens all doors*. Yes, Uncle Fonzo was succinct.

But never this abrupt.

Yuri scowled at the Crafting I'd found in the factory. The Seen was a gray squiggle. The Scrivening was just one word.

Parsimonious.

"What does this mean?" he finally asked.

"That you're right," I admitted. "My uncle has definitely been Crafting here."

He quelled a sigh. "Not the situation—the word. What is the meaning?"

"Maybe we should look it up," I said. "Just so I don't steer you wrong." I called up the definition on my phone and read...with a growing sense of relief. Because, come on, that word really did sound like it couldn't possibly be anything good. The initial few definitions were incriminating, meanings like *cheap* and *stingy*, but it was the lengthier explanation that caught my eye—and not solely because it cast my uncle in a more flattering light. "Parsimony is the principal of getting the most results from the fewest resources. That's exactly what the Crafting did—it made more snow globes with less plastic."

Yuri didn't seem quite as relieved as I was, probably because he still had adobe-mouth. I tilted the water bottle his way and gave it a little wag. When he reached up to take it, the corner of a piece of hot-pressed cotton rag peeked from his cuff.

"Hey!" I yanked the bottle out of reach and pointed. "What's that?"

He shook his head and released the sigh he'd been trying so hard to hold back, grumbling in Russian, then plucked the Crafting from his sleeve. Another Rufus Clahd special—a lopsided circular orangey-red blob that could be anything from a deflating basketball to a distorted sunset...to a freakishly overripe tomato. Scribed over it was the word *Fecund.*

I called up the definition and read, "Fruitful, productive, flourishing."

"Why would he not use a common word?" Yuri asked.

"And why limit himself to a single word at all?" Whatever had prompted Uncle Fonzo to adopt this new aesthetic, it obviously hadn't done him any favors.

"Can you Uncraft them?"

Parsimonious made my eyes cross, and I was still worried that *Revivify* might end up making our brains look a little too tasty. But maybe I could do something with *Fecund.* I held up the Crafting and squinted. Daylight was the best light for studying Spellcraft. Some folks say the devil is in the details. I'm not convinced there is such a thing as Satan, but I do know that the details are what holds the Spellcraft mojo—and the broad, pure spectrum of sunlight brought out the most detail.

The familiar paper was quite heavy. When I held it up, it only let the slightest bit of light through. But that bit was enough for me to see the single word was poorly inked. The margins of the stroke were rough, with a wispy gap in the center. Not only that, but faint spatters marred the Crafting where a ragged quill had caught the paper surface. And with the quality of the stock my family used, that hardly ever happened.

It looked as if the strokes had been made with a poorly-trimmed quill. Strange. Unlike regular feather pens, Spellcraft quills don't wear down. And yet, this had to be a magical quill. Otherwise, the Scrivening wouldn't work.

Although the strokes were janky, since there was only the single word on the page, at least the lettering was large and well-spaced. For Uncrafting, the space in which to slide additional letters, to re-harness the Spellcraft and change its trajectory, was what mattered the most. Not the look of the calligraphy.

I cleared my mind and focused on the orangey blob—Yuri's painting was so much more inspiring—and thought about Vanessa and her greenhouses. Obviously, I still wanted her plants to be fruitful. But not to the point where they'd explode on impact.

Could I squeeze another letter into the current Crafting? I thought so.

I visualized the words re-tooled as *PerFECt, UNDamaged Tomatoes*, and excitement coiled in my belly as the Spellcraft began to flow. My heartbeat quickened and my fingertips tingled.

I could fit those letters in.

I could make it work.

Yes—I could reshape the Spellcraft.

I just *knew* it.

The anticipation of the feel of inking the letterforms was palpable in my hand as I unstoppered my ink and dipped my handsome white quill. I saw how to slant the letter t that would break the two words just so, to make the calligraphy appear almost natural. I imagined the flourish I'd add to the final sweep of my pen. I squirmed, just a little, at the thought of Uncrafting something Scribed not only by a family member, but by Uncle Fonzo—the strongest of us all.

With a deep breath, I steeled myself, imagined my Scrivening one more time to fix words and letters in my mind, then set quill to paper and inked the stem of the letter P.

But by the time I finished, lifted the nib, and set it down again to add the bowl of the letter, the stem contracted into a dozen small beads of ink. They scattered like a spill of black pepper in the midst of a powerful sneeze.

Anyone who's written their name on Easter eggs with a white crayon before dyeing them is familiar with the concept of resist. The wax is invisible until the egg meets its dye bath, and the color shrinks away from the crayon marks. (A great many years ago, I may or may not have written "poo face" on Sabina's egg. After my caption appeared beneath her name, she threw it at me and splattered half the kitchen purple.) But when I ran my thumb along the paper, it didn't feel any different from our normal stock. Smooth, yes, from the quality finish. But still absorbent.

I tried to draw the P again. And again the ink beaded up and scattered.

Yuri pulled a pair of glasses out of the glovebox, perched them on his nose, held out a hand and said, "Show me."

I handed over the Crafting and he held it up for scrutiny. Whereas I'd looked at it face-on, analyzing the character of the ink, he held it sideways as if he could see the Spellcraft wafting off it. He studied it a good long while, then set it carefully on the dashboard and told me, "It doesn't look right. Don't touch it—don't touch any of them."

"We can't just ignore the Crafting. Maybe the town could survive without snow globes, and no doubt they could import their tomatoes. But if the Big Taco falls apart...that's it. A member of my family made this mistake, Yuri, so it's my responsibility to set it right."

"You can't layer a good Crafting over a bad one. You might as well perfume a turd."

"If only we knew what to do." I looked at Yuri pointedly.

"What are you thinking?"

"Obviously, it's too risky to tinker with anything that's been touched by the funky Crafting. But if there's anything we know for sure wasn't in town when the Spellcraft was put in place, it's us."

YURI

11

I had never worked with a Scrivener willing to Craft anything for me as a gift—and I'd certainly never *paid* for Crafting to be made on my behalf. I wanted to feel leery of the idea, and frankly, I realized, I didn't much trust Scriveners in general...but this was Dixon. And he was bursting with sincerity.

We stashed Fonzo's tainted Spellcraft in the truck bed to keep it as far away from us as possible. I was already worried the Crafting we'd done to reveal the nasty little things would make them stick to us for the rest of our lives. And yet, the moment Dixon suggested we Craft yet another piece, the urge to paint began welling up inside. It felt like hunger. Or, more accurately, it felt like the food must feel when it's about to be eaten. A queasy excitement mingled with dread. All bound together in a net of inevitability.

My eyes were open, but only dimly did I see. My attention was focused instead on the landscape of my mind—and even that was more instinctive than deliberate. Dixon tipped water into a bottle cap, then held it for me. I dipped my brush. I became the brush, and the water drawing up into the fibers was like a balm creeping through my veins. If this was how drugs felt, I understood how addicts were made.

The brush was not moving of its own accord, but it was certainly some primal part of me that moved it, with only enough conscious control to hold on. When I daubed the wetness into the pigment, my brush swept through multiple pans of color. Sometimes this left an ombre of varying hues, and sometimes the paints mingled in the brush to become muted and neutral. When I touched brush to paper this time, it was a bit of each. Rounded, cottony forms where the paint mingled toward gray, and a hint of a prismatic arch in the sweep of the stroke.

I turned up the defroster and held the wet painting to the air, then slid it across the dash to Dixon, who dumped the last few drops of water from the bottle cap out the window, then turned his full attention to the Seen.

I held the inkwell as he'd held the water, and when he dipped his quill, his gaze turned inward. Did we search for our Spellcraft in the same place, I wondered—some mystical bit of nowhere in which the *volshebstvo* lived? Or were we opposites, drawing from two distinct sources of energy that only rarely combined?

Even written on the dashboard, Dixon's handwriting was hypnotic and elegant. With room enough to write as he pleased, without needing to fit letters within and around another Scrivener's lettering, he began with a flourish so graceful it made my breath catch. And then the rest of the Scrivening flowed from his pen.

A silver lining, every cloud

Inspiration has endowed

After the Crafting was penned—after *volshebstvo* lit across the back of my neck like a playful breath—Dixon scanned the words as if he had no memory of writing them. "I, ah...didn't mean to be quite so literal. Or so cliche." He blushed. "But, look. It's a cloud with a cute little rainbow. See?" He shielded his eyes and peered through the window. "You don't suppose it will change the weather, do you?"

"Is that what you meant for it to do?"

"That would be awesome! But no. I'm sure those clouds are

entirely too far away—we'd have to send it up on a rocket launcher to make anything happen so high in the sky. I was just thinking that in any given situation, there's always an action that'll lead to the best outcome, even when it looks like every possible option is a bad one. Trying to change Spellcraft that clearly doesn't want to be altered might only make things worse. But you and I could be inspired to make the best of a bad situation, regardless of what else was going on. So I focused on us instead."

He tucked the Crafting onto the passenger visor with an embarrassed little laugh. "Old habit—I never carry Spellcraft on my person."

"Bad luck?"

"No—in case I get arrested." As if the truck would not be searched as well. "So, what now? We've got a bunch of funky Craftings that won't let us change them. Quick, don't think too hard—what's the best course of action?"

"Get rid of them."

"Mom always says that destroying an active Crafting is like trying to wash blood out of your clothes in hot water. All it does is set the stain."

That, I definitely could hear Florica Penn saying. "If they can't be destroyed, then we take them somewhere far away from here and let the town recover."

Dixon brightened. "Whaddaya know? Being in the middle of nowhere can actually work to our advantage. We make a final sweep to be sure we have everything, then drive the Craftings halfway to Grimford and bury them under a rock. That should keep the influence of the Spellcraft to a minimum while the magic eventually dissipates. We'll just need to make sure it's not a dairy farm. I'd hate to make anyone's cows explode." He leaned across the seat, nuzzled my cheek, and said, "Who knows...maybe the motel in Grimford has a jacuzzi tub, too." He quelled his perpetual smile only long enough to brush a kiss across my lips.

I found myself unexpectedly optimistic about the trip. A pleasant drive with pleasant company, a good supper and a warm bed at the end of the day—one I would not fall into alone. What more could we really want?

I pulled away from the Big Taco and headed down Salsa Lane, wondering if we'd need to buy a shovel, or if the hunting knife in my toolbox would suffice. We were almost to the foot of the hill when a figure in khaki stepped into the road, waving her hands. I pulled to the gravel shoulder and unrolled the window.

It was the woman we'd met last night in the motel lobby—and she was too winded to speak. As she caught her breath, Dixon greeted her with, "If it isn't Buggin'!" And, "Was your bathtub everything it was cracked up to be?" And, "Where's your adorable orange Bug?"

"I'm Genevieve—Buggin's my car." She planted her hands on her knees and drank in a few more deep breaths, then said, "And she's not starting, poor baby. I turn the key, and nothing! Hopefully the garage can figure it out. But in the meantime, I need to get to the top of the hill. Give me a lift?"

If Dixon were not in the truck, would I have done so? Who knows. It was unlikely I would have stopped for the woman at all. But Dixon was there, and naturally, he shoved open his door and said, "No problem. Hop in!"

Once introductions were made and Genevieve was situated, with Dixon in the middle snuggling happily against me, I pulled a U-turn and headed back up the hill.

"I'm sure you're excited to see the Big Taco up close," Dixon told her, "but be sure not to judge it too harshly. It's been through some tough times lately."

Genevieve seemed excited to talk about the Taco—but whatever her reply might have been, it was drowned out by a thunderous bang. Instinctively, I ducked to avoid oncoming bullets, but soon registered that the sound had come from underneath the rear of the truck.

Apparently, tomatoes and cows were not the only things in danger of exploding.

Dixon craned his neck to look behind us and said, "Quick, Yuri, turn around. The muffler's getting away!"

Normally, I'd leave the exhaust system where it landed and drop off our passenger. After all, we were the only ones around. But since we were on a hill, not only was the muffler rolling...it was picking up speed. I spun the steering wheel. With a noise like a jet pulling out of a hangar, the truck swung around yet again, only for us to see the muffler pitch toward the foot of the hill, bounce twice, then somersault around the nearest turn.

"Wow!" Dixon said. "Look at that muffler go."

We roared down the hill in pursuit. I turned the corner. Late night traffic was just as sparse as any in Taco Town, but a few curious bystanders had paused in front of the diner to puzzle over the automobile part rolling down the street with the very loud truck right behind it. The ground was level now, but somehow, the muffler kept right on going. It rolled through Taco Town's single stoplight—which, of course, turned red before we could make it through. Small town police being what they were, I didn't dare floor it. Especially with a piece of Spellcraft in the truck.

But Taco Town being the size it was, there just weren't that many places for the muffler to go. And given that it had traveled so much farther than any normal object might, we could only presume it was Spellcraft at work.

That muffler wanted to be followed.

It curved gracefully around one more corner, and when I pulled up behind it, I realized we'd been there before: the You-Make-Um factory. And the muffler rolled to a stop right at the foot of the wooden Indian. Stunned, baffled, bemused, the three of us climbed out of the cab and assessed the truck. "You should really get that looked at," Genevieve said. "But not until Buggin' is fixed. There's only one mechanic in town."

Dixon rounded the back of the truck. The duct tape hung in long streamers. Where they dragged behind, they'd picked up a few empty cans along the way—despite the fact that there'd been no trash in the road. "It looks like someone's getting married," Dixon chortled. "Do they do that in Russia?"

I was beginning to suspect he didn't actually want answers when he asked me these things. I ignored the question and peered through the factory window instead where, despite how late it was, a light still shone.

When Dixon pressed his face to the glass beside me, the shouting began.

"Hello? Who's out there? Help!"

We let ourselves in and made our way to the Globe-o-Matic snow globe maker...only to find Wendall dangling by the collar of his shirt from an articulating arm at the top of the machine. His toes hovered inches off the ground, and his arms were hitched up at an awkward angle on either side of his head.

"Help me," he cried. "I can't feel my arms."

A taller man would not have been lifted off the ground. And a slimmer man would not have been caught around the belly by the hem and slid right out. But Spellcraft was involved—and I was not the least bit surprised. While Dixon took stock of the situation, clearly wondering if it was best to unbutton Wendall's shirt top to bottom or bottom to top, I walked over and simply lifted him off the hook.

"Have you seen my son?" he asked as he flapped his arms, hoping to regain sensation. "Hooray for hands-free dialing, right? But I've been calling and texting him all afternoon, and no answer. What a relief you guys came along. Who knows how long I would've been trapped."

"Talk about getting hung up!" Dixon said. "What happened?"

"I was trying to fix the Globe-O-Matic by figuring out which calibrations the traveling mechanic changed. But I got too close to the robotic arm and it snagged me by the collar. I knew better, darn it. I'm usually more careful. This hasn't happened in nearly a month!"

While Dixon suggested Wendall install a workplace sign—*X Number of Days Without Being Strung Up by the Machine*—Genevieve was looking more closely at the contraption. I came up beside her and followed her gaze. "What is it?" I asked.

"See these dials?" She ran her finger along the control panel. "If you look very close, you can tell where they used to be set. The off-gassing in the atmosphere tarnished this plate just a little, and now there's a tiny notch where the knob used to cover the metal."

It was faint, but when I looked very closely, I did see it. The previous settings were there, you just needed to really look. Wendall was thrilled. He dug up a very bright flashlight and magnifying glass to restore the settings to their prior positions as precisely as possible. Dixon found the whole procedure fascinating—then again, he was easily entertained.

"The proof is in the pudding," Wendall said.

Dixon rubbed his hands together expectantly. "I love pudding!"

"Ahem. Let's see what magic we can make." Wendall flicked on the power and pulled the giant lever. The Globe-O-Matic powered up with a cacophony of whirs, buzzes and crackles. And as the scent of melting plastic filled the air, the machine lumbered into action.

Just moments later, a snow globe rolled through the curtains and hobbled off the end of the conveyor belt. But there was no box of packing foam to collect it. We all turned toward the globe—I thought Dixon would dive across the machine to catch it and adjusted my trajectory to catch him instead before the Globe-O-Matic minced him into glitter. I snagged him by the belt loop before he dove within range of any indiscriminating robotic arms. Besides, Genevieve was closer—and thankfully, she was quick on her feet. She snatched the globe just before it hit the concrete floor... and then she shook it and held it up to the light.

Even from where I stood, it was plain that the figure in the globe was decidedly vaginal.

"Don't worry," Wendall called out over the noise of the machine. "That one was leftover from before. It's the next globe we want to check."

A few moments later, the curtain at the end of the chute parted, and another snow globe rolled off the line. Wendall plucked it from the conveyor belt and held it up to scrutiny. His breath caught. The rest of us all move closer and squinted. On first glance, it looked the same as the one Genevieve was holding. But, looking closer, it became clear that what we were seeing inside was definitely a taco.

"Perfect!" Wendall cried. "Just perfect. Even better than before, in fact. What a relief."

"Maybe you can recycle all the misfired globes," Dixon suggested.

Wendall shook his head. "Not with my fully automated system. I'll need to figure out another way to get rid of them. Maybe we can raffle them off."

"Misfires?" Genevieve held up the malformed globe. "You mean these?"

"Those are the ones," Wendall said with a rueful sigh.

"If you're unloading these, I definitely know someone who'd be interested. My sister would love them."

"Is your sister a lesbian?" Dixon asked.

"My sister is a gynecologist!" Genevieve turned her attention back to the misfire and gave it another hearty shake. Dixon wagged his eyebrows at me as if to say, *Oops*. Once the glitter settled, Genevieve added, "I don't see what her being a lesbian has to do with it."

"What a relief," Wendall said. "We'll negotiate a nice price, and be back in production by tomorrow morning. My son will be thrilled to hear it." He pulled out his phone. "Funny, he's still not answering."

"Try the greenhouse," Dixon suggested. "That's the last place we saw him."

Wendall tried another call. "Vanessa isn't answering, either."

Goosebumps rippled up the backs of my arms as I imagined the tainted Spellcraft taken hold, exploding the two of them in a garish echo of the overripe tomatoes. Casually, so as not to panic the rest of the group, I said, "We should go check on them."

"Field trip!" Dixon said happily. "Let's go!"

DIXON

12

Squeezing Genevieve into the cab was a challenge—not that I'm complaining, since it was a great excuse to mash myself against Yuri while he drove. But cramming Wendall in, too? Wasn't gonna happen.

I could tell by the look on Yuri's face that he was tempted to invite the guy to walk, since it was so healthy and all. But Wendall was happy enough to ride in the truck bed with the muffler, so we hit the road without comment.

"That was really cool what you did back there," I called to Genevieve over the roar of unmuffled exhaust. "How do you know so much about manufacturing? Are you an engineer?"

"Not at all, that would be my baby brother. I just helped him study when he was getting his degree. My real interest lies in—"

Whatever those proclivities might've been, they were lost in the dramatic gasp Genevieve made when we rounded the bend and saw the greenhouse. The tomato explosion from that morning had gone leathery in the day's sun. It had darkened into a particularly bloody shade of scarlet. "Don't worry," I told her. "That's just tomato."

"Obviously. What did you think I thought?"

"Never mind," Yuri said. "Let's go see what's become of the photographer and the gardener."

"A little help?" Wendall called from the back. He acted like it was just some lingering numbness in his arms, even though it was clear he didn't trust his stumpy little legs to hit the ground safely if he leapt the few inches to the pavement. I gave him a hand down without comment, and the four of us approached the "bloody" greenhouse.

It was even warmer inside than before, and just as humid, but the scent had changed. Whereas it was green before all the tomatoes exploded, now it was vibrantly red. I was just about to ask Yuri if he thought it was possible to smell a color when a sultry, feminine giggle reached our ears from the far end of the greenhouse.

It didn't sound like anyone was in trouble. But before I could announce that we were there, I caught a flash of movement. If the plants hadn't all been destroyed, it's possible someone's modesty might've been spared. But between the few remaining battered tomato stalks, we couldn't help but notice that Vanessa and Harvey weren't just hale and hearty...they were naked.

Butt naked.

Vanessa was on her back—but she wasn't doing quite what that you'd guess. She was posing. And Harvey was down on his elbows and knees between her legs—again, not what it sounded like. He had his camera in hand, and was coaching her through a vampy, naked, tomato-covered photo shoot. The two of them lolled around without a care in the world, murmuring soft encouragement to each other as they shared a bizarre and secret diversion. They were so focused on the camera it was a real shame to interrupt.

But Harvey's father apparently didn't share that sentiment. "Harvey! You're butt naked!"

At that, the young photographer scrambled up from the floor and began yanking on his clothes. Vanessa was clearly none too pleased, but she drew her once-white lab coat around her bare body with the grace and aplomb of royalty.

"Harvey?" Genevieve asked. "From Harvey's Haven?"

Harvey was blushing to high heaven and his T-shirt was on backwards, but he rallied and said, "That's me!"

"I'm staying in your coach house. I've messaged you half a dozen times on YourBNB."

His father said, "And I've been calling you all day."

Harvey glanced over at his tweedy jacket, which lay discarded in a heap with his sweater vest and his underpants. "Sorry—I guess my phone was on vibrate."

The tomato-covered gardener eyed the jacket as if she was cooking up some ideas for later.

"The room," Genevieve prompted.

"You found parking okay?" Harvey asked. "The bed was soft enough? The coffee was good?"

"And the tub...?" I added.

Genevieve waved it all off. "Yes, yes, those things were fine. But I hardly slept a wink. It was just too quiet."

Yuri narrowed his eyes.

"Here's an idea," I told Genevieve. "Maybe we could trade rooms!"

"You found a room at the Motel after all?"

"Oh. Uh, no...actually, we slept at the souvenir shop. What time is it, Yuri? Maybe we can make it to Minneapolis before the health food store closes and grab those tortillas."

"Minneapolis?" Vanessa said sharply. "That reminds me—there's an overnight delivery in the truck."

The fact that she'd shirked her postal duties to enjoy a roll in the hay—or more accurately, in tomato guts—prompted the sort of chagrin that the exposure of her personal assets hadn't. While Genevieve eyed a bunch of vigorous-looking tomato seedlings that had sprouted up in a random spill of dirt, Vanessa slipped on her gardening clogs and buttoned her lab coat crookedly. When she dashed out of the greenhouse, the rest of us followed.

The mail truck was still right where we'd seen it last time. Vanessa swung open the back to reveal a prominent package sitting atop the other mail: A medium-sized box from Healthy Belly in Minneapolis. And it was addressed to the Masa Motel.

Everything happens for a reason—that's what Uncle Fonzo always told us. Maybe it was just the fortune cookie way he had of seeing the world...but there was a grain of truth in it, too. Maybe it was Spellcraft that prompted the urgent package to be ignored for the better part of the day. Or maybe Vanessa was just delightfully distracted by the stamina demonstrated by a guy half her age—after all, the Crafting wasn't so much as a twinkle in my eye when the tomatoes blew up and the clothes came off.

I turned to Genevieve and said, "I'll bet that box is full of gluten-free tortillas. And I know for a fact that if you bring it over to the motel, the owner will give you the best room in the house!" Okay, maybe that was an exaggeration, but I'd wager the owner's personal quarters were at least passable.

Genevieve hoisted the package out of the truck and set it right back down. "It's too heavy to carry."

"We will drive," Yuri declared, and hefted the box as easily as if it was empty. We piled into the truck with Genevieve and left the three blushing redheads behind to sort out who was more mortified, father or son.

13

꿈

I've never claimed to possess any great mechanical aptitude, but I realized I wasn't exactly sure what purpose a muffler served when the smell of burning rubber tickled my senses. "Are we on fire?" I shouted over the engine.

"It's not us," Yuri shouted back.

"Look!" Genevieve pointed.

We rounded the souvenir factory and the motel came into view—with a thin column of oily smoke threading up from behind the office. Yuri floored it, and the truck burst forward with a fierce roar. We screeched to a stop right in front and piled out of the truck, then dashed around the corner of the building to see what was going on...only to find Olive sprawled in a covered deck chair beside a fitfully smoldering planter with a half-empty bottle of tequila in her hand. She was wearing the same pantsuit as yesterday, and it looked like she hadn't slept a wink.

"This is horrible," she moaned. "I thought I was doing myself a favor when I bought planters made from recycled tires instead of wood. And now look where my lofty ideals got me."

Stunned, I said, "I had no idea rubber could just randomly burst into flames." Yuri nudged my ribs and pointed to an empty tin of lighter fluid beside the planter, then I noticed the green plastic lighter in Olive's other hand and I realized what I was seeing. "Oh."

Genevieve was less worried about sparing anyone's feelings. "Why on earth would you set your own place on fire?"

"I'm going to lose it anyway. Might as well collect the insurance."

"But you can't burn this place down," Genevieve said. "It's gorgeous. A shining example of midcentury Americana. There's got to be another way."

"The food. The linens. The incidentals. I've done the math. It's no use. Once payday comes around—once I pay everyone for all the overtime they've had to work, cleaning up after the freeloaders—that's it. I'm done."

"But we have your tortillas," I said.

Olive moaned. "Get them out of my sight."

Genevieve casually took the lighter from Olive's unresisting hand. "What you need is an infusion of cash. One that'll still leave your motel standing."

"Taco eating contest?" I suggested.

No one else seemed to hear—sometimes that happens when an idea is just too good. But before I could repeat myself, Genevieve glanced around the motor court and said, "How many rooms are in this place? Thirty?"

Olive sighed dramatically. "Unfortunately, yes. You wouldn't think there'd be that many unethical birders around—but you'd be wrong. And now that the titmouses are gone, all of them are empty."

"But this is perfect! My family reunion is coming up next week, and our venue fell through. I need thirty rooms."

Olive fanned the grudgingly smoldering rubber planter. "Then you'll have to go to Grimford. By this time next week, the Masa Motel will be nothing but a toasty memory."

Luckily, at this rate, it would take all week for the place to burn down.

"I won't take no for an answer," Genevieve said, in that stunningly confident way in which she pronounced all the things she was entirely sure of. "In fact, if you stop fanning that flame, I'll put down a deposit right this minute."

At the promise of money, Olive perked up. "Fifty percent?"

"Done." Genevieve snatched away the paper Olive had been using to fan the flames and handed it to me...and a tingle shot up my arm so sharply it made me stagger.

Watercolor. India ink. Hot-pressed cotton rag. The Seen was a bunch of flesh-colored dots that looked like they'd been doodled by a bored kindergartener. Over the Seen, inked in ragged lettering—the word *Plethoric*.

I cut my eyes to Yuri. He scowled at the Crafting and gave his head a subtle shake.

At least I wasn't the only one who'd never encountered that particular word before. We'd need to get rid of the Crafting before flaming dinosaurs popped out of the planter. But as I turned to stow it in the truck bed with all the others, a bit of dried ink flaked off the paper and fell away. I gave it a shake, and more ink came loose. It crumbled before my eyes and dropped off, leaving me with nothing but a dumb little painting...and a lot of questions.

Olivia let Genevieve walk her back to the office to make that deposit, leaving Yuri and me beside the planter. Although the fire was pretty much done, I pulled out my water bottle and doused what was left. The smoldering died with a grateful hiss.

"Now we know what happened to the motel," Yuri said triumphantly.

I was as glad to find stray bits of Spellcraft as anyone else. "But I've never heard of a Scrivening *falling off*. Is it even a Crafting anymore without the words?"

Yuri held up the painting horizontally and scrutinized the surface. "I think it is just a Seen now. Potential Spellcraft—like gasoline without a car. I made many of these in Russia to work off my debt. But I would not risk re-using this particular piece."

I shuddered vigorously. "Me neither—especially when I could get a much more appealing one from you. Let's put it with the rest of the screwy Spellcraft."

We headed back to the truck. Once we ditched the ugly painting, Genevieve came out to meet us. "I thought I'd started off this trip on the wrong foot," she told us, "but it just goes to show that every cloud has a silver lining."

The echo of the Crafting I'd penned earlier rippled across my shoulder blades. Sure, it was a common enough expression— unlike the word *Plethoric*—but, still.

"Come, Genevieve," Yuri said. "We will fetch your luggage."

"But I never got to take an up-close look at the Big Taco. Can we swing by there first?"

Yuri wanted to say no, I could tell. Probably tired from running around all day—and eager to take advantage of the jacuzzi tub. But since Genevieve was nice enough to give us her room.... "Please, Yuri? It won't take long. It's just a few minutes away."

Yuri grumbled something in Russian—but in English, what he eventually said was, "Fine."

Conversation over the roar of the engine was difficult, to say the least, but I managed to call out, "Why are you so interested in the Big Taco? Are you a roadside attraction enthusiast?"

"Not at all—I think they're eyesores. But I'm interested in what's inside."

Yuri cut his eyes to me. I think he was still a little spooked by that clown. He turned onto Salsa Lane and we began our ascent, and the engine cranked up its volume to extra-loud, discouraging all further attempts at conversation.

We climbed out of the cab and silence rang in our ears. That, and the distant sound of chirping.

"Hear that?" Genevieve asked. "Long-tailed field cricket. Common from here to North Dakota." She whipped out a pair of impressively long tweezers.

The past day had not been kind to the Taco. Even in the starlight, the holes pecked by the titmice were apparent. The yellow-pigmented adobe was more brownish-gray inside, and the whole Taco looked sad and moldy. Probably like the gluten-free tortillas would soon, unless someone put them in the fridge.

Genevieve started digging in one of the titmouse holes with great purpose. I got up close and personal to see what she might find, while Yuri fell back a few paces looking vaguely ill.

"Aha!" Genevieve plucked something from the hole with evident relish. It was fascinating—in the way those YouTube pimple popping videos are fascinating. "Just as I suspected! An articulated mudmucker. Do you know what this means?"

"Honestly? No idea."

"This is the first sighting north of Kansas. What are the odds?"

Given the crumbling, messed-up Spellcraft in the truck bed, probably pretty good.

"Is that bug still alive?" Yuri said queasily.

"This?" Genevieve brandished the insect heartily. "This is just a discarded pupa." She waved the thing under Yuri's nose. "See? No more larva."

Yuri looked a bit green in the starlight.

"If that's just a shell," I asked, "where's the bug?"

"In the belly of a very satisfied crested carrion titmouse, no doubt. Those birds will definitely pick at carrion till the cows come home. But they have a field day when the articulated mudmuckers pupate."

One can only absorb so many new words in a day, and my head was feeling alarmingly full. Even so, I had to ask. "These bug things... they wouldn't happen to be endangered too, would they?"

"Heck, no! Articulated mudmuckers are an invasive species, like zebra mussels or brown marmorated stinkbugs." Wait, that wasn't a real thing, was it? She had to be pulling my leg. I waited for the punchline, but it never came. "The mudmucker eggs spread through clay soil. In this case—the authentic Arizona adobe clay."

"But I don't get it," I said. "The Big Taco has been around for years, and the mudmuckers are only now a problem?"

"It's one of the few species with a proto-periodical life cycle—like the cicada, only invasive, and without the pretty nighttime mating call. Every thirteen years—bam."

That didn't surprise me. Everyone knows the number thirteen

is terrible luck.

Genevieve dropped the bug-shaped casing in a plastic baggie and tucked it into one of her many cargo pockets. "I was worried they'd got a toehold in Minnesota, so I came out to see if we should do a mass fumigation—which can wreak havoc on beneficial pollinators, too. I'm thrilled to find the titmice handled it. They really did this town a favor."

I gave the Big Taco a critical once-over. "Too bad it left the town's main attraction in such a sorry state."

"This? No big deal. My brother-in-law teaches natural building techniques for the state extension. He's crazy good with adobe. I'll have him take a look at it when he comes in for the reunion. But my guess is that a minor skim-coat will have the Big Taco looking good as new in no time. Especially with all the perforations the titmice left behind." She gave the adobe an affectionate pat. "It'll give the new finish something to hold on to."

I peered into one of the titmouse holes to see if I could spot the pupa inside. "You never mentioned which member of your family is into bugs."

"That would be me. Oh, I know a little bit about everything, but insects are my main field of expertise. My bread and butter, so to speak."

I personally wouldn't use the term "bread-and-butter" to describe creepy crawlies...but, to each his own. "How do you make money with bugs?"

"I'm an entomologist, of course." She gave me a meaningful look and added, "A *traveling* entomologist."

YURI

14

Staying in the motel would have been fine by me, but Dixon had his heart set on this YourBNB. The room was in a remodeled coach house not much bigger than my off-season cabin. Judging by the property's condition, very little of Harvey's remodeling budget was spent on the main house. The rental coach house, in comparison, was brimming with upgrades.

So many upgrades.

"Ooh, look," Dixon said. "A built in humidor. Too bad I don't smoke."

While Dixon explored the room—all three hundred square feet of it—I pondered the cargo weighing down the back of my truck. Not the carton of gluten free tortillas Olive had insisted we keep, but the bits of painted paper beneath it.

I was troubled. Spellcraft should not act this way...but that was not what bothered me.

Dixon came back outside once he realized I was still looking at the truck. He slipped his arms around me from behind, went up on tiptoe, and rested his chin on my shoulder. "Thinking about where we can bury the old Seens?"

I shook my head. "We don't need to."

Dixon gave me an extra squeeze, then caught my hand. "Perfect. Then stop worrying about it and come in out of the cold."

It wasn't the leftover Seens that disturbed me; it was the fact that, in the long run, Fonzo's Craftings hadn't sabotaged the town after all. True, they'd helped it only in the most painful and convoluted way. But the Spellcraft was not ultimately as malicious as I'd initially thought.

I should have been relieved.

Yet, I wasn't.

I allowed Dixon to draw me inside where the bath was running and the air smelled like the pine-scented potpourri that decorated every flat surface, from the windowsill to the countertop to the nightstand. Dixon plundered the small refrigerator and dredged up a jar of peanut butter, and we dined on gluten free tortilla roll-ups and tap water. It was not the most elegant meal, but it was satisfying...and nearly impossible to speak around, for which I was profoundly grateful.

I had imagined I would confront Dixon and force him to see his uncle was a fraud, a greedy charlatan who went from town to town, bilking people of their money and bringing shame to the family. Who can say what Fonzo's motives might be? I thought I knew, but I was no longer so sure. One thing I couldn't deny: his *volshebstvo* held great power.

By the time we'd managed to swallow the gluey peanut-butter-laced tortillas, the bath was full. Whether it was full of water or simply foam was another matter. Bubbles mounded the oversized bathtub in dome of white froth, swelling halfway to the ceiling—the *mirrored* ceiling.

Dixon glanced up and quipped, "That's certainly one way to double check that you're clean." He turned to me and unbuttoned my shirt while I stood like a stone, overwhelmed by the day's events and unsure what anything even meant anymore. "Do they have mirrored ceilings in Russia? I'm sure *someone* does—Russia's a huge country—but you never know, what's porn-tastic in one culture might be nothing special in another."

Dixon doesn't seem to expect answers to these questions of his. I'd always thought it was because his mind had leapt to the next topic before I'd figured out the best way to explain. But now I saw there was something much deeper at play. Maybe he was curious, maybe not. Mostly, he was just acknowledging the fact that I was there with him—and our experience of whatever was going on might be vastly different.

He eased my shirt down to my elbows and followed with a brush of his lips over my bare shoulder, accentuated by the scrape of stubble. Emotions welled up inside me, so sharp it felt as if my insides must be shredded. For such a ridiculous man, he made me experience all the deep and complex feelings I'd thus far successfully managed to avoid. The raw hurt of self-awareness. The sting of knowing I always presumed the worst. The dull ache of knowledge that I was unlikely to shed my suspicious nature anytime soon. And the bittersweet throb of hoping that perhaps he knew all this, and accepted me in all my flaws.

No, Dixon more than accepted me. He *cherished* me.

He pulled off my clothes, then his, then led me toward the bath. I gestured to the foam, which smelled like a cheap confection. "What scent is this?"

Dixon thrust a hand through the cloud of foam and groped for the bubble bath. He blew a wad of froth off the bottle and read. "Always Almond. Say, Yuri, do you pronounce it ALL-mond or AHH-mond?" Before I could answer, he read, "Lose yourself in field of delicious sun-ripened almonds as our delectably creamy bath foam floats your troubles away." He gave the bottle a sniff. "Smells more like pistachio ice cream to me."

Better than smelling like tacos, I supposed. Dixon stepped back into the tub, then held out his hands for me. I took them and allowed him to draw me in beside him. The cloud of almond-scented bath foam was nearly up to my waist. It parted for us with a crackle.

"Don't worry," Dixon said. "You can never add too many bubbles.

They always go flat before you know it."

I would have to take his word for it. In the meantime, our elbows and knees took a beating as we groped our way around and settled in. Our bodies knocked holes in the foam, but the jets stirring up the water soon plumped them back up. The cloying cloud engulfed us, not in darkness, but in light.

A puff of breath tickled my nose as Dixon blew an air pocket between us. Foam clung to his long, dark eyelashes. He pressed his forehead to mine to give the bubbles less opportunity to fill in, and treated me to a slippery nuzzle.

It would have been perfect—as close to perfect as he and I ever got—if not for the fact that when things were all said and done, I still didn't know what to make of the Craftings. Had our "silver lining" turned things around? Or had it simply kept us in place to witness the eventual outcome of the Spellcraft already in play?

"I don't know what's wrong with your uncle's Spellcraft—why it would be so rough and strange. But it looks like the people here will end up getting what they want...eventually." And it pained me to admit, "It seems as though he really might have been trying to help."

Dixon smiled wide enough to displace the nearby bubbles with a gentle crackle. "I accept your apology."

"I was not apologizing—"

"Shh...." He pressed a wet, almond-scented finger to my lips. "Don't kill the mood."

While I was tempted to insist, it was difficult to argue when his lips pressed against mine. We floundered together in the tub, which was squeaky in some places and slick in others. Dixon was convinced the water jets would help us reach new peaks, but the only thing peaking in that bathtub was the foamy white cloud. Regretfully, he conceded defeat once the water grew tepid, and we moved to the bed. And at least there, we could please each other without choking on the foam...which, since we'd left the jets running in our distraction, had only continued to expand and was now creeping steadily across the bathroom floor.

"We'll deal with it in the morning," Dixon mumbled into his pillow.

I turned off the jacuzzi so as not to suffer the most bizarre death in Taco Town history—suffocation by almond foam—but decided Dixon was right. I'd deal with the rest tomorrow.

I was drifting off when he spoke again. "All's well that ends well, but I'm not sure exactly how proud of myself I should be. Genevieve was the *deus ex machina* after all, not us, and she was already in Taco Town before we made our Crafting—which only should have affected us, regardless. It's confusing, you know? What came first, the chicken or the egg—is that a saying in Russia? When Spellcraft makes a series of events come to a head—an outcome that has more moving parts than the Globe-O-Matic—I can't help but wonder if the magic's got anything to do with it, or if we Spellcrafters are just taking credit for something that would've happened anyhow."

Knowing what I knew and feeling what I felt, being well acquainted with the *volshebstvo* flitting across the back of my scalp, I was fairly certain Spellcraft reached even deeper than we realized—even if the timing made it seem unlikely.

No matter that I couldn't find the right words. Dixon didn't seem to want an answer. He often doesn't. Then his voice turned uncharacteristically fragile when he said, "If Uncle Fonzo had wrecked this town with his Crafting, I don't know what I would have done."

"You're fine. So is the town."

And before we rolled out of town, I'd bury the Crafting with the silver lining at the foot of Salsa Lane, just to be sure.

Dixon and I slept nestled together in a strange bed in an even stranger town, and woke ravenous to the smell of marzipan and the taste of peanut butter tortillas. We washed it down with coffee from mugs shaped like tacos which, once you got the hang of them, only dribbled a bit. The foam had settled overnight, and though the bathroom floor was now slippery, it wouldn't be too much work for Harvey to mop up.

We moved through our morning routines more easily than we

usually did in my cabin, where the furniture was all bolted to the walls and the bathroom was smaller than the closet. When I finished shaving my head, I found Dixon sitting cross-legged on the rumpled sheets, fully dressed. He was just getting off the phone. "The garage will take us just as soon as you're ready." He waggled his eyebrows and considered my scalp, which he claimed, newly shorn, felt like velvet when it brushed the insides of his thighs. "Too bad it's almost checkout time."

It was tempting to linger, particularly when he was giving me that smoldering look. But the room was already booked for the night, and not by Genevieve. We packed up our few belongings. While Dixon refilled his water bottle, I paused beside the door where a blank journal sat open with a pen in the crease between the pages. A log of some sort. Date, name, comments, filled out in the hands of dozens of different people. I flipped back through a year's worth of entries. A few months ago, the couple Jason and Becky had put the word *Newlyweds!* in the comment field. And every guest thereafter had felt the need to follow suit in defining their relationship.

Clara and Ed - Just engaged.

Walter and Stella - Golden anniversary.

Kelsey and Peyton - Best Friends.

Dixon caught up with me as I scanned the entries, picked up the ballpoint pen and began to write. No surprise. Scriveners will scrawl their names on any blank surface, every chance they get. "Have you seen my signature? Not to brag, but it would give John Hancock a run for his...money." Only then, when he paused to dot the "i", did he take note of the running theme in the comment section. He carried on as if nothing had happened, but I'm well acquainted with the way that man handles a pen. Even the small hesitation was telling.

With an outlandish flourish of the capital Y, he inked my name beside his. And then he leveled a deliberately too-casual look at me. "Funny thing about setting something down in black and white. It makes it feel so official."

His gaze turned challenging...and I tipped up my chin resolutely in return. "Then, write."

"I will." He grazed the paper with the ballpoint, then drew back and looked at me again, less sure. "Boyfriends?"

"We are grown men, not boys."

"Grown-men-friends doesn't have quite the same ring, does it? And *partners* seems kind of businesslike...."

Doubt cut a furrow between his brows as the possibility that he'd misread our relationship occurred to him. But before he made things more awkward by trying to back out of the situation gracefully, I took the pen from his grasp.

"It sounds better in Russian." In my blocky left-handed Cyrillic, I added the word *vozljublennyj*. "Beloved."

Translating a street sign into my native language was enough to give Dixon the shivers. The frisson of this new word coursed over him—and through me—like Spellcraft. And the tingle it left behind echoed between us as Dixon tipped his head up for a kiss.

I never cared much for kissing...until I met Dixon. I always thought the act too intimate. Too soft. But he showed me how kisses could range from tender to fierce—now, especially, as he clung to my lapels with both fists until the shoulder seams of my jacket made a sound of protest. His lips were bold but his tongue was gentle, almost teasing. And when I tasted him in return, he gave a breathy moan that left me calculating whether or not I could pin him to door well enough to keep anyone from disturbing us—though nothing we got up to would be any more scandalous than the scene we'd witnessed back at the greenhouse.

But while our kiss grew more heated, Dixon's phone chimed the arrival of a new text. And then another. And another. He pushed off me gently with a rueful shake of his head, looking even more alluring than usual, breathless and rumpled, with lips flushed from kissing. I was tempted to grab the phone and toss it toward the bed, but figured it was best to first make sure no one had died.

"It's my cousin." He scrolled, and scrolled, and scrolled some more. Then he put his phone back in his bag and added, "She says another postcard just showed up." Dixon was still breathless...but his eagerness was no longer for me.

I said nothing.

He flung open the door, caught me by the wrist, and pulled. "It's from a hot spring less than half a day's drive from here, too. That's the attraction, I mean—of course, the postcard is from Uncle Fonzo, not the water. Do they have hot springs in Russia? Do people soak in them totally naked, or do they leave on their underwear? Y'know, if the garage can take care of us right now, we'll be there by dinner." He gave my arm another enthusiastic yank. "Isn't that exciting?"

Undoubtedly it was.

For him.

As I stood in the doorway while he scampered out to the truck, I paused for a moment and glanced down at the registry. Dixon's signature truly was a work of art—as was the way he'd written my name. But my eyes were drawn to the word I'd penned in ungainly, utilitarian letters.

Beloved.

This was what happened when you grew attached to someone else—you set aside your own trepidations, and you did whatever it took to fend off their suffering, and if possible, bring them a glimmer of joy. I might have said I'd always feared this was how being half of a couple would be...if I'd ever entertained the notion at all.

I looked from the book to Dixon, who beamed at me from the passenger seat of the old truck, then gave me a delighted thumbs-up. Despite myself, I felt my frigid armor thaw, just a bit.

It didn't sting quite as much as I thought it might.

We pulled out onto the road. When Dixon opened the window to brush a stray mudmucker casing from his jacket sleeve, a sudden gust of wind plucked our Crafting from the visor and sent it fluttering away into the pines. Most Handless would demand I pull over and hunt it down, but Dixon and I just exchanged a look and kept on going. Both of us understood that the *volshebstvo* can be harnessed for a time, but in the end, it belongs to no one.

SOMETHING STINKS
AT THE SPA

DIXON

1

I've always adored a good road trip. And taking one with Yuri, the man who made my heart go pitter-patter? Best adventure ever. After a lengthy drive that was rife with potholes, country music radio stations, and a particularly baffling detour, we'd finally made it. Mostly, I was excited to track down my Uncle Fonzo. Excited, and a little nervous, too...which was totally crazy. He was family.

And nothing was more important than family.

We rolled into town well after midnight. The place was famous for its mineral waters, and a series of increasingly emphatic signage encouraged us toward the city's main attraction. And there, at the center of the town where all the signage converged, we discovered a resort built around a pond that was scarcely big enough for Yuri and me to lie down head-to-toe without touching. Not that I ever mind touching Yuri.

As we approached, I tilted my head to see if I could detect any steam rising from the waters. "Is that a tendril?" I asked.

Yuri pulled into a parking spot and squinted through the truck's windshield. "Maybe. Or maybe our eyes only show us what we're hoping to see."

I checked the postcard my cousin Sabina had messaged me—the one she'd received that very morning. *Soak Away Your Troubles at the Spring Falls Hot Springs!* I'd say calling the mineral spa a "hot spring" was quite a stretch. From what I could tell, at best, the waters were tepid.

The spring-fed pool sat at the bottom of a natural depression, and we looked down into it from the cab of the truck. Irregular stone walls sloped down toward the water. One side was cut into a broad staircase. The other had a trickle of water snaking down the stone.

We both stared for a long moment, and eventually I decided, "No, there's definitely a wisp. C'mon, Yuri. Let's go see if they can spare a room."

Yuri cut the engine, and his hand dropped to the door latch. "Judging by how few are in the parking lot, I'd say...ugh! What is that *smell?*"

"It wasn't me!"

When the door opened, a massive stink rushed in to fill the cab like a garden hose filling a water balloon—from a tap with incredibly good water pressure. And it didn't just fill the truck—it filled my senses. A noxious reek, like the whole town had been subsisting on sauerkraut and beans, then let loose in one great, coordinated release of human-produced methane. It coated the inside of every mucous membrane in my head. It was so substantial, it seemed like it should cloud my vision and stop up my ears. So tangible I had to fight my way through it.

"Sulfur," Yuri said.

The witty retort would've been *Sulfur? I hardly know 'er!* But I didn't think I could make the quip without throwing up a little in my mouth.

I wished I could say the Spring Falls Hot Spring Spa at least looked a lot better than it smelled...but that would be a pretty big fib. In person, it was nowhere near as scenic as the postcard. The spa was a turn-of-the-century resort that might not've seen a new paint job since it was built. Unless you counted the corners of the building's foundation where something had been painted over in a slightly different color. That looked pretty fresh.

I clapped my hand over my nose and mouth. Breathing through my fingers didn't really help, but hey, I had to do something. Yuri squinted even harder than usual, and said decisively, "We will get used to it." But his voice sounded pretty thick.

I wasn't so sure...but if we wanted to find Uncle Fonzo, we couldn't exactly start looking somewhere else. Besides, it was really late, and there were no other motels for miles around. We'd have to buck up and try. I hoisted my bag on my shoulder, and the two of us high-tailed it inside.

I hoped that the HVAC system would filter out some of the stink, but the air in the lobby was even worse. Not only did it reek like a baboon's hind end, but it was overlaid with the cloying smell of flowers. Not any specific flower, like lilacs or jasmine or roses, but a generic "floral" scent that smelled like old-lady perfume.

The door chimed shut behind us, and a sprightly blue-haired woman dashed up to the counter to greet us. She had a can of air freshener in her hand, and the aerosol streamed behind her like the exhaust of a steam locomotive all the way across the expanse of the room. Once she got up close enough to get a good look at her, though, I realized that she wasn't sprightly at all. In fact, she was young enough to not take too kindly to being called "sprightly"—as butch as a female trucker, or maybe a phys ed instructor—and her close-cropped hair was actually more like a pastel dye job of pale aqua and violet and periwinkle.

"Cute hair color," I said. "Very chic—very edgy."

She stopped her spraying, blinked at me, then touched her hair as if she'd forgotten it was on her head. "This?" Even her voice was husky. "Uh, thanks. It's...totally intentional. One hundred percent. Anyhow, welcome to Spring Falls Hot Spring Spa. I'm Janet. How may I facilitate your delightful stay?"

Yuri slid me a look as if to double-check that I was truly willing to bed down amid the butt-and-fake-flower atmosphere when the door burst open behind us, and a sobbing woman staggered in.

As she walked, her path wove in a serpentine line and her breath hitched with every inhalation. Her blonde hair was in an updo that must've been elaborate at some point, but now was mostly down. Tears cut through heavily applied foundation, leaving her with twin tracks of paleness streaking down each cheek. The collar of her lacy white top was stained orange with diluted makeup.

Yuri backpedaled. For such a big guy, he can move pretty quick when emotional displays are involved. I stepped aside as the crying woman made her way up to the desk, giving her a wide berth. When she reached the counter, I told Janet, "Go ahead and facilitate her first. We can wait."

Janet didn't look any more comfortable with the weeping than Yuri, but she had a job to do, so she slid a tiny box of tissues across the counter and said, "Welcome to the Spring Falls Hot Spring Spa."

But before she could offer to facilitate a delightful anything, the crying woman said, "I have a reservation. For the...the...." She choked, snuffled, gathered herself, and finally bellowed, "The Honeymoon Suite!"

"Oh," Janet said. "Mr. and Mrs...?"

"Just me: Liza. Do you hear me? Just. Me."

"Of...course," Janet said, none too smoothly, though Liza had started crying again in earnest and probably didn't much notice.

Janet soldiered on with her spiel. Only louder. "The Spring Falls Hot Springs have been a fixture of the community since they were discovered by a turnip farmer in 1910. The building we're standing in right now is the original Spring Falls Hot Springs Spa, and in fact, you won't find anything like it anywhere else in the Midwest. Your stay comes with a complimentary relaxation massage." She glanced at the clock. It was well past midnight. "Between the hours of nine and five, of course. Our sauna is located on the lower level. Rejuvenating mineral soak, highly recommended. And, naturally, no stay would be complete without the Spring Falls Hot Springs Spa gift basket."

She hauled out a massive crate from under the welcome desk—a goodie box clearly created with a newly hitched couple in mind, given the prominent fancy ice bucket and champagne glasses inside, not to mention the chocolates, massage oil and naughty dice game. The impulse to swap it out with a standard welcome gift played across Janet's expression like a tickertape, but before she could switch it, Liza stopped her sobbing, latched onto the wedding-themed welcome gift, and yanked it possessively across the countertop. "I take it this comes with a bottle of champagne?"

"Of course," Janet said, almost naturally, and produced said bottle from a nearby mini fridge.

I eyed the crate. It was filled with shredded paper, mostly, but nestled among that and all the kitschy wedding stuff were all kinds of product—lotions and soaps and a stunning variety of scented candles. I always love a good freebie, and I could hardly wait for my turn to be facilitated.

Once Liza headed off to her room with her welcome box and her champagne, Janet turned to Yuri and me and said, "Thank you so much for your patience, how can I help you?"

I said, "We were hoping to facilitate a room, of course!"

"Just one room?"

"Yep, that'll do."

Janet hesitated like she was trying to feel us out, then said, "The businessman double?"

How intriguing that she pegged us for businessmen. I'm a flashy dresser, so I suppose I could be taken for an advertising rep, or maybe a talent agent. But even in a suit, Yuri looked more like someone who broke kneecaps for a living. Maybe she took him for my bodyguard...and wouldn't *that* make for some interesting roleplay later? "Businessman double, you say? Does that involve a different sort of gift basket, or—?"

"How many beds in room?" Yuri demanded.

"Two. Full-sized. Very comfortable."

"One bed," Yuri said. Such a turn-on when he got all assertive!

"And your most romantic welcome basket," I added.

Janet tittered a bit huskily, but at least now that she knew the score, she had a clear course of facilitation laid out in front of her.

"Our honeymoon suite is taken, obviously." She clicked around on her computer at great length, then said, "But our Romantic Recharge package is available. That comes with all the perks of the honeymoon suite, minus the champagne. Which is available for purchase separately."

When I got a load of the price of the room alone, I thought better about adding a thirty-dollar bottle of bubbly. Lucky thing I was punch-drunk enough that even a fizzy-water would leave me feeling a little giddy. "We'll take a pass on the booze, but one more thing...."

I pulled out my phone to call up the Uncle Fonzo picture I'd been showing around. But before I could even open the app, the door burst open yet again and a blindingly blond man strode in. He was wearing a suit—a power suit—and he strode across the lobby like a man on a mission. "Name's Quint," he announced, even though it was clear Janet was still facilitating us. "I've got a reservation. The *premium* businessman suite."

Dang. I guess the second full-sized bed was for his massive ego. No way could it possibly fit in the same bed with him.

Yuri bristled as if he might teach the guy some manners, but as much as I would've loved to see it, we couldn't afford to wear out our welcome before we tracked down Uncle Fonzo. And if my uncle was there, we'd see him at breakfast—all the Penns were keen on a hearty breakfast. I grabbed the room key, stuck the welcome basket in Yuri's arms, and said, "Thank you so much for all your help, Janet!"

Yuri knows when to take a hint. He grumbled something in Russian—some of those words were starting to sound kind of familiar—but he let me guide him away from that Quint guy and his obnoxious display of self-importance. With Yuri hauling our welcome basket, we made our way to the charming old elevator— the kind with an elaborate gate to keep us from tumbling out between floors, and controls like an old steamship—and headed off toward our room.

YURI

2

"Businessmen!" Dixon exclaimed—he exclaimed the majority of things he said. "She actually took us for businessmen. Imagine that. Parading around like you're the most important guy in the room. Buying trades and trading stocks and selling short and shorting sales. What do you think?"

"I know nothing about business."

"Me neither. But I gather businessmen get to drink pretty heavily at lunchtime. Do you like martinis, Yuri?"

As if anyone didn't care for vodka. I gave him a look, but I doubted he saw it around the towering gift basket.

While Dixon threw around a bunch of meaningless terminology, I pondered the conversation we'd just had at the front desk. It never felt like coming out was an option for me. In the old country, even with another man's hand down the front of my trousers, I would have denied being gay.

But here, I'd been outed by the Spellcraft.

It was surprisingly liberating.

And yet, I was starting to see you don't just come out once. You do it over and over, in every new situation, with each person you meet.

Hopefully someday it would get easier.

The lift stopped, mostly on our floor, and with a lot of elaborate rattling and further exclamations, Dixon opened the gate. Our room was at the end of a narrow hall with worn carpets and yellowed wallpaper—a hall which stunk of air freshener and sulfur. It had been overly optimistic of me to decide we would get used to the stink, but there was no leaving Spring Falls until we found out if Fonzo was still there.

All the way to Spring Falls, I turned around his Craftings in my mind—whether they would have resolved themselves in the end, or whether it was only our interference that turned things around. I still had not settled on an answer. Spellcraft has a funny way of threading back and forth through time, blurring the relationship between cause and effect. And my own experience was limited; my mentor had not been exactly forthcoming in explaining the process.

Dixon unlocked the hotel room and held the door open for me. The room wasn't bad. It was done up in muted shades of white, with hints of neutral blues, khakis and greens—spa colors—but it still reeked of sulfur. I set the basket on the dresser. By the time I locked and deadbolted our door, Dixon was already rifling through the crate.

"Shampoo, conditioner...I don't suppose you're too picky about either of those. Body butter—*caution, do not eat*. What the hey? If you're not supposed to eat it, why call it *butter*? Soy candles. Maybe the candles *are* edible. Huh, doesn't say. And how do you suppose they make candles out of beans, anyway? However they manage to do it, I bet soybeans are easier to harvest than beeswax...unless soybeans have stingers, and I've just never heard about it...."

While Dixon called out the names of all the ridiculous candle scents, sniffed them, and declared they all smelled like rotten eggs to him, I found my gaze pulled to the shredded paper fluff he'd tossed aside. It was just filler. And yet, when I allowed my focus to soften, it seemed as though I could find shapes within the randomness, like I was gazing at clouds. There were colors in the shred. Cool aquas, bluish grays. And when I focused on those, specifically—and especially on the tiny flecks of black—it seemed like the wad of shredded paper was actually alive. The paper itself did not move. But my eyes couldn't settle on any one place, and as a result, the shred seemed to have its own pulse.

Volshebstvo. It took me a moment. But when I saw it for what it was, the influence of Spellcraft couldn't have been more obvious. "Dixon," I said, and he paused to listen. "This place is under the influence of a Crafting."

"I'd be surprised if it wasn't. Businesses who don't add a lucky piece of Spellcraft to their marketing plan are just leaving money on the table. Hey, maybe I know more about business than I realized!"

It was true. Here in America, where Spellcraft had never been exactly illegal, it wasn't uncommon to spot the occasional Crafting passing itself off as a framed poem or inspirational saying. But this was not a charm to make the customers happy. This was... convoluted. And not only that, I recognized the tangled energy.

If ever there were any doubt that we were on the right track, I now knew for certain that Fonzo Penn had been here.

While Dixon watched—momentarily too distracted to speak—I grabbed a handful of shredded paper and dropped it on the white duvet. It wasn't moving. Its outline hadn't changed. And yet, to my eyes, it squirmed like a nest of slender, papery vipers. "Do you see that?" I asked him.

"Unfortunately not...but it's obvious that you do." Dixon crouched beside the bed and pushed his face up close to the shredded wad. "I've seen lots of things over the course of my life—but never once have I seen anyone shred a Crafting. D'you suppose it was intentional? Or a matter of the Crafting being in the wrong place at the wrong time?"

"Since when does a Crafting end up anywhere it was not intended to be?"

"True enough." Dixon poked the shred gingerly, as if he was worried it might shock him. But the only shocking thing was the fact that the Spellcraft had contrived to put itself through the shredder, and thereby stamp its magic on Spring Falls indelibly.

With the delicacy of a surgeon, Dixon teased out one strand of paper, then another, and another. He was going to try to put the Crafting back together. Anyone could see it was a fool's errand—but I doubted that knowledge had any chance of stopping Dixon.

"Why?" I asked.

"What else have we got to go on? Besides, if it's a one-word wonder, like the Craftings in the last town, we could potentially reconstruct it well enough to at least deduce what it said. A little knowledge is better than none." He fluttered his thick, dark lashes at me. "Right?"

A little knowledge was all I ever seemed to have, but unfortunately, I couldn't disagree. Though as we picked apart the paper shreds on our duvet to reassemble the world's least engaging jigsaw puzzle, I found myself thinking an extra businessman bed wouldn't have been a bad idea after all.

DIXON

3

Once I realized I should separate the shredded paper by weight, things went a lot faster. It was easier to do it by touch than sight. Office paper had a limp, fettuccine-like quality, while the rest of it was markedly al dente.

There are only so many kinds of paper in this world, but the stock the Penn family uses is thirty-pound, hot-pressed, acid-free archival block. I wouldn't have thought I could recognize it in tiny little strips. But I guess you never know until you try.

By the time I picked out all the good-quality paper, I wasn't left with all that many shreds. I counted them. Twenty-two. And some of them were clearly edge pieces with no paint or ink. I didn't bother with those just yet. I was more interested in seeing how much of a Crafting there was to salvage.

Unfortunately, not much. I definitively found an F. That was my biggest triumph.

I put the rest of the shreds back in the welcome basket and moved the fragmented Spellcraft to the dresser. But by then, Yuri was already asleep on the couch. I sometimes envy his ability to fall asleep anywhere—until it's time to drag him to bed. At least now I know to back up a few steps after I poke him.

The room could've used some sprucing up—flocked wallpaper, maybe, with a colorful accent wall—but I definitely couldn't find fault with the mattress...even though Yuri claimed it was "too soft." After a good night's sleep, we made our way down to the continental breakfast to situate ourselves and look for Uncle Fonzo.

And eat bacon. Nice and bendy, just like I liked it. I would have liked it even better if there'd been more. But as Janet puttered around refilling the spread, she'd only put out three strips at a time. Yuri was the sort of guy who'd eat whatever you put in front of him, as evidenced by the fact that he could even look at a hard-boiled egg despite waking up with the taste of sulfur on his tongue. Not me. I wanted my floppy bacon—and even more than that, I wanted to know if she'd seen my Uncle Fonzo

Janet must have sensed my hunger. Every time I tried to approach her, she dodged me like a runningback to whisk herself off to the staff-only area before I made my way through the maze of tables and chairs. Once Yuri had eaten his fill of hard-boiled eggs, though, he kenned to the situation. And the next time Janet tried to ghost me, she found herself facing a wall of intimidating tattooed muscle.

Yuri crossed his arms, looking all big and stern. I went giddy inside at the sight of him, but did my best not to show it.

"There's only so much bacon," Janet said defensively.

I had my phone in hand, ready to flash Uncle Fonzo's picture... but I couldn't help but ask. "You're short on bacon? How come?"

Janet slumped into the nearest chair. The breakfast nook had a countertop filled with your typical continental fare—minus bacon—and a dozen tiny round tables with filigreed chairs that creaked when Yuri sat on them, though this particular chair didn't creak for Janet. She planted her elbows on the tiny tabletop, put her face in her hands, and said, "I'm short on everything. The welcome baskets are filled with random samples I found in the storeroom and paper I salvaged from the shredder. There's no more mints for the pillows. And I've had to lay off both my esthetician and my masseuse. All because of the weather. I'm surprised you hadn't heard—we had a record low snowfall this past winter, and the spring thaw that usually brings up the water table seriously underperformed.

"The Spring Falls Hot Spring ran dry. And so did our customers."

No wonder parking was so ample.

"It was easy enough to fill the soaker tubs in the spa with municipal water and add some epsom salts," she said. "But the big draw is the grotto out front—you can't miss the falls." I take it she meant the trickle. "And the level kept getting lower and lower. I tried running a hose out there in the middle of the night, but any water I added would only drain away faster than it could be replenished. Pretty soon I was five figures in debt to the water utility. I took out a loan on the spa, but now I can't even manage a single repayment, since I spent what was left of the loan on the traveling volcanologist."

Oh geez. I slipped my phone back into my pocket.

Yuri shot me a look. The sternness was no longer all that sexy. He murmured, "You don't say."

"The volcanologist knew all about geysers and springs. He told me he could seed the underground stream and get it to produce. In just a couple of days, the water was flowing again."

"And this volcanologist," I said cautiously. "Do you remember his name?"

"I sure do. It was Fonzo. Great guy—very knowledgeable. Very efficient. Whatever he did worked like a charm." She slumped forward and mashed her face into her crossed arms. Her spiky hair ruffled to reveal several more shades of blue. "Too bad he didn't warn me about the sulfur."

Worked like a charm? No doubt! Me? I couldn't fathom Crafting something intended to raise the water table. It simply isn't done. Not in the way a butterfly flapping its wings could kill a dinosaur—or however that old saw goes—but the amount of power it would take to influence something so pervasive and far-reaching boggled my mind.

Then again, no one ever disputed the fact that Uncle Fonzo knew his way around Spellcraft.

You don't get to be the Hand of the Family by scrawling wimpy Scrivenings. The Hand isn't the eldest member of a clan—it's the strongest. I'd heard stories about Spellcraft families who had no clear frontrunner for the position. And I'd heard of Spellcrafters trying to attempt things that were too big for any one person to handle.

Things like changing the weather.

Usually, when a Crafting misfires, it's basically a dud. Nothing happens. But every once in a while—like, once in a generation—a botched Crafting goes horribly wrong, drains the Scrivener, and leaves behind nothing but a drooling husk. And the way Spellcraft families tell the tales, it's always the result of a Scrivener getting too big for their britches and overreaching the unspoken limits of the Craft.

By doing things like shifting the weather.

I would have thought I'd be disappointed that Uncle Fonzo had already moved along. Now I was just relieved he'd managed to do it in one piece. With any luck, we'd find some clue as to where he went next. But for now—we could do worse than to have ourselves a little vacation.

"I'm sure business will turn around once the spring has a chance to air out a little."

Janet shook her head sadly. "This resort has been in my family for three generations. I'm the first woman ever to run it. Hah. Run it into the ground."

"You can't lose the spa!" I told her. "Don't worry—we'll help you."

As Yuri accidentally kicked my foot, Janet looked up pitifully and said, "I don't see how there's anything you can do."

"Where there's a will, there's a way."

Yuri kicked me again. I sidled over a bit to give him more room.

"No," Janet sighed, "it's no use. There's a critic from Vacation Nation who'll be here in just a few hours. Even if I could find some way to explain the smell, once he sees my staff is gone, I'm sunk."

"What is it you need?" I asked. "An esthetician? A masseuse? Look no further! I clearly have the skin of a guy who knows his product—and Yuri has very strong hands."

She wanted to poke holes in my fabulous idea, I could tell. But one look at Yuri's massive paws convinced her otherwise. "But what about the sulfur?"

"A mere detail. We'll leave the critic so relaxed and supple, he won't know the difference between a sweet rose and some stinky toes. What have you got to lose?"

Janet considered my offer, then shrugged and said, "You know what? You're *right*. This is my resort, and I'm not going down without a *fight*."

The urge to Craft something prickled across the little hairs on the backs of my hands—noticing inadvertent rhymes tends to do that to me—but on principle, we Spellcrafters avoid giving our work away for free. "Since we'd be part of the staff, why don't you comp our room?"

"Rooms cost money—just look at how much bacon you ate! And then there's the laundry, and the toilet paper, and the welcome basket. I can't possibly comp you."

"Okay...how about a discount?"

"Fine. Twenty percent."

"Fifty?"

"Thirty. And I swear, that's the very best I can do."

It was better than nothing. Still.... "Are you sure there's no more bacon?"

Janet shook her head in resignation. Her pastel curls bounced. "You win. I'll put on one more batch."

Once Janet was busy in the kitchen, we planted ourselves at a tiny round table to wait for the bacon. Yuri leaned in close and said, "This plan of yours will never work. No one will ever take me for a masseuse."

"Relax, Yuri, watch a couple of YouTube videos and I'm sure you'll do fine. And you can practice on me. Win-win."

Yuri got himself another boiled egg and peeled it very assertively.

"The minute anyone mentions their family, you're putty in their hands."

I couldn't argue there. Especially since I'd been blessed with the best family ever, and Yuri never even mentioned his. "I know, I can be a big softie...but how much does that matter if I'm *firm* when it really counts?"

Yuri wanted to roll his eyes, I could tell. But instead, he said, "Do you want to play make-believe, or do you want to find your uncle?"

"Of course I want to track down Uncle Fonzo. But it won't do us any good to set off in the wrong direction. Besides, I have a feeling about this place...like it needs us. I know it doesn't sound entirely rational, but when I heard Janet's story, I knew I couldn't just sit on my hands and do nothing."

Yuri gazed out the window, where the sulfurous pool at the bottom of the grotto steamed gently in the early morning sun while water from the Spring Falls trickle dripped in. "Rationality is fine for figuring out who to punch first," he said, "but when Spellcraft is involved, it will do you no good to be rational."

"Before you pooh-pooh my idea, at least give it a try."

Yuri swept eggshell fragments into his palm, stood, and dumped them in the trash, and then the two of us headed outside to get a better look at the spring.

The water level in the thermal pool was still fairly low, but by day, we could see the water was a vibrant, unnatural-looking blue, like the milk left in the bowl after I'd finished my favorite sugary blueberry-flavored cereal. "You have to admit," I said. "It might stink. But it's kind of pretty."

While Yuri gazed at the water as if he could store the peculiar color in his memory banks for later use, I poked around the edge of the grotto. The stone walls were pale gray at ground level, but lower down, where the water had touched them, they'd turned all sorts of odd pastel colors. Must've been the inspiration for Janet's hair. I'd touched up my mom's roots a time or two, so I knew my way around a bottle of hair color. But hopefully no one would expect such a complicated dye-job from me.

"Yuri, would you say that's cobalt or periwinkle—?" before I could finish naming any other shades of blue, movement over by the office snagged my attention. What I initially took for a miniature tumbleweed lifted its leg and relieved itself on the corner of the stucco wall...directly on the mismatched paint job.

I crouched down, pitched my voice high, and said, "Hey there— hey buddy—what're you doing out here all alone?"

The scruffy little dog perked up at the sound of my voice, looked at me, and cocked his head. Dogs always seem to know when you're talking specifically to them.

"Ignore it," Yuri said. "It probably has worms."

"He," I corrected him. Because only male dogs peed like that. "And even if he is wormy, that only means he needs someone to take care of him."

"You can't be serious. We just dropped off *how* many animals at your parents' house, and now you're angling for a dog?"

I wiggled my fingers. "C'mon, little guy. I just want to say hello...."

The dog crept forward. I don't know much about dog breeds, but even if I did, I doubted I'd be able to pinpoint this animal's specific lineage. Maybe part poodle. Or part terrier. Or part bouffant wig. Its whitish fur was wilder than my cousin Sabina's teased peroxide-blonde hair when she went through her 80's phase, and its eyes were lost under a crazy poof of dog-bangs. I was losing track of which end was which. Until a tail popped up from one side...and cautiously wagged.

"That's it," I crooned. "C'mon, boy, you're safe with me...."

And just as the little dust mop took a tentative step in my direction, the office door banged open and Janet stormed out, brandishing a set of metal salad tongs like a weapon. "Twinkle! Don't you dare!"

The dog gave a saucy yip, turned tail, and scampered off into the bushes.

"Is that your dog?" I asked.

"Not a chance. If I had a dog, I wouldn't let it use my building for a urinal. Twinkle's owner moved away and left him behind—a real piece of work, that guy—and Twinkle's been on his own ever since. Everyone in Spring Falls knows Twinkle. But no one's been able to catch him."

I glanced back where I'd seen the dog sneak away, but already I couldn't quite recall exactly which two bushes he'd ducked between. Janet scrutinized the corner of her building with a defeated sigh. "Pee stains are bad enough. But the minerals in the atmosphere combine with the uric acid. Once it soaks in, it'll turn all sorts of vivid colors. Hopefully this is fresh enough to hose off." She gestured vaguely at the front door. "No sense in all of us standing around out here—it's not like I need you to supervise. Might as well go eat your bacon while it's still hot."

4

Since there really wasn't much else to see outside, we headed back in. The breakfast nook was no longer empty. By the coffee urn, the blond businessman Quint was pumping vigorously at the vacuum thermos as if he couldn't fill his gigantic travel mug quick enough. Meanwhile, Liza the jilted bride was gazing out the window with an empty plate on her table glistening with something that looked suspiciously like bacon grease.

When I lifted up the cover on the chafing dish, I found it empty.

"They're out of bacon," Liza informed me.

"Dang it!"

"Forget about the bacon," Yuri said. "You can get bacon anywhere."

True. But maybe I wanted *spa* bacon.

"Believe me," Liza said, "it was limp and soggy. Totally not worth the calories. But that's okay. My parents paid for this honeymoon, and I intend to squeeze every last bit of vacation out of it. So...do you guys know where I sign up for the spa treatment?"

Yuri shot me a fierce look. I could barely stop myself from blurting out, *I know, right? What luck!* Because *of course* I needed someone to practice on before I spa'd the hotel critic! "I can *totally* help you with that—I'm the official esthetician of the Spring Falls Hot Spring Spa."

Liza blinked. "You are?"

"Absolutely."

"Then why was it you were just checking in last night?"

The thing about creating your own story is that it goes well as long as people are buying it, but when they challenge the narrative, things get weird. Fortunately for me, Yuri was quick on the uptake. "He is a traveling esthetician."

"Oh. Well...great. Sign me up. I want the works—the full spa package: Sugar scrub. Mineral wrap. Mani/pedi. And mimosas. Lots and lots of mimosas."

Wow, talk about getting thrown in the deep end. But if I got Liza tipsy enough, she'd make an awesome guinea pig. "The works, it is! Buckle in and hang on to your seat—you're about to get a spa treatment you'll never forget."

Yuri coughed. I gave him a good pound on the back to make sure he wasn't choking on any lingering egg crumbs, then escorted Liza downstairs. We ended up taking a little tour of the meeting room, the linen storage and the kitchen first. Luckily, I was able to pass it off as picking up some towels, glasses, OJ and champagne, and eventually we found our way to the treatment rooms.

I've had my fair share of pampering over the years—I've never been averse to showing myself a little TLC—but the equipment at this particular spa wasn't ringing any bells. I did my best to keep up my esthetic charm while I got Liza settled. It was just a matter of figuring out where to settle her. The treatment room at the Spring Falls was nothing like I'd ever seen before. Instead of linen and bamboo, it was all decked out in polished concrete and stainless steel. There was a brutalist severity to the decor, evocative of cleanliness and vigor. Yuri would probably be more at home with it than I was. But I was the one who'd promised Liza an experience...and it looked like she was going to get one. I opened the champagne with a flourish and a pop and poured her a nice mimosa—heavy on the bubbly—while I tried to get the lay of the land. But apparently the offerings in such a fancy resort were nothing like the simple treatments I was used to.

"Just getting the lay of the land," I told her as I tried to figure out what was what without looking too obviously panicked. "Every spa I've worked at in my, er, extensive career has been a little different."

"No worries," she said forlornly, then downed half the mimosa in one gulp. "I've got nowhere better to be."

"That's the spirit!" I topped off her glass, then realized there was nowhere to sit. So I improvised. "Unlike traditional spa treatments, the Spring Falls experience takes place standing up, which allows gravity to work with your own circulatory and lymphatic system."

"Oh. Uh…okay."

I looked to see what skin care products I'd have to work with. They must've all been private label, with names like Citrus Fresh and Eco Scrub I didn't quite recognize. Frankly, I couldn't tell the cleanser from the toner. While I puzzled through various over-sized bottles and jars, Liza slurped her mimosa. Once her glass was empty, she asked, "When do I take off my clothes?"

Now, that was something I didn't often hear—from women, anyhow—but I figured I should roll with the punches. "It's not strictly necessary to completely disrobe."

"It's fine," she sighed. "You're obviously a professional, and I'm sure it's nothing you haven't seen before." Not since I was a fumbling teenager—but that little detail was better left unspoken if I hoped to pass myself off as the pro she thought I was. "It's hardly a honeymoon weekend if I'm dressed the entire time."

"Well, whatever makes you comfortable." I cast around for something to help me avoid being in the presence of utter nakedness, and spotted a pile of sheets. "But I'd be remiss if I didn't mention the recent studies about the health benefits of cotton touching your skin."

"But don't most of us have cotton touching our skin a majority of the time? I practically live in jeans."

"I'm not talking just any old run-of-the-mill cotton…." I poured her another mimosa to keep her distracted. "But luxurious, 100% long-staple, extra-high-quality organic supima cotton." My intent was to shake out the sheet with a dramatic and satisfying snap... but instead it just unfurled like a roll of paper towels into a long, narrow strip.

Liza looked very puzzled.

I gave her my winningest smile.

Before she could ask any questions—or worse, start moaning about her honeymoon again—I shoved the material into her free hand and said, "I'll just let you finish that drink and get changed. And make sure you cover all the most delicate parts. We wouldn't want them to get chafed."

While Liza figured out what to do with that long, narrow strip of fabric, I stepped out into the hall with my phone, intending to look up exactly how all the various unfamiliar cleansers and scrubs worked. But I found a new text from Sabina waiting for me, and by the time I determined there was no new news from Uncle Fonzo and finished the quiz she'd sent me on which Backstreet Boy I should be dating, Liza called out, "Dixon? I'm ready."

I stepped back into the room and found Liza standing right there in the middle of it, haphazardly wrapped like a clumsy mummy. She'd managed to cover her assets—more or less. She took a swig of champagne directly from the bottle and said, "What about the Gentle Exfoliating Dry Brush Treatment I read about in the brochure?" There was a brochure? "My elbows are kinda scaly."

"Absolutely. First step is to close your eyes and center yourself. Breathe in, breathe out." While Liza stood there in her mummy getup and breathed, I pulled up dry brushing on my phone and gave myself a two-second crash course. "Don't stop breathing," I warned.

Liza gave a wan giggle. I supposed it was better than obsessing about the creep who jilted her.

While Liza breathed, I pawed through the shelves until I found some brushes. They were a lot bigger than I thought they'd be—and some of them looked very well-used. I picked one up and sniffed—citrus and sulfur—and decided to go for one of the newer ones in back.

Well, I thought. *Here goes nothing.* I knelt down behind Liza and started brushing her toes.

She squirmed a bit, ticklish, but didn't pull away. "You must get your hands on a lot of new brides."

"Fewer than you'd think."

"I'll bet they're all aglow to begin with. Happy and content. I'd been looking forward to this for the better part of the year. But I thought I'd get to share it with my soulmate. And now...."

"No crying allowed," I said, gently but firmly. "I can hardly dry-brush you if you're all wet."

She snuffled, but managed to stem the waterworks.

I've never understood why marriage was such a big deal among the Handless. We Spellcrafters aren't churchy types, and we prefer to keep the government out of our intimate relationships, thank you very much. Mom says the only reason she and dad made it official was that it was the easiest way to get rid of the unfortunate surname Pidgley—and who could blame her? All the other kids called her "Piggy" until she finally dropped out of school when she was barely old enough to drive. And while Dixon Pidgley might've had a certain odd storybook flair, as a guy who made his living writing things, I was definitely partial to the name Dixon Penn.

I dry-brushed my way up Liza's legs, and slipped in a few scrubs in the gaps between the swaddling, too. I paid particular attention to her elbows, then lingered on her back. Because who doesn't love a good back-scratch? Liza was pink, rosy, and a lot less maudlin once I was done. I said, "We've increased the circulation, exfoliated, and released toxins." According to the first paragraph on the website I'd glanced at, anyhow. "You'll want to make sure you drink plenty of water."

"Does champagne count?"

"Sure. Wine is made from fruit, after all—and everyone knows fruit is good for you." Should I nip back to the kitchen for another bottle? It seemed like an awfully long way to go—and if I left Liza unoccupied for too long, she'd have time to realize I had absolutely zero clue.

Four louvered doors spanned the far wall. Maybe there'd be more champagne in there.

I tried door #1. The closet beyond was definitely full of supplies, but unfortunately, none of them were of the fermented grape variety. Cases of Citrus Fresh and Eco Scrub were stacked high, as well as rolls of paper towels and TP. And there was enough bleach in there to sterilize the floor of a gentleman's club. I guess one can never underestimate how important it is to keep the treatment rooms squeaky clean.

"Hang tight," I told Eliza. "You need to give the dry brush some time to set before you proceed with any further treatment."

"Oh, that makes sense."

I opened door #2. The closet beyond hadn't come into the twenty-first century with the rest of the hotel. The walls were rough, original, handcrafted plaster, and the floors were flagstone. But the coolest part was the old brass pump sprouting up from the far corner. It looked like something out of a Wild West reenactment, or maybe a cowboy movie where a bunch of studly ranch hands would pause to quench their thirst—with a metal ladle, naturally—and proceed to pour water down their sweating bodies so their clothing clung to every well-sculpted muscle. And then take off their damp clothes and do other things.... Okay, I'm really not much for Westerns unless plenty of gratuitous nakedness is involved.

The smell of sulfur was strong in that room. I'm no traveling aquatic engineer, but it didn't take much common sense to figure out that this particular pump tapped directly into the Spring Falls hot spring. I grabbed a bucket from a teetering pile and placed it under the spigot. It took some elbow grease, but I got the water flowing.

Now it was just a matter of figuring out what to do with it. I couldn't very well just throw a bucket of warmish sulfur water at Liza. "How's that dry brushing settling in?" I asked her.

"Good. I guess."

"Just a little bit longer—you don't want to rush these things." I checked door #3. Jackpot! The floor inside was old concrete set with a drain. It almost looked like a shower stall, but without the shower. Who knows how old-timey people took their ablutions... but who needs a shower when you have a bucket? With a flourish, I spun around and told Liza, "It's time."

Her eyes widened.

I gestured to the shower stall like I was presenting a game show prize. A new washer/dryer set. Or maybe even a speedboat. "Now that you're good and exfoliated, you're ready for the ultimate Spring Falls Hot Spring Spa treatment: the proprietary mineral rinse."

"I didn't see that on the brochure."

I pitched my voice low, like I was sharing a big secret, and said, "Because it's proprietary."

"...oh."

Ceremoniously, I ushered Liza onto the concrete slab and positioned her over the drain. I told her, "Now, it's important that you approach this treatment in the right frame of mind. As we move through our days, we pick up different energies. They're not negative, not necessarily. But that doesn't mean that every single vibe you find yourself resonating with is a good fit." Obviously, I was dumbing down what I actually knew to make it accessible to a Handless. There are plenty of woo-woo New Age types out there with a lot of far-out ideas—and we Spellcrafters don't pay them any more mind than we do the church crowd. Our brand of energy might be unpredictable, but it definitely shows results. One thing I knew, though. Energy was real. And you could definitely do worse than to shift your mindset.

Would a little positive thinking change Liza's circumstance? Not in a tangible and decisive way like Spellcraft. But it might at least bring her some comfort.

"Feeling peaceful?" I asked.

"Peaceful...ish."

"Fantastic." I took her hand and helped her step onto the floor drain.

"It's rough."

"All the better to smooth out any calluses. Now, like I told you, put your troubles out of your mind and focus on the present while you steep in tradition." I dipped behind the second door and hauled out my bucket of mineral water, fresh from the pump. The sulfur smell was strong, like a roll of caps, still smoking, that had been pounded flat with a handy rock. But the water was warm-ish and blue.

Especially blue.

When I tipped the bucket over Liza's head, I realized it wasn't just the blue of water optical illusion, but the tint of minerals pushed up to the surface from deep underground. As the water flowed over her in thin blue rivulets, her white mummy wrappings turned a fetching shade of aquamarine.

"I was a little dubious," Liza said. "What with the smell and all. But, y'know what? That felt pretty good. Can we do it again?"

"Sure we can. It's your special day. Just you. Whether or not some guy's ring is on your finger."

In the end, I pumped and poured six more buckets of stinky water. My arms would be looking pretty buff—hopefully I'd get a chance to show off my guns for Yuri. With each bucket I drew, it felt like I was sucking up water from deeper and deeper underground. And by the end of the treatment, the water was no less stinky, but delightfully steamy.

Best of all, though, was that after the last of the pretty blue water swirled down the drain, Liza was actually smiling.

"I think the champagne might've gone to my head," she told me. "I'm going to go have a little nap before you do my mani/pedi."

I wasn't entirely sure I was the best guy for the job, since according to Sabina, I always got more nail polish on her toes than her toenails—which never stopped her from plunking her bare feet in my lap while we binged baking shows on Netflix—but I'd be willing to give it a shot. While Liza wrung out the hem of her sodden mummy wrap minidress, I opened door #4 and poked my head in, hoping to scare up a fluffy terrycloth robe.

What I found were mops. String mops and dust mops and the little sponge mops too. And squeegees and brooms and....

Uh oh.

This was no treatment room—it was a janitorial closet. Not only had I wrapped the poor girl in shop rags, but I'd scrubbed her down like stained grout.

I hastily shut the final door and said with all the authority I could muster, "The thing about the Spring Falls Hot Springs mineral rinse is that you can't just towel it all off. To get the full effect, you'll need to let the treatment air dry on your skin." I led her out into the main room—suddenly all the industrial looking stainless steel made a lot more sense.

Taking her by the shoulders, I faced her away from the doors and said, "Proper alignment. Shoulders back. Clear your mind. Soak in the mineral. And I'll be back with your robe in a jiffy."

I closed the door gently behind me...then tore off down the hall in search of an actual bathrobe.

The treatment level of the spa was a warren of confusing hallways, but pretty soon I figured out that while I'd been chatting up Liza and trying to make myself sound like an esthetician, we'd overshot a turn. The real treatment rooms were a lot more like I'd initially imagined, with massage tables and muted lighting and photographs of stacked rocks on the walls.

I scooped up a robe and hurried back to the janitorial room before Liza got too curious about what was behind those louvered doors...and I hoped Janet wouldn't get too fussy over another appropriated bottle of champagne.

YURI

5

Undoubtedly, Dixon was having a fine time buffing fingernails and dabbing on lipstick. But what he failed to realize was that mangled Spellcraft was serious business. He had been trained by his loving family. My mentor in St. Petersburg was nowhere near as gentle. The old hag once showed me how the *volshebstvo* could go wrong by Crafting me a charm for luck, on which she dumped a glass of water before the ink was fully dry. A few days later, a boxing match I'd bet on won by a long-shot, leaving me with more money than I'd seen in ages. I thought she was trying to demonstrate the persistence of the *volshebstvo*...until I was beaten senseless on the way home, probably by the bookmaker's own sons.

So much for luck.

I gave back the Crafting without a word, though with the split lip and bruises, I hadn't needed to say a thing.

Never again did I allow that bitter old woman to Craft for me.

Perhaps I should have. It had never occurred to me that I would someday deal with Spellcraft gone so bafflingly wrong.

I found Janet outside behind the office, staring at the building with her head cocked and her arms crossed. She acknowledged me with a short nod and said, "Does that corner look discolored to you?"

I followed her gaze. Hard to tell between the patchy paint jobs and streaks of mineral stains. "It's fine," I said. "So. I have been wondering about this volcanologist...."

"Fonzo—such a positive person. I think that's important, don't you? A good attitude makes all the difference in the world."

It was such an American thing to say, the best I could do was to not actively disagree. Though it wasn't easy. "I know he didn't tell you specifically where he was going, but if you could think back on the things he told you, maybe there was some detail you didn't mention."

Janet frowned in thought. "Nope. Nothing. But there aren't many active volcanoes in the mainland states. Heck, I didn't even know there were traces of volcanic activity beneath Spring Falls. Maybe he was on his way to Yosemite."

That would be a very logical guess...if Fonzo actually were a volcanologist.

I followed her back inside. "I hope you're not looking for any more bacon," she said. "That was well and truly the last batch. If you don't believe me, I can show you the empty wrapper."

"Not necessary." But the mention of the wrapper brought another problem to mind. "The shredded paper from the welcome baskets. Can you give me more of that?"

If it was a strange request, it didn't seem to faze her. In her business dealing with the public, she must've heard a lot of strange requests. "It's all used up. But I can make more."

"Never mind." Could I search Liza's room while she was occupied with Dixon? Unlikely, without breaking down the door. Unless.... "I will need a master key, since I am posing as part of your staff."

Janet clearly wanted to refuse. But then she looked at my imposing knuckles and gave a resigned sigh. "Fine. But if anyone calls you on your massage technique, just say whatever you're doing is European."

I could hardly believe my good fortune. But as Janet turned

toward the safe to retrieve the key card, the doors behind me whooshed open with a fresh blast of sulfur.

A man in a brown suit stood in the doorway. His hair was a non-color, not quite light, not quite dark. He was neither young nor old, ugly nor handsome. In fact, he had the sort of face you'd forget the moment you looked away. He walked up to the front of the empty queue and politely waited his turn.

"Welcome to the Spring Falls Hot Spring Spa," Janet said with forced, mannish enthusiasm as she waved him forward. "I'm Janet, and this is my internationally-renowned Russian masseuse, Yuri. How may we facilitate your delightful stay?"

The forgettable man approached and looked me up and down. He said, "You're from Russia?"

His nose was so congested, it very nearly created a dialect of its own.

He went on stuffily, "Did you know that a quarter of the world's water reserves are in Russia, but the National Resources Ministry allows the majority of polluting violations to go unchecked?"

No big surprise. But since I had no desire to get sidetracked into a discussion about it, I answered with my most cryptic shrug.

"No polluting violations here!" Janet declared with forced brightness.

At that point, most people would make a smart remark about the smell. But the forgettable man seemed far too serious for flatulence jokes. He pulled a business card from his wallet and slid it across the desk. "I'm sure Vacation Nation wouldn't have sent me on assignment anywhere significant pollution was an issue."

Janet picked up the card and read his name aloud. "Woodrow. Is that your first or last name?"

"For security reasons, I'm not required to disclose that information. Vacation Nation representatives can't be too careful. You'd be surprised how far some resort owners will go to ensure a favorable review."

One hardly needed a last name to follow a man down a dark hallway and kick out his kneecap, but I kept that observation to myself.

Janet said, "That's fine, Mr. Woodrow. We've been expecting you." She keyed something into her computer and said, "All checked in. You'll find your welcome basket waiting for you in your room."

"And what about breakfast?"

"Available between 7 and 10:30 am."

We all glanced at the clock behind the check-in desk. It was nearly 11.

"Hm," Woodrow said.

Janet watched in alarm as he pulled out a tiny pad of paper and jotted down a notation. She hastened to add, "Our world-class room service is at your disposal 24-7. Would you like some bacon? I can make you a fresh batch of bacon." It was tempting to remind her she'd just offered to prove its non-existence by showing me an empty wrapper. But she sounded so flustered, I settled for a raised eyebrow instead.

Woodrow was no more impressed by the offer than I. "Heavens, no. Do you know how much sodium there is in bacon? Send up two slices of white toast, dry, and a bottle of room-temperature water."

"Water? Certainly. Sparkling or still?"

Woodrow looked scandalized. "It's not even noon yet!"

"Uh...right. Still water it is."

"In the meanwhile, I'll be up in my room, settling in."

I was unsure if his gift basket had been put together before or after the Spellcraft was shredded—so I'd need to get a look for myself. "I will carry your bag."

"No need."

"I insist."

"Only the one valise." He picked up his room key, hoisted a small bag, and said, "Helpful is one thing—overbearing is another. I'll be awaiting my toast." And with that, he stepped into the elevator and pulled out his pad. He was jotting another note as the doors pulled shut.

Janet flung herself across the desk and clutched my arm. My biceps seemed to startle her, but only for a moment. "Did you get a load of that guy?" she said in a desperate squeak. "He's drearier than a month of rainy Mondays. He was supposed to help me get back on my feet after the big drought—but what could ever hope to make him happy?"

"Toast?"

"I'll bet if he ever smiled, his lips would flop right off like two strips of bacon." She buried her face in her hands. "I'm so dead."

I have never inherited anything of value from my family, not like Janet. And yet, I could not help but admire the fact that she was willing to keep trying to salvage it.

What I could do to help her, I wasn't sure. I hadn't met many Scriveners over the course of my life I could actually trust, so my initial solution to any given problem is not usually Spellcraft. However, the declining resort was the ideal place to use our magic—so, naturally, it was the one avenue I could not pursue. Not with bits of mangled Spellcraft still on the loose.

I wouldn't even attempt to sweeten the outcome of the critic's visit until whatever bizarre Crafting Fonzo Penn had left behind was retrieved and disposed of. But first, I had to find the shreds. And that meant searching the rooms—not that I'd announce that plan to Janet. "Give me the staff key. I will go ready the treatment room in case Woodrow insists on a massage."

As we spoke, a door marked Business Center swung open, and out strode the Aryan idiot who'd shown up in his power suit the night before. Quint was dressed in resort wear now, unbleached linen from head to toe with strappy leather sandals, but he still looked every inch the corporate pawn. "Did you say massage? What perfect timing. I'm in definite need of some myofascial release."

I was guessing that even if I knew how that phrase translated, it wouldn't have done me much good. Janet did her best not to sound alarmed. "You'll note on your check-in form that not all techniques are available during all time slots. I'll just check the schedules and see if we can fit in your treatment—though I should warn you, our massage books out awfully far in advance."

She clicked around on her keyboard—which may or may not

have been hooked up to anything—but before she could inform Quint that he'd need to wait his turn, he said, "Don't worry about squeezing me in. I booked ahead online."

Janet cut her eyes to me, silently begging.

I held out my hand and said, "The key."

She whispered, "Room 102," and held out the keycard. Her hand shook ever so slightly.

I took it from her, drew myself up to my full height, gave Quint my most withering look, and said, "Follow me."

I turned on my heel and strode down the hall as if I knew exactly where I was going, and followed the numbers. The resort was mostly empty and the hallway felt abandoned, other than some splashing coming from the janitor's closet. Before long, we came upon Room 102.

There was a sign on the door that read, *Quiet, Please! Massage Zone.* The words were painted in girlish calligraphy on a slice of wood stained pastel grayish blue, hung with a gold organza bow. Spellcraft? I'd never painted a Seen on wood—but that didn't mean it couldn't be done. And a pale enough Seen could easily be camouflaged with decorative stain. But when I squinted at the sign to try and catch sight of any *volshebstvo*, it remained only that. A tacky, handcrafted sign.

My experience with massage was limited to a big-boned woman named Hilda at my gym in St. Petersburg who left me feeling like I'd been run over by a truck, but I doubted people came to the resort hoping to be so thoroughly worked over. I didn't expect the "spa" particulars to be entirely like what I was used to...but I certainly didn't expect to turn on the light and find myself in the gaze of dozens upon dozens of tiny glass eyes.

The walls were covered with shelves crowded with fuzzy animals: bears and cats, penguins and pigs. And between those animals were ceramic figurines of angels with oversized heads and comical faces...and family photos of smiling children...and tiny framed cross-stitch embroideries of words like *Love* and *Joy* and *Namaste.*

"This is your room?" Quint asked.

I did my best to restrain myself from tearing the nearest stuffed bulldog in half, and leveled him my most intimidating look.

"And you're going to do the massage in a suit?"

True, I didn't want oil on my jacket. I took it off and folded it. Dixon claims I look like I'm about to inflict some serious damage when I do so. I may quell a smile when he says this. Here, now, in the closed, quiet room, Quint seemed nearly as fascinated as Dixon always did when I unbuttoned my cuffs and rolled up my sleeves. I indicated a changing screen with a jut of my chin and said, "Undress."

"I have a standing appointment with the best bodyworker in Wichita," Quint informed me, as if the safety of the screen between us allowed the braggart in him to feel brave. "I've had deep tissue massage and shiatsu, trigger point and hot stone. It would take a lot to impress me."

I didn't dignify that with a reply, but I did cross my arms. A few threads snapped in my shoulder seams. The next time Dixon bet me I couldn't do a hundred push-ups with him sitting on my back, I'd first have him buy me some new shirts.

Quint emerged from behind the screen in a robe. "My body-worker usually leaves the room while I get situated."

"I am not your bodyworker." And neither was I interested in his nakedness. Frankly, the thought of touching him left me vaguely repulsed, though I could hardly pass myself off as a masseuse without doing so.

As he climbed on the table, nervously relating stories of his superlative Kansas bodyworker, I searched the room for some sort of massage tool to use as a buffer between his flesh and mine, but found nothing. Whoever had come before me must have seen the spa going downhill and taken her personal equipment the last time she left. Too bad she hadn't removed some of the unsettling dolls.

"I have trigger points behind my shoulder blades that are nearly impossible to release," he said into the table. "It's the price I pay for having such a fast-paced, high-stress career. It's challenging to set ambitious benchmarks for success without burning yourself out."

"And yet you insist on reliving the experience."

"What's that supposed to mean?"

"You are not at work right now." Would he notice if I massaged him with a plush toy? Maybe not, if I greased it up well enough. "You have come to the spa to enjoy a vacation. So, enjoy it."

"Oh. I, uh, never really thought about it that way...."

I was considering which stuffed animal would do the job when I spotted a small wooden rolling pin among all the kitsch. It was glued to a lace-bordered plaque that read: *I sugar-coat everything!* I popped it off the mount and gave it an experimental slap against my palm.

It would do.

I poured the massage oil directly onto his back.

"Yikes! My bodyworker warms the oil first."

"We have already established I am not your bodyworker." I slapped down the rolling pin and began rolling him out like a stubborn batch of *vatrushka*.

It was strangely satisfying. Not the moaning and groaning sounds I squeezed out of him with each push of the rolling pin, and not even the occasional startling crack that sounded from his body. It was simply a relief to be doing something. Given the choice between talking and doing, I would always prefer to use my hands.

I worked him like a ball of dough. The room was small and close, and smelled of almond oil and sulfur. But soon it smelled of sweat, too, both his and mine. No doubt Dixon would have something salacious to say about it.

No doubt I should introduce him to the creative use of a rolling pin at some point in the future.

But Quint was not Dixon. Perhaps he was even the opposite. Dixon was brilliant—creative, disciplined, and most importantly, humble. I had no idea whether or not Quint was as successful as he claimed to be. But in my experience, men who need to brag about their accomplishments only do it because there are so few of them to be proud of.

I rolled the obnoxious businessman until I'd practically flattened him. His groans of both pain and pleasure grew faint. My own muscles ached as if I'd taken on his pain and absorbed it into myself—even without touching him.

Good thing I have never been afraid of pain.

I dropped the greased rolling pin with a clatter—and Quint didn't even flinch. Had I killed him? No—still breathing. But very, very relaxed.

"Your massage is finished," I announced.

"That was...mfnmmmbbb." The non-word was delivered with an abundance of drool.

"Go, now." I poked him. "Go back to your room."

He levered himself up off the massage table and pulled a towel around his waist. His face looked dreamy and a bit squashed. "I've never experienced anything like that."

Unless he was a pastry, I would expect not. I crossed my arms and shrugged.

"If you could pass along the name of the technique to my bodyworker for reference—"

"You have your trade secrets, I have mine. Get moving, and don't make me tell you again." The longer we dallied, the more destruction the malfunctioning Spellcraft would exact on the spa.

Quint staggered away from the table and slipped behind the screen to dress. Meanwhile, I pondered whether Dixon and I should reconstruct the Crafting once we found all the pieces, or simply burn them and hope for the best. When Quint reappeared from behind the screen, he was loose-limbed and wobbly, and smiling like an imbecile.

"Don't go pestering me for another massage," I told him. "My methods are thorough and the results will last for at least a week." By which time, we should be long gone.

"Yeah—no—I get it—absolutely." He reached into his pocket and pulled out a bill, then stuffed it into a black-and-white painted jar that read, *Tipping: Not Just for Cows Anymore*. I loathe tipping—a ridiculous practice, like delayed bribery—but I had never been on the receiving end. I plucked out the bill. A hundred.

Not bad for an hour's work.

Quint was busy pawing at the doorknob with fingers too greasy to turn it. I picked up a towel and opened it for him, then realized maybe I could recoup the time I'd just spent on him in more ways than just the money. I blocked the door with my arm. He nearly garroted himself on my elbow, but managed to stagger back and remain upright. "One more thing," I told him.

"Yes?" he asked vacantly.

"Did you get a welcome basket when you checked in?"

"Uh, yeah, I suppose I did."

"Then before you do anything else...bring it to me."

DIXON

6

Helping Liza forget about the jerk who stranded her at the altar was definitely a worthwhile way to spend my morning, and thankfully, she was grateful enough to hand over her shred without much more than a curious look. I headed back to our room with her paper-filled ice bucket and found Yuri seated by the window in his tank top, with his slightly crooked glasses perched on the edge of his nose and a shirt in his hand. If anyone could make mending a shoulder seam look masculine, it was him. He filled the clingy rib knit of his undershirt in all the best ways. His hands seemed like they should've been too big to handle that tiny little sewing needle, but as with everything he did, he handled it with deftness and precision.

I was about to suggest something else he could deftly handle when I spied a big wad of paper on the dresser. "You found more shred? Me too! This is fantastic! Now we'll see what's what."

Yuri grunted, knotted the thread, and clipped it with his teeth.

"Do they have jigsaw puzzles in Russia? I'm sure they do. This is kind of like a jigsaw puzzle. Except instead of all those crazy, wiggly shapes, we have strips. And instead of pictures of flowers or cottages or puppies or kittens, we have Spellcraft."

While Yuri reinforced one of his buttons, I dumped all the shred together, sorted through it, and plucked out the Spellcrafty bits. A particular tangle of lettering glommed together and I arranged it into the letters "ffl." Baffle? Scuffle? Waffle? Waffles sounded pretty tempting, even if the spa was out of bacon. But none of those words seemed like they'd help a business in serious financial trouble. My gaze followed the loops of Uncle Fonzo's ascenders, which I could still make out despite the fact that the lines were ragged and the nib looked worn. A reimagined Crafting flitted through my mind.

IF FLowers grew
They would be rare
And perfume the air
Anew

Weird cadence and not my usual rhyme scheme, though none of that really mattered. Not if I couldn't find the rest of the word. I went through everything again, but came up empty-handed. "There's got to be more shred around here somewhere," I said. "The beginning and end of the word are all spotty."

"And what if there is no more? What if the remaining pieces are in a dumpster somewhere, dissolving in a stew of rotting garbage?"

"I'm not sure," I admitted. "Mom always told me not to let the Spellcraft wear out its welcome. Once it does its job, she sets it free."

"Once it does its job." Yuri cut his eyes to the shred. "And what if the Crafting is ruined *before* then?"

I gave a helpless shrug. "No clue. All we can do is try to put it back together and hope for the best."

Yuri slipped into his shirt then pulled on his jacket. "I will leave the hoping to you—I'm terrible at such things." He drew a keycard from his jacket pocket. "But I will try to find the rest of the Crafting."

There was still one guest whose welcome basket we hadn't plumbed—the critic—and he was staying in the Presidential Suite. We headed up to the top floor where the rooms cost twice as much and paused at the three doors with "do not disturb" signs on the doorknobs. Unfortunately, we couldn't tell the Presidential Suite from the Businessman Deluxe...and, frankly, I was no longer so sure which room was Liza's, either.

Eeny, meenie, meiney, moe.

But before I could knock, a door swung open and—what luck!—a completely nondescript man stepped out. Unless he'd been in someone's luggage, he could only be—

"Mr. Woodrow," Yuri said smoothly. Even charmingly. Which was how I knew it was a total put-on, because Yuri only likes to be smooth and charming inadvertently. "I have come to see that your stay so far is meeting your expectations."

I had to admit, Yuri did a pretty convincing job of selling himself as an employee of the spa. But before he could angle his way into the room, the critic shut the door behind him with a firm click. "The hot water in my bath is three degrees cooler than I'd prefer, but the thread count in the bedding was adequate." The words were spoken around a nose so stuffed-up, I had to check to see if he even had nostrils. "I'm off to check the sauna, if you'd care to join me." When Yuri looked as if he was about to refuse, Mr. Woodrow added, "I've always been keen on experiencing an authentic *vasta*. Surely, you'll indulge me."

I had no idea what any of that meant—but luckily, Yuri did. He nodded once and said, "I will meet you there." While the critic's back was turned, he flashed a key card. What a thrill! I'd always wanted to be a decoy.

I looped my arm through Mr. Woodrow's to propel him toward the spa posthaste while Yuri went hunting for shred. "Hard to beat a good *vasta*," I said. Agreeing with people is easy. Even if you don't really know what you're talking about.

"Northern Europe has a great tradition of sauna," the critic informed me, while I tried to make it look like I knew exactly where we were going, seeing as how I worked there and all. "So it's exciting to be in the company of your Russian masseuse."

And he'd never seen Yuri doing pull-ups in nothing but a clingy undershirt and a pair of boxers.

"Did you know most saunas in Europe are co-ed?" Woodrow

asked. "American saunas are such a poor facsimile of true Finnish *sudatory*. The human body is used to sell everything from teabags to timeshares, but we're separated for something as innocent and healthful as a steam bath."

We followed the hall past the treatment rooms—and a particular janitorial closet—and came upon two doors: Men's Sauna - Women's Sauna. Woodrow rapped on the Women's door and announced, "Male entering!"

It wasn't easy to stop myself from snerking, but I managed. The only two women at the resort had pressing business elsewhere— Janet was running the front desk and Liza was sleeping off her mimosas—so no one answered. He went in. Since I was "staff," I followed.

We made a circuit of the changing room where Mr. Woodrow gave all the surfaces the white-glove test, dipped litmus test strips in all the water, took its temperature, and jotted a bunch of notes. And then we moved on to the Men's changing rooms. Once Mr. Woodrow did all his temperatures and tests, he stepped into a changing booth and shut the canvas curtain with a whisk. "You'll be joining us?" he asked me.

"I wouldn't miss it for the world."

I stripped down to a towel and met the critic by the sauna door. Of course, I'd sat in my share of gym or hotel saunas—usually with much shameless flirting all around—but never in such a fancy spa setting. The Spring Falls Hot Spring Spa did its best to live up to the unattainable Finnish standards while still keeping its liability insurance from the good old U S of A. Walls and seats were smooth wooden slats, hot stones smoldered in the center of the room, temperatures were steamy...and the smell of sulfur permeated everything.

It was about the size of Yuri's cabin, with relaxing mood lighting and three tiers of benches. There was a thermometer and humidity gauge combo in the room, but apparently Mr. Woodrow didn't trust it. He did a circuit of the space, poking his thermometer into the corners, taking notes.

"You can tell some work has gone into this particular sauna. See here? You can vent the steam if it gets too intense." He tried the lever to see if it was working, and made a note. Then he grabbed a hand-towel from a neatly folded pile and draped it over his head. "But it's better sauna etiquette to control your own temperature by adjusting your position in the room, or protecting your head."

Who knew when I woke up that morning, I'd be subjected to the world's most stuffed-up mansplaining?

"Some American saunas even require their users to wear bathing suits, if you can believe such puritanical nonsense."

And with that, he whipped off the towel around his waist. Luckily, he turned toward the benches to spread it out without looking at my expression.

I'm told my poker face needs work. And let's just say the fancy thermometer wasn't the only serious equipment Mr. Woodrow was packing.

I couldn't very well keep my own towel on without looking like a prude—not that I was worried about anything perking up that shouldn't. I've been a big fan of the male form ever since I could remember, but the third limb Mr. Woodrow was hauling around with him went beyond impressive and into the realm of grotesque. Heck, I hardly knew how much room I'd need to give him. Maybe the whole bench.

I settled myself a good several feet away and searched desperately for something to look at other than Mr. Woodrow's lap. I was studying the far wall very carefully—in fact, I'd counted the slats at least three times—when Yuri finally joined us. Wearing only a towel. And holding a bundle of pussy willows he'd glommed from a vase out in the hallway.

His gaze flicked to Mr. Woodrow's nakedness and his eyebrow twitched. But other than that, he carried on without acknowledging the elephant in the room. I was dying to ask how much shred he'd managed to score, but some things aren't so easy to communicate with a meaningful look.

"*Vastas* are used to increase circulation," Mr. Woodrow informed me, then turned to Yuri and said, "I thought they were traditionally made from leafy birch twigs."

Yuri looked down his nose at the disturbingly naked man—who was now turning a bit pink from the steamy heat and glistening with a sheen of sweat. "The birch is not in leaf. The spirit of tradition is to use materials that are seasonal and local. It would be a shame to give you a false experience instead of the one which embraces the spirit of the tradition."

Yuri sure did sound like an imposing Russian masseuse. Even I was nodding along with his explanation—and I knew darn well he was not an employee, but a Seer. And Mr. Woodrow seemed just as taken with his logic.

Yuri spread a towel on one of the benches and gestured for Mr. Woodrow to climb on. Once the critic was all...tucked in...Yuri dipped a ladle of spring water onto the hot stones. It hit with a sulfurous hiss, enfolding the scene in a cloud of steam. He took up the pussy willow, and began tapping up and down Woodrow's back. Some of the fuzzy gray buds fell off and rolled to the floor, as they were long-dried, and most definitely not in season.

"Is that the normal amount of force?" he asked through the wooden slats.

"Of course," Yuri said authoritatively. "You must take care not to irritate the skin in such a hot environment."

"Ah." And for the first time since I'd met him, Woodrow stopped spewing stuffy facts and went quiet.

Yuri locked eyes with me across the critic's prone body while he tap-tap-tapped with the shedding pussy willow. Yuri's not much for improvisation, so I was pretty darn impressed with the lengths he was willing to go to in convincing Mr. Woodrow he was a capable Russian masseuse. I wasn't sure why he was so inspired—but I was definitely impressed.

Before long, the steam got to the desiccated pussy willows, and all the little buds gave up the ghost in a tiny shower of fuzz. "And now the *vasta* is complete," Mr. Woodrow announced, then pushed himself up from the wooden bench. I scrambled back before I got kneecapped by any wayward body parts. "Although I hardly felt a thing."

"Of course," Yuri said. "It is the mark of a true master...to not leave a mark. Your circulation is enhanced. You feel nothing but the benefits."

"If only dealing with my allergies could be so easy. I'd hoped the steam would get things flowing, but no such luck. Even so, I'm sure your *vasta* will be a highlight of my article. Now, for the grand finale—a plunge into a cold pool. In Finland, it's customary to dive into a frozen lake or roll around in the snow."

Yuri narrowed his eyes shrewdly and said, "That may be true— but these things you speak of are modern ways. In the most traditional Russian *banyas*—in the farthest Siberian villages—a person would douse the sweat from his body in a tepid bath. In his room. With his masseuse in attendance."

"You know, now that you mention it, I have indeed heard of a moderate follow-up soak. That would be why the lounge just beyond the treatment rooms opens out to the grotto. To follow the sauna with a nourishing mineral soak!"

YURI

7

I'd almost had him...and then he slipped through my fingers. Dixon had done an adequate job of distracting Woodrow in the sauna while I went to search the man's room, but all the distraction in the world wouldn't have done me any good. I went through everything twice, and eventually resigned myself to the fact that he must have thrown his welcome basket away...when I noticed a scrap of shredded paper sticking out from the safe.

He'd locked a basket of toiletries *in the safe*.

Because he was worried someone would take them? Or because he was bending to a strange compulsion ignited by the Spellcraft?

And now we'd be stuck visiting the grotto—in nothing but towels—when we should have been talking Woodrow into opening that safe.

As far as I was concerned, only a fool would go roll in the snow, covered in sweat or not. But the cool springtime air was deliciously bracing on our skin. It might have even been enjoyable, had it not been for the stench in the air...and the fact that some mangled magic was responsible for it. The three of us traipsed out to the grotto. When Woodrow dropped his towel, he cast a shadow like a tripod, but we were spared the sight of his nakedness soon enough. The waters in the thermal pool were opaque with mineral concentration.

"Are you going to test that with your portable chemistry lab?" Dixon teetered on the edge of the pool, dipping nothing but his toes.

"The first thing I did when I got here," Woodrow proclaimed. "Magnesium. Copper. Sulfur. Extremely therapeutic."

Dixon and I looked at one another, shrugged, shed our towels and joined him.

Woodrow scooped up a palmful of the water and splashed it on his chest. "Waters with a high mineral concentration relieve muscular tension, reduce blood pressure, and relieve myriad skin conditions."

He continued to wax eloquent about the origins and notable instances of various thermal spas from beneath the veil of the small towel draped over his head. He dominated the conversation—and not many people can manage that around Dixon.

While he droned on like a living, breathing Wikipedia, I pondered how best to relieve him of his gift basket. Surely there was a way in which I could maneuver the critic back to his room and get the shredded paper. Inventing some new Russian tradition would be best, though one in which a hotel guest must open his safe in front of his masseuse would be a pretty hard sell. Perhaps if I claimed to need a particular balm or lotion from his basket.... The plan took shape in my mind, but as it did, the sun glinted off something reflective. Across the parking lot and the boulevard beyond, set back from the road, a large public building of some sort was nestled behind a neatly ordered stand of evergreens. And on the roof of that building, several people clustered.

With binoculars.

Trained on us.

When I turned to get a better look at them, the cluster of heads ducked away.

Woodrow was busy pontificating on the merits of iodine when I broke in with, "You seem very prepared. Have your notes indicated what that building across the way might be?"

"Certainly. It's the Spring Falls Retirement Home. Quiet neighbors make for a peaceful spa."

He turned back to Dixon and began regaling him with tales of calcium carbonate while I kept one surreptitious eye on the old folks' home. After a few minutes, a head was again visible over the parapet. A gray-haired head. Soon joined by another, and another. I double checked that my private parts were still private. Luckily the preponderance of magnesium, iodine and sulfur were serving my modesty well.

Once I was sick of listening to Woodrow blather on, I declared, "Time for the *reven*. Which is traditionally performed in the subject's private quarters."

"I've never heard of the *reven*," Woodrow said, part challenging, part intrigued. And no, he wouldn't have heard of it. Not unless he spoke Russian—and he had reason to discuss *rhubarb*.

"A very carefully guarded tradition among the people of the steppes," I claimed. "I would not perform the *reven* for just anybody. But you, my friend, are clearly a man of discerning taste."

As I grabbed my own towel, Dixon reached for his. We stood and quickly fastened them at the waist while a few gray-haired heads popped up to observe. They wouldn't have seen much, if anything...if a ragged little mop of a canine had not darted up and snagged the corner of Woodrow's towel.

Woodrow yelped in shock. "What is that thing?"

"Just a little dog," Dixon said.

Woodrow didn't look like he believed him. I added, "A dog in dire need of a bath."

"Twinkle, stop!" Dixon scolded. "Let go of that!"

But Twinkle was having none of it. He dug in his paws, growling. He gave his furry head a violent shake, and the towel slid from Woodrow's startled grasp. Dixon and I both made a grab for it, bounced off one another, and splashed down into the water. Woodrow leapt up out of the pool, snatching at the terrycloth. His foot slipped on wet stone, and he spun around, full circle, waving all three arms to keep from toppling over. Across the lane, a gaggle of old women whooped in glee.

Dixon bobbed up, spitting sulfurous water. "You can have my towel," he offered hastily. "You're the guest, after all."

Woodrow planted his hands on his hips as Twinkle wrangled the towel into some undergrowth and slipped away. Dixon and I both looked up at the sky for fear of finding something awkward looking back at us. Someone across the street gave a wolf-whistle, though it was mostly carried away by the wind, and Woodrow didn't seem to notice. "No, no, it's not sanitary to share towels. You should know that."

"Just testing you!" Dixon said gamely.

Woodrow removed the hand-towel from his head and attempted to wrap it around his waist...and if anything, the fact that it showed at least as much as it concealed made his endowments seem twice as unavoidable. "I don't suppose the resort can be held responsible for the actions of an animal," he said philosophically. "Though if it's a known issue, one could argue that a fence might be in order."

On the roof across the way, more gray-haired heads peeked over the edge. The sound of appreciative tittering threaded through the distant birdsong.

"Forget about the fence," I said. "That dog just did you a favor. For full effect, we must perform the *reven* while your skin is still damp."

Not one to miss out on some obscure vacation experience, Woodrow stopped grousing about the dog and hurried back to the building, clutching the slip of a towel ineffectively around himself. "I will meet you in your room in five minutes," I said. "Do not rinse yourself. Do not dry yourself. Lie quietly in your bathtub, face down, and leave your door unlocked. And have the basket of products you were given available for my use—the *whole* basket. Any deviation from my instructions will taint the treatment. Am I clear?"

"Absolutely! Five minutes it is."

He gave a jaunty salute and his meager towel flapped open. I did my best not to shudder. I probably should not have chosen the word *taint*.

As we retrieved our clothes from the massage chambers, Dixon whispered, "What's the, uh, *raven?*"

"Whatever we need it to be—it was all I could think of to get him to unlock his basket. Just play along—and when you see your chance, grab the paper."

Dixon and I hastily rinsed off the sulfur, pulled on our clothes, and headed for Woodrow's room. We found the critic lying face-down in his bathtub as instructed, though now that I thought my directive through, I wasn't sure how long he could hold the position. Maybe the trapped body part was providing cushioning for the rest of him. Most importantly, also as instructed, he'd brought out his gift basket and left it sitting on the bathroom counter.

I squinted at the shredded paper—not long enough to actually see the *volshebstvo* coursing through the shreds, but certainly long enough to feel the elusive pull of its presence.

"Is this right?" Woodrow's voice echoed against the porcelain. "You didn't mention whether or not I should keep my towel on."

Thankfully, he'd erred on the side of caution and left it on. "Did I tell you to remove the towel? I did not. So—we begin." I pointed to the basket and Dixon gave a nod. He'd brought the paper that had already been picked through from our basket, bundled in a pillowcase. Together, we pulled out the various tiny samples from the basket, but none of them seemed like anything I could use to create a plausible ritual. Not one that was strange enough to satisfy Woodrow's love of all things obscure. "It is important to focus inside yourself while I finish your *vasta* with the *reven.*"

"Got it."

It seemed prudent to start by rinsing the minerals from his body. "First, water." I sprayed him with the hand-nozzle, though the water started out cold enough to make him yelp, then immediately went too hot while I struggled to figure out the tap. "Alternating temperatures to stimulate the circulation."

"I see," he burbled stuffily into the water, while Dixon stuffed his shreds into the pillowcase.

I finished hosing off the reeking mineral water. "Then, oil." I shook out a spatter of lotion from the minuscule bottle and swiped it across his back. Dixon turned the basket upside down and gave it a few shakes for good measure. Once he was sure it was empty, he replaced the stolen shreds with the paper from our room, then gave me the thumbs-up.

Good. The sooner I could stop playing nice, the better.

"Is that all?" the critic asked against the floor of the tub. "Water and some lotion? Not much of a ritual, if you ask me."

While I was eager to tell this stuffy little man exactly what he could do with his rituals, when I thought of Janet's distress over the thought of losing her business, I knew I'd have to restrain myself.

I motioned for Dixon to make off with the paper. He gave me an even more vigorous thumbs-up, then hurried away with the shreds while I cast around for some other prop to employ.

Unfortunately, there was no rhubarb in the man's bathroom. But there was a ridiculous Zen garden: basically, a pan of white sand, a tiny rake, and a handful of smooth stones. It was tempting to dump the sand over his body—really let it mingle with his wet hair and lotion-sticky back—but I supposed it would only clog the pipes and saddle Janet with yet another expense she couldn't afford.

If not the sand...then the rocks. "You have heard of a hot stone treatment," I said.

"Of course."

"What most people don't know is that the rocks are only heated for dramatic effect." I scooped up the stones from the Zen garden and held them in my palms to bring them to body temperature. "In the *reven*, we have no use for such theatrics. Now, you absorb the power of the tepid stone."

I placed the rocks on his back.

I stared for a moment, reveling in the stupidity of the whole situation. As I considered rearranging them to make it seem like I was actually doing something, Woodrow said, "I think I feel something."

"Very well. Now, I must leave you with the *reven* stones—for the conversation is best kept to yourselves. Stay there until the stones tell you the *reven* is complete."

8
~

I hurried back to our room and found Dixon standing amid a riot of shredded paper that extended from one end of the room to the other. He whirled around to face me, cheeks flushed. And not just from the sauna, either. "Yuri Volnikov," he said. "What you did back there, handling that self-important pseudo-intellectual so-and-so? Never in my life have I seen someone be so deliciously butch."

I crossed my arms...and felt thread snapping again. With a sigh, I dropped my arms to my sides. "All the playacting in the world won't help us if we can't find that paper." I turned toward the shreds to comb through them for bits of Spellcraft. I could feel Dixon watching me, but pretended I was unaware. Because it was unlike me to not only agree to such a bizarre scheme as this "masseuse" business, but to embrace it. It felt vulnerable, in a way, committing to helping this resort, these people. And vulnerability is something I avoid all cost.

Dixon wasn't buying the ruse of me not paying him any attention. He sidled up to me, hooked his fingers through my belt loops, and turned me to face him. "When this is all over," he said, "I'm eager to enjoy a private *pasta*, or *raven*, or whatever."

When it was over. *If* it was ever over.

With an alluring flutter of his eyelashes, Dixon said, "I have it on good authority that the masseuse is an expert all the way from Europe...and he's well-versed in some very exotic techniques."

I sighed.

Dixon tugged himself up against me and bumped our pelvises together. "Look at it this way. How many people can say they impressed a critic from Vacation Nation with nothing but a few twigs and a whole lot of heart? I have to admit, though, I'm surprised to see you throwing yourself into the role. Don't get me wrong, I'm utterly delighted—"

"It's Janet," I admitted. "She tries so hard. It would be a shame for all her effort to be for nothing." It seemed unfair that a year of unexpected weather and a single damaged Spellcraft could ruin a business that took generations to build. Not that I took any stock in the concept of fairness.

"You and me? We're obviously meant to solve his riddle."

I scoffed.

"It's true." Dixon guided my hands around his waist, then released them to loop his arms around my neck as he melted up against me. "If anyone can figure this out, it's us. A Scrivener and a Seer—the right hand of Spellcraft and the left—drawn together, against all odds, across the very ocean. If that's not a stunning example of Kismet, I don't know what is." His mouth pressed to mine and his tongue toyed at the seam of my lips. Playfully—yet with utmost seriousness. I understood, now, in a way I hadn't really considered before, that while ignorance might be bliss, Dixon's happiness didn't mean he was floundering in the dark.

No. It meant that he himself shone with enough brightness to illuminate the darkness.

His kiss was self-assured, yet not forceful. He didn't need force when he was dripping with charm. While my gut instinct was to force him to acknowledge grim reality for once, when his tongue slid against mine—full of promises and need—I understood that it was Dixon who was changing me.

We kissed. Thoroughly. Even indulgently. But eventually, he pulled away, a bit breathless and utterly beguiling with his lips ripe from kissing. His hands lingered briefly on my chest as he looked up into my eyes and said, "I'm all for less doom and gloom...but I need you to level with me if reconstructing the Crafting is an exercise in futility."

I crouched down and studied the shreds of paper, looking not just with my physical eyes, but my inner eye. I felt the moment my perception shifted. It was the moment the paper began to writhe, with the flecks of Scrivened ink jumping among the seething pile like fleas.

I blinked. The paper was still.

I stood and said, "The *volshebstvo* is still active."

Dixon brightened. "Fabulous! Then all we need to do is patch it back up!"

And so...we worked. I pulled on my glasses, and the two of us searched through each strip of paper for the telltale watercolor stock that was so much thicker than the rest. It was easy enough, plunging your hand into the raveled mess, to feel the strips. But the sight of the Spellcraft seething through the paper made my skin crawl, and I would be just as eager to stuff my hand into a sock full of ants.

Dixon was immune to such notions. He teased apart the paper. The flimsy office paper tore. The watercolor block did not. And soon we had combed through it thoroughly enough to glean all the Spellcraft from the shred. But when Dixon tried to match the edges of the letters together, he had a difficult time. "I wish there were some way of knowing right-side-up from upside-down."

He hadn't actually been expecting anything more from me than a show of commiseration, and yet, I did have a way of knowing. Dixon had been trying to line up the Scrivening. But the trick was all in reconstructing the Seen.

The watercolor beneath the Scrivening was a lopsided wash of uninspired blue straight from the pan. One side was more opaque than the other, and by that, I could match up the orientation of the strands. Once Dixon saw which way was up, he shuffled the shreds into place. He may have thought he was going by the visual look of the letterforms, but I suspected the Spellcraft, now within reach of its adjacent part, was now calling to itself. The pieces slid into place with a snap. Not any physical or audible snap, but a magical one.

More of the Crafting took shape. The FFL became EFFL...T. Progress. But it was clear we did not have all of the pieces. A gap remained before the letter T. And though my English vocabulary was reasonably good, for the life of me, I had no idea what Fonzo had written.

Neither did Dixon.

"This is worse than an itch you can't scratch. You know, like when the bottom of your foot is bugging you, and you're wearing two pairs of socks and a pair of boots, and your boots have, like, twenty eyelets and take tons of time to lace up. You've had Doc Martens, Yuri, haven't you? You seem like the type. I'll bet they'd look hot on you—"

While Dixon rambled, I let my gaze turn soft and squinted at the *volshebstvo* roiling just above the surface of the paper strips. It felt incomplete. It felt *wrong*. Potentially, the final piece was irrevocably lost. And yet, given the way the Spellcraft had called to the adjacent pieces as if it *wanted* to be solved, I suspected the key bit was not far away.

"We are missing this critical piece. We must search this place from top to bottom until it is found."

"Absolutely. If it's here to find, then we'll find it."

We pulled out our basket and searched it thoroughly to make sure no paper fragments were hidden within the reeds. No luck. We moved on to our trashcan, finding some crumbs and a wad of dried gum, but no shreds.

We were just about to hatch an elaborate plan to get the other guests out of their rooms when we discovered they were having a wine sociable in the lobby. None of them looked terribly enthused, holding their small plastic cups. Quint, the insufferable business-man, was pontificating about something. I didn't even need to hear him to know this was the case—his body language was evidence enough. Woodrow had recovered from his *reven* and was scrutiniz-ing the wine, likely preparing to launch into an in-depth analysis of its origins that no one cared to hear. Liza downed what was in her glass in one gulp, then held it out to Janet for another shot. Dixon and I saw all of this in a glance as the elevator door opened. Before he could dash off to join them, I snagged him by the back of the shirt and hit the close-door button.

"What did you do that for? Free wine!"

"Free wine..." I flashed my key card, "means free rooms. But we had better be quick about searching their trash. I doubt Janet can afford to open too many bottles."

"And Liza is drinking harder than a sailor on shore leave. Let's go."

We started in Quint's room. It was obsessively clean, though Dixon was quick to point out that for such a supposedly fancy guy, all his neatly folded underwear was a bargain-basement brand.

Woodrow had cleaned up after the *reven*. His basket was once more stowed in the safe, I presumed, and the rocks from the treat-ment stood in a neat line on his flat-raked Zen garden. No more shreds lingered in any crevices or corners.

Liza's bridal suite was next. Our first thought was that it had been ransacked, but then we realized that was just the way she'd unpacked. Frilly, lacy undergarments were strewn from one side of the room to the other. But the T-shirt she had slept in was a boxy, oversized thing from the Spring Falls Hot Springs gift shop. I felt apprehensive about touching a stranger's underwear. But we did what we had to do.

And came up with nothing.

"Well," Dixon said, "there's no avoiding it. Next up is the dumpster."

While I wasn't exactly looking forward to going through a bin full of garbage, it wouldn't be the first objectionable thing I'd handled in my life. We went downstairs and skirted around the wine tasting--now Woodrow and Quint, each with some alcohol in them, were involved in a grand debate about the origin of the word *spa*. Janet seemed like she was worried the debate would turn into a full-fledged argument, but Liza, sprawled sideways on a stiff looking divan, was clearly enjoying the show.

We slipped outside and went around back. In bigger cities, dumpsters were often locked. But in small towns with nothing potentially valuable or sensitive to dispose of, such security measures were unnecessary. Dixon and I approached the dumpster with some trepidation. "I suppose if you gave me a boost, I could fit inside," he said, in a tone of voice that conveyed it was perhaps the last thing in the world he wished to do. But as I opened the lid, something in the nearby undergrowth moved. I jerked back, and the lid fell shut with a muted plastic clatter.

"Don't worry, Yuri—hey, that rhymed!—it's just Twinkle. And the poor thing's got all kinds of stuff stuck in his fur." Dixon went down on one knee and extended a hand. "Hi, little cutie. Here, boy. It's okay. I won't hurt you. Promise—I'm officially an esthetician now, so you can trust me one hundred percent."

The dog cocked his head as if he actually understood what Dixon was saying, but didn't necessarily believe it. Or maybe animals could just sense he was as dangerous as a half-toasted marshmallow. The dog wavered for a moment...and then took a tentative step forward.

When he emerged fully from the undergrowth, we got a good look at his coat. This dog was clearly not meant for living rough. His fur was speckled with litter: brambles, twigs, a twist-tie.

"That's a good boy," Dixon crooned.

Tentatively, his tail perked up behind him. He gave it a single shy wag....

And a fleck of bluish paper on the top of the dog's head caught my eye.

As surely as if I'd studied the thing under a magnifying glass, even from several paces away, I knew I could be looking at only one thing: the missing piece of Spellcraft.

DIXON

9

I'd never been one for keggers. Too jockish for me. But once, in college, my roomies threw a wine tasting that got a little out of control—probably went overboard spiking the fondue—and I woke up the next morning in a puddle of sticky, dried Chardonnay with a coaster glued to my forehead. I could only imagine how uncomfortable Twinkle must've felt with all that random stuff stuck all over him.

I waggled my fingers and said, "C'mon, sweetie pie. I can help...."

Twinkle's tail gave a tentative wag, then another. He crept forward a few feet, then raised his head and sniffed the air—though how he could discern anything over the rotten-egg stink, I had no idea. They say dogs have an incredible sense of smell, though, and Twinkle must've liked what he was sniffing. Another yard or so...tail wagging away, now...just a few more feet....

And the door behind us banged open. Twinkle startled, planting his scruffy little paws wide, but he didn't run.

Not until Liza staggered outside and let out a piercing wail. As soon as Twinkle got a load of that, he ducked back into the bushes faster than you could say *jilted bride*.

Would it have been too much to ask for Liza to be a happy drunk, not a weepy one?

Yuri muttered something in Russian and headed toward the bushes, but it was obvious Twinkle was long gone. Liza was in such a bad way, I figured she could really use my help instead. I steadied her before she pitched into a deck table, and in the same tone I'd taken with the dog, said, "It's okay, Liza. I'm sure things will look a heck of a lot better in the morning."

"No...they...won't!" she bellowed—she really did have an impressive set of pipes.

"I thought you were having fun at the wine sociable."

"I was! Until I checked my social media. It's bad enough that creep waited until our wedding day to call things off—at the very last second, leaving me with the cake and the guests and all those gifts to return. But he took off with one of my bridesmaids!"

Of all the nerve! I gave her a supportive squeeze.

"At least it wasn't anyone I *liked*—an old friend I don't actually talk to these days, but I felt like I needed to reciprocate because I'd stood up for her at her first wedding. But then pictures started showing up. They're feeding each other his groom cake!"

Yuri cracked his knuckles. "I could teach this miserable excuse for a man some manners...."

"That's the nicest thing anyone's ever offered to do for me," Liza wailed between long, heaving sobs. "But it's not worth it. He's a lawyer—an honest-to-goodness ambulance chaser—and he'd sue your pants off before his nose even stopped bleeding."

If ever there was a profession viewed with as much disdain as Spellcraft, it was personal injury litigation. "Forget about your ex," I said. "Who's enjoying a fabulous getaway in Spring Falls, complete with wine, and cutting-edge spa treatments, and...wine?"

Liza snuffled. "I am?"

"That's right—you are! And you've got a big day ahead of you tomorrow." I'd figure out what this "big day" might entail later. "So let's go up to your room and get you all tucky-innish so you're nice and fresh in the morning."

Despite Liza's efforts to roll back out of bed, I managed to get her situated smack-dab in the middle of the king-sized mattress while Yuri shored her up with pillows on either side. She fussed a bit, but drifted off just as soon as Yuri tucked the covers around her. I parked her empty wastebasket right beside the bed just in case some of that wine decided to double-back the way it came.

I stepped back and considered her. In sleep, Liza still looked troubled. Having your wedding tank at the eleventh hour wasn't the type of thing you just brush off and walk away from, even if you are better off in the long run not being hitched to an ambulance chaser. Even though I personally didn't have much use for weddings, I could see she'd been totally on board. I bent over her and whispered, "Everything will work out, Liza—you'll see. Sweet dreams."

It might be unprofessional for me to kiss my clientele goodnight—but, hey, I'm not a real esthetician. When I got close enough to her hair, though, I realized I saw a glimpse of the unexpected. Gingerly, I parted her hair. Liza didn't stir—she'd had *a lot* of wine. And lo and behold, there inside her honey-colored locks were streaks of bluish green and greenish blue. And I'd bet cash money her stylist hadn't put them there.

I rearranged her hair so the pastel colors weren't showing quite so obviously, then whispered to Yuri, "Let's go find that dog."

We headed back to the spot we'd last seen Twinkle, but even in the daytime it would've been hard to pick him out among the local flora. At night? We had a better chance of finding a lead slug in a jarful of quarters. "Twinkle! Here, boy! Twi-i-inkle!"

Nothing.

I elbowed Yuri. "Why aren't you calling him? Maybe if you joined in, he'd hear us."

"It is useless to try and coax the dog out of hiding by calling his name. He has no great love of people."

Which was why I knew he and Yuri would get along famously, if they ever gave each other half a chance. However.... "You just might be on to something. Maybe Twinkle *is* a little skittish. But what can we bribe him with that smells savory and smoky and drool-worthy enough to carry even over the stink of rotten eggs?"

Yuri gave me a look.

"That's right!" I pointed him toward the doors and gave him a playful shove. "Let's go get some!"

We found Janet in the kitchen scooping seeds out of a cantaloupe. I didn't know it was possible to butcher a melon fretfully, but she was managing to do it. "Say, Janet," I said in my charmingest voice. "We've figured out exactly how to get Twinkle to stop peeing on your building." Yuri slid me a look that said, *Oh, did we?* I ignored it. "All I'll need is a nice, salty strip of—"

"Again with the bacon!" Janet cried. "There is no bacon, do you hear me?"

"But it's for a good cause."

"I can't give you what I don't have—and there is zero bacon in this building. Zip. Zilch. Nada. The last of it was eaten today, and the check for this week's grocery delivery bounced. They won't resume my service until I get caught up. Not only is there no bacon, but no lemon wedges for the water in the lobby. No cucumber slices to put over people's eyes. No mints for the pillows. You know what our continental breakfast is going to be tomorrow? A box of stale donuts from the gas station I pay for with change I found in the couch cushions and a dusty old can of pineapple."

Actually, if she had a tub of whipped topping, she could make one of my mother's signature parfaits. But before I could suggest hunting for more spare change to make it a meal, Yuri was reaching inside his coat. He pulled out a single bill, crisp from the ATM, and handed it to Janet. I didn't recognize the dead president. Hopefully he wasn't trying to pass off counterfeit money. "If you can't pay your debt," he told her, "at least you can take a trip to the market and see yourself through the rest of the critic's visit."

Janet blinked at the bill, wide-eyed and baffled. I began edging toward the door, just in case she had the Spring Falls police on speed-dial. But instead of throwing the book at Yuri, she flung herself into his brawny arms, hugged him soundly, and whispered, "Thank you."

10

It was hard to tell if the pineapple passed the sniff-test or not, what with all the sulfur in the air. But my mom always says, if the can's not bulging, it's still good. We headed back, yet again, to the spot where we'd last seen Twinkle. "Why d'you suppose pineapple is cut in rings," I wondered, "but they don't do it for other fruit? Maybe canned peaches would taste better as circles. Or canned pears. And what do they do with the pineapple pieces that made up the negative space? Is there a pineapple equivalent to the donut hole?"

Yuri looked at me blankly. Maybe they didn't sell donut holes in Russia. Or if they did, they called them something Russian.

I waved the pineapple ring. Juice ran up my arm—how was it that liquid could run *up* sometimes?—and said, "I've never had a dog. Do they eat pineapple?"

Yuri shrugged. "Only a spoiled American dog could afford to be so choosy."

"Well, Twinkle hasn't exactly been living high on the hog. Hopefully he's a fan of tropical fruit." I inched toward the bushes.

"Here, Twinkle! I've got something for you. Even better than bacon...."

"What's going on out there?" called a voice from the resort. We turned and found Quint standing on the balcony of his deluxe businessman accommodations. He wasn't quite as corporate in a fluffy white robe...but he still came off just as douchey. "What's happening—is there some sort of resort activity going on? Why wasn't I informed?"

Before I could ask what kind of "resort activity" involved tromping around outside after dark with an open can of pineapple, Quint had already made up his mind. He whisked back inside, full of purpose.

"He will help us catch dog," Yuri said. He doesn't often drop his articles...but when he does, it's beyond hot.

"You think he will? He seems like he only cares about one thing—himself."

"He will do as I tell him. Men like him are always eager to please."

When they encounter someone as alphatastic as Yuri, probably so.

Quint flerp-flerped outside in a pair of one-size-fits-all slippers and his white terrycloth robe. "So, fill me in. What're we doing out here?"

Deadpan, Yuri said, "Dog hunt."

Quint inhaled the beginning of a laugh, then realized Yuri was serious, and went puzzled instead. "Dog...hunt?"

"Was I not clear? We capture dog. You do not do this in Wichita?"

"Can't say that we do."

"It's a regional activity," I explained, and handed him a pineapple ring. "More of a dog taming, really. It's all kind of Zen. The dog's pretty skittish, so you'll need to bring down your heart rate and modulate your vibe, otherwise he'll just run away."

Quint's wheels were clearly turning now. "Is there a prize?"

"Self-satisfaction," Yuri said decisively. "Now stop talking and go."

Quint shuffled off in the direction we pointed him. "He's making an awful lot of noise," I observed.

"And he will drive Twinkle toward us."

Brilliant! While Quint flerped around at the far end of the yard, Yuri and I delved into the undergrowth. We followed the sound of rustling branches, and were occasionally rewarded with glimpses of Twinkle's matted white coat. "Here boy," I said. "Look what we've got for you—some ripe, juicy pineapple. Yum, yum."

But the dog must not have been a big fan of canned fruit. Every time it looked like we had him, he managed to slip farther into the bushes. The undergrowth was giving way to trees now, and it was harder for the two of us to follow. Yuri spread a couple of saplings apart, just short of snapping them off, and a dusting of dainty bluish petals rained down on the two of us—and not a negligible amount of pollen, too. It was tempting to tell him how adorable he looked covered in flowers. But I resisted.

With Yuri holding apart the young trees, I finally spotted our quarry cowering in a thicket of brambles too dense to slip through. Poor little guy! I crouched low to the ground to make myself smaller and held out the pineapple. "It's okay," I crooned. "I'm not gonna hurt you. I just need to pluck the shred out of your fur—you'll hardly feel a thing, I promise. And you can have *all* the pineapple."

I'm not sure whether or not animals understand us when we talk. Sometimes it seemed like Meringue the cockatoo knew exactly what she was saying, and if she were able to smile, I think she would look even more pleased with herself than usual when she called Yuri and me Scribblers and Hacks. But I'm sure critters at least pick up on our tone—plus our body language, anxiety level, and overall demeanor. Lucky for me I'm the opposite of scary, and as I murmured sweet nothings to Twinkle, eventually he came to see I was harmless.

Crouching low to the ground, he crept forward one inch, and then another, until he was close enough to that pineapple ring to lick it. As smoothly as possible, I crept back. Twinkle wasn't keen on following me, but now that he had his eyes on the prize, he shed some of his caution—if not the Spellcraft caught in his fur.

He was just about in shred-plucking range...when, off in the distance, Quint sneezed. The sound was so startling, even Yuri flinched. Twinkle skittered back a few feet. I did my best to stay calm. "Nothing to worry about, buddy...just a sneeze...."

Achoo!

Achoo!

Achoo!

I'd never heard anything like it. It was as if Quint was literally screaming the word *achoo*. Repeatedly. Did they say "achoo" in Russian, or something else? I'd have to remember to ask—but not until I got hold of that final bit of shred.

Lucky for us, the repetition of the sneezes actually made Twinkle feel braver as he habituated to the goofy noises. Either that, or now that he'd got a lick of the pineapple, he just couldn't resist.

"Little bit more," Yuri told me. "Back out far enough so I can let go, and I will grab."

"Thaaat's right," I told the dog. "All this ripe, juicy pineapple can be yours." Inch by excruciating inch, I begged and cajoled, until eventually, we emerged from the trees. Yuri eased the saplings back together and turned to gently scoop Twinkle off the ground... when the sound of sneezing suddenly closed in on us.

Flerp - flerp - flerp - flerp - flerp.

"I caught it!" *Achoo!* "I caught the dog!"

I'm not gonna say Yuri screamed like a little girl...but that doesn't mean it didn't happen.

Twinkle took off like a bottle rocket. But the creature dangling from Quint's outstretched grasp—a thirty-pound opossum— remained totally unfazed. It was too busy chomping on a pineapple ring to let a little screaming hamper the enjoyment of its dessert.

Like Yuri, Quint was covered in flower petals and pollen. Unlike Yuri, his eyes were swollen practically shut. This was probably for the best. As harmless as the opossum appeared to be, it had a startling arsenal of teeth. "Great!" I declared. "Super! You caught the...dog. Now, let him get back to what he was doing, take an antihistamine and go to bed."

"That's it? That's the prize?"

"Self-satisfaction," Yuri repeated.

"Oh, right." Quint set down the opossum. It waddled into the undergrowth, still chomping. "Just wait till those idiots in accounting hear about this!"

Still a d-bag. Even in victory.

Once the rustling in the undergrowth grew distant and Quint *flerp-flerped* away, we looked at each other ruefully, Yuri and me. Pollen dusted the stubble of his hair, and a tiny flower petal had caught in the scruff of the corner of his mouth. I took him by the lapels and drew him down toward me—first catching the petal between my teeth, then going in for the kiss.

For all that Yuri can be a bull in a china shop, when he kisses me, he's practically demure. It's like he's worried I'll change my mind halfway through. One of these days he's bound to figure out I'm all in. But maybe these early times are precious for what they are.

The skim of his tongue across my lips was tentative and adorable. It shouldn't have been romantic, the two of us covered in tree gunk and surrounded by the waftings of a stinky sulfur pond. But Yuri, and moonlight, and the most fragile of kisses?

Most romantic night ever.

Once we'd had our share of kissing, we strolled together side by side, listening for rustlings in the undergrowth. Hard to tell if it was Twinkle or the opossum—I would wager that the opossum made more noise—but both of them were pretty scarce. When we settled into a couple of loungers by the grotto, just to rest our eyes, sleep came over us, sneaky and sudden.

I woke at dawn, confused as to why I was covered in dew, and wondering what that strange sound might be. Carefully, I cracked open one eye and saw Twinkle with his nose buried in the pineapple can, licking at it so vigorously it was scooting across the fieldstone patio with a metallic scrape. A telltale bit of paper glinted bluish-white in his tangled coat. A few feet away, Yuri was quietly rousing himself too. We locked eyes and he gave his head a subtle shake. Between him and me and the stinky blue pond, if we angled ourselves just right, one of us was bound to catch the dog. All it would take was delicacy and patience. I could hardly contain myself as Twinkle inched closer, and closer, and—

"*Ya yem reven'!*" someone bellowed in a bizarre minor key, like a dirge, but vigorous and forceful. "*PROTIVEN' PROTIVEN'!*"

The pineapple can pitched up into the air as Twinkle jumped, spun, and plunged into the pond. He doggy-paddled to the other side with impressive speed, launched out of the water, gave himself a thorough shake, then disappeared around the corner of the building.

Meanwhile, Woodrow the critic strode out from the resort, looking very well-pleased with himself. In the daylight, his ash blond hair had an interesting sheen of purple. He wore his brown suit again, though now that we'd seen exactly what he was packing inside those boring old trousers, it was kind of hard to look at him quite the same. He announced, "I've been boning up on the *reven*." Boning! Meep. "Though it's hard to say if I've got the song right, since all the webpages were in Russian. How's my accent?"

"Passable," Yuri told him. "You may join us for the *bumaga*."

Woodrow went all aflutter. "*Bumaga*...that wasn't in any of my research. What is it?"

"A traditional Balkan scavenger hunt for a small piece of paper."

"How small?"

"Minuscule. Start down in the grotto and we will catch up."

As Woodrow made his way over to the water humming his strange little dirge, I whispered to Yuri, "What was he singing about anyway?"

"A baking dish—or maybe a subversive protest song. Who knows?"

Woodrow poked through some reedy planters around the perimeter of the pool. Who were we kidding—that fleck of paper could be anywhere now, from the bottom of the grotto to the acre of undergrowth surrounding the resort. Frustrated, I said, "If the Spellcraft doesn't want to be found, it won't matter how many people are looking for it."

Yuri took my hand in his and smoothed my writing callus with his thumb. I felt a gentle tingle—not of Spellcraft, but of affection. "I often think the *volshebstvo* just wants to make sure we work for it. Otherwise, it would not have revealed itself to begin with. Just humor it until we come up with a better plan."

As we poked around the grotto, I came to realize tiny bluish flower petals looked a heck of a lot like little shreds of paper, and they didn't seem nearly as romantic anymore.

Despite Yuri's words of encouragement, I found my enthusiasm flagging when Janet came and found us. Her unbleached linen resort outfit was shapeless and frumpy, but her lavender- and aquamarine-streaked hair jazzed it up. "There you guys are, what a relief! Our local meditation group is starting in five minutes, but I called in an order at the grocery store—seriously, thanks again—and need to go pick it up."

Anything to get out of looking for a fleck of paper among a gazillion tiny flower petals. "Meditation? I've never been much good at sitting still, but I'm happy to give it a shot."

"Not that I don't appreciate your offer," Janet said with some chagrin, "but the group specifically requested Yuri."

YURI

11

"I know nothing about meditation," I told Janet.

"Don't worry, we use a free app. All you'll need to do is pop in some earbuds, listen to the recording, and repeat what they say. Couldn't be easier. Give me your phone and I'll set you up."

While Janet downloaded the app, I wondered how it was that a local group could request me specifically, given that I'd only been in Spring Falls a day—and I didn't actually work there. Maybe she was just worried Dixon was too hyper to lead a meditation and was too polite to come right out and say it. Or maybe she didn't trust me to work the front desk in her absence. That might be for the best. I doubted I could offer to facilitate anyone's stay without scaring them off.

Once the download was done, Janet whisked me off to a conference room, opened the door with a flourish and said, "Okay, gang—here's Yuri!"

A dozen conference chairs were arranged in a semicircle. A dozen fluffy, permed, gray-haired heads swiveled in my direction. Through thick bifocal lenses, a dozen pairs of eyes widened eagerly. A dozen wrinkled faces grinned, flashing dentures.

"Don't go too easy on them," Janet told me playfully, then abandoned me to their unflinching scrutiny.

I stomped to the front of the room and said, "Close your eyes," but I was used to giving orders, not suggestions. My voice felt too big in the neutral, subdued room, too forceful, but the old women did as they were told...smiling to themselves all the while.

I checked the app. Thirty minutes. I could force myself to repeat some words for thirty minutes. I hit the play button and began.

"Take a deep breath and release any cares or concerns as you gently bring your focus to your breath. Breathe in. Hold. Breathe out."

I told the group to breathe. They breathed. As practices went, the meditation was...unobjectionable. The quiet, the stillness, the focus. Was it not the very thing I did when I cleared my mind and called up my Seens?

Maybe I was not entirely unfamiliar with meditation after all.

"Now bring your focus to the place in your body where you feel the emotion of...anger." I hesitated as I wondered if there was any cell in the body where anger was absent, then pushed the thought aside and carried on.

"It may be a sensation of heat in your belly. It may be the feeling of tension in your muscles. It may be a nagging, persistent itch that erodes your happiness."

It may be a stupid meditation you've agreed to deliver.

The app guided the group to breathe through it and let go, but I could barely force out the words. Only a fool released their anger when they should harness it instead.

"Imagine yourself free from anger."

I shuddered.

"Visualize your heart opening."

Bone saw? Or machete?

"Know that you are surrounded by unconditional love."

My initial impulse was to scoff—because of course all love is conditional. But then I considered Dixon. His presumption about everything he encountered was positive until proven otherwise.

Even then, he'd go to great lengths to see the good in everything. A liability, obviously. Yet, I was willing to entertain the possibility that his optimism smacked of unconditional love.

"Now take a deep, cleansing breath, open your eyes, and go forth with your day."

Namaste.

I didn't repeat that. A man must have some self-respect.

I thought the room would clear. Instead, the old women all stared at me expectantly. I'd given them what they came for, so if they weren't about to leave, I would. I strode toward the door, and a woman with a silvery-blue poof of hair caught me by the sleeve. "That was delightful," she gushed, "so much more serious than Marilee always was."

If Marilee was the massage therapist with the fetish for stuffed animals, I didn't doubt it.

"Just one thing before you go. We noticed you hanging around yesterday with a couple of other fellas."

Noticed...with binoculars. I narrowed my eyes.

"The one with the, uh...lighter hair. D'you know if he's single?"

A woman with a large mole on her chin cackled. "Who cares if he's single—what happens at the spa stays in the spa. I just wanna know if he's free tonight."

Another one piped in, "And I'd like to know how he gets his pants on."

"Ask him yourself," I told the women. "He is down by the grotto."

That pronouncement cleared the room faster than any "namaste" could hope to. But before the final meditator slipped away—clumping forward on a walker with tennis balls fixed over its legs—I caught up to her and said, "Tell me, when you were...stargazing... last night, did you happen to notice a dog?"

"You mean Twinkle? Sure. You wouldn't know it to look at the little scamp, but under all that hair, he's actually not that big. I've seen cats bigger than that. In fact, just the other day, I heard some cats fighting outside my window. Or maybe it was Verna singing in the shower—"

"Did you see where he went?"

"All over the west corner of the resort!" Once she was done chortling over her own wit, she said, "Twinkle's got his routines down pat." Dogs had routines? "When it rains, he hides in the municipal garage. When it's picnic weather, he heads over to the park and begs for scraps. On garbage day, he rips open the bags and rolls around in the trash. Why, just last week I heard Rita from the QuikMart complain about the beer cans all over her lawn, but I wonder if the real culprit was her deadbeat brother-in-law—"

"Do you know where he might be now?"

"Probably down at the Spring Falls Saloon waiting for happy hour."

"Not the brother-in-law. The dog!"

"It's right about the time Mr. Pope feeds the pigeons in the Geyser Garden. He's been a widower coming on five years now, but no one's willing to pass the time with him, on account of his crippling halitosis—"

I restrained myself from shaking her. Barely. "What about *the dog*?"

"Oh, Twinkle usually manages to steal a crust of bread or two."

"How far is this Geyser Garden?"

The woman looked as if she was doing calculus in her mind— or searching it for another tedious story about a person I would never meet—but before I burst out of my own skin, she tipped back her walker, pointed with the tennis balls, and said, "It's right through that door."

I side-stepped the walker and rushed out the door. It led to a small hallway, with Dixon approaching from a side branch. "Janet's back," he said. "I think she got a pretty good deal on the bacon—"

"Forget about the bacon." I motioned for him to hurry. "Let's go grab the dog."

I dashed out into the garden, fully expecting to settle this whole Spellcraft fiasco once and for all...only to find it deserted, save for a pair of scruffy pigeons squabbling over half a bagel.

The bird match took place in a ring of stone benches surrounding a hole the earth from which an occasional spit of water sputtered. I dropped down on to one of the benches and planted my face in my hands. I had told Dixon the *volshebstvo* wanted to be found, but maybe that had been wishful thinking on my part. Maybe its real motive was to make a fool of me.

"What now?" Dixon said gamely.

I gave a humorless laugh. "Now? We quit. The Spellcraft is too damaged, and we have done all we can do. We pack our things, dispose of the fragments as far away from people as we can, and head back to Pinyin Bay."

I expected an argument from Dixon, since not only does he believe his uncle is redeemable, but his optimism knows no bounds. But when no disagreement was offered, I looked up, curious, and found him gazing off into the surrounding hedge.

"I could be wrong," he murmured, "but I think I know what happened to Mr. Woodrow's towel."

DIXON

12

Yuri and I went silent. The bushes trembled. We exchanged a meaningful look, then split up to approach the spot from oblique angles. At the last moment, as we zeroed in on the corner of a towel poking out, it occurred to me that we could very well be barging in on the opossum. But I kept that notion to myself as Yuri parted the branches, and held myself poised to spring into action....

Only to find a dog. *The* dog. And Twinkle was so busy licking his own butt—and I mean, *really* going to town—he took no mind of a couple of Spellcrafters barging in on his nest. He did make a startled sound as I grabbed him. Even though he wriggled for all he was worth, since he was mostly fur, he was a lot lighter than he looked. "Do you see it?" I asked Yuri. "Is it there?"

Up close, there was a lot more than just a potential fleck of Spellcraft in the dog's matted fur. Twigs and grass, burrs and leaves. Even a wad of gum. Yuri's face scrunched up in that adorable way it does when something really squicks him out—no doubt it would be even worse if he had his glasses on and got the full gist of the pooch's accessories—but he steeled himself, plucked something off Twinkle's forehead, and said, "I have it."

When I set Twinkle back down, I attempted to pluck off one of the burrs, but he was off like a shot before I could even try. "Leave the dog," Yuri said. "We can deal with it later. Right now, we must finish this."

Gotta love how Yuri sounds all action-hero whenever he talks. Like the Terminator...if the Terminator were from Russia, not Austria. Or is he from the future...or from California? At any rate, I was just as eager as he was to plug in the last piece of the puzzle.

We hurried back to the room, and the Crafting was there waiting for us. Now that we had the keystone in our grasp, the letters on shredded Scrivening were hard for me to even look at as they seemed to shift and blur. Before, when I was matching up the edges of the letters to one another, it was a challenge to keep my focus in one place. My gaze kept trying to jump around the calligraphy. But now, it was as if the Spellcraft was calling to itself, it was veritably vibrating with anticipation of that final piece sliding into place.

The gap in the letters EFFL_T waited like an eager mouth grinning to flash a single missing tooth. At the last moment, I wondered what would happen if I messed up. The gap was rectangular, but there was always a fifty-fifty chance I'd place the piece upside down. And the penmanship was so ragged—the word choice so strange—even with the stray bit in my hand, I wasn't quite sure what I was looking at and I felt myself spin into a loop of self-doubt....

Until Yuri's hand settled between my shoulder blades—big, and warm, and strong. "You can do this," he murmured. "If anyone can, it is you."

I steeled myself, ignored the fact that the lettering was really hard to see, and went with my gut. And when I eased the remaining shred into place, the Spellcraft lit up to my inner eye like a disco ball.

I backed into Yuri. "Sparkly."

He tensed. "Wavery."

His hands were on my shoulders as if he was ready to pick me up and deposit me somewhere else, but I shrugged him off, blinked away nonexistent afterimages, and took a good hard look at the Crafting.

"Effluent," I declared. And then I admitted, "Can't say I know *precisely* what it means."

Yuri pulled out his phone. As we were consulting his dictionary app, something in our bathroom gurgled. The plumbing in my converted attic apartment complained all the time, so I didn't think much of it. Not until a sound like distant thunder rumbled through the floorboards.

"Earthquake!" I said—and I didn't know whether or not they had earthquakes in Russia, but there was no time to ask. "Follow me."

I hurried into the bathroom with Yuri right on my heels. As we crowded in, I realized the bathtub might actually be the place you were supposed to sit out a tornado, not an earthquake, and maybe we were supposed to stay under the doorframe instead. Or was it stop, drop and roll? No, that couldn't be right. Look both ways? Stranger danger? Righty-tighty, leftie-loosie? Argh! What the heck was the protocol for—?

The sink let out a long, low, echoing belch. The bathtub did the same. And I must've been more inured to the smell of sulfur than I realized, because the reek that followed was so palpable, it wrapped around my head like a mildewy towel—one that had been lying outside overnight and was slept on by a filthy, wet dog.

Yuri retched. I swallowed down the part of my breakfast that was trying to repeat—just toast, thankfully, since bacon might've had some sharp edges I'd regret. I wasn't keen on making an offering to the porcelain god in front of Yuri, but hopefully it was just a right of relationship passage we'd laugh about it someday. Or I'd laugh and he'd scowl a bit differently than usual. But as I flipped up the toilet seat, the floor rumbled again. Yuri caught me by the shirt and tugged. My arms pinwheeled as I tipped back against his chest—just as a spume of water sprayed up out of the bowl. Clean water, I hoped, given that I hadn't entirely escaped the spray. When it settled back down, I risked a peek.

The water was Technicolor.

Blue and green and purple and black swirled in the bowl as if a giant, invisible Seer had just cleaned his paintbrush. It was hypnotic, almost beautiful.

If not for the stench.

Yuri read aloud from his phone. "*Effluent*: sewage. Liquid waste discharged into a body of water."

I craned my neck to squint across the bedroom and look down on the grotto through the tall windows. Not only was the spring-fed pool now swirling with various colors, but it was bubbling away like a witch's cauldron. It was obvious the Spellcraft had run amok—the rumbling began the moment I slid the final scrap into place.

Oh no! We'd thought that by putting Uncle Fonzo's Crafting back together, we were helping it. But what if its trip through the shredder had been the only thing stopping Spring Falls from filling with sewage?

The plumbing groaned. A huge bubble swelled from our bathtub drain, with vivid colors swirling through it like an oily kaleidoscope. Suddenly, the bathroom didn't seem like a very safe place to be, after all. I hooked an arm through Yuri's and dragged him away from the fixtures as the sink let loose a diabolical chuckle.

I slammed the door shut and pressed my back against it, but even so, the cacophony of gaseous noises grew louder. And the stink?

Overwhelming.

And that wasn't the only overwhelming part. Most upsetting of all was the thought that this "effluent" thing was no normal piece of Spellcraft. I hated to say it—heck, I hated to even so much as *think* it, but.... "Yuri? What if Uncle Fonzo cursed this resort?"

One of the drains behind the closed door belched its assent. A chorus of answering burps resonated up and down the hall.

"No," Yuri said simply.

"But look around you—and listen, and smell! What else could it be?"

"Have you ever seen a curse?"

"Of course not. Cursed Spellcraft is a felony. Once, someone brought a curse into the shop to try and have it Re-Crafted, and my mother chased him right back out the door with a dustmop—and even swatted him a few times for good measure. Family talked about it for years. No one had ever seen Mom move so fast. Before, or since."

"I...have seen curse. In Russia." There Yuri was, dropping his articles again. Only this time, it wasn't sexy. It was chilling. He raised his voice over the plumbing chorus and said, "This writing is rough, but it flows together. The letters of a curse are each different, like a ransom note. And the *volshebstvo* is so twisted you can feel it in your bowels."

I crept up to the shreddy Crafting, which was sparkling so hard to my Scrivener sight now I could barely make out the letters—but I had to try. If it wasn't a curse, then maybe the word *effluent* wasn't what had originally been Scribed.

"Then, what if it's not the Crafting—what if it's me? Maybe I put it back together wrong."

"Dixon—"

"No, look, the edges of the strips are straight, I could've easily mixed them up." I scrambled to come up with some other arrangement of the letters. *Fen flute? Fun felt?*

I reached for the Crafting, and Yuri struck like a viper, grabbing my wrist so hard it hurt. "Don't touch that!"

"But I can fix it!"

"There is no fixing. This is the only way the letters fit."

I tried to shrug out of his grasp, though it was like trying to rip the fender off a Buick with my bare hands. "But, *effluent?*" I yelled over the glugging and gurgling and geysering that echoed through the resort. Pretty soon the plumbing wouldn't be the only place the waterworks were wonky. "Tell me how that can be anything other than a curse?"

But before I could add to the wayward wetness, Yuri set his jaw, squared his shoulders, and said, "There is another definition of the word. An adjective, to describe a thing that is flowing. No sewage.

Just flow. A reasonable enough Crafting to put on a dry spring."

He crouched in front of the bureau to look at the reconstructed Crafting from the side, squinting as if he was trying to stare at the sun. "The ink is rough," he said. "It's true. But that's not the problem."

YURI

13

My mentor back in St. Petersburg was a woman of few words. But during my time with her, in which I paid for my apprenticeship with a thousand small watercolors, she made sure to demonstrate how a Seen could cause a Crafting to misfire. Early on, she taught me the importance of the Seen being flawless. The image need not be pretty—in all honesty, the paintings at Practical Penn were some of the clumsiest paintings I had ever seen—but they must not be damaged.

I presented the old hag with a torn Seen once—and only once. What difference would a small tear make, I thought, since her Craftings were always hidden, so as not to give the police any evidence to find.

When I presented her with the pile of Seens, she picked the torn painting out of the pile immediately, held it up for inspection, and said, "I suppose you'd like to know how it feels to be given a Crafting of your own."

She had never offered such a thing before, so of course, I was leery. But I could hardly aspire to be a Spellcrafter without being the subject at least once. I nodded.

"Then, tell me, what is your biggest problem?"

"My flat," I answered immediately. I was living in a gray, Soviet-era apartment block where the radiators knocked all night and mold grew around the windows. In America, there would be someone to complain to, but not in Russia. I would either need to fix it myself or move. And how could I earn enough money to move when I spent all my free time learning Spellcraft?

The old woman drew her quill out from its hiding place in a false compartment at the back of her desk. She thought for a moment, and over the top of the torn Seen, inked in the Cyrillic alphabet, "Problems at home are resolved." She handed the paper back to me and said, "I don't need to tell you to keep it somewhere safe."

I shook my head mutely, holding the Crafting by the corner for fear of smearing the ink.

Once it dried, I smuggled it home in my coat as if I was hiding a contraband German porn magazine, worried all the while that policemen would invent some reason to stop and frisk me. But I made it home without incident. Once there, I was unsure where to put it, and eventually settled for hiding it under my doormat.

It took me a while to fall asleep that night, but when I slept, I slept soundly....

And was woken by the smell of burning plastic.

As fires go, it was a small one, confined to my apartment only, more smoke than flame. I could have suffocated, if not for the sickening smell the old light fixture made as it melted. No one was hurt, though I had a rattling cough for the rest of the winter. And the sickening, burnt smell never washed out of my clothing.

I didn't tell the old woman what had happened—wouldn't give her the satisfaction. But in the weeks that followed, I spent a lot of time thinking in a cramped, rented room in an even worse part of town, wondering why the *volshebstvo* had done what it did.

Now I know. Because now that I have been a Seer for so many years, my eyes have been opened. It was a gradual process, and there was always something new to figure out for myself—because I had no one to ask. But the integrity of the Seen? That, I understood.

I focused on the shredded Crafting.

The paper had weight to it, and where the shredder dragged through the fibers, it created thousands—maybe millions—of microscopic tears. The purpose of the Seen is to harness the *volshebstvo*, to hold it in place while the Scrivening directs the power. In the shredded Crafting we were dealing with now, the letters were eager to reconnect. But the Seen was too damaged to contain the magic. When I focused, I could feel the Spellcraft stuttering across the surface like a restless leg at midnight, jerking this way and that to the tune of a misfiring nerve.

Fonzo's rough, strange, one-word Crafting would have been bad enough when it was whole. Now, on a ruined Seen?

A recipe for disaster.

It was obvious Dixon was incapable of letting things lie. Even more obvious that I was unwilling to let him tackle the problem alone. A smart man knows when to walk away...so, clearly, love had made me a fool.

But at least I was no longer alone.

Tears glittered on Dixon's sable eyelashes as he struggled with this urge to repair something that was broken in a way he had no chance of fixing. I cradled both his hands in mine, holding tight to stop him from rearranging the letters and making it even worse. "The Scrivening may have sparked whatever is happening here, but right now, the bigger problem is the Seen. It's too damaged. And the magic is running wild."

Dixon went still, then slowly turned to look at me. His ebony eyes were wide, fringed by the gleaming, wet points of his lashes. Those eyes begged me to do something. But he didn't say the words. Not aloud.

He knew what he'd be asking. He'd grown up dealing with a Seer, after all.

If I told him it was too dangerous, he would agree to find another way. But there *was* no other way. Even if we could afford to pay, no other Seer would touch this. While the plumbing around us gurgled and groaned—while the earth disgorged a reeking stew of minerals into the resort—I made my decision.

With great solemnity, I drew his hands to my lips and brushed a kiss across his knuckles, which smelled faintly of sulfur. "I will fix. Find paper."

My pocket notepad was too small to contain the broken Spellcraft. But a hasty search of the drawers turned up a room service menu, a brochure on the various spa packages, and a pad of lined paper. The back of the paper was blank. Flimsy...but it would do.

I had never before Re-Crafted a Seen. As far as I knew, it simply wasn't done. But if Dixon could slide letters in and around the Craftings of other Scriveners, it stood to reason I could do the same for a Seen.

At least, I hoped so.

Seeing is taxing, and it is important to rest between paintings, but I'd had more than enough time to recover since my last Seen. I gathered myself, and focused my thoughts on the Crafting. All other thoughts—Janet's desperate need, Dixon's heartbreaking distress—could not be allowed to distract me. My mind had to be on the Craft. Nothing else.

I took a glass off the nightstand, removed its fussy paper wrapper, but stopped short of going to fill it in the bathroom. If the Spellcraft was determined to prevent me from cleaning up the mess the shredder had left behind, it would be a bad idea for me to make myself such an easy target by getting within range of the spewing drains. Luckily, Dixon kept a water bottle in his bag. Before I even needed to ask, he was there, filling the glass.

I have painted Seens in many distracting places. In the bathroom of a transatlantic flight. Huddled under a tarp while the rain poured down. Crammed in the back seat of a Volkswagen doing eighty. But never have I Crafted to repair something, and I was desperate to concentrate. Take a breath. Clear my mind. Maybe there was something to be said for the meditation I led earlier. Calm did not come naturally to me, but at least I had this recent experience to call upon.

I didn't need to sustain the moment. A single flash of

inspiration—this was all it took for the magic to seed itself. My arm moved as if controlled by something else, something greater. I dipped my brush in the clean water, and despite the distraction of the churning and burbling that rang through the resort, I felt the Seen take hold.

The impulse coalesced somewhere deep in my chest, then rolled down my left arm like an artistic coronary. I found the colors with the brush, and water wicked out of the bristles to fill the tiny square pans. Purple and black, blue and green. Wet on wet on wet. My Seen was not just wetter than usual, it was sodden. And still, I returned my brush to the water, again and again and again. The paper buckled and sagged. A pool formed in the center—a depression that looked suspiciously like the grotto outside—and as pigment swirled through the water, the sensation of *volshebstvo* burned down my arm with even more force.

I wanted to resist, but instead, I somehow forced myself to give over. And in a sudden, startling movement, I dropped the brush, scooped up the sopping wet Seen...and slammed it, upside down, on top of the shredded Spellcraft with a resounding splat.

The chorus of groaning drainpipes went silent—and then shrieked in a sudden crescendo. Water geysered from our tub, toilet and sink. And outside, gaily colored water erupted from the grotto in a plume two stories high. The ground under our feet trembled and groaned....

And gradually...went still.

The gurgles in the plumbing grew father away as whatever strange waters had been dredged up retreated back the way they'd come. Down in the grotto, the single trickle that fed the pool from above sputtered a few times, like a water line flushing out a pocket of air. Moments later, Spring Falls flowed—clean and clear.

I was momentarily panicked by the darkness that rolled through the landscape, but only until I understood it was not some unscheduled eclipse come to mark the ruination of the natural order of things. Rather, it was just the toll the *volshebstvo* took on me as consciousness began to ebb.

Dixon got a shoulder under my armpit and managed to swing me around to the bed before my knees gave out, then he climbed up on top of me and cupped my face in both hands.

"That was the most selfless display of Spellcrafting mastery I've ever seen." His breath tickled my stubble as he trailed tender wisps of kisses over my brow and cheekbones, but I was too drained to even lean into his mouth. He settled, finally, on my lips, where he whispered, "How cruel would it be for me to drop a massive L-bomb on you when you're pretty much out for the count?"

Not just cruel...but vicious. There was no denying it—Dixon Penn was my biggest weakness.

I wouldn't have it any other way.

As things went dark, I strongly suspected I slipped away with a smile.

14

I woke to the smell of freshly cooked bacon, and noted it was hardly contaminated at all with the scent of sulfur. "You're up!" Dixon cried as my eyelids fluttered. The box spring squealed as he dive-bombed the bed, bounced, then sprawled inelegantly across my chest. He wriggled an elbow out from my ribs, propped his chin on one fist, then walked his fingers up my sternum—grinning all the while. "You've been out like a light, but I know how it is with Seers. Rufus Clahd has a Murphy bed in his office so he can take a nap between every single Seen—and I'll bet he's never done anything nearly as taxing as you did!"

In a single Seen? I'd be surprised if any Seer had. My eyes felt like sandpaper and my body ached like I'd gone a dozen rounds in an underground cage match. But I supposed if I were to See myself to exhaustion in any particular location, a spa filled with liniments and lotions and mineral soaks was probably the best place to do it.

I ran a hand over my head. I'd shaved it recently enough, though I might consider doing it again to ensure the stubble didn't come in blue. But not just yet. It might be tempting fate to revel too deeply in Dixon's admiration...but in that particular moment, I felt I deserved it.

Unfortunately, my stomach only let me revel for so long. I was ravenous. But like he'd anticipated my exhaustion, Dixon had anticipated my hunger, too. And though I strongly suspected my room service breakfast had come with more than two strips of bacon, it was good of him to have it waiting for me nevertheless.

"It looks like Spring Falls just needed to move past some kind of blockage," he told me. "Have you ever watched those pimple-popper videos online? No? Oh man, the ick just keeps coming and coming and coming like you wouldn't believe. Anyway, once the hot spring was done *effluenting* the big glob of whatnot that was holding everything back, it all started flowing again. It still smells a little bit like rotten eggs. But Janet says that's normal."

Janet. Hopefully this new development would be enough to save her resort from ruin. "What about the critic?"

"Mr. Woodrow is set to check out at noon, so once he's gone, she can work on hiring back her old staff, and you and I can get going...."

His patter trailed off for an unusually long moment. I forced myself more fully awake, caressed the scruff on his jaw with my knuckle, and said, "What is it?"

"She said we could stay, if we wanted. As in, live here. We'd need to do some actual training, mind you, but the feedback from the customers was absolutely glowing. Free room and board. Flexible hours. Not really sure exactly how much bacon would be included...."

The old resort was a much nicer place than either of us currently called home, but I could tell that while Dixon felt obligated to relay the offer to me, his heart wasn't in it. Dixon had done plenty of wandering, and now he wanted to settle down. With his family.

And who could blame him?

"It is a good offer," I said. "But I was just getting used to Pinyin Bay."

We made love in the big, soft bed, and though my body was still recovering from the paces the *volshebstvo* had put it through the night before, Dixon was happy to straddle me and do all the work while I laid back and reveled in his enthusiasm.

Afterwards, he nestled into the crook of my arm with a contented sigh. "Even if we're not planning to make it permanent," he said dreamily as he drew flourishes in my chest hair, "maybe we could stay an extra couple of days. I'm starting to suspect you've never had a vacation."

"Is that so?"

"Sexytimes with you are usually so intense—and, don't get me wrong, I'm down with it, a thousand percent—but it's nice to see you relax into things for a change."

Maybe it was the fatigue. Maybe the decadent bed. Or maybe it was just me getting accustomed to the fact that whatever transpired between Dixon and me was more than some furtive, shameful aberration.

We headed downstairs for fresh coffee and found Liza sitting alone by the continental breakfast, thumbing through her phone. She had on a stylish sarong skirt topped by a wrinkled Spring Falls T-shirt she'd likely slept in. Her blonde hair hung loose around her shoulders, vividly streaked with blue. She still seemed fragile... but not quite as miserable as she'd been when she first checked in.

"Oh, hey guys—did you notice anything strange last night? I thought I heard a really big eighteen-wheeler rolling by. They really should regulate that kind of thing."

"Crazy, right?" Dixon said—neither confirming nor denying, I noted—as he pawed through the buffet and I poured myself a coffee.

"I was thinking about doing a little sightseeing while I'm out this way." Liza was definitely in a better state of mind. Her stint at the spa had done her good. "I've got the time off work, anyhow. Might as well take advantage. Hit a few swap meets to do some antiquing and...." Her phone dinged as she spoke, and she took a few leisurely swipes...then went still.

"And?" Dixon twirled around with a huge muffin precariously perched on a tiny saucer. "Liza?"

I looked up from the sugar packets and saw that Liza had gone white, and her eyes were bigger than Dixon's plate. She scanned whatever was on her phone, back and forth, back and forth, like she was reading and re-reading the same bit of information. And then she drew in a sudden, startling breath...and wailed like a banshee.

Dixon jammed the muffin into my hand and hurried over to Liza. He went down on one knee beside her and threw an arm around the back of her chair. "What is it? Is it your despicable lawyer ex? He's not trumping up some crazy reason to sue you, is he?"

Liza's wail died down to a warble, and then ended in a hearty, fluid-filled sniff. "They have a HASHTAG!" she sputtered wetly.

I presumed "they" could only be the renegade groom and the traitorous bridesmaid.

Dixon took the phone from Liza's unprotesting hand. "#tradingup? Are you kidding me?" He flashed the phone at me. I caught a glimpse of a pasty man in a selfie with a very self-satisfied woman. "The nerve!"

"I am still willing to make him pay," I said with a shrug. It would feel good to snap those soft, white fingers backward. At least one or two.

Liza didn't acknowledge my offer. She just planted her forehead on her placemat and wept. Dixon locked eyes with me from across the table, wagged the phone a few times, and shook his head slowly. As much as he usually barraged me with talking, he didn't need to say a word for me to know what he was thinking. He wouldn't rest until we made things right for Liza.

Crafting a solution wouldn't be quite as satisfying as wrenching a bone out of its socket. But it would suffice.

Dixon patted Liza on the shoulder, set down her phone, then came over to me and whispered in my ear, "Can you do it, Yuri? Or are you all used up?"

I narrowed my eyes and said, "There's plenty of fuel in the tank."

Dixon did an eager little shoulder shimmy. He's a real sucker for innuendo.

We keep the tools of our trade close at hand—Dixon because his quill is irreplaceable, me because it's simply my habit. But when I pulled out the travel paintbox that has worn a rectangular mark in the left leg of every pair of my trousers, I discovered that while I myself might have enough fuel, my gouache was practically gone. In my painting trance, I'd used most of my color to bind together the shredded spell. Purple, blue, green and black, all gone. And the red had been running on fumes anyhow. Unless I wanted to paint yellow on yellow—and even my yellow was down to a sliver—I would need to top off after all.

An art supply store would be ideal, but even a child's drugstore watercolor set would suffice for the time being. But before I could track down Janet and figure out where to refill my paints, the tell-tale call of the *volshebstvo* prickled down my left arm.

How it is for Dixon when the urge to Craft comes over him, I do not know. It is an urge for me, like hunger or sleep or even sex. Something that that can be denied...but not forever. Maybe once, before I painted a thousand Seens. And now, I felt the need to Craft.

The urge was familiar, but the particulars were strange. Because usually when I felt the need to paint, touching the paintbox in my pocket brought me the sort of relief an alcoholic must feel when he pours his first drink of the night. But I felt no relief. Instead, the pull intensified I glanced up at the French doors leading out to the grotto. There. My addiction's relief was there.

I stepped outside and Dixon followed, silent. He knew something was going on. As a Spellcrafter, he most likely felt it himself.

The water level in the thermal pool was high. Whereas before we had to sit on a rocky bench, now we could have stood and still been mostly submerged. But I wasn't being pulled down those fieldstone steps to take the waters. I was drawn to dip my brush.

Effluent marbled the surface of the pool in hypnotic patterns. Striking, vivid whorls in cobalt, obsidian and aquamarine swirled through the fresh spring water, undulating. Beckoning. Some primal urge deep within me wondered what it would be like to sink in and lose myself in the color. But I understood that being a Seer meant keeping some small piece of myself in the here and now. To be not the painting, but the hand that guides the brush.

And yet, there was no way to reach the streaks of mineral without sinking in.

"Yuri?"

I blinked, surprised that Dixon had managed to hold his tongue for this long. I turned and found him with one hand planted on a wrought iron railing, the other beckoning to me. "Give me your hand. I'll anchor you."

I can't say if it was the *volshebstvo* flowing between us or not. It was not unusual for Dixon's touch to leave a wave of goosebumps in its wake. But between the two of us, I was able to reach out over the waters far enough for my paintbrush to pierce the surface. And when it did, both of us let out a groan of relief.

Was my need for control actually an asset? Maybe a better Seer would have actually strode into that pool and allowed himself to be consumed. I was still drained from repairing the shredded Crafting, and giving my trust to Dixon had opened an inroad to allowing. When brush met paper, for just a moment, that slip of awareness that usually observes the proceedings ebbed.

And when I came back to myself, the Seen was complete.

Even Dixon couldn't figure out what to say.

My work is loose, but not entirely abstract. This hypnotic swirl of colors and rhythm, however, was unlike anything I'd ever painted. The minerals had created their own distinct layers and cells. The effect was stunning.

Eventually, Dixon tugged at my arm to encourage me to come up out of the grotto. The *volshebstvo* no longer sparked between us. And I felt as though I could go right back to bed.

We settled at a table on the patio, and Dixon brought out his quill. "I figured I'd Scribe something that rhymed—there's an extra kick to the Spellcraft when you can make it happen—but looking at this image, I'm not so sure anymore." He reached across the table, took my left hand in his right, and turned my palm face up to draw a flourish on my skin with his fingertip.

I'd been wrong. The *volshebstvo* was definitely still sparking.

Dixon smiled at me, looking uncharacteristically thoughtful. "I guess they don't call it a comfort zone for nothing. But if you can step outside it, so can I."

His gaze went distant as he uncapped his ink and dipped his quill. He stilled for a moment, then wrote.

Happiness

In whatever form

It takes

He looped a final flourish under the letter *s*, and then his gaze shifted as he came back to himself. He cocked his head and considered his writing. The words were simple, but the ink work was even more elaborate than usual. It swooped and bent, flowing through the marbled painting in a dance of confident calligraphy. It was modern and fresh, and stunning in its elegant freedom.

I'm never sure how people will react to Spellcraft in this country. "What will you do? Slip it into Liza's welcome basket?"

"It would be a real shame if she took it for some kind of generic pre-printed verse and left it behind." Dixon blew gently across the ink to dry the thickest parts of the flourishes. "C'mon, let's go find her. I'll think of a plausible excuse on the way."

Excuse—good euphemism for a lie. Scriveners can be a slippery bunch. That was probably why I felt so much at home among them.

DIXON

15

We found Liza in the lobby with a mimosa in her hand. Another wine sociable? Evidently—a sociable of one. And that one was already tipsy.

"There you are," I said brightly. "What sorts of pampering are on the agenda for today?"

"Why bother?" she snuffled. "Who cares if my toenails are painted or my elbows are rough? It doesn't matter what I look or smell or feel like if I'm all alone."

I hate other people's sadness—it's my Achille's heel. "Of course it matters. Look." I shoved the Spellcraft into her free hand. "We made you something."

She scowled at it. "What do you mean? Made it, how?"

"With brush and ink."

"That's...interesting." She seemed confused. "Thanks."

"You need to hold onto it. For luck. At least a week." That should be enough time to turn around her sorry situation and get her pointed in the right direction. "Promise me."

"Okay." She shrugged and tucked it into her T-shirt pocket. "I promise."

As Liza gave her word, a frisson played across the back of my neck like an unexpected blast from the HVAC system. Only I wasn't standing under a vent. And once I registered that, two doors banged open, both at the same time.

At one end of the room, Quint the businessman strode through in a slouchy linen outfit that probably cost more than my entire wardrobe. He looked tan and fit, and even kind of edgy with his platinum blond hair gone robin's egg blue.

At the other, Mr. Woodrow shouldered in with a brochure in one hand and a thermometer gizmo in the other. His hair had gone a strange, mottled aquamarine. His clothes were nowhere near as fancy as Quint's, but half the town knew what he was packing in those unassuming trousers.

Once they crossed the threshold, the clouds outside parted. A fractured beam of sunlight flooded through the windows and illuminated each guy like a spotlight. Both men were on a trajectory that converged on Liza. And both of them barreled toward her like they were being led by a homing device.

Or a particularly potent bit of Spellcraft.

Liza looked up from her mimosa and cocked her head, sensing blearily that something was going on. One smile from her, one bit of encouragement, and her life would career off in an entirely new direction. She'd shown up for her honeymoon alone, but wouldn't leave that way.

But who would she pick? Successful, wealthy Quint? Or Mr. Woodrow and his generous endowments?

Both guys staggered to a stop just a few feet away from Liza—close enough for her to reach out and touch them—and as I held my breath, squirming with anticipation of which guy would tickle her fancy...I realized, with a growing apprehension, that neither one of them was a particularly good catch.

Quint might have money, but he reveled in rubbing everyone's nose in it. He was the epitome of entitlement—a braggart and a jerk. And while Mr. Woodrow was a smart guy who was open to new experiences, he was horribly pedantic, and managed to render even the most exotic things boring. Plus, eventually, his other particular asset was bound to chafe.

My family's always had a saying—*better single than sorry*. And I was starting to wonder if maybe *that* was what I should have Scribed. Liza looked from one blue-haired man to the other, sizing up each one, and I gathered myself for a dramatic tackle to thwart my own Spellcraft and stop her from making a massive mistake. It probably wouldn't happen in slow motion like it does in the movies—and I'd likely regret it. But I couldn't let one of these men latch onto her just so she didn't have to be alone.

But as I dove for her, something snagged my foot. I figured it was just Yuri being too cautious, but then I realized Yuri wasn't behind me—he was over by the coffee urn. And before I could make sense of what was happening, I found myself covered in yards of sulfur-smelling fabric as an entire bank of curtains engulfed me.

I poked my head free. The room was blindingly bright now, and it took me a good few seconds of blinking to make sense of what was going on.

One end of the drapery rod I'd dislodged had launched a pitcher of cranberry juice at Quint, and his trendy linen outfit was now tie-dyed pink. Kind of festive with his blue hair, but I doubted it was the look he was actually going for. Meanwhile, Mr. Woodrow had pulled out a notepad and was scribbling furiously. "Shoddy workmanship," he declared. "That could have hurt someone."

In the eye of the storm, Liza squinted against the dazzling sunlight, staring out into the courtyard. She swayed on her feet, mesmerized, while Quint carried on about his wardrobe malfunction and Mr. Woodrow pontificated on some obscure drapery requirements. Was it the Spellcraft holding her in place for one of the two undesirable men to come and get her? If so, there was no way I could let her keep that Crafting. No matter how well-intended it might have been.

But as my eyes adjusted to the brightness, I realized it wasn't Spellcraft holding her riveted to the spot. It was the sight of one very filthy, bluish dog.

Out on the patio, Twinkle stood with his head cocked, looking on as the humans inside emerged from the fallen drapery.

Liza cocked her head at the same angle as the dog's. "I heard you guys stomping around outside last night. Was this who you were looking for?"

"In the flesh," I said. "Or fur." Or...whatever was stuck to that fur.

A pair of glass doors bisected the wall of windows. Liza took one step toward them. Then another. And I was positive that any minute, Twinkle would perform his disappearing act.

Except, he didn't.

Even as Liza swung open the doors, and cried, "Ooooh, lookit the boo-boo puppy snoo-choo!" the dog stood stock still.

"He's kinda skittish," I cautioned.

Which Liza ignored. "Oo da good boo-boo?" She dropped to her knees and threw her arms wide. "*Oo da boo-boo?*"

His tail perked up...and gave a tentative wag.

"Come eer lil' snoochie-poo," Liza hollered.

And still, the dog didn't bail.

"What was his name again? You were calling it out half the night. Oh wait, I remember! It's Tinkle."

"Actually," I said. "It's...."

"C'mere, Tinkle! C'mere, boy!"

"Eh, never mind."

The wagging grew more confident, and so did the scrappy little dog. He crept a few inches toward Liza, then Liza shuffled forward on her knees, crooning adorable nonsense...and beyond all odds, the two came together in a whirlwind of babbling and tail-wagging and pink-tongue doggy kisses.

But the mood inside the dining room was nowhere near as prosaic.

"This is unacceptable!" Quint declared, dripping with pink. But before he could start spewing any businessman threats, a single bumblebee meandered in through the open door, and made a *bee*-line right for him. (Like, seriously, I had no idea that was an actual thing.)

I'd never seen anyone backpedal as fast as Quint. "I'm allergic to bees! Why is it coming straight for me?"

The bumblebee wasn't exactly a heat-seeking missile—more of a disoriented wiffleball—so it was unlikely Quint would get stung unless he insisted on standing around swatting himself. "It's the juice," I told him. "You'll want to go up to your room and change."

Well...that was one way to get rid of an annoying businessman.

Yuri hauled aside a curtain so I could step out, and while he did, he leaned in and said, "I will go speak to the critic."

I snagged him by the lapel and pulled him in to brush a kiss across his lips. "But aren't you going to revel in what we did for Liza?" I nodded toward the yard, where she and *Tinkle* were lolling together joyously on the lawn. The jilted bride had blades of grass and clover stuck in her messy, blue streaked hair—they were already starting to look alike. "You've got to admit...it was one heck of a Crafting."

Yuri did his best to look entirely unmoved. "The Crafting was fine." Yeah. He was into it. "But Woodrow had better not write up these curtains. His review must be glowing—all those ridiculous treatments I've done can't be for nothing."

I smoothed down his jacket and gave his massive pecs an appreciative pat. "Take Mr. Woodrow aside and tell him about some obscure Russian custom where it's good luck to pull down the drapes." Yuri looked dubious, and I added, "He loves your crazy made-up customs. And who'd ever be mopey about an extra bit of luck?"

Yuri ran the backs of his paint-stained fingers down my cheek. "Who, indeed?"

While Yuri headed off to fill Mr. Woodrow's head with invented traditions, Janet passed him in the hallway carrying a covered tray. I edged away from the curtains so I didn't need to take all the blame for pulling them down.

"What happened in here?" Janet sounded dazed.

"Funniest thing...." I began, scrambling to come up with some positive spin on the situation. But of everyone we'd met in Spring

Falls, Janet was our toughest customer—the sort of no-nonsense person who'd be really hard to bamboozle.

Weirdly enough, though, she wasn't angry. She trudged across the old curtains and looked out through the glass as if she was seeing her resort for the very first time. "I didn't realize how much light those curtains were blocking. Look at this place—it feels twice as big. And that's a real nice view of the grotto." Sunlight played over her features as she gazed down at the healthy trickle, which now ran into the pool sparkling clear, and only smelled slightly of sulfur.

She turned to me. "The offer still stands, y'know. You're welcome to stay."

"We appreciate it," I said warmly. "But Yuri and I...." Huh. There was nothing we urgently needed to do, now that Uncle Fonzo's trail had gone cold.

I took the tray from Janet's unresisting hands, set it down and cracked the lid, hoping for bacon...and found, instead, little cups of whipped topping and pineapple sprinkled with crushed cookies—just like Mom used to make. It was the sight of those awesome desserts that made me come to a realization. While my family was accustomed to me coming and going, maybe I wasn't. Not anymore. Truth be told, I was even a little bit homesick. No doubt it wasn't the same there without Uncle Fonzo. But until there was something more to go on, there was no sense in just wandering around aimlessly, hoping to cross his path.

Yuri and I had a life waiting for us back in Pinyin Bay. A pretty darn good life. And now I was ready to go home.

I scooped up a parfait for myself and another for Yuri. I was considering whether or not to try balancing a third cup in the crook of my elbow—just in case Yuri didn't let me eat his—when my phone rang.

Since I didn't recognize the number, I let it go to voicemail. But when I got up to our room, it started ringing again. I tapped the door with my foot. Yuri opened it and took the parfaits without a word. The ringing stopped...but before I could get the lowdown on what new and exotic Russian curtain-pulling tradition he'd managed to cook up, the phone rang yet again.

I'm as glad as the next guy to brighten a telemarketer's day, but sometimes they've just gotta learn to take *no* for an answer. I grabbed the call and said, "Sorry to disappoint you, but whatever it is you're selling, I'm not your guy."

Through the ambient noise of a raucous crowd, I had the distinct impression of hearing someone smile.

And then a familiar voice rang out.

"Dixon Penn...." My heart skipped a beat, then started pounding. Hard. "Is that any way to greet your favorite uncle?"

DEAD MAN'S QUILL

DIXON

1

"Dixon Penn.... Is that any way to greet your favorite uncle?"

It takes a heck of a lot to render me speechless. But after all this time? The sound of my uncle's voice left me too baffled to form a coherent thought. I was in our hotel room at the spa, in the midst of picking up a pineapple parfait when I'd answered the phone, and the dessert was now face-down between my feet. I was so stunned, I had no memory of how it even got there. Yuri squinted at me from the bathroom sink where he'd returned to washing out his socks, completely unaware than my world was tilting on its axis...or, at least, just beginning to suspect.

"Listen," Uncle Fonzo told me. "I know it's been a while—"

"It's been a year," I managed.

"I know, kiddo. And I feel pretty lousy about falling off the radar. So, why don't you come see me—and you can read me the riot act in person?"

After a year of searching—of wondering and worrying—it hardly seemed real that it would be as simple as that. Even so, my heart was racing with the anticipation of finally bringing my uncle home. "Okay. Yeah. *Definitely.* Just tell me where you are."

"I'll do you one better and tell you where I'm going to be. I've hooked up with the Big Fun Traveling Carnival, and we're heading for a three-day stint in Mount Valley. It's just a day's drive from Pinyin Bay."

I mapped it on my phone—a day's drive from Spring Falls, too. "Then I'll see you tomorrow."

"That's my boy! Oh...and one more thing. Before you head out, I'll need to you swing by Rufus Clahd's office and grab me a fresh Seen."

Given how Yuri felt about clowns, no doubt he would've preferred to drive *away* from the carnival, not toward it. And I was too hopped up to be my normal, soothing self.

I also had a sneaking suspicion Yuri was none too thrilled to meet my uncle, either...judging by the way he accidentally knocked the hotel room door off its hinges on the way out.

Good thing I'd paraphrased the conversation about meeting Uncle Fonzo at the carnival, and left out the part where we were supposed to bring him a fresh Seen. Hoping Yuri could offer a few civil niceties to my uncle was one thing. Expecting him to turn over something as intimate as a Seen was another.

We reached the Big Fun Traveling Carnival at dusk, when the sky was streaked the color of strawberry jam and the lights on the midway came to life with only the occasional burned-out bulb interrupting the pattern. A teenage girl chewing a huge mouthful of gum took our admission, and listlessly upsold the all-you-can-ride wristband around the gum wad. "No thanks," I told her. "We're not actually here to ride the rides."

"Food-and-game tickets are a fun-filled bargain at thirteen tickets for ten dollars," she said with zero inflection, parroting a script she'd been forced to memorize. "And be sure to check out our deep-fried frozen cotton candy."

I paused for a moment to try and imagine how a frozen anything would survive a dunk in the deep-fryer, but only for a moment. "Actually, I'm looking for someone on the crew." I flashed the photo of my Uncle Fonzo. "Maybe you can point me in the right direction."

The girl gave a few juicy mastications, then shrugged. "I just started today, and I've been in the ticket booth the whole time. Sorry."

I thanked her and bought a strip of food tickets even though my stomach was in knots. No sense in starving to death when tents full of shaved ice, candy apples and funnel cake were just a ping-pong ball's throw away—even when everything cost three or six tickets, and no matter how you sliced it, you'd never use up ticket number thirteen without buying two more strips.

We asked around, or at least we tried. Safety regulations didn't allow the ride operators to talk while their rides were running. The game barkers were too busy calling out patter. Eventually, a guy on the cleaning crew seemed eager to talk to us—but only for the purposes of selling some "bargain" tickets he'd clearly pilfered... which I bought, since Yuri was looking kind of hungry.

Eventually, we finally found someone who recognized my uncle—the lady stuck stirring the kettle corn, a hot and thankless task. "Oh, I met him. Friendly guy. But I think it's been a day or two since—"

She went back to her stirring, mid-sentence, and twice as hard.

A day or two since what? I was about to ask, but Yuri nudged me and drew my attention toward a towering figure all in black. He was a homely middle-aged man, rawboned and angular, with per-manently etched frown lines and a home haircut—the lovechild of Abraham Lincoln and Frankenstein. As he strode through the carnival, a pall of discomfort spread around him like ink furling away from the tip of a quill plunged in water. Even the customers went silent and shrank away.

Once he'd turned the corner of the plywood haunted house, Kettle Corn Lady loud-whispered, "That's Reverend Fun. You don't want to end up on his you-know-what list."

Reverend *Fun?* If ever there was a walking oxymoron.... "And here I thought the Big Fun Traveling Carnival was named that way because it was enjoyable. Is he actually a holy man?"

"Not that anyone here can tell. I heard it was a vanity mail-order license he's using to get a tax break."

Hmm...Reverend *Penn* might have an interesting ring to it. But my family wasn't keen on organized religion, so I shelved that idea without much serious thought.

The kettle corn was starting to singe, so we thanked the sweaty lady and left her to her stirring. We asked around for a few more hours, but unfortunately, no one else knew any more than she did. If I'd been discouraged by not knowing where Uncle Fonzo was all this time, after a couple fruitless hours trying to talk to the carnies, I was on tenterhooks wondering if this trip would turn out to be a big, fat dead-end.

The midway held all the usual carnival games. Water gun races. Goldfish bowls. Duck pond. But it was the balloon pop where Yuri froze in his tracks, then did a double-take. Maybe they didn't have balloon pop games in Russia. But before I could ask, I saw that he wasn't focused on the game, but rather the prizes. The assortment was just as kitschy as game itself. Fake nose with glasses, paddleball, potato gun, itching powder. I was about to inform Yuri that the X-ray specs didn't really work when he shoved some tickets into the host's hand and said, "Darts."

The stoned guy behind the counter handed over three darts with a vague half-grin on his squinty-eyed face. "Reveal a star and win yourself a prize."

"Where is star?"

"Hey, man, that's not how the game—ulp!"

Yuri dragged him forward by the shirt and said, "Where...is...star?"

The guy nodded toward the board and said, "That red balloon up in the corner is a good bet."

Before I could mention that I would occasionally win a com-plimentary well drink playing darts at Bar None, Yuri had fired the three darts in rapid succession—*Pop! Pop! Pop!*—annihilating every red balloon on that side of the board. Not only one, but *two* of them had been hiding stars.

"Two stars," the stoner declared as he flapped his hand at a tier of awkward-looking stuffed animals. The cartoon knockoffs were so bad they were almost cute, though I doubted Yuri would be eager to wake up to the cross-eyed gaze of a pale blue Porky Pig. "Pick a prize!"

Yuri squinted, then jabbed a finger at the tier below it—the one-star stuff that was so cheap it was nothing more than a consolation prize, and a lousy one at that. "Give me the paint."

The stoner swayed on his feet, staring in the direction Yuri was pointing as if he was trying to see the hidden picture in a Magic Eye painting. After an awkward pause, he said, "But, like, you can have one of the *good* prizes."

Yuri dropped his voice low and dangerous, and repeated, "Give me the paint."

"Chill, dude—you want the Pretty Princess Glitter Face Paint so bad? You got it!" He turned to the display and pulled off a glitzy pink card with a minuscule children's paint set attached. I personally wouldn't get that stuff anywhere near my face, since it was clearly so cheap, the sparkle was probably all floor-sweepings from a glass-grinding factory. But I guess kids have pretty resilient skin. The stoner also threw in the next prize over, a pink glow stick bracelet, to sweeten the pot and make sure Yuri was well and truly satisfied...and didn't come back an hour later with buyer's remorse.

Yuri snatched the toys and crammed them into his pocket. For reasons unknown, the stoner was compelled to try and sustain the conversation. "So. Who's the lucky little lady?"

Yuri gave him a look that could wilt a Sequoia. "I am."

Well...at least, one of us had found something he was looking for.

The longer we picked through the carnival without spotting Uncle Fonzo, the more nervous I grew. It had been so long since I'd seen him, being without him had become my new normal.

Eventually, my growling stomach got the best of me, and we paused for a break, perched at a sticky-topped picnic table. I picked at my deep-fried cotton candy (the middle had not only thawed, but melted to a sugary syrup, leaving a hollow shell of fried batter that looked unappetizingly like a cow flop) while Yuri inhaled a fried dough, then tried out his new paints on the wrapper. I was just about to ask him whether he thought the word "tenterhooks" had its origin in the carnival when he looked up from his painting and went very still. He squinted into the visual cacophony of the midway and said, "What is *that*?"

YURI

2

American carnivals were nothing like the ones I'd been to as a young man outside St. Petersburg. There were no snowball fights...in fact, no snow at all. No straw effigies burning in the square. No blini, though the fried dough was not bad.

And no expectation that I would return home, as was the tradition, with a fiancée.

Even better, I determined there were no puppet shows at this traveling carnival, and the only clowns in sight were merely images printed on the popcorn boxes. Even those images were cartoonish enough to not strike me as particularly disturbing.

While many of the amusements had a Russian equivalent, those that did not were easy enough to figure out, even though the prizes were more garish, the rides were more thrilling, and every food option was deep-fried. But the huge water tank painted with the words Dunk the Skunk?

I could think of no counterpart for that.

But while I scanned the amusement with mild curiosity, Dixon froze in his tracks.

Which could only mean one thing.

I looked closer and saw that inside the tank, a man wearing a skunk costume perched, shivering and damp, on a thin wooden ledge. Beside him, a barker called out, "No one likes a stinker! Five balls for three tickets—can't beat that with a stick! Come on now, little missy," he called out to a teenage girl in earbuds, "you know you want a shot!"

The girl seemed unimpressed once she saw there was no prize other than the satisfaction of seeing a man suffer hypothermia. But the game made quite the impression on me. Because behind the animal nose and ears, the wet hair and the miserable expression, was none other than the Hand of Dixon's family, Fonzo Penn.

I thought he'd be taller.

It is rare indeed for Dixon to be at a loss for words. I marched up past the Barker and peered into the tank—or at least, I tried. The Barker, an elderly man with massive dentures and a well-worn wooden cane, poked me in the knee and said, "Now now, Sonny, you know what happens when you spook a skunk." He gestured with his cane and said, "No crossing the red line. No exceptions."

If push came to shove, he could probably do some damage with that cane. I backed up a few paces until I crossed the red strip of tape stretched across the asphalt. I stared. Dixon stared. And eventually the barker made a "gimme" motion with his hand and said, "Three tickets. Are you slow?" He held up three fingers, and slowly articulated, "One...two...three."

I tore three tickets off our strip and shoved them into his arthritic hand.

The skunk in the tank had been staring at his own knees, but at the pause in the barker's patter, his curiosity got the best of him. When he looked up and locked eyes with his nephew, both of them went wide-eyed and stunned—and while Fonzo's features were a generation older (not to mention half-covered with a felt skunk nose) no one could possibly miss the family resemblance.

The barker handed me a baseball. It felt too light, but what did I know? He jabbed his cane toward the center of the target and said, "Here ya go, ball number one. Hit the bullseye and dunk the skunk!"

The girl in the earbuds might not have found the prize particularly appealing...but I did.

Unfortunately, my first pitch bounced harmlessly off the edge of the target.

"So close—but no cigar!" The barker jammed another ball into my hands.

I hefted the ball. Definitely too light for its size. But while I took its measure, I glanced up and noticed that Fonzo was making a signal of some kind with his far hand, where the barker couldn't see it, but Dixon could. Not sign language, exactly. Numbers. Directions.

"Come on, now, Jumbo," the barker told me, "I don't have all day. Take your shot."

I pitched the second ball. It bounced off the other side of the target.

"Big, strong guy like you," the old man said. "I'm sure you can do better." He gave me another ball. Dixon gestured to his uncle. Fonzo gestured back. They both nodded.

Something was settled, then. Good.

I took aim at the target...and threw hard.

The ball went wide, hit the side of the tank, and dropped to the pavement.

"And a miss! Two more tries—better make 'em count."

As the barker gave me my fourth ball, I glanced up at Fonzo. He was watching me intently now. I met his gaze, narrowed my eyes, and threw.

The lightweight ball arced over the top.

Obviously, the game was rigged—but it couldn't have been entirely impossible to hit the mark. The most successful ploys at parting people from their money needed to offer at least some margin of hope, however slim. Otherwise no one would play.

"Put your back into it!" The barker handed me the final ball.

I squinted at the target—really got the feel for it—but as I wound up my throw, Dixon tugged at my sleeve, then wordlessly held out a hand.

Dixon claimed he was more of an athletic supporter than an athlete, but if he wanted a shot, who was I to deny him? As satisfying as it would be to send his uncle plunging into a tank of water, I couldn't possibly resist that big-eyed look. Our fingers brushed when I handed him the ball. He held it for an extra moment, allowing the touch to linger...then without even bothering to aim, turned and flung a wild pitch at the target.

It hit, dead center, with a hollow smack.

I'm not sure who was more surprised. The barker? Me? Dixon himself?

Or Fonzo Penn...as he was dumped unceremoniously into the water.

DIXON

3

Our meeting was set for ten o'clock at the northwest corner of the grounds. I killed time waiting for the carnival to wind down by watching Yuri eat fried dough and trying to imagine how on earth Uncle Fonzo had ended up in this predicament. I have a pretty active imagination. And I couldn't think of a single darn thing.

The rendezvous point was well-chosen. Dark. Secluded. And not particularly comfortable. No one would have any reason to find us lingering out back behind the maintenance truck unless they were in dire need of toilet paper, or maybe some of that vomit-soaker-upper.

Ten o'clock came...and ten o'clock went. And as it did, it dawned on me that my uncle could have sent me to the spot where I was waiting so he could slip out the other side of the carnival before I was any the wiser. And never mind that it would've been totally illogical, since he was the one who'd asked me to come in the first place. Hopefully he wasn't ticked off about the baseball. I couldn't really explain what had come over me back there at the Skunk Dunk myself, and anyone who's talked to me for more than five minutes would surely know that any success I might have in throwing a ball was purely coincidental. But just as I was about to ask Yuri to split up and do a sweep of the grounds, I heard the thready sound of whistling in the dark.

Not just any song, but the one my uncle had sung when he tucked me into bed—a nonsense ditty about trolls stealing your toes unless you allow your eyes to close—that never failed to catapult me straight into dreamland. In the dim glow of the distant carnival lights, my eyes played tricks on me. For just a moment, as he rounded the maintenance truck, Uncle Fonzo looked like he did when I was still a kid who tucked his blankets tight around his feet so as not to make it any easier for the underbed trolls to have their way with me. But then he smiled, and I saw the pronounced lines around his mouth. And sagging jowls. And receding widow's peaks. And it was obvious the years had changed him. Just like they'd changed all of us.

"Dixon, my boy. Aren't you a sight for sore eyes?" He opened his arms. "Come and give your ol' Uncle Fonzo a hug."

I flung my arms around him. His sweater smelled like chlorine, and words tumbled out of me, too eager to form real sentences. "I...you...we...I'm so sorry for dunking you."

Yuri made a scoffing sound. "*You* are apologizing to *him?*"

Uncle Fonzo gave me an extra-hard squeeze. "A lucky shot! Remember, I know full well how quickly you can run *away* from a baseball." Once the hug was all hugged out, he landed a few good claps on my back. He wore thin leather gloves, like Yuri, like lots of old-school Spellcrafters, so the claps were more of a muted *thwack*. He then pushed me to arms' length, gave my shoulders a squeeze, and said, "It's been too long."

Yuri crossed his arms and said, "And whose fault is that?"

Undaunted, Uncle Fonzo craned his neck to peer up at Yuri through the darkness, and said, "You brought a friend. A boyfriend?"

"Grown man friend," I said. "His name is Yuri."

"Guess where the two of us met," Yuri said.

"Well, the Pinyin Bay Pride Parade isn't for another couple of months. Did the gin mill on Stump Street take my advice and put together a disco-themed Thursday?"

"Precious Greetings." He sounded kind of hostile—even for Yuri. "We met at Precious Greetings."

My uncle's smile turned pained...then dropped away completely. He looked from Yuri to me. "Oh, Dixon...what were you doing in that awful place?"

Before I could figure out where to begin, Yuri said, "He was doing what you could not. He stopped Emery Flint from trapping any more Spellcrafters in his web."

"Flint is gone?"

"Neutralized, more like it," I said eagerly. "Last I heard, Precious Greetings was being renovated into a build-your-own yogurt bar. And the old full-time Scrivener, Dolores Tran, put out the word that Flint tried to bilk her into signing a bum contract—so nobody in the circuit is likely to Scribe for him again."

"If they can help it," my uncle added.

"Spellcraft compulsion is gone." Yuri's accent had gone thicker and he'd dropped his article, so he was obviously feeling nowhere near as calm, cool and collected as he made out. "You can stop hiding now."

Uncle Fonzo took it all in stride. "Hiding? Is that what you think? Well, who can blame you? It's not as if you know me."

Yuri didn't disagree—but his thin smile spoke volumes.

"I wasn't hiding. I was making sure the rest of the family didn't suffer from the fallout of my mistake. Dixon is resilient—always lands on his feet—but he's got nothing Flint would want. My daughter, though? I couldn't just sit by and let that predator scoop her up. Look, everything's under control, I've just got a score to settle here before I wrap everything up. Can't Craft something for nothing, it upsets the natural order. And this surly old carny owes me a whole lot of somethings. I bought out the last Dunk Skunk so I could take his place, tag along and keep an eye on things. I know where Fun is keeping my money. I've got a plan. All I need is a Seen—you did bring me a Seen, Dixon, right?"

"Actually...I didn't."

Uncle Fonzo's smile shifted into a wince.

"Dixon did not bring Seen," Yuri announced. "He brought Seer."

"He...? You...?" Uncle Fonzo slapped his knee. "Well, how about that? Snagged yourself a Seer—not that I'm surprised, handsome young buck like you. Quite the catch. Florica must be so proud."

She was over the moon—practically orbiting Venus—but I knew flattery when I heard it, and I had the sneaking suspicion there was more to the story he was avoiding. "Mom's tickled pink—but let's stick to the topic at hand. Why do you care so much about your payday? I get that you need some kind of compensation, but there's something funny about this carnival—funny-weird, not funny-ha-ha. Why not pocket a prize from the midway, call it even, and come back to Pinyin Bay?"

Uncle Fonzo's shoulders slumped. "I'd love to—more than anything. Especially hearing that Flint's been taken care of. But the truth is, now I've got a debt to settle, and the clock's ticking. I can't come home empty-handed. And, for your own protection, that's as much as you need to know. So, about that Seen...."

"I never agreed to paint for you," Yuri said. "You need money, Fun has money, we take it, we leave. You don't need Seen."

"Sure, in an ideal world, that's exactly what we would do. But there's rumors flying left and right that his stash is *protected*."

"How so?" I asked.

Uncle Fonzo lowered his voice dramatically. "No one knows. But carnies are hard to impress—they've seen it all, and then some—and if they're all too spooked to even *think* about robbing Reverend Fun, I'm not about to find out the hard way exactly what his protections...entail. Erm...Dixon?"

"Yes?"

"You're standing on my foot."

Of course I wasn't...oh. "Oops. Sorry."

My uncle fixed me with a very serious look. "If there's anything you want to say to me, kiddo, I'm all ears."

"I dunno. Welcome back?"

Abruptly, Yuri said, "I will get crowbar from truck," and strode off. Because he needed a crowbar? Or because he wanted to give me some time alone with my uncle?

"Listen," Uncle Fonzo said. "I get that you might be a little ticked off."

"Me? No way! I'm totally jazzed to see you."

"I know I've been MIA, but like I was saying, I had to keep contact to a minimum, in case whatever Spellcraft Flint used on me got its hooks into any of you. The way it all went down, I thought the best course of action would be to regroup and deal with Precious Greetings myself before anyone else got hurt. And I want you to know that even though I wasn't with you guys, I thought of you all each and every day. It was a strategic retreat, that's all."

A strategy that somehow involved finding another quill...but before I could ask about that, Yuri slipped from the shadows with a crowbar in his hand and said, "Now we go get money."

4

The days of carnivals coming to town in brightly painted caravans were long gone...if all that pageantry had ever happened anywhere besides the silver screen to begin with. The Big Fun Traveling Carnival made its way across the country in a series of dilapidated campers, a graffiti-covered eighteen-wheeler, and a pair of repurposed school buses. One of those buses was the private sanctum of Reverend Fun himself. It bore little resemblance to the vehicle that transported groups of eager children to and from the local establishments of learning. The (once) cheese-colored exterior had been painted dull black, and the banks of windows along the sides were bolted over with thin sheets of corrugated aluminum, which left it looking like a charter bus to Hell...or maybe a thrash-metal concert. The only thing that differentiated it from a post-apocalyptic prison van was the black-painted calliope welded to the back.

"I can't say I recommend taking the short way in," Uncle Fonzo said as he cut his eyes from the bus door to Yuri's crowbar. "If there's an alarm system, that's where it'll be rigged."

Yuri tapped the crowbar against his palm as he weighed his options. He had on his leather gloves, so the iron tool made a satisfying *thwack* with each strike. After several good thwacks, he nodded and said, "We go through metal window."

There's never a convenient stepladder around when you need one, so my uncle and I got down on hands and knees to form a pyramid base for Yuri to stand on. Uncle Fonzo made an "oof" sound as Yuri stepped onto his back, then muttered, "I still think it would've made more sense for you or me to climb up top."

"But Yuri's the one with all the upper-body strength. And besides, it's just like my days on the cheerleading squad." Which most definitely qualified as a sport—and was also the best way to ogle the football team running around in their skin-tight leggings.

While Yuri grumbled in Russian as he tried to wedge in the crowbar, my uncle told me, "Still...a Scrivener needs to be serious about protecting his greatest asset—his hands."

He was totally right. I'd need to start thinking about it myself. Lots of Spellcrafters wore gloves, including Yuri. But I'd never developed the knack for having gloves on all the time. They felt sweaty, and the stunted sense of touch was annoying.

As I pondered, yet again, whether a stylish pair of gloves, maybe in a cute paisley, would make me change my mind, Yuri's crowbar hit home. With a shriek of stripping bolts, the corrugated metal peeled up like the top of a sardine can. Unfortunately, he'd underestimated exactly how wide his shoulders were. He tried every which way, but couldn't manage to wedge himself through the window. Uttering a few choice Russian expletives, he climbed down and said, "I will wait here."

He knelt in the dirt, wove his fingers together and gave my uncle an alley-oop. He was none too keen on me following, but he must've known there'd be no stopping me. As Uncle Fonzo wriggled his butt through the peeled-up window, Yuri pressed something into my hand. Something small. And glittery. And vibrating with Spellcraft.

He brushed his lips against my ear and said, "I would not paint for him...but for you? Always."

That elusive whisper of magic shivered through my body and coalesced in my right hand. But it would have to wait until I had some idea what I might need to Scribe.

With Yuri pushing and Uncle Fonzo pulling, I was up and into the big black bus in no time...despite the fact that it was so full, we could hardly cram ourselves in. The seats had been removed, and the big bus was filled, floor to ceiling, with balloons.

I can hardly think of anything more harmless than a balloon— but apparently I'd never imagined I'd have to wedge myself into a confined space so full of them I couldn't even turn around. The latex creaked alarmingly as it rubbed against itself. My hair follicles tingled with static. And I experienced the disconcerting sensation of being pressed into from every conceivable angle.

"Dixon?" My uncle's voice echoed oddly around the latex, as the membranes all reverberated with the sound of his voice like several thousand ginormous eardrums. "Whatever you do...don't pop anything."

Cautiously, I squeezed a hand into the balloon avalanche and eased open a springy crevasse to walk in. I became profoundly aware of anything on my person that might be even remotely sharp, from my tie tack to my cufflinks. "Any idea where your money is?" I asked.

"If it were me, I'd stash it at the point farthest from the door."

A logical notion—though I wasn't sure logic necessarily prevailed with someone who guarded his hoard with a bumper crop of inflated rubber. "Good thing I'm not allergic to latex." D'oh... probably something I didn't need to announce to *my uncle*. "Maybe we can let the air out of some gradually and free up a little elbow room."

I picked apart the knot on the nearest balloon and deflated it with a *squee-ee-ee*, but it was such a delicate and time-consuming task, we'd be at it all night if we ever hoped to make any headway. I said, "As much as I love hearing a balloon sing the song of its people, this'll take forever. And the squeak it makes is just as loud as a pop—so we might as well start stomping."

My uncle put a steadying hand on my shoulder. "Hold up there, kiddo. Human Behavior 101—people don't do things for no good reason. If the Reverend took the time to blow up all these balloons, they serve some kind of purpose."

"A carny alarm system?" I guessed. "And something to keep us in place while security shows up."

"Security consists of a couple of unenthused rent-a-cops and a retired lunch lady named Bernice. Keep your eyes on the prize and we'll be just fine."

Eyes on the prize. Easier said than done wallowing in balloons. "If I were a stack of money, where would I be?" My mom kept her secret stash inside a fake lettuce in the crisper drawer—because everyone knows lettuce is for rabbits, or maybe garnish, if you're being fancy. But unless the converted bus was tricked out with a kitchenette, we were probably looking for a safe. Most non-professional burglars would be foiled by a safe. But, lucky for me, I just so happened to have a fresh Seen and a quill.

"We'll cover more ground if we split up," I decided. "You take the back end of the bus, I'll take the front." Despite the gentle illumination of the exit signs over the doors, within moments I was disoriented, but I did my best to press forward. Good thing I wasn't claustrophobic. Step by step, inch by inch, I squeezed my body through. All around me, the balloons marked my progress with a symphony of squeaks.

I banked off the sides of the bus a few times, but eventually I found the driver's seat. And built into the back of it was a secure panel with an urgent-looking sign that proclaimed in bold, red letters, *Authorized Persons Only*.

How nonspecific. Undoubtedly, at some point in my life, I'd been authorized by *someone* to do *something*. With that settled, I went about prying the panel open with my trusty knockoff Swiss army knife. Most of the blades had snapped off years ago. But the toothpick was surprisingly sturdy.

It was like trying to unseal a can of house paint that's been moldering in the basement for years, but eventually, my persistence paid off. I plucked open the door in triumph, fully expecting to find stacks of greenbacks. Or diamonds. Or even gold doubloons. So I was puzzled to find, instead....

A stapler.

Not one of those hand-held staplers you'd use to organize your personal magazine clippings or receipts, but the big, hulking, automatic kind you'd find in a hardcore office environment. It was lying on its back. Odd. I cocked my head to get a better look, and noticed, stranger still, that a thin line of filament connected it to the metal door I was holding open.

And also, that a tiny lever had sprung out to keep the door open. *Ca-chunk.*

It wasn't so much that the staple hurt—it bounced off my lapel—but it sure was startling. I backed away quickly as the staples picked up steam. *Ca-chunk-ca-chunk-ca-chunk.* And before I knew it, I had plenty of room to flail around—as the balloons all around me detonated.

Once I got over my startlement, it was kind of festive, actually, since the balloons were all filled with glitter. When they popped, they gave off a sparkly spray.

As the balloons around me let loose, other balloons sank down to take their place as airborne glitter rained down. And within moments, the sparkly surface had lowered to eye-level. Loud? From where I stood, yes. But the joke was on Reverend Fun, because the bus was so trussed up so tight, it would effectively muffle all that popping. I scrambled around and found Uncle Fonzo looking at me, alarmed, from the opposite end of the bus. The balloons kept on popping, and soon the surface level reached my shoulders, then my chest. Across the length of the bus, more of my uncle was revealed as the balloons around him gently rolled away to fill the void. He'd found a hatch just like the one I'd pried open. But before I could warn him about the staples, he pulled his little door open.

There was no stapler inside his.

Instead, it was hooked up to the massive calliope.

The steam-powered instrument wheezed to life. It was like a giant's pan-pipes on steroids, blasting out a cheerful carnival tune with enough decibels to shake the whole bus, and the parking lot all around it, too. If the security staff didn't hear the balloons popping, they'd sure as heck hear that calliope playing...all the way from Poughkeepsie.

The entirety of the bus was tricked out with hatches and doors, I realized—and any of them could be hiding the money. If it was even there at all. As the balloons around me continued to burst, dousing me with glitter, I felt a telltale tingle in my hand and decided that enough was enough. Spellcraft wasn't guaranteed to work instantaneously. But when all you've got is a hammer, everything looks like a nail.

Actually, that probably wasn't exactly the expression I was looking for.

Anyhoo.

I whipped out Yuri's Seen...and did a double-take. He'd used the glitter face-paint he'd won on the midway, and his abstract design was a bunch of circles that could easily represent balloons—*glittery* balloons. Trying to figure out which came first—the chicken or the glitter-filled egg—was enough to make my head hurt, so I set those considerations aside and focused instead on Scribing my way out of there.

I slipped my quill from my pocket and opened my ink with my teeth, hoping I didn't end up wearing it. Juggling quill, ink and Seen was a challenge—but if you're gonna juggle, what better place to do it than in a bus full of glittery balloons?

Since Uncle Fonzo wouldn't leave without his payout, *show me the money* came to mind, but I quelled the impulse to Scribe something that specific. If Reverend Fun had made a bank deposit, I could end up wasting my Spellcraft on a deposit slip or a few nickels that slipped behind the seat cushion. I discarded my initial idea and did my best to clear my mind. As the balloons popped glitter and the calliope blasted, what came to me would need to be good enough.

Fair is fair.

Carnival. *Fair.* Get it?

It was hasty calligraphy, no doubt, scrawled on my knee while my ink splattered the popping balloons. But I felt that old Spellcraftian tingle anyhow. Or...did I? Because my left hand was tingling now, too.

That was different.

"I've got it," Uncle Fonzo hollered over the off-kilter music, and I saw him, covered in glitter, pulling a gigantic plushy walrus from the guts of the calliope. "Let's get out of here!"

He high-tailed it to the window and tossed the walrus to Yuri. I waded toward our exit through balloons that were just thigh-high now. The stapler was still ca-chunking, but the staples were over-shooting the balloons, and soon the strip ran out. I thought I was home free, but then the tingling morphed into an itch. I realized it wasn't just glitter filling the balloons—but itching powder. Panic flooded me. I might've been raised in the Craft, but I was still relatively new to Scrivening. What if I'd botched the job by Crafting for fairness instead of money?

And what if it wasn't Yuri outside the bus waiting for us...but Reverend Fun?

This couldn't be happening—I was *way* too pretty for prison. But as I scrambled to follow my uncle—terrified of what I'd find once I looked out that window—my elbow jostled a switch on the wall.

Overhead, a dome light blazed to life, revealing the balloonish wreckage in all its colorful, glittery glory.

I raised a hand to shield my eyes from the sudden onslaught of light, and realized there was something stuck inside the dome. Something small and papery.

Something the exact same size as all the other wonky bits of Spellcraft we'd been trailing.

Something with a single, ragged word Scribed on it.

Remunerate.

YURI

5

Outside, on the outskirts of the fairgrounds, the festive blinking carnival lights had long since been extinguished. But when the thunderous music started playing, a distant searchlight blazed to life. It swept the grounds around the black bus, and though I tried to avoid looking directly at it, my eyes were dazzled by the glare.

The corrugated sheet metal covering the window pried open and an ugly stuffed animal dropped out, followed by Fonzo Penn. A few balloons drifted out behind him. To his credit, he didn't immediately dash off into the night with his prize, but instead planted himself beside the bus and waited for Dixon.

Hard to say what was happening in there over the earth-shaking racket of the great pipe-organ in back blasting out its creepy circus tune. As the searchlight swept away from us, I stole a glance at the fairgrounds. A single, tall figure strode toward us, backlit and menacing. And it was holding something that looked suspiciously like an elephant rifle.

I was just about ready to pry off the entire side of the bus and retrieve Dixon myself when he slid feet-first from the window and dropped awkwardly to the ground. He hastily looped an arm through mine and hollered over the music, "Let's go!"

The three of us zig-zagged through the parked vans, but everywhere we turned, the tall, dark figure was not only right behind us, but gaining ground. He lurched along like an animated scarecrow, closing in, silhouetted against the lazy strobe of the searchlight.

Hastily, we ducked around a corner and found a small mob running toward us—only to realize, when we all staggered to a stop, it was nothing but a stack of funhouse mirrors from a disassembled attraction leaning against the side of a truck.

We dodged the mirrors, careened around the skunk tank, then found ourselves at the edge of the parking lot. It had a dark, weedy, deserted feel with all the other customers long gone. Only one truck remained.

Ours.

With Reverend Fun and his great big gun behind us, we broke into an all-out run. Dixon let go of me, and instinctively, the three of us fanned apart, weaving as we ran. We might be easy targets out in the open with nothing to hide behind. But hopefully he couldn't reload fast enough to get us all.

We were far enough from the black bus that the music had faded into the distance. Still audible. But quiet enough to hear the meaty thump made by the Reverend's gun.

"Oof!" Dixon went down, rolled in the dust, then sprang back up with a wad of material in his hand. "T-shirt cannon!"

I was relieved—mostly—until a shirt smacked me between the shoulders. I staggered, but kept on running.

Another thump and a shirt arched over Fonzo's head...and finally, we were at the truck. We scrambled in. Another T-shirt bounced off the rear window and dropped into the truck bed as, with a gritty spin of the balding tires, we left the Big Fun Traveling Carnival receding in the taillights.

Fonzo craned his neck to look back on the latest snare he'd managed to slip. With a whoop of triumph, he turned his attention to Dixon—who was wedged between us, scratching furiously at the backs of his hands. "Whoo—wasn't that something?" Fonzo cried. "Were my eyes dazzled back there, kiddo, or did I actually see you Scribe?"

"It wasn't the balloon-glitter. It was me."

"No thanks to you," I muttered. In English.

"I knew you had it in you," Fonzo said. "Tell me all about it. Who decided to do another Quilling? Whose pen did you use? It wasn't Johnny's turkey feather, was it? Your old man'll never live that one down."

"There was no Quilling Ceremony. Turns out I'm such a sparkly Spellcrafter, a bird went out of its way to Quill me on its own." Dixon pulled a Crafting from his pocket. I'd just painted the thing, so the *volshebstvo* still resonated, but it was weak now, mostly spent. He tore it up and released it through the passenger window before the magic could sour. It doesn't pay to be greedy where Spellcraft is concerned.

Fonzo itched at his neck. "Kinda makes you wonder, doesn't it? How many Spellcrafters throughout history had a feather dropped on their heads before one of them picked it up and Crafted with it?"

Probably a few. The real game-changer was the first one who'd penned his magic on a Seen. I had no desire to hold a philosophical discussion with Dixon's uncle, though, so while they enthused about Dixon's newfound Scribing ability, I held my tongue and simply drove.

My objective was to put as many miles as I could, as fast as I could, between us and the carnival. I didn't think Fun would get the law involved, but you never know. And even though we weren't carrying any Spellcraft, I wouldn't trust a superstitious policeman to not "accidentally" snap Dixon's delicate cockatoo quill in half. I focused on the road. But the road was not enough to distract me from the light banter shared by nephew and uncle.

Fonzo spun tales about how many people he'd "helped." Dixon regaled him with the story of the demise of Precious Greetings. They filled the cab with enthusiastic chatter...but neither of them voiced what was really going on. When, finally, we decided we'd taken enough turns to throw an angry carnival owner off our trail—and when their itching became too great—we found a 24-hour gym, where Fonzo talked the sleepy attendant into letting us "try out" the facilities. While Dixon and Fonzo hit the showers to scrub away the itching powder, I soothed myself with bench-presses.

Even that did little to curb my annoyance.

The Penns emerged from the locker room, pink-cheeked and steamy, in matching Big Fun T-shirts. "...and so I told Mom, 'Maybe the Oreo cake didn't rise, but how many people can say they've met a paramedic *and* a fireman on the *same day*?' Oh, hey Yuri." Dixon came over to where I stood, looked me up and down, then melted up against me. He slung his arms over my shoulders, pulled my forehead to his, and whispered playfully, "The veins in your neck are all bulge-y! You know what that does to me."

My impulse was to shrug him off. Because he was shamelessly flirting with me in public? Or because he did it in front of his uncle? It wasn't easy, but I stayed right where I was and let Dixon have his flirty moment. And I made myself enjoy the fact that Fonzo couldn't help but see it.

The hot shower must have been soothing, because as soon as we hit the road again, the two of them nodded off. It was disturbing, to say the least. They were more like one another than I was my own parents, from the pattern of their facial hair to the way they both smirked ever so slightly in their sleep.

They even breathed in tandem.

There was no question of Dixon's paternity. His father had proudly regaled me with the story of the month-long honeymoon in Schenectady that resulted in a bouncing baby boy nine months later. So, it wasn't the physical resemblance that bothered me, but how easy it would be for Dixon to someday disappear, as Fonzo had done to Sabina, and leave me with nothing but an occasional jaunty postcard.

I drove until sunup, then pulled into a roadside diner to quell my hunger pangs and spur myself onto the last leg of the journey with an infusion of caffeine.

We ordered our food and the inane chatter resumed. I sipped my coffee, fuming. The food came. Both of them hacked up their pancakes in the same haphazard way. Each shoved a forkful of syrup-soaked flapjack into his mouth at the very same time. It was all too much. When they were both chewing—to the same rhythm—I heard myself say, "Why don't we talk about what's really going on?"

Even the bewildered, chipmunk-cheeked looks of confusion were identical. "Wrr?" Dixon said through a mouthful of breakfast.

I looked Fonzo in the eye and said, "What was the real reason you didn't just walk away from Reverend Fun?"

He swallowed once, twice, then gave me a grin that I would have found perfectly charming...on his nephew. "Come on, now, everyone knows it's lousy luck to let someone bilk you out of what's rightfully yours. Fun owed me big—we had an agreement. And now, thanks to you boys, everything's copacetic."

"Very logical. Too bad you are lying."

Dixon nearly choked on his milkshake. Fonzo was the picture of affronted innocence. The Penns don't handle directness very well. That's what makes it such a good weapon.

I said, "Money is everywhere. What Spellcrafters value more than any amount of cash is their freedom. Yet you attached yourself to the carnival without even knowing that Dixon could Craft you out of your predicament. What have you conveniently neglected to tell us?"

Fonzo heaved a sigh of resignation. "You got me there. I would have loved nothing more than to ditch that old miser, Fun. Unfortunately, money wasn't the only thing I was short on, but time. The clock's ticking." He patted the stuffed walrus. "And if I don't get this wad of cash back to Pinyin Bay by midnight, I can never show my face there again."

"Sure you can," Dixon exclaimed. He pitched his voice to an urgent whisper and added, "No one knows you leaked our secrets to the Handless...no one but us. Emery Flint is under house arrest for tax evasion. And with all that money, you can pay off the second mortgage, we'll send our nasty tenant packing, and everything can go back to the way it was before!"

A fine fantasy. Too bad there was more to the story than a debt. "But it's not that simple," I said. "Isn't that right?"

"Everything's under control. Just as soon as I get this curse lifted—"

At the mention of the word "curse," the *volshebstvo* tingled across my scalp.

"A curse?" Dixon squeaked, then looked around to make sure the truckers in the corner weren't listening in. He hunched into the table and hissed, "Uncle Fonzo!"

"Listen, boys, it sounds wa-a-ay worse than it is. All I need to do is make the final installment on my payment plan and I'm in the clear. And anyway, as curses go, it's not even that big a deal. In fact, I've found a good stopgap solution, so it's honestly nothing to get all worked up about. "

The trail of strange Craftings we'd been following was beginning to make a lot more sense. "Let me guess," I said. "Your solution is to Craft only a single word."

"Brawn *and* brains!" Fonzo exclaimed to Dixon. "Not to mention the fact that he's a Seer. No wonder you picked him. Yep, it's true—for the time being, I'm operating under some pretty harsh restrictions. I can only Craft with new words I've never Scribed before, otherwise a piece of the nib crumbles off." In all Fonzo's years of Scribing, I'd imagine the total vocabulary added up to a good number of words. "Even so, I've managed to help small business owners far and wide be more profitable than ever before... thanks to this handy thesaurus." With a wag of his heavy eyebrows, he flashed us the cover of a tattered book from the inner pocket of his coat. "Pretty darn clever, if I do say so myself!"

We regarded the book. Then, with a wince, Dixon drew something from his own coat pocket and slid it onto the table: a piece of Spellcraft that bore a single, ragged word.

Remunerate.

Fonzo's eyes went wide, and at first I thought he was horrified by the sight of what he'd wrought. But then he broke into a wide

smile of delight. "And you took back the Crafting! What a grati-
fying turn of fortune! Reverend Fun weaseled out of his end of
the bargain—he didn't deserve to keep on reaping the benefit of
my magic."

I have learned to only trust a dictionary as a starting point.
English is a tricky language, and the same word can have shades
of meaning in direct opposition to one another. And that's not
even taking into account the possibility of saying something in a
sarcastic tone. I pulled up the word *remuneration* on my dictionary
app and read, "Requital for a loss."

Fonzo blinked. "Pretty sure it's the same thing as *payment.*"

"To remunerate is to make up for," I read. "To compensate."

"Like I said, guys. Payment. Commerce. Tit for tat. The exchange
of goods and services makes the world go 'round—that's why so
many different words for it exist, and they're all saying the same
exact thing."

Truly spoken like one who has never had to master a foreign
tongue and wade through all the various shades of meaning. Not
only did the word have the potential to signify something damaged
that needed to be paid for, but thanks to the lack of a full sentence
to support the intended meaning, it could have applied to anyone.

It was we who were in possession of that particular piece of
Spellcraft. Were we the ones to be remunerated? Or would we now
do the remunerating?

One thing was for certain...no doubt we'd find plenty of damage
to rectify.

We finished our food, and I went outside to warm up the truck
while Dixon and his uncle used the facilities. I was joined shortly
by Dixon, who climbed in, fastened his seatbelt, and gave me an
expectant look like he was ready to hit the road. "Shouldn't I wait
for your uncle?" I asked.

Dixon smacked himself in the forehead. "Wow. I must've slept
funny. Totally slipped my mind. Good thing you said something—
that would've been awkward!"

He unbuckled himself and shifted toward the center of the seat while Fonzo strolled out to the passenger door and heaved himself in. As I put the truck in gear, I double-checked Dixon from the corner of my eye for any telltale signs of wayward Spellcraft at work. But there was nothing magical to be found...just the cheerful enigma that was Dixon.

DIXON

6

On one hand, it was a relief to find out there was a logical reason behind Uncle Fonzo's weird string of Craftings. But on the other...a curse?

Shudder.

Obviously, I wanted to know every last detail about this curse, but my uncle dozed off the second we hit the road. He's always claimed he was capable of falling asleep standing up, and that might not have been an exaggeration.

Yuri was understandably concerned about the whole *curse* business. I could tell by the way the steering wheel creaked beneath his leather gloves. "Look at it this way," I told him. "We found my uncle. We've got enough money to lift whatever curse might be on him. And that Reverend Fun guy really didn't deserve to keep the profit he'd tried to bilk from Uncle Fonzo, so it's all fair and square."

With a grunt, Yuri spun the wheel and careened off onto a side road, where he pulled over amid a sorry little stand of trees. "Then the Crafting has done its job, and we get rid of it. Here. Now."

"But what if it brings us additional remuneration?" I asked. "After all, Reverend Fun kind of owes me for that itching powder discomfort." Yuri gave me a Very Stern Look. I sighed. "Okay, fine. If you insist, we'll ditch the Spellcraft."

Uncle Fonzo had clearly been through some stuff, so we left him snoring in the truck...though when Yuri pocketed the keys, I knew better than to suggest leaving them behind in case my uncle woke up and wanted to listen to the radio. With the crowbar in hand, we headed off into the trees.

I know Yuri doesn't mean for it look like a seductive striptease when he takes off his jacket—it's just the slow deliberation of someone who's packed in tightly and doesn't want to convert the outfit to tear-away sleeves. Still...it never gets old. He stripped down to his clingy undershirt, handed me his shirt and jacket for safekeeping, and then began hacking at the hard earth. His labor was a symphony of muscle. Bulging biceps. Pulsing pecs. All of it adorned with Russian tattoos and glistening with the faintest sheen of sweat.

Once the hole was finished, Yuri dropped the crowbar, looked at me, and snapped, "Stop fanning yourself with the cursed Crafting!"

Whoops. I handed over the paper. Yuri dropped it in the hole, kicked the rocky pile of dirt on top, and gave it a few solid stomps. Then he shoved a huge fallen log over it for good measure.

He pulled out a handkerchief and mopped his perspiring face, then gestured for his shirt. Instead of handing it over, I held it up for him with an inviting shake. Yuri isn't used to anyone doing nice things for him...but he's getting better at letting me try. He slid one arm into its sleeve, then the other—and he didn't even remark that it would've been quicker for him to simply put it on himself. I swung around the front and nudged his hands away before he could button it up himself. I worked my way up, brushing my knuckles against every defined swell of his musculature. Eventually, I came to the point on his formidable neck where even the most valiant of buttons wouldn't manage to stay unpopped for long. I smoothed the fabric over his broad shoulders...then I took his collar in both hands and pulled him in for a kiss.

His lips held the tantalizing whisper of salt. I slicked it away with my tongue. He sighed against my mouth—part resignation, part desire. Tongue played against tongue. Our kisses grew more fervent, until finally I had to come up for air with a gasp. Yuri's brows were still drawn together in a fierce scowl, but we'd spent enough time together that I knew the difference between his angry scowls and his thoughtful ones. (Plus, I think there may be some truth to the old saw, "Stop making that face or it'll freeze that way.")

"It's okay if you're angry," he told me.

Clearly, he was projecting. I caressed his scruffy jaw and said, "Everything's fine." Having Uncle Fonzo along changed the dynamic more than I thought it might, but I was confident everything would eventually work out. I cupped his damp face in my hands and said, "And it makes no sense for you to be jealous of my family."

"I'm not—" he began to protest.

"Shh." I pressed the fingertip of my Scribing hand to his lips, and the Spellcraft tingled between us. "There's no reason for you to feel threatened. You're family now, too."

People think Spellcrafters play fast and loose with the definition of "family," but that's only when we're claiming exemptions on our income taxes or trying to get into a restricted VIP area. Otherwise, it's more of an elite club where only the most desirable of candidates makes the cut. Yuri's a perceptive guy, and despite the fact that we'd grown up on entirely different continents, hundreds... thousands of miles—hundreds of thousands?—I should probably look at a map one of these days. Anyway, however far apart it might have been, Yuri fit in with the Penns like he was born into the clan.

Though, thankfully, he wasn't. With all the naked hijinks the two of us got up to, that would've been creepy.

With the unfortunate Spellcraft good and buried, we piled back into the truck and set a course for Pinyin Bay. Eventually, I nodded off again, though thankfully I managed not to drool on anyone. Sometimes I'm not sure exactly when Yuri sleeps. A micro-nap on the side of the road? Or the capacity to sleep one brain hemisphere at a time, like a shark who can't stop swimming? Either way, when I woke, it was nighttime again and we were practically home.

My jostling woke up Uncle Fonzo, who snorfled awake, took a bleary look at the highway signs, and said, "Up there—hang a right and go around Pinyin Bay to the opposite side of the water."

"But our exit is the next one up," I said. "This one would take us to Strangeberg."

"And not a minute too soon. My payment's due at midnight. And the Stranges have one heck of a long driveway."

"The *Strange* family cursed you?" That couldn't be. The Stranges and the Penns were all in the same Spellcraft circuit. We were invited to all the same quilling ceremonies. On a clear night, we could see their patio lights across the bay. Heck, I'd even gone to summer camp with the Strange twins. It seemed impossible that they would have cursed someone—especially one of our own.

Especially Uncle Fonzo.

Everyone loves Uncle Fonzo.

"There must be some mistake," I said. "The Penns go way back with the Stranges. I'm sure this is all just a big misunderstanding."

"Dixon—" my uncle said.

"I'll even talk to them for you. They're important so-and-sos these days, but I'll bet Violet Strange will see me."

"Dixon, hold on."

"We actually dated for a week—nothing to be jealous about, Yuri, we were only twelve, and I was more curious than enamored. Sure, we did make out that one time, but there was hardly any tongue involved. Once I tell her Uncle Fonzo's side of the story—"

"Dixon!" my uncle snapped, and I lost track of the point I'd been about to make. "There is no misunderstanding. I'm cursed—and it was the Stranges who cursed me."

"I don't get it," I admitted. "What reason would they possibly have to curse you?"

My uncle let out a gusty sigh. "Before you jump to any conclusions, keep in mind that if everything had gone to plan, this whole rigmarole would be entirely unnecessary. Emery Flint pulled me into a poker game I never had any chance of winning."

"But you've got such a good poker face!"

"Didn't matter—the game was rigged, in more ways than one. A marked deck, and a line of Spellcraft inked on one of his cards. Normally, I have enough sense to walk away when Lady Luck is giving me the cold shoulder. But not that night. The more I lost, the more I bet."

Magic draws Magic. Disturbing how versatile that three-word bit of Spellcraft had been.

Uncle Fonzo went on. "Pretty soon, the only thing of value I had left was my quill. If I'd been in my right mind, I never would have upped the ante. But I wasn't thinking straight—I actually thought it was *lucky* that he'd let me throw it in the pot at all, since the Handless think our quills are just any old feather. I didn't realize he knew all about Spellcraft, and that my quill had been his target all along."

I gave my uncle's hand an encouraging squeeze. He looked weary. And when he went on, his tone was uncharacteristically serious. "Losing my quill was bad enough. Once he had that, the blackmail began. Flint forced me to supply him with Seens. He was convinced it was possible to *teach* him to Craft. The Handless always think we're hiding something." Probably because we usually are. "And he spent every spare moment forcing lessons out of me. It was only when one of our lessons blew up hard enough to knock him out that I was able to shake the hold he had on me and get away. But he'd had my quill on him at the time, and somehow it ended up in the hospital with him. I tried to charm it out of the nurses on staff—I just about had one of 'em convinced to give me his personal belongings—when Flint woke up. All I could do was get out of there before he saw me and sucked me back under his thrall."

I'd felt the compulsion of Mr. Flint's Spellcraft, but lucky for me he'd never seen me as a real Spellcrafter and given me any direct orders. Even Yuri had been unable to resist his commands—and Yuri's strong enough to open the pickled egg jar at Bar None...and dauntless enough to eat one.

"But you found another quill eventually," I said. "Did you run across a helpful bird, like I did?"

"Unfortunately, no." Uncle Fonzo turned to face the passenger door. It was dark in the little subdivision of Strangeberg, where streetlights are few and far between. The light of the persistent Check Oil warning lamp illuminated his reflection in the window... where he looked even more weary than before. "But the quill's prior owner didn't need it anymore."

I said, "I've heard of Spellcrafters swearing off Crafting, but I always figured they were just trying to sell autobiographies."

"Not exactly..." my uncle sighed.

Before he could find more words to explain, Yuri said, "Whoever this Crafter was, they didn't need it because they were dead. He is Crafting with a dead man's quill."

I laughed. Yuri's sense of humor can be pretty peculiar...but my laughter died abruptly when neither of them joined in. Scandalized (and, believe me, it takes a lot to scandalize me) I gasped, "Uncle Fonzo!"

"It's not like he was using it!" my uncle declared. "Desperate times call for desperate measures."

"But...*grave robbing*?"

"Mausoleum robbing, if we're being technical. That's why I picked the Stranges—they've got that big ol' marble monstrosity out back where they keep their stiffs...er, their dearly departed family members."

Yuri said, "More efficient than digging around in a cemetery."

"Exactly! And far less likely to get caught. I would've returned it once I got my own quill back and no one would be any the wiser, if not for the curse." Uncle Fonzo shook his head ruefully. "Who *curses* things anymore in this day and age?"

Apparently, the Strange family did.

While there was nothing particularly *strange* about the tidy subdivision of Strangeberg—other than the name, and the fact that their recyclables were on a bi-weekly pickup schedule—the manor at the top of the hill that overlooked the place was another story. The sprawling building had been a mental asylum back when the

Model T was all the rage and women weren't allowed to vote. Later, in the Reagan era, the residents were turned onto the street and the asylum became a boarding house for the awkward single men involved in the fledgling computer programming industry...one that eventually relocated to the West Coast, which let the Strange family acquire the place for pennies on the dollar.

A cunning bit of Spellcraft was probably involved, too, though none of us other practitioners would have dreamed of remarking about it to the Handless.

Strange Manor, as it was re-christened, not only featured a hedge maze, an exercise yard, and a shallow pond full of bloated, slow-moving goldfish...but an honest-to-goodness cemetery out back. The graveyard housed several generations of residents unfortunate enough to die in the old asylum's dubious care—and it contained a mausoleum in which the Stranges' late family members now rested as well.

One of whom was now missing a quill.

It was a bright, waxing moon that night, nearly full, and it illuminated Strange Manor in all its semi-dilapidated, asylum-esque glory. The cobblestone drive was doing a number on the truck's suspension, and the three of us bounced along in the cab, too jostled to attempt to speak. And even if we could, what was there to say? Uncle Fonzo was in a real pickle, but thankfully, once we paid the final installment, all of that would be water under the bridge. Or maybe more like sour green juice swirling down the drain, if one were to extend the pickle metaphor. Or maybe—

Yuri's hand fell on my knee and I snapped into the present.

"We will handle this," he said firmly.

Some people have boyfriends who buy them cute trinkets or laugh at their jokes. Some people have men who serenade them badly, though it's mostly off-key on purpose. Some people receive near-constant declarations of undying love. But at that particular moment, I wouldn't have traded Yuri for any other man in the world.

We approached the front door with some trepidation, but Yuri gave me enough strength to pass along to my uncle. "You can do it, Uncle Fonzo. I have faith in you."

"Right." He squared his shoulders and pressed the doorbell. "And we made it with plenty of time to spare."

He plastered on his winningest smile as, with an ominous creak, the door swung open.

7

〜

Violet Strange and her twin sister Pansy were identical, right down to the tiny, pale scar each girl bore high on her left cheekbone. Back when we were kids, I'm not sure if their parents purposely dressed them alike. Since everyone wore an Ink-a-Dink Calligraphy Camp T-shirt the summer we met, the wardrobe was no help in telling them apart.

If you observed the two of them for any length of time, though, it couldn't have been more obvious who was who.

While Violet drifted unobtrusively to the back row and never raised her hand, Pansy volunteered to clean the dry-erase board after lessons and made herself the teacher's pet. While Violet spent her free time down by the pond trying to coax frogs out of the water, Pansy nearly fainted at the sight of a tadpole. And when Violet announced, quietly and firmly, that I should be her boyfriend (because my penmanship was, by and far, the most ornate) no one scoffed louder than Pansy.

That was a long time ago, and neither one of us was still a pre-pubescent Scribbler. But despite the fact that we'd both developed secondary sex characteristics, we still looked enough like our younger selves. Violet's mannerisms were the same—the way she brushed her thumb over the pads of her fingers as if to double-check that they were still safe and sound. The way she took a half-step back to get a broader view of the situation. The delicate furrow in her brow.

But the way the iris of one of her mahogany brown eyes was now a startling purple? *That* was new.

"Dixon," she said blandly. "I hadn't realized you'd be here."

If my uncle hadn't run afoul of Reverend Fun and needed to call in for reinforcements, no doubt I wouldn't be. Lucky thing he'd needed my help. "Great to see you," I said. "In person, I mean. I sent you a friendvitation on Friendlike a few years back—maybe you're not much for social media."

I'd seen recent pictures of Violet—the ones that weren't set to friends-only, anyhow—so it wasn't really a shock to see her all grown up. Aside from that odd eye, anyhow. It was like the brown-eyed guy in Brussels I'd dated who wore colored contacts. I'd thought his eyes were pale blue until one contact fell out after a vigorous shag and he popped up out of the sheets looking like a disconcertingly preppie Marilyn Manson.

Violet must've been pretty good at Photoshop these days. Either that or the purple eye was a fairly recent occurrence.

As I congratulated myself for being tactful enough not to mention it, she stepped aside. "Come in," she said, stilted and formal. "We've been expecting you. Well, your uncle, anyhow. But leave the hired muscle outside."

"Yuri's not my bodyguard." I waggled my eyebrows. "And I get all the muscle I can handle for free!"

Violet looked puzzled—until she realized what I'd meant, and an adorable blush colored her pale cheeks. I hadn't dated many women, back while I was still figuring myself out, but the ones I eventually came out to were never particularly surprised. Violet didn't seem too shocked, once she figured out the score. She simply stole another glance at Yuri, then gave a quick nod and said, "Right this way."

Strange Manor had been redecorated since its days as an asylum, but here and there you'd glimpse something—like the sturdy hardware on every door—that served as a pervasive reminder of the building's origins. Violet led us into a dining room that would've been cramped for a few dozen convalescing patients, but was outrageously large for a family of three. Even the twelve-seated dining table was dwarfed in the cavernous space. Massive family portraits were hung throughout the room in an attempt to break up the vast expanses of wall. I couldn't tell Violet's portrait from Pansy's, since the subject of each painting had two brown eyes.

As I tried to deduce which twin portrait was which, a towering grandfather clock at the far end of the hall let out a startling *clong*, followed by ten more. "I hate that thing," Violet said. And then, "Have you eaten?"

At eleven o'clock at night? It was awfully late for dinner, but Uncle Fonzo and I had slept right through mealtime while Yuri drove. And even if we hadn't, it's not like me to turn down free grub. The table was set for four—the Strange Family and Uncle Fonzo—so, Violet grabbed a couple of plates from the sideboard for Yuri and me before she buzzed an intercom and announced, "We've got company."

The Strange twins' mother hadn't aged quite as gracefully as her children. Dahlia Strange was the Hand of the family. While I found her tall and stately when I was young, now she just seemed a little too thin, and as brittle as her smile.

Violet's twin, Pansy, was still her sister's spitting image—or vice versa (though, thankfully, neither of them actually spat.) Both her eyes were brown, and even if the twins didn't quite match anymore, I'd still be able to tell the two of them apart. Pansy didn't simply walk into a room—she sashayed. And when her brown eyes fell on me, a smile crept across her face that was equal parts pleased...and predatory. "Well, who have we here? If it isn't Little Dix."

"People don't call me that."

"I haven't seen you in ages."

"Really. They don't."

"How long has it been, fifteen years? No, even more than that."

"And if they did, it would be ironically."

Pansy tittered. "It's only a name. You always were such a *sensitive* boy." We took our places at the table. She sat directly across from me. "Such a shame to hear about your Quilling Ceremony."

My knee-jerk impulse was to inform her in no uncertain terms that the botched ceremony'd had zero to do with my Spellcrafting ability—but under the table, Yuri kicked the side of one foot just as Uncle Fonzo kicked the other. I couldn't rise to my own defense without letting on that my uncle had been duped by the Handless. So, I did the next best thing and tried to change the subject.

"Oh, you know what they say about ceremonies—they make a serum out of moan and knee. Not that knees moan, but people take a lot of creative license where idioms are concerned. Anyway, there's more to life than Spellcrafting. Scuba diving, for instance."

"Scuba diving," Pansy repeated blandly.

"Sure. I'm told I look absolutely fetching in a wetsuit." Which was a bald-faced lie, since the closest I usually got to the water was checking out guys on the beach. But before I could dig my hole any deeper, Violet appeared, pushing a rolling cart full of covered platters—just like you see in the movies, where dinner is served by butlers in tuxedos and white gloves. I'd been ruing my decision to accompany my uncle to Strange Manor, what with the whole "Little Dix" thing, but maybe my discomfort would turn out to be worth it after all.

The family's Hand, Dahlia, indicated the rolling cart with a gesture that was meant to be gracious, but mostly came off as stilted. She flashed her brittle smile. "I'd been hoping you'd come to settle your business in person tonight," she told my uncle. "In fact, I've spent all day slaving in the kitchen to make you my signature dish."

Oh boy—what would it be? Mac and cheese with chopped baloney? Baloney roll-ups? Baked bean surprise? (The surprise was baloney.) Actually, though, it smelled more like fish. Maybe it was tuna casserole. I could go for a nice tuna casserole with frozen peas, cream of mushroom soup, and big, squishy egg noodles. Hopefully Dahlia knew enough to top it off with crushed potato chips, preferably ranch-flavored....

The twins set a covered plate in front of everyone. It was Violet who served Yuri and me. I tried to catch her eye—either one—to nod my thanks, but she didn't meet my gaze. Maybe she was put out because using the good china meant more domes to wash later. I was practically bubbling over with anticipation waiting for the countdown reveal, but the Strange family apparently had no sense of drama. When Dahlia lifted her dome, everyone else just followed suit.

I'd been so sure there'd be a nice big scoop of tuna casserole under mine, I hardly knew what to make of the grayish-whitish lump on my plate.

Dahlia bared her teeth in the semblance of a smile. "Pinyin eel," she announced. "Quite the delicacy."

Was this some kind of joke? Eels weren't food—they were over-blown sea-worms.

Pansy shaved a sliver of eel off her lump with the precision of a surgeon. "Maybe you've seen them in the bay," she said. "Scuba diving."

I gave a noncommittal head-bobble, since I was too busy trying to keep from throwing up in my mouth to actually answer.

Her mother said, "Most people think Pinyin Bay is just a moder-ately-priced resort area. A harmless diversion. A lark. But there are depths to the bay that are completely underestimated by outsiders."

I was fairly sure we were no longer talking about tourism. What the actual subtext might be, though, I had no idea. I was far too distracted by the lima beans on my plate.

Lima beans.

I just...couldn't.

"Try the dandelion greens," Pansy suggested. "I made them myself."

Surely this was some kind of farce, and the Stranges were in possession of a truly *strange* sense of humor. Any minute now, they'd haul out a tuna casserole while we all shared a good laugh. Except that everyone at the table was actually tucking in. Especially Yuri—in fact, I'd never seen him attack a plate with such gusto. Either he didn't know what *eel* meant in English, or he hadn't actually stopped anywhere for dinner on the way home.

"Or don't try the greens," Violet said. "And go hungry."

I forced down a few mouthfuls. Maybe if they'd told me it was spinach, I would have managed more than that—because my mom's bread-bowl spinach dip was a mainstay of our annual Cyber Monday feast, and I always consumed so much of the green stuff, it was a wonder I didn't turn into Popeye. But as it was, I could only choke down enough of the greens to keep my stomach from announcing my ravenous hunger to everyone at the dinner table with a loud, empty gurgle.

My uncle was making good progress on his plate. But my uncle also had a stunted sense of taste, thanks to an irate customer, years ago, who'd broken his nose with a stiff whack of her purse. Uncle Fonzo always claimed he was glad all the damage was on the inside, so as not to detract from his dashing good looks. But now I suspected that having a compromised nose came with other, less obvious benefits—such as being able to swallow lima beans.

And eel.

Yuri cleaned his entire plate, right down to the very last bite, then looked at my mostly-untouched food and said, "Are you going to eat that?"

I shook my head queasily, attempting to convey that he didn't have to fall on the sword on my account. Yuri must've taken it as a plea for help, because he immediately picked up my plate and shoveled the yucky excuse for food onto his, then proceeded to wolf it all down.

As Yuri chased a final lima bean around his dish, my uncle plucked the cloth napkin off his lap, dabbed his mouth with the corner, and declared, "It's very civil of you all to treat us to a meal, all things considered. I wish we'd broken bread under less trying circumstances. I'd like you to know that I had the utmost respect for Hawthorn Strange."

"You knew grandpa?" Violet asked.

"Indeed, I did. A truly stand-up guy—even if he had the penman-ship of a doctor and his flourishes were atrocious. As the Hand of the family, he always did the Stranges proud. He was the first to bring a bottle of top-shelf whiskey to a card game, and the last to whine about it when the booze ran out. I was proud to call him a friend. And I had every intention of returning his quill, just as soon as I was done with it."

Dahlia arched a penciled eyebrow. "I hope this song and dance isn't just some attempt to get us to lower the bounty."

"Of course not." Uncle Fonzo hefted the lumpy walrus that hadn't left his side and gave it a pat. "Just hoping that once this is all squared away, we can let bygones be bygones, preserve our families' alliance, and put the whole affair to rest once and for all." He stole a look at the grandfather clock that had been overseeing dinner from the foot of the table like a judgmentally dyspeptic relative. Twelve *clongs* would ensue shortly, and my uncle wanted to make sure he fulfilled his contract to the letter of the law.

We Spellcrafters are well aware precisely how much power words can hold.

"It's all there." Uncle Fonzo thrust his hand into a seam in the animal's belly and came up with a neat bundle of twenties. He rif-fled it meaningfully, basking in the sweet smell of currency, then quickly dealt out twenty-five bundles from the dwindling walrus and shoved them across the table toward Dahlia. There were even a few bundles left over—but not many. "I'll entreat you to lay a hand on the payment," he told her. "Before the clock strikes midnight."

"Oh, there's no need for that." It seemed as if Dahlia was about to tease Fonzo for being such a stickler for the rules...until I realized there was something malignant lurking in her smile. "Midnight has come and gone."

We all did a double take at the clock, which hadn't yet begun *clonging*.

"Don't trust that old thing," Dahlia purred. "It's deplorably slow.

One day it will stop running altogether. At least then it will be right twice a day."

At my side, Yuri went rigid while Uncle Fonzo threw down the deflated walrus. "This isn't fair!"

"Come now," Dahlia said. "You can hardly take the moral high ground when you robbed my father's grave. Your installment is overdue. Now you owe interest."

"This wasn't what we agreed."

"Perhaps not—but Strange curse, Strange rules."

Uncle Fonzo squeezed the few bundles of currency that remained. He wanted to keep them—but it was more important to have the curse lifted. He slid the walrus puddle across the table. "Fine."

Dahlia peered in and gave the remaining bundles a quick scan. "That will do...for tonight."

"What? That's an outrage. What we have here would easily cover 8% interest."

"Do I look like Pinyin Savings and Loan? My rate isn't 8%, it's a hundred—so I'd recommend you come up with the rest before your final installment doubles again tomorrow at midnight."

The initial impression I had of the Strange family having no sense of drama?

Untrue.

There was more than enough drama here to last us all a lifetime.

YURI

We retreated to the truck. Fonzo muttered angrily, while Dixon was uncharacteristically silent.

"I should've known the Stranges would pull something like this," Fonzo declared. "Dahlia always was a nasty piece of work."

It was tempting to mention that she'd have nothing to hold over his head if he hadn't stolen her dead father's quill, but the Strange woman reminded me so much of my old mentor in St. Petersburg that my sympathies were, surprisingly enough, with Fonzo.

"Lottery tickets," Fonzo decided. "Between the business loans outstanding on Practical Penn and the second mortgage on my house, it's the only way. But not a single big win—that would take too much time to pay out, more time than we have. A bunch of scattered winning scratch-offs throughout the city, though, a few hundred bucks at a crack...."

Dixon shook his head wearily. "Don't rig the lottery, they'll throw the book at you—that's Spellcraft 101."

Only if you get caught. I met Fonzo's eyes. He was thinking the same thing. But before he could try to coerce Dixon and me into Crafting him a small windfall, I said, "I have dealt with plenty of people like the Hand of the Strange family. Even if we came up with the money, she would simply keep raising the bar. The only way to get out from their blackmail is to ensure they have nothing to hold over your head."

Dixon swallowed nervously. "What are you saying?"

"We must steal curse."

Before Dixon could protest that it was too dangerous, Fonzo agreed. "He's right. It's the only way."

"Is it?" Dixon looked to each of us earnestly, one, then the other. "Because usually, when a situation is all screwed up, the more you try to finagle your way through the minefield, the deeper of a pit you dig for yourself. Uh...that metaphor doesn't really hold up, but you get the gist. We steal the curse, and maybe that activates another curse, and suddenly it's an infinite loop of itching powder balloons all the way down. But what if you just set aside the dead man's quill, walk away and get a fresh start?"

Although Dixon was raised in the Craft, somehow he'd also managed to pick up an unhealthy sense of trust. In himself. In others. In the notion that good luck existed and the world was somehow fair, and that pluck and perseverance would ultimately be rewarded. And who had filled his head with such ridiculous ideas? His family. And even though Fonzo Penn was as slippery as an eel and twice as tough, I suspected he, too, carried within him that insidious seed of hope—so, I was surprised when he merely sighed and shook his head.

"Dixon, there is no starting over for me." He tugged at the index finger of the glove on his right hand. "Not until the curse is lifted."

It was late, and it was dark. But even by the moonlight that filtered through a canopy of trees, the true measure of the Strange curse was revealed when Fonzo exposed his Scribing hand.

And what I saw? Something that would surely haunt my dreams for the rest of my days.

At first, I thought he was merely holding the cursed quill inside his glove for safe-keeping. He'd lost one magic quill already, after all, and he couldn't be eager to lose another. But then I saw the black quill was not merely flattened against Fonzo's hand...but instead, it had merged with his very flesh.

The feather covered him from the tip of his forefinger, across the entire length of his palm, and beyond—several centimeters past his wrist, up into his forearm. It looked like a stark, ugly tattoo. But unlike body art, this cursed black feather was in motion, writhing beneath the man's skin like a parasite. The mere sight of it made my vision tunnel...and then a smell arose from the cursed quill. The stench of death. I felt so light-headed, I might have even blacked out, if not for Dixon's fingers digging into my knee hard enough to bruise. A high-pitched whine escaped his throat: the only sound I could hear over the panicked pounding of my own heart.

"Yeah..." Fonzo nodded ruefully. "It ain't pretty."

Pretty? If that *thing* were on me, I'd be sorely tempted to saw off my own arm. I had no great love of Fonzo Penn, and would like nothing more than to leave him to his own devices. But even I was not cold-hearted enough to walk away now.

"So," he said, "now you boys know what we're up against. Come hell or high water, I have to break the curse."

Indeed he did—and failure was not an option.

I turned the key, gunned the engine and peeled away. The cobblestone drive felt twice as jarring coming back down—then again, we were probably going twice as fast. So fast that I had to slam on the brakes when a figure stepped into the driveway and motioned for me to stop. The truck skidded on its balding tires and arced in a perfect circle, coming to rest an arm's length away from one of the twins.

"Violet," Dixon gasped. Given their history, I shouldn't have been surprised that he could tell one from another just by glancing at them—but I *was* impressed. I needed to watch them interact to know one from another. Pansy was the one who took pleasure in goading Dixon, and Violet was harboring an old grudge. We piled out of the truck and approached her.

The moonlight painted Violet in cool tones of indigo and slate, and lit her single violet iris an unnatural shade of purple. Her expression was cold and stern. She planted her hands on her hips and said, "Don't bother trying to steal the curse. Dahlia has been up to something in the crypt and she's been really secretive about the whole thing. I'm sure it's a trap, and if you break in, you'll be walking right into it."

"You call your mother by her first name?" Dixon asked.

Violet acknowledged the question only with a roll of her eyes, then said to Fonzo, "When you stole the quill, you left grubby footprints all over my Great Uncle Rowan's sarcophagus. Don't think she'll let you get away with the same thing twice."

He scratched his chin. "So you're saying, bring a step-stool next time?"

"What I'm saying is, you need to back off and wait for a better opening."

"Is this some kind of reverse psychology?" Dixon asked.

"Not at all. I adored my grandfather, and frankly, I think your uncle got what he deserved. At least...I did." She turned to Fonzo. "But those things you said about Grandpa...they really rang true. And if the two of you were as close as you say, I don't think he would have signed off on all this. He'd take your money, sure—we all know you don't get something for nothing—but he wouldn't ruin you. If you keep messing with Dahlia, though, that's exactly what will happen. Give it some time. Let me work on my mother. And whatever you do, stay away from the mausoleum. It's just not worth the risk."

Dixon and I climbed into the truck. Dixon slammed his door, leaving Fonzo outside. It was tempting to play innocent and pull away without the man, but I did him the favor of waiting until he'd rapped on the window and been let in. We drove to my cabin in silence. As we pulled up alongside it, Fonzo said, "I'm sure Violet means well, but she wasn't on the receiving end of that little love note. Besides, it's not like my curse can get any cursier."

I didn't care for his logic. Things can *always* get worse. But exhaustion had finally sunk its claws into me. My traitorous body would no longer allow me to remain conscious, and I was out before my head hit the pillow.

DIXON

9

Normally, I can sleep through pretty much anything—but I'd dozed off and on all the way from Spring Falls to Pinyin Bay, and in the still of the night, I woke to my phone chiming with an incoming Friendlike alert. I reached across Yuri's broad chest and grabbed it off the built-in nightstand.

Violet Strange has accepted your friendvitation.

Huh! I must've made a pretty good impression forcing down those dandelion greens. I gave the action a thumbs-up. The number 2 appeared beside the thumb icon as Violet did the same.

And here I thought she'd been kinda chilly at dinner, and unduly ominous when she met us by the crypt. She probably just needed time to process me coming out to her. Of course, if she'd accepted my friendvitation years ago, my gayness wouldn't have been any big revelation. But better late than never.

If Friendlike had existed back when I was in high school, it's possible Violet would've been one of the first people to know when I kissed Braden Harvey in the Haunted House at Pinyin Beach Park. I'd never found that attraction particularly scary, since the skeletons were clearly spring-loaded and the ghosts were pretty tattered. But my heart nearly hammered out of my chest when I realized Braden's mouth was actually pressing against mine. It was a few more years before my cousin Sabina seemed old enough to regale with the sordid details, once I'd blurted out my big announcement to my family at the dinner table. But Violet was my age. And if she'd been the first person I'd told...I'd like to think she might've understood.

Now, though, I wasn't so sure exactly how much of our old history she wanted to dredge up. Our fateful kissing experiment at Ink-a-Dink Calligraphy Camp was pretty adorable in retrospect. A few days after she'd deemed me her boyfriend, she slipped me a note asking me to meet her alone by the pier—with a little Y/N for my reply. Of course I circled Y. The thought of doing something clandestine was a thrill. And it would still be a few years until Braden Harvey demonstrated exactly how thrilling it could actually be.

I'd thought I was a pretty good kisser. If not experienced, then at least enthusiastic. But the next day, I couldn't find her at breakfast, or sing-along, or the advanced letterform workshop. In fact, I didn't see her until her mom came to pick her up and she made a dash for the station wagon. And until my first (and hopefully only) eel dinner, that was the last I'd seen of Violet Strange.

I'd always figured she was just embarrassed we'd swapped spit. Kids will fart proudly at the drop of a hat, but they find certain other natural urges profoundly shameful. Did any of this matter anymore? Was it too late to bring it up now? Heck, did she even remember? Before I could figure out how to broach the subject, the little pulsing dot icon told me Violet was typing, so I waited to see what she had to say.

Meet me alone by the bier - Y/N

Hooray—that was quick! Not only did she remember our note—but she was cool about it. And her sense of humor was adorably punny.

Best gal-pal ever.

I messaged back—Y. As I hit *send*, Yuri rolled onto his side. It was a really narrow bed for two grown men, but we'd adapted. Normally, I'd roll right along with him and nestle my rump up against his business. But not now. There was no time to be the little spoon—not when I had to go meet Violet and break that curse.

As I extricated myself from the bed with the skill of an expert Twister champion, I knew full well Yuri would insist on going with me, were I to wake him. But Violet's message had said to come alone. And I wasn't about to give her any reasons to change her mind about helping us.

Normally, I'd worry about waking up Yuri by starting the truck. Its engine isn't exactly subtle. But luck was on my side, since my uncle had bedded down in the shower stall, which was the only free floor space in the dinky cabin. The fiberglass walls reverberated with the sounds of his snoring, and amplified them into a drone loud enough to cover the sound of the pickup truck, and then some.

The moon had set. The water of Pinyin Bay was still and dark. As I drove off and looped around the shoreline toward Strangeberg, I was the only one on the road. I hadn't realized exactly how much noise people make, even when they're not talking, until I took the trip alone. The creak of Yuri's leather driving gloves on the steering wheel. His occasional annoyed huff. My uncle's nose whistle. All of that was absent, which left me alone with my thoughts, and the churning anticipation of being the one to break Uncle Fonzo's curse once and for all.

The Strange Family mausoleum was a low marble building surrounded by columns and covered in ivy. Like so much cemetery architecture, it was designed to look Grecian—if something from ancient Greece had been miniaturized, teleported across the ocean, and dropped into the graveyard behind a Midwestern mental asylum. I parked a respectful distance away, not wanting to roll over anyone's grave, and hurried up the path to meet Violet.

The gate to the mausoleum stood open. In the archway, a figure stood, backlit by the dim orange light of a single guttering candle. I was breathless by the time I reached her. "I got your message," I said. "That was some serious wordplay!"

"You always did have a soft spot for things like that." She stepped aside and motioned for me to come in.

I'd never been inside a mausoleum before—my grandparents were buried in the perfectly normal cemetery out by the interstate—so I guess I expected something spooky.

The Strange family crypt didn't disappoint.

The candle cast ominous shadows, and when Violet stepped aside to let me in, another figure stood beside her, arms stretched wide. She'd hired some muscle of her own! I curled up to protect my vital organs, then realized her thug hadn't moved. Because he was no thug at all, but a marble likeness of Hawthorn Strange.

In all fairness, though, Hawthorn really had looked like he'd been a brawler, back in his day. What a relief to learn I wouldn't need to dodge any punches.

Statue-Hawthorn held a tiny slip of marble paper in one hand. A marble likeness of his quill in the other.

Funny to think it had once been a regular old Spellcrafting quill before the family'd cursed it.

The statue was poised in front of a vault, set high in the wall, with *Hawthorn Strange* engraved in elaborate lettering on a bronze plate. There were a few scratches where my uncle had pried the door open, and off to one side was the smaller crypt he'd stood on top of to do it.

I was eager to get down to business and break the curse. Unfortunately, Violet was more interested in catching up on old times. "It was such a shame about your Quilling Ceremony. Your uncle invited us, you know."

He'd invited every Spellcrafter within a hundred miles, and even a few from out of town. I knew. Every last wide-eyed face was etched into the memory of my greatest failure...one which no longer stung that much, seeing as how I did turn out to be a Scrivener after all. I was just about to say as much, when Violet surprised me by pulling me into a hug. "It must have been horrible."

"Not my greatest moment." I patted her on the back and disengaged. Not that I have anything against hugging, I was just eager to put the curse to bed. "But it all worked out in the end. So, the curse...."

"So horrible. Pansy and I always thought it was paranoid of Mother to place the curse—as if there were vagabond Spellcrafters roaming the moors in search of an unattended quill. We had no idea we'd be violated by a Scrivener from our own circuit."

"Violation is a pretty strong word."

My gal-pal eased up closer and dropped her voice low, and a little sultry. "And we had no idea it would be Fonzo Penn...or that he needed that quill for *you*."

I shuddered and thanked my lucky starts Uncle Fonzo hadn't pressed that gnarly black quill into my Scribing hand. Seeing the thing melded into him was bad enough. I couldn't fathom how nasty it would feel to be stuck to it myself. No, Uncle Fonzo had just wanted his own quill back, and was hoping to Spellcraft it out of Emery Flint without involving any of the rest of us.

Not that I was at liberty to tell her that.

Violet moved closer still and patted my chest with the flat of her palm. "Your uncle should have asked instead. The Penns and the Stranges weren't particularly close, it's true, but I would've argued on your behalf." Her pat turned into more of a caress. "Given our history."

If I didn't know better, I'd think Violet was coming on to me. Which was pretty *strange*, given everything I told her last night when I introduced her to Yuri. I took her by the wrist and gently settled her hand at a more comfortable distance, down at her side. "That was a long time ago. And like I always say, all's well that ends well."

It wasn't easy to see by dim, flickering candlelight, but Violet's brow definitely furrowed. "In what way has this ended even remotely well?"

"Wrong idiom," I said, with a growing sense of unease. The Stranges were angry enough about the quill. I couldn't afford to have Violet think I'd been leading her on. "It's not over till the fat lady sings? A stitch in time saves nine? Wait, I know—curses and promises are made to be broken!"

"That's not an expression."

"It isn't?" I hadn't realized I'd been backpedaling till I butted up (literally) against Statue-Hawthorn. His marble arms hovered like they were about to wrap the two of us in a stony embrace. "If not, it should be." I flailed for a change of subject. "Say, if you don't mind my asking, what happened to your eye?"

Although it was too dark to get a good look at her one purple iris, she tipped her head aside as if it embarrassed her. "A misguided attempt to differentiate myself from my sister. And you, of all people, know how capricious Spellcraft can be." Violet draped herself against my chest, and there was no doubt left in my mind that when she'd asked me to meet her, it hadn't been to deal with any curse. "Don't worry, Dixon. You might have failed your Quilling Ceremony, but I won't hold it against you."

How was it that she hadn't heard of my new Uncrafting venture? I definitely needed more aggressive marketing. But before I could ask if she knew anything about running Friendlike ads, she'd dragged me down by the front of my shirt and pressed her mouth against mine.

Wrong. On *so* many levels. Not just because said mouth had recently been chewing up lima beans—and *eel*—and not just because it was a woman's mouth. But because I couldn't imagine anyone's lips pressing into mine but Yuri's.

I eluded Violet like a dog on bath day, ducked under Hawthorn's Scribing hand, and slipped around the sarcophagus that still bore the faint outline of my uncle's wingtip shoe tread.

"Cold feet?" she asked flirtatiously. "I'm sure you've had ample opportunities to practice your kissing since then."

"Look, even if I wasn't 100% gay, like I said, I'm head over heels for Yuri. Him and me—it's not just a fling. It's the real deal. So don't take it personally, Vi, but I really can't be anything more than friends."

"You...? Oh." She seemed surprised. Not that I blamed her. I could see where she'd take me for the type of guy who liked to play the field. Before Yuri came along, I had a serious case of shiny object syndrome, and the men I dated were quick to tarnish. I was always wondering if I'd find a sexier smile, a more exotic accent, or a naughtier repertoire of bedroom tricks just around the corner.

These days, it didn't even occur to me to check.

"Wait!" Violet lunged at me, but I dodged her again—though I had to push off the low sarcophagus this time to do it. I'd expected the marble to be solid under my hands. But instead of supporting my weight, it fell in with a click as a hinge mechanism engaged. Violet made a grab to stop me from taking a header, but all she managed to do was pull off one of my shoes. And as I tumbled down the chute just as precipitously as my uncle had dropped into the tank at Dunk the Skunk, it occurred to me that the reason Violet was so shocked about Yuri was that it *wasn't* Violet who'd tried to kiss me just now—it was Pansy.

YURI
10

A foul odor intruded into my dreams. It roused me, and good thing. Sleep was a luxury I simply could not afford. Early morning light filled the cabin. Dixon was off doing whatever Dixon did, and Fonzo was perched at the narrow table folded down from the wall, poised over a Seen I'd painted. Scriveners shape magic into spells to release into the world, but it's the Seer who fixes the magic onto the page for them to work with. I might not be able to see it, flat on the table, from the angle at which I lay. But I felt the Seen pulsing with *volshebstvo*.

I sat bolt upright and flung myself out of bed. Fonzo had removed his glove, and his right hand was black and twisted. The feather had merged with it even more fully, and instead of a fingernail, his index finger terminated with the crumbling nib of a quill. One that dripped stinking black ichor like ink.

I snatched away my Seen before he could foul it with his cursed Scrivening, and snapped, "This is *not* yours to Scribe."

I tore it in two. Such a waste. But I had a point to prove.

Fonzo threw up his hands in desperation and reeking black fluid spattered the table. "Desperate times call for desperate measures.

We need to dredge up that money and appease the Stranges, and it can't wait another night. Not only will Dahlia double the price again." He massaged his wrist gingerly. "But it's getting worse."

I lowered my voice, so as not to be overheard—and, frankly, I seem more threatening when I speak deliberate and low. "Do you think I care about your discomfort? If not for your nephew, I'd happily leave you to your own devices. It was your greed that got you into this situation to begin with."

Fonzo leveled me a shrewd look. "Greed? Show me a man who doesn't strive for more—for his family, for himself—and I'll show you a man who doesn't deserve to be successful. If anyone should understand, it's an immigrant like you."

That might be true, had I come to America looking for a better future, and not simply to escape my past. I elbowed past Fonzo and checked the bathroom, but Dixon wasn't there. What a relief. I'd never met a man so enamored of his own family. I'd be stupid to give him any reason to reconsider my honorary position in it.

I forced myself to look at the cursed quill. Its tattered shape pulsed against Fonzo's palm, and the veins on the back of his right hand ran dark with ink. It seemed even more malignant in the cold light of day than it had the night before. "If Crafting is your best bet at getting out of this mess, fine. But not with your tainted Scribing. Dixon might not have your experience. But even so...he's talented, and he's clever. If anyone should Craft my Seens, it's him."

No one gets to be the Hand of a family by letting others order them around, but I glared at Fonzo until he relented. "Fine. But only because I have just as much confidence in Dixon as you obviously do." He crammed his hand—and the dead man's quill—into his glove, looked around expectantly, and said, "So, where is he?"

How would I know? I was asleep. "Didn't he tell you where he was going?"

"He was gone when I woke up."

"How long ago was that?"

"An hour?"

Or more. That Seen had been well-hidden in a pair of socks at the bottom of my suitcase.

"Maybe he went out for a walk," Fonzo suggested. "This cabin's smaller than a wiener in an ice water bath. There's hardly enough room to change your mind."

There was plenty of room when it was just Dixon and me, but I wasted no time arguing. I knew Dixon—and he'd never walk far, especially at this hour, unless we ran out of gas on the way to an all-you-can-eat breakfast buffet. I picked up my phone and called him, half-expecting to hear the jaunty trill of the ridiculous ringtone he'd selected for me just outside. I heard nothing but the waves lapping against the shore and the sound of Fonzo's annoying nose-whistle.

No answer. Dixon might be ignoring me. Or, possibly, his phone was dead. But when I threw open the door and found my truck was gone, I knew it could only mean one thing: that brave, gullible man had gone back to Strange Manor without us.

Unbelievable.

I brandished my phone as Fonzo hurried out behind me. The Spellcrafter is nothing if not observant, and he'd grabbed me by the arm before I could call up my contacts. "Yuri? Don't do it."

"How do you know what I—?"

"You're going to call Sabina to come get us." Observant...and accurate. "Please. I'm begging you. Leave her out of this."

"So, that's how it is? Fine for Dixon to be tangled up in your mess, but not your daughter. He's only your nephew, so he's fair game."

"Is that what you think?" Fonzo made to scrub at his bristly face in frustration, then remembered the quill burrowed into his Scribing hand and thought better of it. "You couldn't possibly be more wrong. The reason I don't protect Dixon is that I don't need to. Even before he was quilled, it was obvious he was the best and brightest of us all. He's clever and creative and stunningly dauntless. Sabina is the apple of my eye, but she's still so young. Not worldly like Dixon. The Strange family? They'd eat her for breakfast. So, please...." He clasped my wrist with his left hand. "Don't throw my little girl to the wolves."

What he said was not wrong—but I feared that one day, Dixon's relentless confidence would be his downfall.

"I'll try my brother," he said. But Dixon's father had no great love of cell phones, and while Fonzo wasted precious time trying to get hold of him, I felt like I would burst out of my own skin. I'd thought watching Dixon plunge into a black bus full of balloons was horrific, but that was nothing compared to the thought of him marching into a repurposed *mental institution* that a set of *identical twins* called home. "Johnny?" Fonzo hollered. "Is that you? Dang it, no one thinks those fake messages that sound like you're answering are funny anymore!"

The urge to punch something (and keep on punching until I'd pummeled it into the ground) seethed through my veins like Spellcraft. I paced back and forth, back and forth on the shore, glaring across Pinyin Bay at Strange Manor, just visible beyond a springtime canopy of budding trees.

"I'll call a cab," Fonzo declared. "They won't know we're too broke to pony up the fare until we get there...."

A cab was unlikely to make it to us in time since the campground's signs were covered for the season, and online maps led people down a road that no longer existed.

I squinted across the water. It felt as though my heart should be able reach across the bay and grab Dixon away from whatever had drawn him into its clutches, but instead it just pounded desperately against my ribcage. It was a straight line between me and Strange Manor. Yet the road around the bay was so convoluted, once a vehicle found us, it would take far too long to get there. I tasted frustration as a bitter tang at the back of my throat—or maybe it was adrenaline. Either way, I was just about to go against Fonzo's wishes and call Sabina when my gaze fell, instead, on a tarp-covered mound by the boat launch...and I realized there was another way.

I tore off the tarp. Three battered rowboats were piled face-down on the gravel. I grabbed the top boat and heaved it toward the water, but I'd overestimated its weight. It was aluminum, and only half as heavy as I'd thought—and I'd flung it so far into the water, we'd need to wade in up to our waists to get to it. Immediately, a current grabbed on and pulled it down the shore.

The second boat might have fared better, were the interior not covered in slugs, which pattered out of the hull like softly falling rain. I pitched the thing in a startled arc, and it landed nose-down in the spongy silt of the bay with its aft protruding like a stunted monolith.

One boat remained. I braced myself for more slugs—and was nearly toppled by a muskrat running between my ankles. It slid into the cold water and was gone. The creature had nearly given me a heart attack...but at least it had eaten most of the slugs. I set the boat (carefully, this time) on the ramp, then turned to see if Fonzo had enjoyed himself watching me do all the work...and was surprised to find him waddling toward me with a heavy outboard motor in his hands. A nearby shed, which had been firmly pad-locked all winter, stood open.

At least he'd made himself useful.

Together, we mounted the motor. "I picked the one with the most gas sloshing around the tank," he said.

That might not even matter. Unless the fuel was treated, it could be unusable after the freeze and thaw. I grabbed a pair of oars, flicked off a stubborn slug, and clambered into the boat as Fonzo gave me a hand up. He liked the sound of his own voice just as much as Dixon did, but I was much less keen to hear him ramble. "Now, the thing about engines is to treat 'em like you would a lady...." He embarked on a running commentary while I fit the oars into place and began to row.

Because doing something, effective or not, was better than doing nothing.

I'm in good condition. Even so, above the urgency and the growing sense of dread, I felt the exertion in my thighs, my arms, my shoulders and back. And especially in my hands, which were naked and exposed since my gloves were still in the truck. I con-sidered asking Fonzo for his, but thought better of thrusting my hand into a glove that had touched the dead man's quill.

"It's a good head start," Fonzo was saying, "but it's not as if anyone can row all the way across Pinyin Bay without the rest of the high school rowing team pitching in. You might want to save your strength." The engine clicked as he tinkered with the starter. "I've almost got it."

My shirt protested. I doubled down and rowed even harder.

"C'mon, c'mon...." Fonzo jiggled the starter. The engine coughed, then went silent. "It must be flooded."

I dug the oars into the water and pulled for all I was worth. Seams split. Buttons popped. But the boat hardly moved at all.

I've never given much thought to the currents in the bay. Not until they were working against me. For every stroke that brought me a meter closer to my goal, the current swept me back half that distance. Each time I took a breath, I found myself closer to our starting point. I leaned into it and rowed faster, as if I could outpace the bay itself.

The engine chugged twice, then fell silent. "Almost got it."

My muscles burned. The palms of my hands were on fire. I doubled down again.

A few more hollow clicks. "I think the spark plug's had it."

My energy flagged. Despite what Dixon thinks, it takes more than pluck and courage to prevail. And if I was attempting something physically impossible, no amount of grit would make any difference.

But.

If I've learned anything in my time with that exasperating man, it's that you can't tell the difference between impossible and merely difficult until you try.

I pulled even harder.

The boat leaped forward with a lurch. The current circled through the bay, and suddenly it was working *with* us, not against. Perhaps I could've eased up and allowed it to carry us to shore—especially when the engine finally caught. But instead I leaned into it and kept on rowing.

There were no boat launches on the edge of Strangeberg, just a rocky coastline. The old rowboat screeched to a halt as submerged stones scraped aluminum and the propeller jammed. I jumped out and sent the boat spinning, and Fonzo tipped over the side, jumped to his feet, and sloshed up onto the shore beside me.

Lucky for us Strange Manor was such an eyesore. Even through the trees, we managed to keep our bearing and hurry, ever upward, to the top of the hill. Undergrowth lashed our faces and we were covered in welts by the time we discovered a road, but Fonzo tugged me away from it. "Not the front door," he said between gasps of air. "Around back, where the curse is. The graveyard."

I ignored the gooseflesh competing for attention among all the welts and forged on.

A dreary dawn was warming the horizon as we stumbled out into the Strange family plot. The approaching sunrise didn't lighten the scene so much as draw attention to the eerie mist that clung to ground. With only the Strange women to look after the place, the grounds were now dilapidated, fuzzed over with moss and choked with weeds. The only spot that had been cared for (and not very well, at that) was the mausoleum.

From which could be heard the thready keen of a woman sobbing.

The *koza*—the sign of the horns—would offer as much protection as a cheap umbrella in a typhoon. Intellectually, I knew that—still, my right hand curled into the protective gesture anyway. But as superstitious as the Penns might be, their sense of danger was horribly askew. Fonzo was already outpacing me to the clearly-haunted crypt.

And so, I forced myself to follow.

His foolhardy lunge into danger wasn't the only thing that was just like Dixon—but his propensity for drama. He didn't slip into the tomb and try to assess the situation. No, that would be too sensible. Instead, he flung the gates wide and declared, "Aha!"

But instead of a group of frightful mages summoning a wailing spirit, inside there was nothing but a single, crying girl kneeling at the foot of a marble statue. She looked up sharply at the two of us, then hiccupped and began crying even harder.

"Violet?" Fonzo asked.

She shook her head, and between sobs, snuffled, "I'm Pansy."

"Where's Dixon? Is he with your sister?"

Apparently, this was the wrong question. The girl cried even harder.

I shouldered Fonzo aside—hysterics would do us no good—and said, "What have you done?"

But before I could shake the girl to her senses, Fonzo got between us, put an arm around her and said, "Don't worry, you're not in this alone. Just tell us what happened and we'll figure it all out."

"I thought he was luring Violet away from me. Again. I was wrong—and now it's too late." She sobbed and pointed with a trembling, pale hand at one of the stone sepulchers. "Mother suspected the thief would come back and try to steal the curse to break it himself, stepping in the same spot he did when he took the quill. So she moved Uncle Rowan and rigged his casket with a trap door. And now Dixon is stuck under the mausoleum."

Fonzo assessed the sarcophagus. "So what do we need to get him out? A rope? A ladder?"

His sensible demeanor rubbed off on Pansy and she began to calm down. "None of that will do him any good unless we get the trap door open. And now that it's been triggered, it's locked shut. Dixon is stuck down there unless he can find the failsafe."

"Everything's fine—we've got plenty of time to figure this out."

"Until the tide comes in," Pansy said. "But he won't panic in the water, will he? Not if he's an experienced scuba diver."

Right.

Fonzo crouched beside the sarcophagus, cupped his hands and yelled, "Find—the—failsafe!"

"He can't hear you," Pansy said. "The stone is too thick." She buried her face in her hands. "This is all my fault!"

It most certainly was, but before I could agree, Fonzo said, "C'mon, now, there's no time for wallowing. Let's focus on the solution. What's the quickest way to get him a message?"

I sent him a text—*Find the failsafe*. Its arrival dinged a few feet away from us, where Dixon had dropped his phone. I tried to pocket my own phone, and found it had stuck to my palm. Evidently, our rowing endeavor had made a casualty of more than just my ruined shirt. I now saw the skin on my palms hung in shreds, weeping with blood-tinged fluid. I carefully peeled off the phone and eased it into my pocket, then retrieved Dixon's with my fingertips and did the same...and did my best to ignore the fact that it now felt as though I was holding my hands in a bonfire.

Fonzo pulled out a pocket knife and wiggled it into the seam of the sarcophagus. "Where there's a will, there's a way."

While I resented his optimism, maybe he was on to something. Will was a useless abstraction, but where there was a mechanism, there was a way to force it open. I staggered out into the early gray dawn and spotted my truck parked haphazardly where Dixon had left it at the side of the path. My gloves sat on the dash, though I was none too keen to pull them on. I grit my teeth and forced myself to work my hands inside while I tried not to think about pulling them back out again. Best not get ahead of myself. Once gloved, I grabbed my crowbar from the back and headed in.

Fonzo was fishing around the hinge with his small, thin blade— completely ineffectively. I shoved him out of the way and drove my crowbar in. The stone lid was rigged like a see-saw. If the front half of the sepulcher dipped down, then the back half should pry up. I jammed the crowbar in again. Shards of granite sprayed as if I was a sculptor, not a painter. I tried not to think about my hands. I tried not to think about the fact that I was desecrating a grave. And I tried not to think about what would happen to Dixon if the tide came in before I got to him. He was no more a scuba diver than I was a motivational speaker.

"Don't worry," Pansy said. "It should be a while before the tide seeps into the hollow. It's mostly blocked by a valve that the excavators installed."

"All this to safeguard an old quill?" Fonzo asked.

"You're the Hand of your family. You more than anyone should know how important it is to protect what's yours."

If he didn't, I certainly did. The palms of my hands were screaming, but I kept on pounding at the stone. It made a sound like a hammer on concrete, the percussion of metal on mineral. Regular. Predictable. Until something gave, the sound changed, and a chunk of stone fell away. I had a momentary flash of the lid falling in and crushing Dixon beneath it. Luckily, though, the shard that broke away was not even the size of my hand. But it did create a very small opening for him to hear us.

"Dixon," I called, and my voice was ragged with exertion. "Are you okay?"

"I'm fine! This big pile of twigs broke my fall. I've been trying to make a fire by rubbing them together, but I can't quite get the hang of it. It's darker than a black cat in a sealed box."

Telling him to find the failsafe would do no good if he couldn't see. If I tossed down his phone, in all likelihood, all I would accomplish was destroying the thing. Besides, it wouldn't fit through the tiny hole. But I had a better idea. I shoved the crowbar into the hole and leaned on it, really leaned on it, and pried the gap open another fraction of a centimeter. "In my pocket," I gasped to Fonzo, straining with exertion with every word. "Pass it to Dixon."

Fonzo hurried around the sepulcher, thrust his hand into my pocket, and pulled out a condom. With a shrug, he slipped it through the hole.

"Not...that." The crowbar was starting to slip. "Glow stick."

They say there is only so much pain a man can bear. If that is true, I have never found the threshold—but not for lack of trying. The pain in my hands was already excruciating. Now it redoubled with every moment I held open that gap. But Fonzo wanted Dixon out of that pit just as much as I did, and while his harebrained schemes so often went wrong, he was not a stupid man. He plucked the glow stick out of my pocket and bent it with a snap. It lit with a wan pink light—much dimmer than I'd hoped.

But it would have to do. He shoved it through the gap, and finally, I could let go of the crowbar.

DIXON

11

The water was up to my knees by the time they started prying the trap sarcophagus open. I couldn't really see much by the light of the tiny opening, just enough to know that I'd fallen a good dozen feet, and I'd definitely have a few choice bruises to show for my adventure. Something dropped on my head and I grabbed it. A condom? My sex drive is pretty healthy, so I'm generally up for anything, anytime, anywhere...but, frankly, I drew the line at getting my jollies in a mausoleum.

And then everything went pink.

Grunting and clattering ensued up above as I blinked away afterimages from my dark-sensitized eyes. After a few blinks, I discovered the glow bracelet from the balloon pop floating by my knees. I plucked it from the water and had a look around.

Those twigs that had broken my fall? Not twigs at all. Unless some of them just so happened to look like femurs. And ribs. And skulls.

"Find the failsafe," Pansy called faintly.

She didn't need to tell me twice. "Got it!" I looked around. Bones and bones and bones. "Uh...what's it look like?"

"There are two levers in the floor," she said. I found them protruding from the bones. "The left lever unlocks the trap door. The right one will flood the chamber. So be sure to pull the right one."

"I thought you said the *left* one would get me out."

Pansy warbled a scream of frustration. "Stop confusing me!"

If there's anything a Scrivener is good at, it's telling right from left. And Scribing, obviously, but only with the right hand. The frigid water crept up my thighs, half submerging both levers. Despite growing up near the shores of Pinyin Bay, I was always more of a sunbather than a swimmer. Good thing I'd be out of there soon. I knew for a fact Yuri kept a clothesline in his truck—weird insistence on hand-washing his clothes, don't ask—and once the trap door was open, he could hoist me out of there, no problem. "Just to be clear, which lever do I—?"

"Left!" Pansy hollered. "Pull the *left* one."

She didn't need to be all huffy about it. I squared myself up to the levers, and I pulled. It was a big, solid thing connected to some major machinery, and I really had to put my back into it. Initially, it seemed like it might not even budge. But I'm nothing if not persistent. Sometimes you need to shove something in the opposite direction to break the seal—case in point, the pickled egg jar at Bar None. So I braced myself and gave the lever a good, solid shove. That seemed to do the trick. In fact, it moved really well in that direction.

There was a distant click.

Followed by a muffled roar.

And then the realization that if I happened to be *facing* Pansy, her left was my right, her pull was my push...and that harmless little lie I told about scuba diving?

It was coming back to bite me square in the butt.

YURI

12

The marble floor rumbled beneath our feet—and the trap door held fast. "Oh no," Pansy said. "He pulled the wrong lever! Now he'll drown—and it's all my fault!"

The pain in my hands? Gone. I hefted the crowbar and began pounding at the sarcophagus for all I was worth. In between clangs, I overheard Fonzo and Pansy yelling over the noise. "How much longer does he have?" Fonzo called out.

"Ten minutes? Maybe five."

Fonzo caught my arm mid-swing. "Then we've gotta work smarter, not harder. It's obvious you'd dig to China if that's what it took, but you've been whacking away at that thing with only a little chip to show for it. We need to Craft."

Good thing Fonzo wasn't the only Scrivener there. I told Pansy, "You can redeem yourself and Scribe him out."

She stood on tiptoe to peer out a decorative window at the bay. "My quill is back in my room, and the water level's too high. We're running out of time. By the time I got to the quill, it would be too late."

I'd thought there couldn't be anything more terrible than

Crafting with that cursed black quill...but the thought of something happening to Dixon was infinitely worse. However, as I resigned myself to letting Fonzo touch one of my Seens with his revolting pen, my hands cramped so fiercely the crowbar clattered to the floor.

I might be willing to paint...but I wasn't so sure I could hold the brush.

Unaware of my struggle, Fonzo was already flipping through his pocket thesaurus. "Which sounds better—*manumit* or *disembarrass*?"

I swatted the book from his hands. "If we do this together, we do it right. Bad enough you'll be using that cursed quill. I will not have you write something ambiguous and cryptic. You Scribe for real." I glanced toward the chipped sarcophagus. "Dixon's life depends on it."

He wanted to bargain with me out of sheer habit, I could tell. But we were out of time. "Fine. Give me a Seen."

"I don't just carry them around with me."

"Could've sworn I saw one just recently—oh, wait, *somebody* tore it up."

I should've known that gesture was too good to be true by how satisfying it felt. I'd need to make another Seen.

A Seer can't paint wearing gloves—they're a barrier to the flow of the magic. Too bad I hadn't realized I'd need to Craft before I forced them on. It had only been a few minutes. Unfortunately, that was long enough for the wreck of my palms to turn gummy and thick.

I grit my teeth, braced myself, and pulled.

The human hand is rich with nerve endings. I often suspect that flowing the *volshebstvo* through them makes them even more acute. A ragged scream tore from my throat as the glove stripped away what little flesh remained on my palm, punctuated by Pansy's horrified yelp. Fonzo just let out a low whistle.

Pain muddled my thoughts. Pain...and fear. Not just the fear of losing Dixon—but the dread of it being *my* failure that condemned him to a watery death.

Fonzo tore a blank page from the back of his thesaurus and slapped it down on the sarcophagus lid. I expected him to tell me I was no good. Worthless. Weak.

But instead?

"You got this, kiddo." He gave me a few solid whacks on the back. "You got this."

You're family now, too.

Maybe I wasn't quite ready to fully accept that. But I was willing to entertain the possibility.

I fumbled the cheap paints from my pocket and opened them with my teeth. Glitter paint spattered from the tiny plastic pot and the brush dropped to the floor and rolled away. I couldn't let it stop me—there was no time to let it stop me. I scooped out what was left with my finger, called in the *volshebstvo*, and forced it onto the page.

I'm not sure I could even call it a painting, this haphazard swipe of glitter and blood. But it pulsed so strongly with Spellcraft that the air all around it wavered to my sight.

Scriveners don't visualize the magic exactly as I do, but they know it when they see it. Pansy gasped and backed away a few steps. Fonzo nodded grimly, then pulled off his own glove.

Black foulness drooled from the tip of the cursed quill—from the tip of Fonzo's index finger—as the dark feather writhed beneath his skin.

Pansy shrieked and flattened herself against the wall, too terrified to even faint.

Fonzo took no notice. He was Crafting even before the leaking nib touched the Seen. Spellcraft originated not on the page, but in the mind. As he touched pen to paper, images of all the cursed Craftings we'd found flashed before my mind's eye. For a terrible moment I thought Fonzo would make another spell just as bad as those, attempting to Scribe words he'd never before written. But then he took a deep breath, gave a preemptive wince, and wrote...a word I'm sure he'd Scribed before. More than once.

Dixon

It is powerful magic to Craft by name. Illegal here, too—though Scriveners followed their own code, and they had no compunctions about naming their own when they Scribed. Fonzo bit back a groan as he finished the word, and something crumbled off the tip of the quill...or maybe his fingernail. Or both. Black ichor spattered.

He caught his breath, then Scribed again.

is

Another chunk dropped off. Fonzo's breathing went ragged and Pansy tried, unsuccessfully, to stifle a moan.

I'd formed plenty of opinions about Fonzo Penn. Con man. Charlatan. Thief. But seeing him Scribe, a bigger picture emerged. Yes, he truly was all those things. But he was also the Hand of his family. And his power was great. Even with the quill fighting against him, Fonzo was strong enough to ink one more word.

free

Now complete, the Crafting pulsed with magic, even as Fonzo's forefinger made a sick crunching sound of joints grinding and bones shifting. An agonized whine escaped him, and he staggered back into the statue that had been presiding over the goings-on. All three of us—Fonzo, Pansy and I—caught our breath. Yes, Fonzo was strong. But what if Dahlia Strange and her curse were stronger? And in the moment of harrowing stillness where I very nearly surrendered to despair, we heard a small click.

Hawthorn Strange's right arm dropped as if to stab himself in the thigh with his stupid marble quill. In the distance, gears ground, then engaged. And with a gritty sigh, the top of the tomb tilted open.

We all dashed toward the opening—Pansy in tears, Fonzo cradling his blackened hand, and me running on pure adrenaline. There was no sarcophagus inside, but instead, a dark shaft with the sound of water lapping at its stony sides. How high was the water level? Too dark—no way to tell. I thought of the parasites that would surely work their way into my flayed palms if I dove in to retrieve Dixon, but only briefly. Before I could plunge in, though, a rosy will-o-the-wisp in the shape of a smile bobbed to the black surface.

Dixon broke the water and his smile broadened, pink as the sunrise, with the glowstick clamped in his teeth.

"You can swim?" Fonzo demanded—evidently shocked.

"Who needs to swim when you can float on a big rubber...balloon. Yep. That's what I'm floating on. *Totally* a balloon."

How he managed to say all that around a pink glow stick was beyond me.

Pansy gave him a hand up, and good thing. I was in no shape to haul Dixon out of the shaft, and neither was Fonzo. Dixon left the inflated condom floating on the dark water and climbed out, soaking wet, and bathed us all in his pink Cheshire Cat smile.

DIXON

13

"I knew you were no scuba diver," Pansy said shakily. "You couldn't even hold a kiss for ten seconds without breathing into my mouth. And it tasted like Bubble Yum."

I spat out the glowstick. "Bubblicious...and I'm more talented than you realize. I've had lots of time to hone my skills. Not *kissing* skills, obviously. A person might get somewhat better with practice, but I think that talent is mostly innate. We're not kids anymore, though. We're grown men—well, not you, Pansy—anyhow, we're all adults. And we're all Spellcrafters. So let's get this curse lifted, once and for all."

Pansy wrung her hands. "But I don't know how."

"Between the four of us, we'll figure it out." We had to. I risked a glance at my uncle's mangled hand and immediately wished I hadn't. "Now, show us the curse."

Carefully avoiding the trapped sarcophagus, Pansy dragged a series of decorative square urns against the wall, forming a set of steps, and climbed up to the fancy metal plaque bearing the name of her grandfather, Hawthorn Strange—the plaque dinged with scratches where Uncle Fonzo had pried it open. She pressed the letter H. The plaque clicked and the vault hinged open.

As secret activations went, not exactly rocket science. Then again, none of us had thought to try it.

Pansy steeled herself and looked down at us. "Are you sure you want to do this?" She sounded scared.

Yuri glanced at my uncle's hand, blanched, and said, "It is the only way."

Pansy probably knew that herself. But hard things are that much easier to accomplish when someone's got your back.

She pressed the letter S. More distant mechanical sounds, and suddenly the wall became a massive Pez dispenser—one that dispensed big black coffins filled with the remains of deceased Spellcrafters instead of candies. The coffin of Hawthorn Strange tilted out, then down, angled like the world's most gruesome recliner. And with an ominous click, the lid swung open.

I must've expected it to be another Reverend Fun type situation. Something that felt super scary when we were all caught up in the hubbub...something that turned out to be nothing more sinister than a burst of itching powder and a T-shirt cannon. But no. We were looking at a real dead body. And an even realer curse.

The Crafting unfurled from the coffin lid like a macabre party banner in a grim, gray scroll. Usually, Spellcraft sparkles to my inner eye. I'm not sure if it's possible for something to nega-tive-sparkle, pulsing with black flashes of light instead of white, but it sure as heck *felt* like that's what was happening.

Scribing is as individual as Scriveners themselves. We pen our own words in our own styles. But there's a certain phrase each and every Scrivener will write at least once, at their Quilling Ceremony: *I choose the quill and the quill chooses me.*

On first glance, that's what I thought was inked on the cursed banner which, in all fairness, was *really* hard to read.

It was the most inharmonious calligraphy I'd ever seen, and given those whackadoodle things my uncle'd been spreading around, that's saying a lot. The letters were big and thick, each one different from the one next door. It would've made a spiffy punk rock album cover. But Spellcraft? The magic wasn't just directed through those letters, it was distorted.

And then I realized the lettering wasn't the only thing that was distorted, but the Scrivening.

THou choSE tHe quiLL aNd
ThE qUiLL CuRseS tHeE

One time, at calligraphy camp, when we were singing this charming (but lengthy) madrigal called the Scrivener and the Cuckoo's Quill, I realized I'd been standing on an anthill for the better part of the song. Maybe if I wasn't a prepubescent boy with legs as smooth as a pantyhose model's, I would've felt them coming before they breeched my underwear. Let's just say the phrase "ants in your pants" had its origin in a very uncomfortable reality.

That's what it felt like to look at the curse.

If I was disturbed by the profaned Spellcrafting, Yuri was downright horrified. But Uncle Fonzo simply shook his head.

"And now you understand," he said. "Some knots are just too tight to untangle. And the only thing left to do is cut them off."

I took that statement to be metaphorical—until it registered that it wasn't a *knot* he was talking about.

Yuri might turn green when he encounters a hair in his food, but he's disturbingly blasé over the sight of blood. "I will do the job," he said calmly. "There's a hacksaw in the truck."

Pansy bit back a sob and said, "You've gotta believe me—I didn't know it would end like this."

"Hold on a sec," I told everybody while I inserted myself between Yuri and the exit. "Maybe it doesn't."

My uncle shook his head with a sad smile. "Dixon...some dark clouds simply don't make it through the storm with their silver lining intact."

"But you won't know until you really look. If there's one thing I've learned about Spellcraft is that there's always another way—it's just a matter of exploiting the loopholes."

"Not this one," Pansy said. "It was inked by my whole family, switching off one letter at a time, with each of us binding the curse to the Seen. Even if you thought of the right phrasing to Uncraft it, three Scriveners penned the curse—and thirty times three would need to reverse it. That's every Spellcrafter in our circuit, and then some. And most of them wouldn't touch a curse with a ten-foot quill."

"Wait a minute," Fonzo said. "How can that be? Dahlia promised to lift the curse."

Pansy shook her head. "It was a lie. She was just stringing you along until all your blood turned to ink."

Oh dang. I had no idea *that* was even a thing.

Neither did Yuri. He was galvanized into action. In an attempt to move me aside, he tried to grab me by the shoulders, then flinched away in pain. His hands were all red and sticky, and his fingers were curled into claws. "I am not able to hold the saw. You need to do it, Dixon. It must be you."

My head swam and I swallowed back the urge to revisit my dandelion greens. There had to be another way—there was *always* another way. Maybe we could steal back the walrus and pay a bunch of Scriveners to do the curse-breaking. I took another look at Uncle Fonzo's right hand. Even in the guttering candle light, I caught a glimpse of black veins creeping up his forearm. Finding eighty-some willing Scriveners outside my own family would take time. Time we didn't have.

Was it possible to Scribe without a hand? After all, my uncle's real quill still functioned even though the nib had been hacked off and jammed into the body of a fountain pen...a topic I still hadn't quite figured out how to broach.

And which...I realized...might actually be the viable loophole I was hoping for.

"Forget about the saw," I told Yuri. "Uncle Fonzo, read those words aloud."

"Dixon, there's no time—"

"Do it!" I insisted. "But read it in first person."

"Fine. *I chose the quill and the quill cursed me.* Is that what you wanted to hear?"

I nodded along with the words as my inspiration took hold. "You chose the quill."

"It's my fault—everything's my fault. You think I don't know that? I'm sorry. More sorry than you'll ever know. And I'd take back every last decision if I could, but I can't."

At my uncle's admission of guilt, something inside me clicked. Yuri hadn't been projecting after all. From the baseball to the foot-stomp to the attempt to leave him at the diner...all this time, I'd truly had been angry with Uncle Fonzo for leaving. I was only able to see it now that he'd apologized.

Now that I was able to forgive him.

"Maybe you can't take it back," I said gently. "But you can make another decision. You chose the quill—a Scrivener can only have one quill—and now you can choose another."

"There's no way I can manage a new Quilling Ceremony." He flailed his right hand in a spray of bleeding ink. "Not with this thing under my skin."

"You don't have to. Emery Flint didn't end up with your original quill. I did."

I could tell him about the state of its condition later.

"Choose it," I said. "Choose your real quill. Just like it chose you, all those years ago."

Emotions played across my uncle's face. Shock. Disbelief. And a grim determination. I'm especially good at figuring out loopholes—that's why I'm such a good Uncrafter—but I'd inherited that knack from him.

He stomped up to the open casket and peered down at the corpse. The old patriarch of the Strange family had never been a handsome man, and aside from the fact that his nose had collapsed, he didn't look much different to me dead than he had when he was alive. "Hawthorn," Uncle Fonzo announced, "I don't need your quill anymore. I've got one of my own."

I swallowed audibly. Pansy sniffled.

Uncle Fonzo looked expectant, then puzzled...and, finally,

alarmed...as nothing at all happened.

"Don't just say the words," I prompted. "You've gotta choose it in your mind, and in your heart."

Because that's where Spellcraft really got its focus. Not from words on a page.

He nodded, then gathered his courage yet again and said, loud and clear, "I choose my own quill."

When the change in the air came, it was so subtle at first, it felt like wishful thinking. But that's the thing about Spellcraft. Once you really spot it in action, you know what to look for. The air in the crypt flexed as dark un-sparkles swarmed at the corners of my vision. Subtly at first, then stronger. Until the whole structure was reverberating with that single note of cursed Spellcraft. Struck. Sustained. And finally...released.

The gray scroll fluttered as if caught by a breeze that none of us could feel, and the malignant lettering pulsed with power. At first I thought it was just the paper trembling that gave the illusion of movement. But soon I couldn't deny that the letterforms themselves were shifting, breaking down into ugly black strokes that crawled across the page like leeches, until they finally reached the bottom, taken by gravity, where they shriveled, died, and fell away. Ash rained on the corpse of Hawthorn Strange. I half expected him to start moving around, too. But thankfully, he just laid there with his squashed nose and allowed the curse's ashes to rain on down.

As the last bit of ink fell from the page, Uncle Fonzo lunged forward, cursed hand outstretched, as if he wanted to catch the ash like snowflakes on a mitten. It wasn't my uncle calling the shots, though, it was the black quill. It dragged him right up to the casket, and for a moment I thought it was yet another elaborate trap, one that would suck him in and pull him into the vault, never to be seen again. But instead it was the horrible cursed feather that was suctioned away. It pulled from his flesh and veins with an appalling, wet sound like you'd hear at the bottom of an overlarge slushy, and it flowed from his body like gravity-defying blood. The blackness was mesmerizing in its intricacy and terrible, dark grace. It spun through the air like a girl changing dance partners. My uncle might've led her on a few spins across the dance floor. But thankfully, she was willing to leave the ball with her original partner.

The blackness coalesced in the right hand of Hawthorn Strange and formed itself into the shape of a vulture's plume. And before it could get any funny ideas about taking a spin with anyone else, Pansy jabbed at the secret buttons on the foot of the casket, the lid ground shut, and the corpse of her grandfather slid back into the wall, taking his quill along with him just as the sun edged over the horizon.

Coral-colored light pinked the mausoleum through the open door, enough to see that Yuri looked like he'd spent the night with his palms pressed against a hot stove. Pansy's eyes were most definitely both the same dark brown. And while my uncle's hand had seen better days, at least it was still attached to the end of his arm. He wasn't relieved, though. He was angry. He turned to Pansy and said, "All that graft I've been giving your mother this past year—she obviously hasn't used it to spruce up the Manor. I hope she's put it in some good investments. She made me a promise she had no intention of fulfilling, and now she owes me. With interest."

Pansy shook her head helplessly. "She spent that money having Great-Uncle Rowan's sarcophagus dug out so no one could use it to get to Grandfather again. All but the cash you brought with you last night."

As the four of us limped through the mausoleum door, soaked and stunned, bruised and beaten, Yuri slipped an arm around my shoulders and guided me toward the truck...then recoiled with a startled gasp.

A slip of paper that was stuck to my back peeled off when he jerked his hand away, and dropped to the ground with a moist pat. Even though it was wet, I still recognized it as the Crafting we'd taken such great care to bury, all to no avail. The watercolor Seen had mostly rinsed away, maybe while I stood in rapidly rising water, desperately trying to tie off the blown-up condom (and that slippery lube coating was definitely no help). Or maybe the whole Crafting had lost its integrity and begun to fade once the black quill returned to its rightful owner.

But the single word, *Remunerate,* was still legible.

Uncle Fonzo thrust his arms out wide as if he was protecting the rest of us from a papery grenade. But I'd been developing a pretty good feel for Spellcraft, so I suspected the detonation had already occurred, and what we were dealing with now was only the aftermath.

"Of all the words in the language you could have picked," I said to him, "the one you chose was a real doozy. Requital for a loss. Make up for. Compensate. Reverend Fun was forced to pay you for your services whether he wanted to or not, while you paid dearly for...uh...*borrowing* Hawthorn Strange's quill. But where does all this titting and tatting end? Dahlia Strange will eventually get what she deserves—miserable people like that usually do—and once your hand heals, you'll Scribe another day. I think it's time to cut your losses and move on."

My uncle is a proud man. Stubborn, too. But even he could see when it was best to put down his cards and walk away from the table, like he sorely wished he'd done a year ago when this whole train wreck began with Emery Flint. He made up his mind, nodded once...and the ragged black word faded from sight.

We left Pansy to make her way back to the manor while we piled into the truck. I hardly ever drove it—I'm told I ride the brakes— but given the fact that I was the only one with two functioning hands, Yuri let me take the wheel without comment. As I turned out of the cemetery gates, I caught one last look at Pansy in the rearview mirror, picking her way through the thorny brambles that passed for landscaping at Strange Manor. She'd really had me fooled. I thought I was so clever, being able to tell the twins apart by their body language alone. But who better to imitate Violet than her twin sister?

"Hold on." I tapped the brakes.

"You see what I mean?" Yuri muttered.

I ignored him. "If that was Pansy...then how'd she know about the bubble gum?"

14

In light of the bubblegum revelation, I realized it was never my girlfriend Violet who'd invited me to the clandestine meeting on the pier all those years ago, but her sister, Pansy. Not because they were in cahoots, either. If Pansy had always been jealous enough to drive us apart, she must've been the one to slip me the note, then let Violet think I was two-timing her.

No wonder Violet thought I was such a heel.

Over the next few days, I debated whether or not to exonerate myself and let Violet know I hadn't intentionally cheated on her that fateful night at Ink-a-Dink Calligraphy Camp, despite whatever Pansy might've told her. But in the end, I decided that it was more important to protect the twins' relationship than to clear my own name. I had an awesome family—including Yuri. Pansy and Violet only had each other, and it would be quite the irony to mess that up by trying to prove I was a nice guy.

And I was most definitely a nice guy. Would I be spending so much time peeling Yuri's hard-boiled eggs for him if I wasn't?

Yuri refused to seek medical attention for his hands—of course he did—but according to the internet, we were just dealing with some really bad blisters. (Pro tip: don't search for blisters online unless you've got a really stunted gag reflex.) Since nothing appeared to be infected, it was just a matter of keeping everything clean and dry while we waited for his hands to heal.

By contrast, Uncle Fonzo was happy enough to see the doctor—probably because she's disproportionately chesty and he's always been into that kind of physique. Fortunately, Dr. Butcher was a reasonably competent medical professional, too.

My uncle claimed to have hurt his forefinger rescuing a trapped bag of chips from a vending machine, and that's how it ended up lacerated, bruised and broken. Dr. Butcher didn't question his story. The Handless can be kind of oblivious that way.

Yuri's main problem these days was boredom. In his little lakeside cabin, he paced in the sliver of floorspace beside his bed, which was clearly unsatisfying. With his long strides, he could only go two steps before he had to turn and go back again. "No push-ups," he grumbled. "No pull-ups. No weights. If I can't exercise, I will grow soft."

Hardly. He must've gone up two shirt sizes rowing across the bay. I didn't mention it—I've learned to be strategic in my compliments with Yuri, since too much affirmation only makes him leery. Distraction, though? I was pretty good at that. I snagged him by his waistband before he could do another two-step pace and pulled him down onto the bolted-down bed. His hands were wrapped loosely in gauze, partly for their protection, and partly to keep them from oozing on everything. It might be awkward trying to figure out how to avoid them, but luckily there was a lot more of Yuri to love besides his hands.

I wriggled out of my clothes in no time flat, but I couldn't pull Yuri's sleeves over his mummy hands. That was fine by me. I settled for unbuttoning his shirt and rucking up the ribbed undershirt to get to that broad, tattooed chest beneath it. It felt naughty for only one of us to be totally naked—and I've never been averse to a little naughtiness.

If Yuri's push-up muscles did end up a smidge atrophied and he had trouble assuming his normal bedroom position in the future, there was no doubt in my mind that we'd figure something out. I'm always happy to do whatever heavy lifting is required of me in the sack. Judging by the way his mesmerizing stomach muscles rippled as I straddled him and rode him like a mechanical bull, he was getting a pretty solid workout, too. Even flat on his back.

The cedar smell of the tiny cabin was soon seasoned with that particular olfactory tang of man-on-man lovin', and it was trippy to press Yuri into the mattress and make him submit to my kisses once we were through. Sure, we both knew he could stand up and brush me off like a crumb...but it gave him a good excuse to let me linger at his mouth even after the fireworks were done exploding.

I wouldn't dream of interrupting a good roll in the hay to check my phone, but with Yuri on his back and the phone on the nightstand, it was right in Yuri's line of sight when a Friendlike notification pinged. He tried to glance over with just his eyes—as if I wouldn't notice. Now *I* was curious. So, I made a mental note to pick up later where we left off—at which point all our bottle rockets and roman candles would be restocked, anyhow, so it was probably for the best—and I pulled the phone into bed.

We read together, with Yuri snugged up to my back, reading over my shoulder. The notification was from Violet—a group selfie with her, Pansy and a male set of identical twins. Given the dark-haired, dark-eyed, five-o'clock-shadow looks of the guys, they were Spellcrafters, too. Not from our circuit, though. I would've remembered them from Calligraphy Camp.

Yuri moved to take the phone from me and thumb through the post, but only succeeded in boffing it with his gauze. I waved him off and flicked open Friendlike myself.

More photos of the four of them. Laughing. Eating. Horsing around. They looked so happy.

They looked like they were in love. Or if not love, at least serious *like*.

There was one particular selfie on the teacup ride that brought a lump to my throat. One of the guys was gazing adoringly at Violet, and the other at Pansy. The Strange twins had sunglasses on, and I could no longer really say which twin was which. But it was more than obvious that those guys totally knew.

Scrolling through the comments, I could see the twin-sets had been courting each other online for quite a while, but had only just met in person. I also realized the teacup ride was not the type of scuffed, dented attraction you'd find at the Big Fun Traveling Carnival, but a fancy teacup ride at WonderWorld Paris.

Yuri reached around me and boffed the phone again with his swaddled hand. He clucked his tongue, then said, "Scroll down farther. There. The harpy mother has something to say."

That, she did. All in caps, too.

COME HOME IMMEDIATELY AND DON'T EITHER OF
YOU DARE SPEND ANOTHER DIME

Blocking her would be easy enough, but either Violet enjoyed the fact that her mother was fuming, or she was having such a good time she simply didn't care. My uncle might've paid off Dahlia Strange for nothing, but at least she wouldn't be able to fund another creepy renovation project with his final installment.

"You are not angry about the money?" Yuri asked.

"How could I begrudge the twins a little vacation? I'm sure they deserve it after living in that asylum with Dahlia for so long."

Money comes and money goes, and, hokey as it may sound, it clearly can't buy happiness. I had my quill now. And, more importantly, I had my family, too—my *whole* family, including Uncle Fonzo...and including Yuri.

Which made me the luckiest guy ever.

ABOUT THE AUTHOR

Jordan Castillo Price thoroughly subscribes to the notion that words hold power. She has submitted verses to greeting card companies...and been rejected. Though invited to resubmit, she was not nearly as persistent as Dixon.

She has a soft spot for carnivals and amusement parks, though her tomfoolery did once knock an old ride off its tracks and cause the entire attraction to back up and shut down.

The wails of the other children trapped in the dark funhouse were particularly satisfying.

www.jordancastilloprice.com

CPSIA information can be obtained
at www.ICGtesting.com
Printed in the USA
BVHW050121061021
618220BV00006B/190